The more I thought about it, the less I understood why I found Ren's smile so scary.

Other than the night she'd smiled at me in the lounge, I couldn't actually remember her doing anything threatening, but thinking about her definitely increased the feeling that I'd forgotten something. I ground my teeth, trying to force my stupid brain to remember. There had to be a reason I was so afraid of her; what was it? What had I forgotten?

I was still trying to figure this out when the hand grabbed my spine.

I shot bolt upright. From the lack of horrible pain, I knew there was no way a hand could *actually* be grabbing my spine, but that was exactly what it felt like. Five fingers and a palm, wrapped around the vertebrae just below my neck. I could even feel the fingers moving inside me, readjusting to get a better grip.

My shock had been enough to flip my suit into combat mode, but when my vitals flashed up, I didn't see anything wrong. My suit had no breaches, and though the panic had elevated my heart rate, I was otherwise fine. I didn't see anything behind me through my rear cameras either. I was about to flip my visor back down and do a full scan when a soft, feminine voice whispered in my mind.

Come.

As the word finished, the hand on my spine jerked, and I popped out of my body like a shucked pea.

BY RACHEL BACH

Paradox
Fortune's Pawn
Honor's Knight
Heaven's Queen

BY RACHEL AARON

The Legend of Eli Monpress
The Spirit Thief
The Spirit Rebellion
The Spirit Eater
The Spirit War
Spirit's End

The Legend of Eli Monpress: Part I, II, & III (omnibus edition)

HONOR'S KNIGHT

RACHEL BACH

www.orbitbooks.net

Orbit
Hachette Book Group
237 Park Avenue, New York, NY 10017
HachetteBookGroup.com

First Edition: February 2014

Orbit is an imprint of Hachette Book Group, Inc. The Orbit name and
logo are trademarks of Little, Brown Book Group Limited.

The Hachette Speakers Bureau provides a wide range of authors
for speaking events. To find out more, go to
www.hachettespeakersbureau.com or call (866) 376-6591.

The publisher is not responsible for websites (or their content) that are not
owned by the publisher.

The characters and events in this book are fictitious. Any similarity to real
persons, living or dead, is coincidental and not intended by the author.

Library of Congress Cataloging-in-Publication Data
Bach, Rachel.
   Honor's knight / Rachel Bach. — First edition.
      pages cm
   ISBN 978-0-316-22108-5 (trade pbk.) — ISBN 978-0-316-22107-8
(ebook) 1. Imaginary wars and battles—Fiction. 2. Space warfare—
Fiction. 3. Science fiction. I. Title.
   PS3601.A26H66 2013
   813'.6—dc23

                                    2012051227

              10 9 8 7 6 5 4 3 2 1

                          RRD-C

         Printed in the United States of America

To the original crew of the Glorious Fool

PROLOGUE

You said *no*?" the girl shrieked, crushing the letter in her fist. "You didn't even think you should ask *me* first?"

Her father folded his arms over and fixed her with the look that used to make his soldiers tremble. "No. It was not your decision."

The girl threw the balled-up letter at him, bouncing it off his chest. "I can't believe you, Papa!" she shouted. "The best plasmex school in the galaxy invites me to be a student, and you ruined it! You don't even ask me what I think, you just said no like you get to talk for me!"

"I do talk for you, Yasmina," her father said calmly. "You are twelve, a child. Children should not go so far from home."

"I'll never go *anywhere*," Yasmina wailed. "I'll be stuck out here in the middle of nowhere *forever*!" She whirled around and ran through the farmhouse to her room. "I hate you!" she screamed.

"You will not speak to me like that!" her father yelled back, but it was too late. The girl had already slammed her door.

He took a step to follow, then stopped, running his hands through his thick, curling black hair, which seemed to be getting grayer by the day. He knew from experience that confronting her now would do nothing but make her angrier. That was natural; Yasmina was young. He was not. It was his responsibility to be calm, to do what was best. But that was cold comfort when he could hear his daughter crying.

The man sighed and sank onto the worn chair beside the picture window that looked out over the open fields that surrounded their sprawling house. Honestly, he didn't like being out here any more than she did. He'd never liked wide open spaces. There was too little cover, too many ways someone could sneak up on them, but he'd had no choice.

Yasmina was plasmex sensitive. It hadn't been so bad when she was young, but with her powers growing every year, they couldn't stay in the city with all its voices. So he'd quit his job with the Terran military and moved his family to the colonies, away from everything that could hurt her. The isolation had been bearable while his wife was alive. Now, things were...less easy. But with just the two of them, it was more important than ever that he keep his Yasmina safe and close at his side.

Something bumped gently against his shoe, and the man looked down to see the balled-up letter his daughter had thrown. He leaned over and picked it up, pressing the crumpled paper flat across his knee. The letter from the plasmex school informing them of Yasmina's acceptance was printed on heavy, old-fashioned paper. A ploy, he was sure, to convey an age and importance he'd seen no sign of when he'd looked the place up. He'd sent his reply on a far less prestigious droid relay, and despite Yasmina's tears, he felt no regret. So long as he breathed, his little girl was not going to a coed school on the other side of the galaxy.

He balled the letter up again, crushing the paper ruthlessly. He was getting up to toss it in the incinerator when he heard a knock on the door.

The man froze. He was not expecting anyone, and you didn't get accidental visitors this far out. More worrisome still, none of his proximity alarms had warned him someone was coming, and he'd bugged his farm very thoroughly. Whoever it was must have flown in, but he had not heard a ship land.

The knock sounded again, louder this time, and the man burst into action. He grabbed his army pistol off its rack above the fieldstone fireplace and loaded it with stun rounds from the box on the mantel. Then, hiding the gun behind his back, he opened the farmhouse's heavy door a crack to reveal two strangers, a woman and a girl.

The man paused. The woman was middle-aged and clearly elite military; no one else could make standing still look so dangerous. The girl was different, though. She couldn't have been more than sixteen, and she was far too thin, with dark brown hair cut flat just above her jutting shoulders, but what worried him even more than her thinness were her eyes. The girl's gaze was glassy and blank, like she was drugged, and the man tightened his grip on the pistol hidden behind his back. "Can I help—"

The words weren't out of his mouth before the woman grabbed him. Her strike was so fast he had no time to think, but he had been a solider himself for many years, and he didn't need to think. Even before her fingers tightened on his wrist, he was swinging his gun out to shoot the stranger in the leg, but as his gun came up, a second hand stopped him.

The grip was so hard, he thought it was the strange woman again, but one look proved him wrong. It was the girl. The strange, blank-faced girl had her thin hand wrapped around his wrist like a vise, and as her fingers dug in, a word spoke in his mind.

Sleep.

The command landed on him like a weight. All at once, he was falling, the gun clattering from his hand as he tumbled to the ground. A second before his shoulder hit the floorboards, he was out.

The man woke with a snort. He was sitting in his chair, staring out the dark window. He blinked groggily and wiped his hands over his face before glancing at the clock. Nearly nine; he must have fallen asleep.

The man stood up, stretching the soreness out of his limbs as he walked to the door. He had a vague feeling that someone had been there, but all was quiet and the bolt was set, just like normal. Shaking his head at old paranoia, the man glanced down the hall toward his daughter's room. It had been hours since their argument, but the sight of the shut door still stung.

With a deep, tired breath, the man set off down the hallway. He knew he was giving in, being soft, but Yasmina was the only one he had left. Fortunately, her light was still shining under her door, so he knocked softly. When she didn't answer, he leaned his head against the cool, painted wood.

"Yasmina," he said quietly. "I'm sorry. I know you feel isolated out here, but you have to understand, we did it to keep you safe. I should have asked you about the school before I turned them down, but I couldn't bear to let you go." His voice began to shake, and he started talking faster. "Now that Mama's gone, you're all I have left. If anything happened to you, I would pull the universe apart."

He stopped, holding his breath, but there was no sound from inside. Scowling, the man knocked again. "Yasmina?"

No answer. Suddenly furious, he reached down and threw open her door. "Yasmina! I know you're angry, but you *will* answer me when—"

He stopped cold. His daughter's room looked just like always—the floor too messy, the walls covered in pictures of places she wanted to go—but there was no one in it. The room was empty. Yasmina was gone.

That was all he saw before he tore back through the house and out into the night, screaming her name into the cold wind that blew across the empty fields.

———

Yasmina made herself as small as possible, hunching her shoulders and keeping her chained hands close against her back. The strange woman walked beside her, tugging her along. The other stranger, the large man in the dark suit, walked behind with the girl. That was good. The adults were scary, but their danger was understandable, like her father when he had his rifle out. The girl was different. Her glassy eyes and blank expression were terrifying in a way Yasmina could not explain. Sometimes it felt like there was nothing inside her at all. Like the strange, silent girl wasn't even human.

It had been two days since the strangers had taken her from the house. Since then, she'd been watched every moment, unable even to use the bathroom alone. The man and the woman treated her like a piece of luggage, refusing to tell her who they were or where they were taking her, and the glassy-eyed girl didn't seem to realize Yasmina existed. She just sat in her chair while they made one hyperspace jump after another, playing her chess game like it was the only thing that mattered in the universe.

By the time they arrived at a huge black space station, Yasmina had grown numb to her own terror. She hadn't even cried when they'd marched her into the hangar like a prisoner. Instead, she'd tried to keep her eyes on her surroundings, looking for some kind of marker, some clue she could use to let her father know where she was. But the station was a blank. There were no markings or logos on the walls, there wasn't even any directional signage. Just a maze of hallways that the strange man and woman navigated as if they'd lived here all their lives. The blank corridors were so bleak, Yasmina had given up hope completely by the time her jailers marched her through a heavy steel door into a large, windowless room that looked like a lab with other people in it. The first people besides her captors she'd seen since they took her from her father.

It was two men, both older, deep in conversation. One, a stern-looking man with a white beard and hair, was dressed like an officer in a military coat and boots, though he wore no insignia and she didn't recognize the uniform. Surprisingly, the other was dressed like a spacer in a worn leather flight vest, ship boots, and a heavy pistol in a leather holster at his hip.

Both men looked up when the door opened, and Yasmina seized

her chance. Since the spacer likely couldn't help, she threw herself at the man in the military coat. After the obedient trip from the ship, her guard was unprepared for the sudden movement, and she actually made it several feet before they caught her.

"Help me!" she cried to the officer as her guard wrestled her back into line. "My father's a very important man! He'll—"

Her words cut off as a gag slid over her mouth. Yasmina screamed in protest, but it did no good. The woman tied the gag tight before lifting Yasmina one-handed, tucking her under her arm like an unruly child. Yasmina screamed against the cloth in her mouth until her throat felt raw, kicking and fighting as hard as she had when they first took her. She even tried to use her plasmex, stabbing at the woman with all her strength, but her captor didn't even seem to notice. Tears of frustration poured down Yasmina's face. If only her father had let her go to school, she wouldn't be weak now. Wouldn't be here at all.

That thought made her cry even harder. "*Papa*," she sobbed against the gag. She'd seen him on the floor when they'd dragged her out. He'd fought for her, she knew, and they'd still gotten through. She'd always thought her papa was invincible. If these people could beat him, what hope did she have?

"You see what I was talking about?"

Yasmina swallowed her cries and looked up. The men who'd been talking when she'd been brought in were walking toward her now. As they approached, her guard saluted and set Yasmina back on her feet, though the woman's hands never left her shoulders. Yasmina knew from days of experience that the woman's iron grip was unbeatable, but she fought against it anyway, scowling up at the men, who were looking down at her with pity.

"She's unstable," the white-bearded man in the officer's coat said. "Rejects influence. They couldn't even sleep her on the way over." He glanced at the second man, the one dressed like a spacer, with a severe frown. "I know you're the expert here, Caldswell, but she'll just be trouble if you try to take her out into the field."

"That's fine," the man called Caldswell replied. "That's why I have the *Fool*, isn't it?"

"Oh yes," the officer said, looking back at Yasmina. "Your little experiment."

"Successful experiment," Caldswell corrected, though his voice wasn't smug. He was merely stating fact. "I've got the numbers to prove it. The crew environment keeps my daughters stable twice as long as the usual setup. Ren lasted almost five years this time. That's a record."

The man in the officer's coat did not look convinced, but Yasmina wasn't paying attention to him anymore, because Caldswell was standing in front of her now. He wasn't a particularly tall man, but he was broad and bulky, and his short, reddish brown hair was going silver at the temples, just like her father's. He was smiling at her as her father used to do, too. None of the others had done that, though his smile was so sad Yasmina wished he'd stop. She didn't want to know what was coming to make him look at her so sadly.

"Hello," he said softly. "I'm Brian Caldswell, and I'm sorry as hell this is happening to you. I'm sure you hate us right now, but you need to know that even though you didn't choose this, what you're doing makes you a hero." He reached out, squeezing her arm softly with his calloused hand. "Thank you. Thank you with all my heart. I swear I won't let your sacrifice be in vain."

The man in the officer's coat scowled as Caldswell finished. "I wish you'd stop doing that," he said coldly. "It's demoralizing for the others, and she won't remember."

"She still deserves to hear it," Caldswell said.

The officer's scowl deepened. "In all likelihood, she won't even make it. She's only a ninety-eight percent match. Maat ate a ninety-nine-percenter just yesterday."

That statement made Yasmina whimper against the gag, but Caldswell shook his head. "She'll make it," he said. "I have a good feeling about this one. Send her in and see."

The officer gave a long-suffering sigh and waved his hand. A second later, Yasmina was nearly taken off her feet as her guard yanked her by the shoulders and began to drag her toward a door on the opposite side of the room.

This door was smaller than the one they'd come in through, but it was heavily reinforced and covered with a thick, glowing shield, the kind banks used to cover vaults. As soon as she saw it, Yasmina began to fight harder than ever. After Caldswell's cryptic remarks, she wanted nothing to do with whatever was in that room, but as always, her struggles did nothing. The woman dragged her across the room like she was a tiny, unruly dog. The shield vanished when they reached it, and the heavy door slid up into the ceiling with a soft hiss to reveal what looked like a white closet. That was all Yasmina could make out before the guard yanked the gag off her mouth and shoved her inside.

She stumbled through the door, tripping on the frame. She caught herself on her hands just before she landed on her face, which was unexpected, since her wrists had been cuffed behind her not a second before. But the strange woman had removed those too, leaving Yasmina unrestrained for the first time since they'd grabbed her. There was no time to do anything with her freedom, though. Already, the heavy door was sliding back into place, sealing her into the white room.

Yasmina ran for it anyway, banging on the metal with her newly freed fists, but her hands barely made a sound. Defeated, she slid down the door, sobbing in great heaves. She wanted her papa, she wanted to go home. She'd never complain about living in the country ever again if only she could get out of here.

She was still crying five minutes later when she heard a soft rumbling. Her head shot up, looking for the next terror, but she couldn't see anything but white. She could feel the vibrations through the floor, though. *Something* was happening.

Yasmina got to her feet, keeping her back to the door. She was trying to figure out if the grinding sound was coming from the floor or the ceiling when it stopped. For one second, the white cell was silent, and then the wall directly across from the door she was cowering against slid up.

The sight was so odd, it took Yasmina several seconds to realize that the interlocking mess of metal joints on the other side was some kind of moveable platform. The rumbling she'd heard had been the huge metal machinery moving it into place. The metal itself was spotless and gleaming, clearly medical, which made sense, because at the center of it all was a person.

It looked like someone had set a hospital bed on its end so that the mattress was vertical. Likewise, the person lying on it was bound upright, held to the bed with so many restraints Yasmina couldn't even tell if it was male or female. The only part not covered by straps was the person's head, which was instead completely encased in a smooth metal mask.

The case covered the person's entire skull starting from the neck just above the shoulders. It had no features, no visor, not even an air vent. Just seeing it made Yasmina claustrophobic and terrified, but the terror was manageable until the blank metal face jerked up to look at her.

Yasmina screamed, her voice breaking in pure panic as she threw herself at the door, clawing at the smooth metal. "Let me out! *Let me out!*"

No one answered. Behind her, she heard the click of something unlocking, and then a crash as the metal mask fell to the hard plastic floor. The sound was so loud Yasmina almost turned on instinct but she caught herself just in time. She didn't want to know what was under that mask. Didn't want to see—

See what?

Yasmina stopped. The voice spoke softly, but she'd heard it clearly even over her panic, because the voice was in her head. At the same time, she felt something brush over her cheek, almost like a gentle hand.

Don't be afraid.

The voice was so soft, so sad and sincere that Yasmina stopped crying and turned. What she saw almost stopped her hammering heart. There, tied to the wall like a mummy, was the girl who'd brought her here. No, that wasn't right. This girl looked exactly like the other one—same delicate features, same olive skin, same dark hair cut straight right above the shoulders—but where the girl on the ship had looked empty, this girl looked full to bursting.

"Who are you?" Yasmina asked, her voice quivering.

The bound girl gave her a sad look. *Poor little rabbit, I'm your death.*

The words were so matter-of-fact, it took Yasmina several seconds to understand what the girl meant. Once she got it, though, she pressed herself so flat against the door she could barely breathe. The bound girl just gave her a pitying look. *Here it comes.*

Yasmina craned her neck, looking every direction, but there was no one in the room but the two of them. Then she caught the sound of something whining somewhere beyond the walls. It was a building pitch, like some huge piece of machinery was charging up. "What's that?" she cried, looking back at the girl as the whining got louder and louder, higher and higher. "Stop it!"

The girl began to laugh, a horrible, mad sound that turned Yasmina's bones to water. *I can't.* Her mouth split into a wide grin, and Yasmina recoiled in terror. In her entire life, including the horrors of the last two days, she had never seen anything as awful as that insane, hopeless smile. *See you on the other side.*

As Yasmina opened her mouth to scream, the whining pitch reached its highest octave. For one painful second, the room was filled with a piercing shriek, like an alarm going off right by her ear, and then all sound stopped as the bound girl began to seize.

She writhed against her restraints, her mouth moving in huge screams, but nothing came out, not even a gasp. Her face was contorted in horrible pain, her brown eyes bulging, and despite her own terror, Yasmina felt a sudden wave of pity. Before she realized what she was doing, she began to move forward, reaching out automatically to help the suffering girl a few feet away.

She'd only made it a step when the hand landed on her spine.

It was the most peculiar sensation, like the invisible touch that had stroked her cheek just a few moments before was now reaching through her skin to grab hold of her vertebrae. For five seconds, Yasmina stood frozen as her mind tried to make sense of the feeling of fingers touching parts of her that had never been touched. Then, like a hand running up a pole, the fingers on her spine slid up her neck to wrap around her brain.

Across the room, the bound girl's convulsions stopped, but Yasmina didn't notice. Her whole world had shrunk to the fingers closing around her brain. And as Yasmina's scream finally broke the silence, the hand began to squeeze.

Brian Caldswell stood inches away from the reinforced door of the conversion chamber, listening. The girl had been in there for a little over an hour. The rules said he couldn't go in to check until the full exposure period had elapsed, but things weren't looking good. In his experience, if it wasn't over by the hour mark, the girl wasn't coming out. He was about to call Commander Martin back in to discuss the next girl on the docket when the door alarm went off.

His hand shot out, punching the button that would close the panel inside. Through the heavy metal, he heard Maat's sobbing cut off as the drugs kicked in, forcing her back into sleep. Crying was a good sign. Maat usually laughed when they died.

Behind him, the two Eyes who'd brought the girl in were restless, watching him for clues. Caldswell ignored them, focusing on the reinforced door until, at last, it opened.

The girl standing in the doorway looked nothing like the girl who had gone in an hour ago. The twelve-year-old the Eyes had dragged off the ship had been brown skinned and tall for her age with wavy, thick dark hair that tangled around her face. The girl who stood before him now was a good six inches shorter with olive skin, straight black hair cut above the shoulders, and calm, empty brown eyes, just like every other daughter of Maat.

11

Caldswell reached out at once, grabbing her hand. With newly imprinted daughters, you had to act fast to ensure obedience. But despite Commander Martin's worries that she'd be trouble, the new daughter accepted his grip meekly, letting him pull her forward until they were standing right in front of each other. When she was in position, Caldswell bent down until he was staring straight into her empty eyes.

"My name is Brian Caldswell," he said firmly. "You are my daughter, Ren Caldswell. Say hello."

"Hello," the girl whispered, her voice little more than air.

Caldswell nodded, adding his other hand so that her thin palm was sandwiched between his fingers. "We're going to do bitter work, Ren," he said softly. "But I'll be with you the whole way. I'll care for you until the end, and when it comes, I'll do it myself. I promise."

The girl didn't answer, but they never did. Caldswell let her go with a sigh and turned around, waving for her to follow as he walked out of the room. Ren obeyed silently, her brown eyes watching nothing as she trailed him through Dark Star Station's blank tunnels to the dock where the little shuttle was waiting to take them back to the *Glorious Fool*.

Behind them, buried beneath the most sophisticated security system in the universe, bound by restraints strong enough to stop enraged symbionts, Maat's silent sobs went on and on and on.

CHAPTER

1

Three years later, present day.

If you asked me how I came to be standing in a baking desert on a half-made Terran colony world trying not to get emotional while I buried a skullhead, I'd be hard-pressed to tell you.

I'd be hard-pressed to tell you a lot of things, actually. Like how I'd broken both my arms, or what had given me the huge gut wound Hyrek had only just okayed me to move around on. I didn't know who had attacked our ship on this rock in the middle of nowhere or why they'd done it. I couldn't even say for certain how I'd ended up outside my armor to get the blow on the head that was the cause of all this not knowing. Still, things could have been worse. After all, I was the one doing the grave digging instead of the grave filling. I bet Cotter would have switched places with me in a heartbeat, though he would have bitched about having to use a borrowed pickax. Skullheads could bitch about anything.

But though I knew I was lucky to be alive, all I could think about as I stood out there in the blazing sun and the gritty wind, pounding a hole into the rocky yellow ground, was that this wasn't right. Skullhead or not, Cotter's ruined armor and empty gun showed that he'd gone down like a Paradoxian should, defying his enemy to the very last. He deserved more than an unmarked grave in the middle of nowhere dug by a girl who couldn't remember.

Unfortunately, an unmarked grave was all I had to offer him, and I'd had to fight just to get that much. Caldswell was chomping at the bit to get off-world. If it had been up to him, we'd have been in space two days ago. The only reason we weren't was because the *Fool* was so banged up it had taken Mabel two days just to get us spaceworthy. That delay was how I'd found out the captain had made arrangements to leave Cotter's body with the terraforming office for disposal like a piece of trash.

Needless to say, I blew up at him so hard I almost reopened my wound. The captain didn't usually pay much attention to my opinions, but he must not have wanted to be down two security guards, because he caved in the end. Ten minutes later, I'd walked into the desert with a borrowed pickax on one shoulder and Cotter slung over the other. I found a good spot with a nice view in minutes, but digging the actual grave took longer than it should have. My pickax wasn't made for armor, and Cotter was a big man. By the time I'd made a hole large enough to fit him, I was thirty minutes past Caldswell's time limit.

Not that I cared. I'm no priest, but I've been in armored combat for nine years. I've buried a lot of partners, and I consider it my business to do a proper job. I took my time getting Cotter's grave arranged just right, using my suit's star map to make sure his feet faced Paradox so he would be ready to stand when the king called and tapping a double measure of salt into each of his hands, a tip for the death guide who would ferry Cotter's soul to the warrior's gate of heaven. Finally, I covered him in a white sheet and reached up to the grave's edge to grab the bottle of whiskey I'd snatched from the kitchen on my way out.

I unscrewed the cap and raised my visor, drinking quick before too much of Falcon 34's thin, hot, dusty air could get into my suit. The dry heat was already evaporating the whiskey in the bottle, but I didn't rush as I poured the remaining liquor up and down Cotter's sheet-covered body while I spoke the ancient prayer that would commit his bones to the dirt. I actually teared up a bit when I got to the part about soft green hills and flowing water, but I kept it together by reminding myself that when the terraforming was eventually completed, Falcon 34 would probably have those, and the last words I spoke to Cotter wouldn't be a lie.

When all the whiskey was gone, I set the empty bottle at his feet and climbed out of the grave. The broken-up rocks and dirt went in much faster than they'd come out, forming a tall mound over my dead partner. He'd have liked that, I thought. A big grave for a big man. When the last of the dirt was back in, I weighed the mound down with small boulders so the wind wouldn't undo my work and headed back to the ship.

Caldswell's *Fool* had never been an impressive piece of machinery, but it was looking especially pathetic now. Whoever had attacked us had done a bang-up job. The *Fool's* nose was blown almost clean off, damaging the bridge beyond repair. Another even larger blast had taken out the side of the cargo bay, slagging the new door we'd just put in plus several inches of hull. Mabel had covered the holes as best she could, overlapping the plasma patches until the ship looked like a pearly white mud wasp nest, but no amount of layering changed the fact that we would be going into space with hardened plasma where metal should be.

Bad as the outside of the ship was, though, the interior was worse, even by the *Fool's* normal bullets-in-the-walls standard. The upper hallway was black with blast shadows from grenades, and the floor had so many shots lodged in it that I could feel the bullets under my boots like pebbles. The lounge took the prize, though, with its huge dents and the terrifying man-sized hole that had been ripped through the blast door. I didn't even know what could do something like that, though I should have since it was my blood that had been smeared over on the battered floor. Whatever had happened here, I'd seen it, but I couldn't remember a damn thing, and since there was no footage, I wasn't going to be getting any hints.

You'd think on a ship with so many cameras there would be something, but the explosion that had taken out the bridge had fried all the feeds, and my own cameras hadn't done any better.

Whatever had happened during that fight that had gotten me out of my armor had also erased my footage. All of it. Even my Final Word Lock and Mercenary's Bargain had been wiped clean, which was blatantly impossible unless I'd colluded with the enemy for some reason, which was a possibility I wasn't willing to consider.

Just thinking about the fight that had taken all my memories and nearly taken my life put me in a terrible mood, so it was good that I didn't have time to brood. I was forty-five minutes later than I'd promised, and the captain must have been waiting with his hand on the launch button, because the thrusters fired the moment I was inside. I barely had time to get to the safety handles in the cargo bay before we launched into the air and away from Falcon 34. Forever, with any luck.

With the bridge unusable, the captain, Nova, and Basil were reduced to flying the ship from the engine room. It was a horribly cramped setup, so rather than call me in and squish things further, the captain came out to the cargo bay as soon as we entered orbit. "Took your sweet time, Morris."

Since I was safely hidden behind my visor, I rolled my eyes. Good old Caldswell, always sensitive. "I did it right, sir."

The captain nodded, looking me up and down. "You good to go back to work?"

"Yes sir." Hyrek hadn't officially cleared me yet, but if I was fit enough to dig graves, I was fit enough to walk in circles.

"We've got a three-day flight to the jump gate," Caldswell warned. "Might be a little rough."

I shrugged. "What else is new?"

The captain actually laughed at that. "Make yourself useful, then. We've got a long night ahead of us."

"Yes sir," I said, jogging to help Mabel, who was already getting the patcher fired up to repair the bits of the ship that had shaken loose during takeoff.

In hindsight, I shouldn't have been so flippant. I'd done hell shifts before, so I thought I knew what I was in for, but nothing could have prepared me for what I'd later come to remember as the worst three days of my life.

It started with the patches. Hardened plasma is meant to fill small holes temporarily, not to be a replacement for a hull. We'd barely cleared Falcon 34's orbit before the plasma shell that kept us spaceworthy started cracking. Since I was the only one strong enough to haul around the patcher, I was the one who ended up following Mabel around the ship like a talking, walking equipment cart. Under better circumstances, this would have been beneath my dignity, but I was too busy trying not to panic over the cracks growing in the brittle layer of hardened gunk that was the only thing separating us from certain death to fret much over my image.

Cracks weren't our only problem, either. Patched as we were, any idiot with a density scanner could see that the *Fool* was heavily damaged, and a damaged freighter is to pirates what a wounded seal is to sharks. It wouldn't be so bad if we were flying through more civilized space, but the Falcon Sector wasn't even half terraformed yet. Other than building a jump gate to haul in supplies, the corps developing this sector hadn't done a thing except bring in a bunch of expensive machinery to an undeveloped, undefended area. I couldn't have invented a better hunting ground for pirates if I'd tried, and we were flying right through the middle of it in a busted trade ship with only one working gun and a single security officer. The situation was so ridiculously bad it could have been the punch line of a joke, and if I hadn't been the one getting punched, I probably would have laughed myself sick.

Between maintaining the patches and keeping an eye out for trouble, I didn't catch more than forty-five minutes of sleep altogether in the three days it took us to reach the gate. My only comfort was that I wasn't suffering alone.

I'd never actually appreciated the work it took to be the engineer on an old junker like the *Fool* until I started following Mabel around. Caldswell's sister-in-law was everywhere at once, applying patches, keeping the engines going, crawling up into the maintenance tunnels with the dexterity of a monkey half her age. Even more impressive was how she stayed cheerful about it. While I was ready to bite off heads by hour two, Mabel never once complained. She just worked, keeping a hundred technical problems in her head so effortlessly I finally broke down and asked.

"Why are you here?"

Mabel looked down at me from where she was perched on a broken beam, spraying down a tangle of blown-out lines that had once gone to the bridge. "Because these wires can't take the exposure," she replied. "The cold will—"

"Not *here*," I clarified. "Why are you on this ship? I understand the captain's your family, but there's got to be something better. You're a good engineer, you could get work anywhere. Why stay on this rust bucket?"

"I've had offers," Mabel said cheerily. "But there's nothing to do on a shiny new ship. Besides, I'm too old to move on. Brian and I have been together for a long time. He's a good captain and a good man who tries hard to do the right thing. It's an honor to serve under him."

I scowled. I had the funniest feeling someone had said that to me before.

"Anyway," Mabel went on, finishing the patch before dropping down beside me. "You'd all die stranded in deep space without me. Now come on, the seal over the engine should be starting to crack right about…." She pulled out her battered handset. "Now."

The word had barely crossed her lips before the hull breach alarm started blaring. I jumped at the sound, but Mabel just grinned and started for the stairs, leaving me no choice but to pick up the patcher and stumble after her.

———

And so it went. The state of constant panic kept my exhaustion at bay for the most part, but whenever I slowed down, the tiredness would kick back in with a vengeance. Still, I was holding together pretty well all things considered, but then, just when I thought I'd found my stride at last, the cook reappeared.

I hadn't seen him since right after I woke up from the attack. Frankly, I was shocked that he was still on board. Considering how the captain had been glaring at him when I saw him last, I wouldn't have been surprised if Cotter's hadn't been the only unmarked grave left in the Falcon 34 desert. But the cook must have only been confined to quarters, because when I came up to scrounge for food while Mabel was refilling the patcher solution, there he was, working in the kitchen like he'd never left.

I was so surprised I actually turned to look at him head-on. Bad decision. The moment my eyes met his, the revulsion hit me so hard I staggered.

It was just as strong now as it had been that first time in the medbay after I'd woken up, an intense mix of nausea, disgust, and revulsion, like realizing your food is rotten only after you've taken a bite. I had no more idea now what caused it than I'd had the first time, but whatever was wrong with me, it clearly wasn't getting better. Anytime I caught so much as a glimpse of the cook, the sickness would hit me like a sucker punch, which was a real bitch when you considered how many times I had to walk through the lounge in a day.

In the end, I just learned not to look. But though I was making a point not to watch him, the cook was constantly watching me. He never leered or did anything I could call him out for, but every time I caught a glimpse of him by accident, he was looking back. I would have confronted him anyway, but there's no law against looking at someone, and he hadn't said anything untoward. He hadn't spoken to me at all.

That actually bugged me more than the staring. The *Fool* wasn't a big enough ship that you could give your crewmates the silent treatment. I didn't know what I'd done to tick the cook off. I couldn't even remember the man's name, actually, and soon I was too tired to care. After seventy-two hours of near panic and constant work, I barely had the brain left to be happy we'd made it to the Falcon Sector hyperspace gate without dying.

Nova and I were helping Mabel redo all the patches one last time before the jump to hyperspace when the captain's voice sounded over the ship's com, ordering me to his quarters. It's a sign of how exhausted I was that the unexpected summons didn't even unnerve me. I just left the patcher chugging and went down to see what he wanted.

I couldn't remember going into the captain's rooms before, but my tiredness must have been playing tricks on me, because I had the strangest sense of déjà vu when I stepped through the door. The captain's quarters were divided into two bedrooms, a private bathroom, and a sitting area dominated by a large window that looked out the front of the ship. He was sitting there now, leaning on the little table with a tired look on his face.

I stopped just inside the door and stood at attention, locking my suit to be sure I wouldn't wobble. "You wanted to see me, sir?"

"Yes," the captain said. "I wanted to thank you for stepping up these last few days."

I blinked. I couldn't actually remember the last time an officer had thanked me. I especially hadn't expected it of Caldswell.

"You don't have to look so surprised," Caldswell said with a sigh. "I like to think I'm a fair man, Morris. You've been doing the work of five mercs in dangerous territory without complaint. I could hardly let that go without thanks, or compensation."

"Compensation?" The word popped out before I could stop it, and Caldswell shot me a wry smile.

"I've already transferred a week's double pay into your account," he said. "I'm also willing to foot the bill on a new blade to replace the one you lost. Just let me know when you find something you like and I'll buy it for you, within reason. Think of it as a bonus for pushing through hard times."

I stared at him wide-eyed. I had no idea why the captain was suddenly being so nice to me, but I wasn't going to jinx it by asking questions. I needed to replace Phoebe badly, but I'd drained all my cash repairing the Lady after that nasty business on the xith'cal ghost ship. Thinking back, I couldn't actually recall how I'd lost my blade. The whole tribe ship mess was a blur, which was strange considering I'd been under the hyperfocus of the battle drugs. I thought about it a moment before I decided I was just too tired to care. My blade was gone, and if Caldswell was willing to pony up for a new one, I certainly wasn't going to turn him down.

"Thank you sir," I said at last. "I'll be getting a new blade as soon as possible then."

"You'll have a chance after we jump," the captain said. "With the ship this damaged, I can't take a risk on some colony repair bay. We're headed to Wuxia. It's not Paradox, I know, but you should be able to find something suitable."

That was an understatement. Wuxia was a Terran Republic core world and one of the biggest trade centers in the universe. If I couldn't find a replacement for Phoebe there, it didn't exist. "Thank you sir," I said again.

Caldswell nodded and turned back to the window. I waited a moment to see if he would dismiss me, but he said nothing. I was about to ask if that was all when he suddenly spoke again.

"Have any of your memories come back?"

"No sir." Hyrek had assured me that my memories would come back in time, but the blank spot in my head was just as empty now as it had been when I'd first woken up in the medbay. Of course, considering the hours I'd been pulling, I was surprised I remembered my name. The captain didn't seem troubled at my answer, though. He just nodded again and told me to get some sleep.

I bowed out of habit and left, stumbling up the stairs to my bunk as Basil's whistling voice came over the com to start the jump countdown.

We entered hyperspace with barely a bump, but we could have crashed into the gate and I don't think I'd have noticed. I was so tired I felt almost feverish, and I fell onto my bunk face-first, diving into my pillow without even saying hello to Nova, who'd come in behind me. I was asleep the second I was flat, and I didn't move again until the alarm sounded to signal our arrival at Wuxia.

Wuxia was deeper into the Terran Republic than I'd ever been. My work in the Blackbirds only took me to the lawless fringes, and now that the war was over, the Paradoxian army never entered Terran space. As such, I'd never set foot on a Republic core world before, but I'd heard a ton about them, especially Wuxia. It was supposed to be one of the oldest human colonies, founded by early jumpers from Old Earth back before the ancient human homeworld had collapsed. After all that buildup, I was expecting something majestic and historic. Something impressive. What I got was a lot of smog.

I couldn't even see the ground as the *Fool* entered the atmosphere, just black clouds and the glow of lights below. The view wasn't much better after we broke through the cloud cover. Being such an old colony, the vast majority of Wuxia's landmass was covered in city. That normally wouldn't have bothered me, but I was used to big, beautiful cities like Kingston. Wuxia just looked decrepit, crowded, and filthy.

The industrial grime was so thick it tinted the air brown, and the buildings, even the newer-looking skyscrapers, were coated in a greasy film. We'd set down on the daylight side of the planet, but thanks to the heavy clouds you couldn't actually tell that from the ground. Between the smog and the huge buildings, the sun didn't have a chance, though it was still plenty bright. Massive projected signs shone in the sky, blanketing the heavy clouds in a wash of glowing advertisements that shed their neon light onto the buzzing city in the sun's stead.

I went outside just long enough to look in a full circle before going back into the ship. I've never cared for Terran cities at my most charitable, and a minute outside on Wuxia had almost been enough to choke my suit's air filter. That, plus the huge traffic jams I could see on the public skyways even at this distance, told me this was no place for sensible people. Hell, it was probably no place for Terrans.

Because of the Terran Republic's draconian armor regulations, I could only legally wear my suit while I was on Caldswell's ship. Since I wasn't planning on going anywhere, that suited me fine, but the Terran work crews who showed up to fix the ship shortly after we landed seemed unnerved to have a Paradoxian in full armor watching them. That suited me fine as well. The war might be over, but scaring Terrans witless is one of life's little joys. These were core worlders, too. Most of them had never even seen a Paradoxian in armor outside of the movies. All I had to do was click Sasha's safety and the whole lot of them would jump like startled rabbits. Quality entertainment at its finest.

Unfortunately, Caldswell, being Terran himself, didn't see it that way. The crews had barely started pulling down Mable's patches before he banished me to my bunk to pick out a replacement for my lost thermite blade. Any other time I would have complained about being sent to my room like a surly teenager, but after the three days of hell I'd put in to get us here, I was more than happy to lie in bed with cold beer and a year's worth of weapons catalogs while someone else worked.

"I'm thinking something that attaches to my armor this time," I said, flipping through the interactive sales display I'd pulled up on my com. "I don't want to lose another blade."

"That sounds wise," Nova replied. My bunkmate was also off duty since there's nothing for a sensors officer to do when the ship's not in the air, but while I was whiling away the time looking at sharp things, she was on the floor digging through drawers filled with her incredibly bright clothing. Finally she pulled out a pretty but completely over-the-top dress spangled with so many metallic gold stars you couldn't see the fabric between them and held it up for me to see.

"Nice," I said.

Nova beamed and started pulling the dress over her head. "Will your new blade light up like your old one?"

"Of course," I said, taking a swig off my beer. "The burning thermite edge is the only way you can get through ballistic plates with a slicing weapon. But I'm thinking of getting something that utilizes my suit more."

Useful as Phoebe's replaceable blades and long reach had been, I was seriously considering a stabbing weapon this time. Something I could throw the Lady's weight and power behind. I was trying to think of a way to explain this to Nova without sounding too bloodthirsty when she pulled out a small mirror and started brushing a thick coat of sparkly silver across her eyelids. That caught me. The star-covered dress was nothing out of the ordinary, but I'd never seen Nova use makeup before.

"So," I said casually, tossing my com on the pillow and rolling onto my side with a grin. "What's the occasion?"

Nova flashed me a huge, excited smile in the mirror. "My brother is on planet! I'm meeting him for dinner."

My face fell. I'd been hoping for something more exciting than a brother. Still, considering how little Caldswell's crew seemed to get out, dinner with your brother was probably a pretty big event on Nova's calendar.

"I haven't seen Copernicus for almost a year," she continued, catching her short, wispy blond hair back with a glittery silver headband. "I write to him every time we land, but I never expected he'd be on Wuxia at the same time as we are. What a perfect alignment!"

"Cheers to you," I said, tipping my beer at her. "I hope that you have a great time."

Nova flashed me a shy smile. "I would be delighted if you would share space with us in harmony as well, Deviana."

It took me a few moments to realize that was Nova-speak for inviting me along. "Thanks for the offer," I said. "But I'd better stick to the ship, and I don't want to go out in that smog again. I think it might be toxic."

"Almost certainly," Nova agreed, adjusting her hair. "Nic promised me we'd go somewhere above the particulate layers."

I frowned. "Nic?"

"Short for Copernicus," Nova explained. "Just like I'm Nova instead of Novascape."

I nodded absently, trying to remember where I'd met a Nic before. Nothing came to mind, but I couldn't shake the nagging feeling that there was something I was supposed to remember. But the harder I tried, the farther the memory ran until I was forced to give up.

"Are you certain you don't wish to come?" Nova asked again, smoothing out her star-spangled dress one last time. "Basil's coming."

If I'd been on the fence, that would have knocked me right off. The last thing I wanted to do was go anywhere on this crowded, dirty world with a picky bird. "Thanks again," I said. "But I'll pass."

Nova's face fell, which made me feel like a jerk. Before I could tell her I was sorry, though, she said, "Maybe I should ask Mr. Charkov?"

I frowned. "Who?"

Nova blinked at me. "Rupert Charkov? The cook?"

"Is that his name?" I said, trying to remember.

Nova stared at me in confusion for a moment, then looked away, her pale cheeks going red. "I'm sorry," she said. "I just thought that you and he were..." She trailed off, going redder still before she turned away and started brushing her hair frantically. "Never mind. It's just, his aura has been even dimmer than usual, and I assumed, well, never mind."

She was talking so fast by the end that the words were running together. I had no idea what she was on about. If the cook's aura was dim, it couldn't be my fault. Other than his seeming inability to keep his eyes to himself, there was less than nothing between me and—

I stopped. Even though Nova had just told me, I couldn't remember the cook's name. It had just slipped through my mind. That was strange; I wasn't usually forgetful about stuff like this. What was his name? I was about to ask Nova to repeat it when Basil squawked from the hallway that they were going to be late.

Nova darted out the door, yelling over her shoulder for me to have a good evening. I didn't feel comfortable with the ship full of strangers, so I got up too, following her into the lounge where Basil was waiting. This dinner must have been quite the thing, because our aeon navigator was dressed up as well. I'd never seen Basil wear anything over his feathers, but tonight he had some kind of black silk cape thing tied over his back and wings. The little square of black cloth on the back of an alien who looked like a giant ostrich was so stupid looking I forgot all about the cook in my struggle not to burst out laughing.

"Is something funny, Morris?" Basil snapped, swiveling his long neck down to put his sharp yellow beak right in my face.

"No sir," I said, trying not to choke. "I was just admiring your cape."

Basil rolled his huge yellow eyes. "It's a mark of *respect*. I'm not about to embarrass myself going out without my black on Remembrance Day."

"What day?"

Basil's beak fell open. "You've worked in the Terran Republic for how many years and you don't know about Remembrance Day?"

"Do I look Terran to you?" I asked, crossing my arms. "The Blackbirds took Republic jobs, but we're a Paradoxian outfit. We celebrated the five high holy days and King Stephen's birthday. Besides, Terrans have like ten thousand holidays. You can't expect me to keep up with all of them."

"There are a lot," Nova admitted. "But Remembrance Day is special. Unlike the regional celebrations, Remembrance Day is one of the thirty-seven mandated holidays celebrated on every planet in the Republic."

I shook my head. Mandated holidays. How Terran. "What are they remembering anyway?" Because if it was some giant defeat at the hands of the Paradoxian army, I was having another beer to celebrate.

"The destruction of Svenya," Basil said, his whistling voice taking on what he probably meant to be a somber tone. "It was a colony world even older and bigger than Wuxia, but sixty-some-odd years ago its orbit spontaneously destabilized and the planet broke apart."

Now that Basil mentioned it, I dimly remembered hearing about the tragedy of Svenya back in school, usually as an example of what happened to those who did not have a living saint to rule them. "Didn't some absurd number of people die?"

"Billions," Nova said sadly. "Scientists still haven't figured out exactly what went wrong, but the holiday makes sure Svenya is never forgotten." Her face fell as she looked down at her sparkling star dress. "Maybe I should go change."

"No way," I said. "I'm sure the ghosts of Sven-whatever won't mind you looking cheerful. Now get out of here." I nodded at the open cargo bay. "You're letting in the dirt."

Nova and Basil hurried down the ramp to their waiting cab. I watched them drive off until the bright blue vehicle disappeared between the hundreds of parked freighters sharing our tiered dock, and then I went back inside to continue the serious work of picking out which new blade I'd be making Caldswell pay for.

———

The repairs to the *Fool* went on all night and into the morning. The captain and Mabel took shifts supervising, and when Nova and Basil got back from dinner, Caldswell pressed them into service setting up the new equipment being loaded into the bridge. Hyrek, of course, stayed in his room. There was nothing for the xith'cal doctor to do, and his presence would only terrify the work crews. I was banished for the same reason, but unlike certain lizards, I can't sit around reading all day. I'd found and ordered my new weapon the night before, and now that I didn't have blade shopping to keep me busy, I was getting bored.

A bored Paradoxian is a dangerous thing. Caldswell knew it, too, and the moment I came out of my room, he'd put me in charge of picking Cotter's replacement. I'd never had a hiring position before, and I was so thrilled at the promotion that I said yes before the captain had finished speaking.

An hour later I'd rewritten Caldswell's grossly inadequate job requirements and put a new ad up on every employment listing I could find with instructions for applicants to send their résumé. The résumé requirement was a risky move since we were leaving tomorrow, but there was no way in hell I was doing a cattle call like Caldswell had used to find Cotter and me. After all, the person I picked would be the one guarding my back. This contract with Caldswell was my ticket to becoming a Devastator, and I'd be damned if I died because I wasn't willing to take the effort to find a partner who could do the job properly.

If the résumé requirement cut into my replies, though, I couldn't tell. Not four hours after I posted the position, I had fifty applications waiting on my com. I rejected most out of hand, but by evening I had a nice pile of potentials. All I needed now was the captain's approval and I could start calling people back, so I hopped out of bed, threw on a long T-shirt over my shorts and tank top so the Terran work crews wouldn't leer, and headed out to find him.

I'd thought Caldswell would be overseeing the work on the bridge, but Mabel was the only one up there when I stuck my head in. The captain wasn't in the lounge either, or the cargo bay. That left his cabin, so I started down the spiral staircase to the lower hallway where the captain kept his rooms. I'd just made it to the second spiral when I heard someone say my name.

The sound stopped me cold. I didn't recognize the voice, but it was masculine, softly accented, and clearly angry. The anger wasn't what stopped me, though. I couldn't actually say what had done it, but something about hearing my name in that soft accent hit me like a shot. But while I was trying to recover, the man was still speaking.

"...can't stay here," he said. "Send her back to Paradox. Leave her on Wuxia if you have to, just get her away."

And with that, shock was replaced by rage. There was only one Paradoxian left on this rig, and that accented idiot was trying to get me kicked off. Applicants forgotten, I dropped into a crouch and peered through the gap in the metal stairs to see who the voice belonged to, though I had a pretty good idea already. Sure enough, the cook was standing at the far end of the hall, talking to the captain.

The cook's back was to me, so I was able to drop my eyes before the revulsion kicked in, but nothing could stop my fury. I don't take well to people bad-mouthing me behind my back to my superiors as a general rule, but after all I'd gone through for this job, the thought of being undermined by a damned potato peeler made me see red. I was one step away from charging down the stairs and laying the cook out for his trouble when Caldswell came to my defense.

"No," the captain said. "She stays and that's the end of it."

"I didn't risk everything so you could keep her here."

Angry as I was, the cold fury in the cook's voice made me flinch. He sounded as ready to kill as I was. Fortunately, Caldswell wasn't taking that shit.

"Then you should have thought about that before you disobeyed orders and put me in this position," the captain said. "You made this mess, you live with it. She stays until I say otherwise, and I don't want to hear a damn peep out of you. Is that understood, soldier?"

The hall went silent. So much so that I thought the cook must have turned tail and run. But then he whispered, "Yes sir."

That sounded like the end of things to me, but Caldswell went on. "I've heard back from command," he said. "Your punishment has been set."

My ears perked up. Punishment for what? And what did Caldswell mean by command? Wasn't he an independent trader? I held my breath, waiting for the cook to give me a clue, but all the horrid man would say was, "Yes sir."

The reply was barely out before I heard Caldswell stomp back into his cabin, leaving the cook alone in the hall. Back on the steps, I stood up silently. Considering I hadn't been a part of it, that exchange had gone remarkably well for me. The captain was clearly on my side, and the cook was going to be punished. For what, I didn't know, but unless it was for talking about crewmates behind their backs, my job wasn't over. I'd been a merc long enough now to know that this sort of thing needed to be nipped in the bud, and since I was headed for the captain's room anyway, now seemed like as good a time as any.

With that, I squared my shoulders and started down the stairs again. I hadn't heard the cook move or the door to his cabin open, so I was pretty sure he was still standing where the captain had left him. You can imagine my surprise, then, when I rounded the final spiral and nearly ran right into his chest.

He was standing at the bottom of the stairs with his head down and his shoulders slumped. Seeing how he'd just gotten chewed out by his captain, I hadn't expected him to be cheerful, but this was different. The cook didn't look upset, he looked devastated, like a gambler who's lost everything and has only just begun to realize it, and for a tiny moment, my heart went out to him. Fortunately, it was a fleeting madness, because as soon as he looked up, the revulsion hit me like a tank.

For one terrible second, I thought I was going to get sick right there and ruin everything. I had a point to make, though, so I swallowed my nausea and forced myself to keep looking. That was how I caught the strange desperation on the cook's face before his expression smoothed over into a calm, polite smile so bland and sudden it was like he'd put on a mask.

Once he'd recovered from my sudden appearance, the cook stepped aside to let me pass. When I didn't move, he asked in a cool, polite voice, "Is something wrong?"

"You could say that," I drawled, resting my hands on my hips. Now, you might think it's hard to look intimidating when you're dressed in a ratty T-shirt, barefoot, and unarmed facing down a man who has a good ten inches on you, but that's bullshit. Intimidation is all about attitude. All you have to do is let just how much you'd love to kick the other guy's ass show on your face and even the biggest skullheads will start backing down. The cook must have been a little dense, though, because he didn't even flinch. Apparently, I'd have to spell it out for him.

"You have a problem with me, you say it to my face," I said, keeping my voice nice and deadly. "I catch you bad-mouthing me behind my back to the captain again, and I'll make sure that whatever punishment he has planned for you seems like a day at the beach by comparison."

To his credit, the cook didn't try to deny what he'd done, though his voice did get colder. "I meant no offense," he said crisply. "It won't happen again."

"You're right it won't," I promised him. "Because if it does, it'll be the last thing you ever do."

His shoulders tensed, and I braced, ready to take him, but the cook didn't swing for me. He didn't turn and walk away either. He just stood there, staring at my face like he was trying to memorize it.

"Stop that," I snarled. "I am so *sick* of you staring at me. You want to ogle someone, find a dock girl, but I catch you looking at me one more time and I'm throwing you out an air lock."

It was a stupid threat to make since we both knew I couldn't make good on it, but the cook didn't call my bluff. He just looked away, his blue eyes falling as he slipped past me. "My apologies, Miss Morris. I won't bother you again."

It might have been my imagination, but that last sentence had sounded almost sad, and that pissed me off even more. Why the hell was he sad about this shit? He'd started it. But even as the thought crossed my mind, I realized I felt sad, too. Sad and guilty, like I'd just done something cruel.

I clenched my fists and stomped down the final stair to the hall. What the hell was wrong with me? What did I care if I hurt someone who never talked to me but thought he could go around behind my back and bad-mouth me to my officer?

I glanced over my shoulder, but the cook was already gone, vanished up the stairs without a sound. *Good riddance*, I thought, jogging the final few feet to the captain's bunk. I didn't need that shit anyway.

I shook my head and raised my fist to knock on Caldswell's door, but as my hand came up, I saw there was something on my fingers. The tips were stained black, like I'd dragged them across something sooty. Cursing this filthy hole of a planet, I wiped my hand on my T-shirt, thankful that I'd picked a black one, but the dirt didn't come off. I scrubbed again, harder this time, but all that did was make my fingers feel funny. All pins and needles, almost like they were asleep.

I gave up after that. I disliked looking unkempt in front of an officer, but I was already all the way down here, and the captain wasn't going to mind a little bit of dirt. Still, once I was done knocking, I moved my hands out of sight when the door opened and Caldswell stuck his head out.

"Morris?"

"Sir," I said, standing at attention. "I have the first candidates for you to look at."

The captain's look brightened at once. "Let me see."

I'd already sent the applications to his com, so we stood together in his door while he looked them over. In the end, he approved the whole lot, and I left to make my callbacks feeling infinitely better than when I'd arrived. There was no way the cook was going to poison the captain against me now, not that he'd had any luck before. Asshole.

It might have been childish, but that thought made me grin as I jogged back upstairs to wash the gunk off my hands. By the time I reached the bathroom, though, the black stuff was gone. I stared at my clean fingers in confusion for a moment, then I shrugged and headed back to my bunk to make my calls, whistling as I stepped around the Terran crew who were hard at work prying the bullets out of the hall ceiling.

CHAPTER

2

The repairs to the ship were due to be finished tomorrow after-noon, so I'd set all our interviews up for that morning. It was short notice, but that was the standard run for armor jobs, and con-sidering the positive response I'd gotten from my callbacks, I had a good feeling about this. At nine sharp, I walked into the lounge suited up and ready to roll. As had become my habit, the first thing I did was glance around for the cook so I could plan where to sit accordingly, but the kitchen was empty. So was the couch. The cook and the captain's daughter must be downstairs, I realized with a relieved sigh.

Caldswell was there, already seated and waiting for me at the table. He did not look happy, though, and my good feeling began to sour. "What happened?"

"Nothing," Caldswell said. "That's the problem. There are only five people in the cargo bay." He glanced at the clock. "This might be a short session."

"Five?" I cried. I'd confirmed interviews for seventeen applicants yesterday. One or two dropping out was expected, but twelve was just ridiculous. "I guess your reputation preceded you," I grumbled.

"More likely your accent scared them off," Caldswell replied drolly.

I rolled my eyes and walked out to see what we had left.

It was slim pickings. Of the seventeen candidates I'd called, only the dregs had bothered to show. We had two idiots in rental armor who, despite what they'd told me over the com, had clearly never been outside of the central Terran systems, and one kid whose "combat experience" turned out to be a medical discharge from Republic Starfleet boot camp. The fourth was a veteran with a solid record I'd had high hopes for, but I could smell the alcohol on her as soon as she came up the stairs, and I didn't even look at Caldswell before I declined her.

Thankfully, the fifth and final applicant looked like a winner. According to his résumé he'd been in the Terran Army for five years as a gunner before moving into private contract work. We didn't really need a gunner since Mabel did all our ship-to-ship shooting, but he had some armor experience as well. Of course, by this point I was ready to take anyone who wasn't a liar or a drunk, but when I stuck my head out the lounge door and peered down into the freshly repaired cargo bay, the man who peered back up at me wasn't the one pictured on the application.

"Who are you?" I demanded.

"I'm here about the job," the man answered.

I scowled. The man standing at the base of the cargo bay stairs was thin and dark skinned with thick, curling black hair going gray at the top and brown, laughing eyes that made him look like he was smiling even when he wasn't. He was older, fifty maybe, but he carried himself like he knew what he was doing, and the gun case strapped across his back looked sleek and expensive. Unlike the others, who'd been almost impossible to understand through their heavy Wuxian accents, this man spoke perfect Universal. He also bore no resemblance to any of the pictures on the applications I'd set aside yesterday afternoon.

"This is a closed interview," I said. "We're not talking walk-ins."

The man looked around at the empty cargo bay. "But it seems I am the only one left," he said. "If the position is not yet filled, surely it would be no trouble to look at my credentials at least?"

My eyes went back to the expensive gun case. "Come on up."

The man gave me a close-lipped smile and trotted up the stairs. I showed him to the interview chair and took a seat at the table beside Caldswell.

"My name is Keno Rashid," the man said.

"Brian Caldswell," the captain replied, holding out his hand. Rashid shook it and then looked at me, but I shook my head.

"Not wise to shake hands with someone in armor," I cautioned. "I could sneeze and break something. I'm Deviana Morris, head of security for the *Glorious Fool*."

Caldswell arched an eyebrow at that, but he didn't say anything. Not that he could. Way I saw it, if I was doing the hiring as well as all the work, that made me the boss, and the earlier you established rank, the easier it was to keep it. Terran mercs might not be as pushy as Paradoxians, but that didn't mean I was going to waste time laying down the rules twice.

"A Paradoxian head of security," Rashid said, eying my armor appreciatively. "In a Verdemont suit, no less. I like this job better and better."

My opinion of him shot up several notches, but I refused to let it show. If the captain found out I could be won over by anyone who knew his armor, he'd never trust my judgment again. But when Rashid set his handset on the table and pulled up his résumé, my opinion only rose higher.

The man's work history read like a military thriller. He'd been in the Republic Starfleet as a combat ops sniper for twelve years before moving on to the Free Guards, the Terran mercenary unit that was the Blackbirds' primary competition. Before that, he'd worked security on a mining station in the K5 asteroid belt, which was about the most dangerous job I could think of. The running gag in the Blackbirds was that the reason the belt was named K5 was because you ran into five thousand pirates every time you went through. If this man had survived three years as guard in *that*, life on the *Fool* would seem almost dull.

Best of all, though, was his equipment. We'd advertised this as an armored position, which usually meant a heavy suit of some sort, but Rashid was packing what the Terrans call tactical armor. *I* called it padded clothes, but it was an intriguing setup nonetheless.

His "suit" was a steel woven polymer lined with ballistic gel instead of plates. It wouldn't stop an ax, but it was light, mostly bullet-proof, and extremely nimble, especially with the reaction net added in. Since it didn't have a real motor or strength augs, the whole thing only weighed about twenty pounds and rolled up small enough to fit in a small duffel, which in my mind put it miles above the hulking idiot boxes Terrans had the nerve to call heavy armor. But interesting as his armor was, what really sealed the deal for me were Rashid's guns.

The sleek, expensive case I'd admired earlier was only the begin-ning. He had four guns in total, starting with a gleaming 5000 Series Jakob's sniper rifle so modded I didn't think a single piece of the original hardware remained. Next he showed us his two pistols, a heavy Republic Army slugger that was nearly as customized as my Sasha and a cannon of an energy weapon I didn't recognize.

"It's called a disrupter pistol," Rashid said when I asked him about it, hefting the big handgun with practiced ease. "And I'm not surprised you haven't seen one before. They used to be the standard anti-xith'cal weapon for the Republic a few decades ago, but they're not used much these days."

My ears pricked up. "Anti-xith'cal? How so?"

Rashid smiled and turned the pistol so I could see the two-notch meter on its side. "It's a heat weapon. Since xith'cal scales are about as easy to shoot through as a ship hull, the idea was to cook them from the inside. Highly accurate and destructive, especially against lizards."

I stared at the gun in his hands. I'd never even heard of a weapon like that, but now that I'd seen it, I wanted one in the worst way. "Why isn't everyone using them?"

"Because they've only got two shots," Caldswell said. I glanced at the captain, but he wasn't even looking. He was still studying

Rashid's résumé, paging through the projected screen thrown up from the merc's handset with his thumb.

"Two shots?" I said, dismayed. "Why?"

"It takes a prohibitive amount of energy to cook a xith'cal warrior," Rashid answered. "Far too much for a sidearm. Two shots are all the battery can manage before the gun needs to recharge."

I sighed. So much for my gun lust. A weapon that could down a lizard in one hit without lining up a head shot was amazing, but with such a small clip, it was practically useless. In my experience, xith'cal came in tens, not twos. "Why bother carrying it, then?"

"Habit and sentimentality," Rashid said as he carefully returned the disrupter pistol to its nook. "It has saved my life enough times that I'm willing to overlook its eccentricities. We are both of us old guns, after all."

Considering that I would probably hold a funeral when Sasha broke, I couldn't argue with that logic. Rashid's final gun was an automatic assault rifle he claimed was for crowd work. I approved of any merc who used the term "crowd work," and by the time we'd moved to his weapon repair kit, a five-tiered behemoth that made my rack look like a toy, I was ready to hire him on the spot.

"You seem to have a gap in your work history," Caldswell said, flicking back to the beginning of Rashid's résumé. "You left active duty with the Free Guards five years ago but stayed on as a special agent and consultant. Then, three years ago, you quit your consultancy contract without notice. According to your record, you haven't had a job since. Why is that? What were you doing these last three years?"

"Taking care of a family emergency," Rashid said calmly. "But I think you'll find my qualifications are still up to date."

Caldswell nodded, waiting for more, but Rashid just smiled. I was about to ask if he wanted to do a combat test when Caldswell suddenly stood up. "Thank you, Mr. Rashid," he said. "Would you mind waiting outside?"

Rashid's smile didn't waver. "Certainly sir," he said, standing in a graceful motion. "I will be happy to wait while you discuss my employment."

Caldswell smiled back, but it didn't reach his eyes. He didn't say anything else until the lounge door was closed and Rashid's footsteps had vanished down the cargo bay stairs.

"Well, seems like we have a winner," I said. "Clearly experienced, fantastic equipment, doesn't seem crazy. If he had a real suit of armor to go with those guns, I'd call him a gift from the king."

"I don't like the gap in his history," the captain said, scratching the stubble on his chin. "And I don't like how much better he is than everyone else. It seems too convenient."

"A family emergency isn't the same as running off to be a pirate," I pointed out. "And with all due respect, sir, perhaps you've gotten a little too used to bad luck. We're in desperate need of another security officer, and you're looking to reject the best candidate because he's too good?"

The captain glared at me, but I held my ground. I couldn't take another round of double shifts like the one I'd done from Falcon 34, and even though hiring a light suit meant I'd be doing the frontline work, Rashid looked like exactly the sort of teammate I loved working with: experienced, polite, and he clearly took great pride and care in his equipment, the surest sign of a true professional. It was wrong to speak ill of the dead, but after three months of dealing with a skull-head like Cotter and all the dominance bullshit that went with it, working with a career soldier who could be trusted to do his job and not make a fight out of every order sounded almost like a vacation.

"A sniper isn't much good inside a ship," Caldswell said.

"But excellent for protecting the ship on planet," I countered. "And he has three other guns."

The captain folded his arms over his chest. "Fine," he said at last. "Call him back up and tell him we'll hire him on a provisional basis. Two months, same terms as you and Cotter."

"Yes sir," I said, grinning.

Caldswell just shook his head and headed for the door. "I'm

going to check to see if they're finished with the bridge. Make sure he fills out all his paperwork, Miss Head of Security."

I grinned wider still. "Yes sir!"

Rashid must have known he'd get the job, because when I went out to get him he was waiting with his duffel, ammo cart, and gun case ready to go. I gave him the same spiel about pay and duties Caldswell had given me. He listened attentively until I was done before asking a few pointed questions about rotations and the cargo checklists that hadn't even occurred to me when I'd signed up.

By the time I'd given him the tour of the ship, which took me less than half the time it had taken Basil back on Paradox, I was more certain than ever we'd made the right choice. Rashid was unfailingly polite and surprisingly knowledgeable about antibreach tactics in older ships. We were talking about how he would have handled the xith'cal raid Cotter and I had held off during our first month on the *Fool* when we walked back into the lounge to see that the cook and Ren had returned to their customary places.

I averted my eyes immediately, letting Rashid introduce himself. Our new security officer greeted the cook politely, but when we got to the captain's daughter, his face lit up in a smile that made all his others look brittle. "Hello," he said softly. "And who are you?"

Since Ren wasn't going to answer, I spoke for her. "This is Ren Caldswell. The captain's daughter."

"Hello, Miss Caldswell," Rashid said, leaning over to catch Ren's eyes. It didn't work. Ren just kept playing her chess game, moving the little plastic pieces with mechanical precision without so much as a glance in our direction.

"Don't mind her," I whispered to Rashid. "She's like that to everyone."

My new partner ignored me and dropped into a squat so that he was peering up at Ren from across the table. "Can you tell me about your game?" he asked sweetly.

Ren's hands didn't slow, and she didn't reply. Rashid asked again, his voice even gentler, but the result was the same. He might as well have been talking to the wall. Eventually, he gave up, giving Ren a final smile before standing with a sigh.

"Sorry," I said awkwardly as we walked out the lounge door.

"For what?" Rashid asked. "She is absorbed in her game. Girls that age are ever too busy. I have a daughter myself."

"Really?" I said. "What's her name?"

"Yasmina," he answered proudly.

I smiled. "That's a pretty name."

"She is a pretty girl," he said. "And very smart."

"Is she here on Wuxia?" I asked as we walked down the hall.

Rashid gave me a smooth smile I couldn't help but think of as fake after seeing how he'd smiled at Ren. "Perhaps."

His strange answer threw me for a second, but then we ran into Nova and Basil and I forgot all about it as we went up to see the newly redone bridge.

Getting blown up might have been the best thing that could have happened to the *Fool*. Caldswell had replaced the entire command deck, and except for the salvaged captain's chair, which was still the same worn, dirty old leather lounger from before, the bridge now looked almost modern. Basil was beside himself with joy. He spent nearly thirty minutes showing us how his maps could now be projected across the whole bridge, filling the room with neatly labeled stars.

When we finally managed to escape the impromptu navigation lesson, I showed Rashid to Cotter's old room so he could start settling in. The captain had shipped all of Cotter's possessions and what was left of his armor back to his family on Paradox when we'd first landed on Wuxia, but with the door closed, I'd still thought of the room as his. Now that Rashid was here, though, Cotter's presence was gone from the ship entirely, and that brought me down a lot more than I'd expected.

I'd lived among strangers ever since I joined the army at eighteen, but I'd always been around Paradoxians. Cotter had annoyed me, true, but he'd been a familiar annoyance. Now that all trace of him was gone, I was starting to realize that I was alone. Truly alone among aliens and off-worlders for the first time in my life.

That realization killed the good mood I'd managed from hiring Rashid. Between the attack on Falcon 34, my missing memories, losing Cotter, and the bullshit with the cook last night, this was shaping up to be a bad month for me. I needed something to get my spirits up. A xith'cal raid maybe, or pirates, something straightforward I could stomp into the ground. But as I entered my room, I realized I was wrong. There *was* something that could cheer me up even more than a good fight, and it was sitting on my bunk.

Perched on my pillow was a rectangular package wrapped in plastic and stamped all over with caution warnings. I sprang on it like a tiger, ripping it open with my suit's strength. The plastic shell was just a covering for another case, a metal one, and inside that was the blade I'd ordered two days ago.

To say it was a thing of beauty would be an insult. My new blade was *breathtaking*. At eleven inches, it was a little smaller than Phoebe's cutting edge had been, but unlike my old blades, which had to be replaced when they burned out, this one had a replenishable thermite edge set into a tungsten steel core. This meant I could actually parry with it, something I'd never been able to do with Phoebe. Also, where Phoebe had been little more than a thermite cutting edge screwed into a handle, my new blade was meant to be integrated into armor, which meant so long as I kept my arm, I'd keep my weapon.

I stared at the thing for a good minute before I grabbed the package and my armor case and ran to the lounge to start installing it.

Two hours later, the lounge table was covered in tools and my new blade was in place. The manufacturer's suggestion had been to embed the blade on top of the arm, but I'd attached mine to the outer side of my right wrist, which allowed me to hold my gun even while the blade was out. The included installation kit was designed for Terran armor, and I'd tossed it without opening the box. Instead, I used the nano-repair in my armor's case to integrate the blade's tiny computer into the Lady's closed gap system so I could control it directly via my neuronet.

Modding a custom suit like my Lady Gray was always a tricky proposition, especially with non-Paradoxian equipment, but the blade I'd picked was high quality, and after a few tweaks, everything snapped into place. When it wasn't in use, my new blade rested in a sheath on the outer side of my right forearm, but with a single thought I could shoot it out like a spike. Another thought would fire the thermite. Even better, now that my blade was hooked directly into my computer, I could set the temperature I wanted the thermite to fire at, lowering the base slightly to extend the burn time by up to five seconds.

"I know each moment contains eternity, Deviana," Nova said when I caught her in the hallway to show her my new lovely. "But five seconds doesn't sound like much time to me."

"It's not," I admitted, retracting the blade and then shooting it out again just for the joy of hearing the razor sharp edge whistle through the air. "But when you've been stuck at eighty seconds forever, five more can be a game changer. Plus, with the tungsten core, the spike will still be useful even after the edge burns out. No more brittle blades. And since it's attached to my suit rather than held in my hands, I can put a lot more power into each swing."

I planted my feet and punched to prove my point, shooting my new blade out as my fist extended while Nova made appropriately impressed noises.

"What are you going to name it?" she asked.

I'd been thinking about that ever since I'd first seen the blade gleaming in its case. I'd considered calling it Phoebe just to keep things simple, but that seemed like a dishonor to the real Phoebe's memory. In the end, I'd gone with an old favorite.

"Elsie," I said proudly. "After Elsievale of Ambermarle. She founded the king's Hidden Guard almost five hundred years ago, and she was the first woman ever to receive a royal knighthood. I wrote a paper about her in school. They used to call her 'the sword you never see.' A perfect namesake for a blade that retracts."

Nova's pale eyebrows shot up. "Are all your weapons named after famous Paradoxians?"

I pulled Elsie back with a laugh. "I wish. I was never that good at history. Mia's called Mia because I liked the sound of it, and Sasha was my grandmother's name."

Nova bit her lip. "You named your gun after your grand-mother?"

"Yep," I said, checking Elsie's sheath to make sure my new baby had gone in snugly, which she had. "She was so proud when I told her that she bought me a whole crate of ammo blessed by the king's monks." I still had a clip left, actually, stowed in my armor case along with the pictures my mother had sent of my sister and her family. You can guess which one I looked at more.

"Come on," I said to Nova, flipping down my visor. "We've got an hour before takeoff. Let's go get a drink and scare some Terrans."

"But I don't drink," Nova protested as I pushed her along. "And *I'm* Terran."

"You can spectate then," I said. "Come on, this will be fun." And if we were quick, we'd be off-planet before the Wuxian cops could give me a ticket for wearing my suit.

Nova didn't look convinced, but I was already escorting her through the lounge to the cargo bay steps. The cook was sitting at the table prepping a pile of vegetables for dinner. Nova said hello to him, but I kept my mouth shut and my eyes down, using my suit to track him just to be sure he was keeping his promise not to stare. It wasn't perfect, but as far as I could tell he kept his eyes on the leaves he was mincing like he was trying to turn them into powder, and that was good enough.

―――――――

We left Wuxia with minimal fanfare. As usual for the *Fool*, the cargo bay was empty, but if Rashid was worried by the lack of actual trading aboard Captain Caldswell's trade ship, he didn't comment. He didn't comment on anything, actually. He was unfailingly polite, but he kept to himself, though not to his room. He followed me on patrol while we were waiting our turn to use the Wuxia gate, but the moment we entered hyperspace, he'd taken off his armor and installed himself on the opposite side of the lounge couch from the captain's daughter with Mabel's fat cat snoring on the cushion between them.

This didn't seem to bother Ren at all, but though I still wasn't looking at the cook directly, I could tell it bothered him. He was glaring at Rashid so hard I could feel it through my suit, but Rashid paid him no mind. He just sat there reading on his handset, never bothering the captain's daughter, never crowding her, and never speaking unless spoken to. He stayed that way all through the jump, and while I thought it was a little odd, he wasn't doing any harm, so I quickly moved on to other, more important things, like seeing just how much metal my new blade could slice through.

By the time I'd pinned it down to six inches of industrial steel, exactly as the brochure promised, Basil was announcing our exit from hyperspace. That surprised me. Last I'd heard we were headed for the Aeon Sevalis, which was a lot farther away than the hour and a half we'd spent in hyperspace. I couldn't see a thing from down in the empty cargo bay where I'd been doing my cutting, though, so I pulled my new baby back into her sheath and trotted up the stairs to see what I was in for.

The answer seemed to be snow. We'd come out of hyperspace in orbit around a small planet that shone blindingly white in the light of its distant sun. Looking down through the lounge windows, I tried to spot the cities, but I couldn't see so much as a shadow through the thick clouds that swathed the planet like a waxy coat. The heavy atmosphere hid everything from mountains to seas, leaving only smooth whiteness, like a pearl floating in space. A very lonely pearl. So far as I could see, we were the only ship in orbit.

"Where the hell are we?" I asked over the com.

"IoFive," Nova replied, her dreamy voice breathless. "Isn't it pretty?"

I scowled at the white clouds. "Looks cold to me." Cold and empty. Forget other ships; I couldn't even see a traffic control satellite. "What are we doing here again?"

"Work," the captain said dryly before cutting off the channel.

Since that was clearly all the answer I'd be getting, I ran Io5 through my suit computer. What I found wasn't reassuring. Io5 was a research planet under the jurisdiction of the Republic Scientific Council, though it wasn't currently in use due to the harshness of the planet's fifty-year winter. Not the sort of place you took an empty trade freighter unless you were shipping snow, but I knew better by now than to question the captain, and I kept my mouth shut as we passed through the cloud cover into the worst blizzard I'd ever seen.

Below the shell of clouds that gave Io5 its smooth, pearl-like appearance, the planet itself was a crag-riddled mass of black rock, ice, wind, and thick, blowing snow. I'll never know how Basil found the ground in that mess, but we made our final descent with only a few hairy spots. Ice pelted our hull the whole way, rattling off the *Fool*'s heavy sides like gunshots.

By the time we finally set down, I was good and ready to be on the ground, snowball planet or not. When the entry shutters rolled away, though, I almost changed my mind. I've been to some dirt-scratch operations before, but this was ridiculous. The "starport" was a stretch of icy cement hidden from the worst of the wind in the lee of a small mountain. There was a generator building, a tiny equipment garage, and one floodlight. Other than that, there was nothing. I didn't even see a signal tower. Though, to be fair, there could have been a thousand signal towers and I wouldn't have known. Even with the mountain to block the worst of the storm, the falling snow was so thick I couldn't see more than a dozen feet in any direction. I was watching drifts pile up against the *Fool*'s side when Caldswell came into the lounge.

The moment I saw him, my heart began to sink. The captain was suited for cold weather in a huge, heavy coat, eye shield, and thick boots. Oddly, the cook was right behind him, dressed the same, but what really blew my mind was Ren. She was standing beside her father, wrapped head to toe in so much snow gear I could barely see her face.

"Going out?" I asked, though the answer was painfully clear.

"Just for a bit," Caldswell replied, putting on his gloves as he walked past me and down the cargo bay stairs. "And you can stop making that face, Morris. You're not coming."

Relief washed over me. Neither my suit nor I like snow. But the feeling left just as quickly when I realized this meant the captain would be going out alone. I followed him down to the cargo bay while I tried to work out a way to tell him how stupid that was without getting yelled at. In the end, though, I didn't have to say anything, because Rashid beat me to it.

"You're not seriously considering going out in that, are you, sir?"

My new partner was standing at attention at the bottom of the stairs in his tactical armor with his pistols at his hips, every inch the good soldier, but the expression on his face was anything but obedient. "It's thirty below with no visibility. That is killing weather. To take a child out in such—"

"I take my daughter anywhere I please," Caldswell said without missing a beat. He walked to the cargo bay door and hit the button to release the lock before looking pointedly at me. "We're meeting a contact. It shouldn't take more than two hours. I want you to keep everyone on the ship and in position. Basil has orders to take off as soon as we get back."

"Yes sir," I said. That wouldn't be hard. Other than Caldswell and whatever insane contact he was meeting out here, I didn't think anyone would be crazy enough to go out in this weather. I was just glad we weren't staying long. The ice was still pelting the *Fool*'s hull like it was the back wall at a firing range, and even though I could see on my suit that the ship's internal temperature hadn't changed, just knowing the snow was out there made me feel wet and cold to my bones. The sooner we left this place, the happier I'd be.

Rashid didn't look like anything would make him happy, but he didn't fight the captain again. When it was clear there would be no more questions, Caldswell hit the switch to open the cargo bay. The new door slid open with a soft rumble, and as the seal cracked, a blast of snow billowed in, dropping a foot of white stuff on the floor before the door had opened halfway. Caldswell shook his head at the snowdrift that was building in the middle of his cargo bay before pulling his scarf down from his mouth. "And clean this up!" he yelled.

"Yes sir," I grumbled, cutting on my suit's heaters. Rashid, whose suit was too thin to have heaters, made do with folding his arms tighter over his chest and glowering.

Caldswell pulled his scarf back up and marched down the ramp, which was already covered in a thick sheet of ice. His daughter walked behind him, fitting her feet into the large holes left by Caldswell's boots. The cook went last.

By this point I was standing by the door with my hand on the switch, ready to close up the cargo bay and cut off the snow the second Caldswell's group was through. Considering my position, I'd thought my intention was obvious, but the cook clearly didn't understand that having three feet of snow in your ship was a bad thing, because he stopped on the threshold. He was so buried in coats, I could actually look at him without feeling too bad, and I used this temporary immunity to glare a warning. When he *still* didn't move, I opened my mouth to tell him to get the lead out, but the words died in my throat, because that was when he turned and stared straight at me.

I was in my suit with my visor down, looking at him through my cameras. Even so, his gaze cut right through me, and the revulsion stabbed me like a blade. I looked away at once, furious. I *hated* when he did that. But though my head was turned, I could still see the cook through my side camera, and that was how I caught the *way* he was looking at me.

Once before, when I'd first woken up on Falcon 34, the cook had looked at me with a strange mix of loss and triumph. The look he gave me now was much the same, only there was no triumph this time. When he stared at me now, all I saw was sadness, like he'd lost something precious. I had no idea why he would look at me like that. He'd made it clear back on Wuxia that he hated me. But as his eyes bored into me, I suddenly had the strangest feeling that I'd forgotten something. Something important.

"Charkov!"

The cook and I both jumped, and I looked to see the captain standing at the bottom of the ramp, glaring murder. "Let's go."

The cook turned without a word, walking down the icy ramp delicately as a cat despite his heavy boots. The moment he was out of the way, I hit the door. But as the metal slid into place, closing off the freezing wind, I couldn't help one last look.

The cook and the captain were both facing away from me now, walking off into the snow with Ren between them. But though neither man was looking at me anymore, Ren was. She was staring over her shoulder, her head turned straight toward me at a painful angle. When she saw me looking, her dark eyes pinned on mine, and she pulled her scarf down to shoot me a smile.

I'd seen Ren smile only once, back in the lounge when I'd first realized she could also see the floating, glowing bugs I'd thought were hallucinations. Now as then, her smile was terrifying, so much so that I took a step back. That only made Ren smile wider, and she watched me like a predator until the closing cargo door hid her behind a wall of steel and ice.

"I cannot believe he would take a child into such weather."

Rashid's voice made me jump. I'd been so caught up in Ren, I hadn't realized he was right behind me until he'd spoken.

"What does he think he is doing?" Rashid snapped, glaring at the closed cargo door like he could burn a hole in it with his disdain. "I don't care whom they're meeting, it is suicidally foolish to go out in such weather."

"The captain does as the captain does," I said, but my heart wasn't in it. I didn't even care about the weather anymore. All I wanted to do was go hide somewhere Ren's smile couldn't find me.

Fortunately, the crazy impulse passed, helped along by the fact that we had a cargo bay full of quickly melting snow to deal with. "All right," I said, walking purposefully over to the closet where Mabel kept the big brooms. "Let's clear this avalanche out before it melts and we have to deal with a flood instead."

After his surliness, I expected an argument, but Rashid did exactly as I asked. We swept all the snow into a big pile at the bay's center, and then, since opening the door again would only let in more, we piled the frozen stuff into ten-gallon buckets and hauled it over to the ship's water tank. By the time the cargo bay was clear, our water was topped off and my arms were aching even in my suit.

But bad as I was, Rashid's suit had no motors to help him. By the time we emptied the last barrel, he looked ready to fall over, so I sent him to the bridge to rest up and keep an eye on the external cameras. I should have gone back on patrol—this was still a hostile planet after all—but there didn't seem to be much point to being on guard when we were sitting with no cargo on an ice ball that even scientists wouldn't live on. But I couldn't bring myself to slack openly, so I grabbed a mop and started swabbing up the water the snow had left behind.

I told myself I was performing a vital service for the safety of the ship. After all, if the floor was wet when the door opened again, it would freeze solid, leaving us with an ice rink. That was a nice cover story, but the truth was, the mopping was busywork, something legitimate looking that didn't require real attention. *That* I saved for my footage of what had happened at the door.

My cameras had caught everything. I didn't dare look at the cook's face directly, even on a recording, but I didn't have to. Just like when I'd woken up in the medbay, his expression was seared into my mind. I didn't know why my brain cared so much about the stupid man, but it seemed like I was stuck with him. All I could do was shove the horrible feeling that I'd forgotten something aside and focus on what was really bothering me: Caldswell's daughter.

The captain couldn't have seen Ren's smile from where he was standing, and from the way the cook had been watching the frozen ground under his feet, I was betting he hadn't either. Her smile had been just for me, but why? What did the captain's crazy daughter want?

I was alone in the cargo bay, so I raised my visor and glanced around surreptitiously. To my great relief, I didn't see a thing. I hadn't seen a glowing bug for a while, actually, not since the one Ren had also seen in the lounge. My private theory was that the knock on the head that had taken my memories had also fixed whatever it was that made me see the hallucinations, which would make it the only good part of the whole mess as far as I was concerned. Then again, whatever the things were, I knew I couldn't see them through my cameras, so there was always the chance that they had been around and I'd just missed them. I had my visor up now, though, and I still saw nothing, but it was starting to be less of a comfort.

I leaned on my mop with a frustrated sigh. The more I thought about it, the less I understood why I found Ren's smile so scary. Other than the night she'd smiled at me in the lounge, I couldn't actually remember her doing anything threatening, but thinking about her definitely increased the feeling that I'd forgotten something. I ground my teeth, trying to force my stupid brain to remember. There had to be a reason I was so afraid of her; what was it? What had I forgotten?

I was still trying to figure this out when the hand grabbed my spine.

I shot bolt upright. From the lack of horrible pain, I knew there was no way a hand could *actually* be grabbing my spine, but that was exactly what it felt like. Five fingers and a palm, wrapped around the vertebrae just below my neck. I could even feel the fingers moving inside me, readjusting to get a better grip.

My shock had been enough to flip my suit into combat mode, but when my vitals flashed up, I didn't see anything wrong. My suit had no breaches, and though the panic had elevated my heart rate, I was otherwise fine. I didn't see anything behind me through my rear cameras either. I was about to flip my visor back down and do a full scan when a soft, feminine voice whispered in my mind.

Come.

As the word finished, the hand on my spine jerked, and I popped out of my body like a shucked pea.

CHAPTER
3

When the hand on my spine let go, I was no longer on the ship.
I wasn't even in my armor, just the thin shirt and pants I'd been wearing under it, which was pretty sad coverage against the blizzard I was standing in. Snow was blowing so thickly I couldn't see more than a few feet in front of my nose. My legs were buried to the knees in it, and I could feel even more beneath my bare feet. For all of this, though, I wasn't cold. I was pretty comfortable, actually, except for my right hand, which hurt like someone was squeezing my fingers in a vise. I looked down in alarm, jerking my hand back at the same time only to find I couldn't. Ren was standing beside me, and my hand was crushed in hers.

I've seen a lot of weird shit in nine years of armored combat, but I was now officially out of my depth. The captain's daughter wasn't wearing the heavy coat I'd seen her leave the ship in twenty minutes ago. Instead, she was dressed in a white cotton hospital gown that tied at her sides. Her feet were bare like mine, but she was standing on top of the drift rather than in it, perched on the crested snow like a bird. Other than that, though, she looked normal: same blank expression, her dark hair hanging still just above her shoulders despite the howling wind. Even her eyes were focused with the same insane attention they had when she was playing her game, only now, instead of staring at a chessboard, Ren was staring at *me*.

I stepped back instinctively, and then yelped when her hand tightened on mine so hard my joints popped. The pain sent a clear message, and I stopped trying to get away, shuffling back to her side. The grip eased up with every inch I neared. By the time I was standing next to her, our locked hands were almost friendly.

I glanced down at thin clothes and then up again at the howling blizzard that wasn't wet or cold. And then, because it was obvious that this was a dream, I asked, "What's going on?"

Instead of answering, Ren just tilted her head, her dark eyes sliding past me. When I turned to follow her gaze, I realized we were no longer alone. Three figures were trudging out of the storm behind me, climbing a steep slope I hadn't seen under all the snow. They were little more than shadows in the blizzard, but I could see enough to make out the shapes of two men and a child.

After that, it was pretty obvious. Caldswell, Ren, and the cook reached the top of the slope and walked past us without a glance. I watched them until they vanished into the snow again, and then I took a deep breath of the snowy air I couldn't taste or feel and closed my eyes, trying to will myself to wake up. If I was dreaming, then I must have nodded off in my suit, which meant I needed to wake myself back up as soon as possible. If Basil caught me snoozing on the job, I would never hear the—

Watch.

I almost jumped out of my skin. The word wasn't a sound. It was a thought, a sharp command that slid through my mind like freezing water, and my eyes popped open to see Ren staring at me.

Standing on top of the snowdrift, she was actually a little taller than I was. She used the height to her advantage, staring down at me until I couldn't look away. When she had my utter and undivided attention, the captain's daughter turned and started walking over the snow toward the trampled path Caldswell's group had left, dragging me behind her.

It was awkward as hell trying to walk through drifts when the person you're trying to keep up with could walk on top of them. I floundered in the deep snow, tripping over hidden rocks and holes every few steps. By the time we reached the path the captain and the others had trodden down, my legs were burning and I was out of breath. I was pretty damn sick of this dream, too, but I couldn't wake up. I'd even tried stumbling deliberately in the hopes that the fall would do it, but all I'd gotten for my trouble was a mouthful of snow I couldn't even taste.

By the time I gave in and let Ren lead me, we'd caught up with the captain. I hadn't noticed before, thanks to the blizzard, but the flat spot we were standing on was actually a plateau nestled in the lee of a taller mountain. Caldswell was at the edge of the cliff where the mountain began to climb again, stomping down the snow in front of what looked like a metal door set into the rock itself.

I rolled my eyes. Leave it to me to dream about bunkers, but at least I'd dreamed up a solid one. The door was heavy enough to take a cannon blast, and now that I was looking for them, I could see little slits set high in the stone beside it, perfect for ventilation and shooting down at an enemy from cover. Not that there would ever be anyone to shoot at out in this wilderness.

When he was done clearing a space to stand, Caldswell walked up to the heavy door and knocked politely, like he was a neighbor come over to pay his respects. I didn't think whoever was inside would be able to hear such a soft sound over the gale, but I was wrong, because the door opened immediately, the heavy metal slab swinging inward to reveal a large, dark room.

From where we were standing, I could see that the bunker stretched back into the mountain for quite a ways, but I didn't want to see any more. The moment the lock on the door clicked open, a painful knot of dread formed in my stomach. Dream or not, I did not want to go into that dark room.

But my opinion didn't matter. Caldswell was going in, and Ren, both the bundled up one I'd seen leaving the ship and the barefoot one with the death grip on my hand, was following him. I tried digging in my heels, but while I could easily have lifted the real Ren over my head even without my suit, dream Ren was strong as a cargo loader. I kept fighting anyway, straining with all my strength until Ren looked over her shoulder.

Don't fight. Watch.

Her face was blank as always, her mouth still, but I felt each word like a slap across my mind. I was still smarting from it when she yanked me forward, dragging me the last few inches through the bunker door, which had already closed. We passed through the heavy steel like ghosts, and I found myself standing right beside the cook.

He was so close, the fog of his breath mixed with mine. I gritted my teeth in preparation for the revulsion, but it didn't come. Confused, I blinked hard and looked again, but the result was the same. The inexplicable nausea was gone.

For a moment, I felt elated, and then I remembered that this was a dream. Still, I wasn't one to waste opportunities, real or not, and I took the chance to actually look at the cook properly for the first time.

To my surprise, he was worth looking at. Even buried under the coats, his body looked tall and graceful. His pale skin was reddened from the cold, but the blush only accented his sleek black hair and blue eyes. If I hadn't caught him trying to kick me off the ship yesterday, I would have called him handsome.

I was so busy studying the cook, I didn't realize the bunker was already occupied until I heard the scrape of boots on the cement floor. A man and a woman were standing on the other side of the bunker from the door where we had come in. They were bundled in the same heavy coats as the captain and the cook, and they held themselves like soldiers. Between them was a smaller figure so wrapped up in winter gear I couldn't see anything until she raised her head. When she did, though, I wished to the king she'd left it down, because the girl standing between the strangers like a shy child between her parents was Ren.

Even covered in coats, there was no doubting it was her, though

I suppose I shouldn't have been so surprised. None of this made sense, anyway. Why not throw in another Ren? This made three of them now: Caldswell's Ren, the barefoot Ren who'd been dragging me around, and the new girl.

No one else in the room seemed to notice my Ren. Or me, for that matter. They could clearly see one another, though, and none of them looked weirded out in the slightest by the two identical girls. In fact, the pair who'd been waiting in the bunker seemed more intimidated by Caldswell than his daughter. They snapped to attention the moment the captain looked up, and the woman, a tall, wiry lady with straight dark hair, gave him a sharp salute.

"Commander Caldswell," she said crisply. "Well met, sir."

"I'd hardly call such business well met, Eye Natalia," Caldswell said. "Do you have what we discussed?"

I winced. The captain's voice was calm, but I could tell from his posture that he was pissed. The lady, Eye Natalia, must have picked that up too, because she cleared her throat and glanced nervously at her partner, a huge brick of a man in a black suit very similar to the ones the cook always wore. "We do," she said. "We can begin at any time."

Caldswell hooked his thumbs in the pockets of his coat and turned his glare to the cook, who'd stayed perfectly still through the whole exchange. "Do it."

Eye Natalia saluted again, but it was her partner who acted. The huge man let go of his Ren's hand and turned away, walking through the shadows to a little door at the bunker's far end. He returned a minute later, dragging something behind him.

The light from the bunker's single lamp was so bad, I couldn't actually make out what it was at first. The cook recognized it, though. His whole body had gone stiff the moment the thing came through the door. But as the big man dragged it closer, I stopped worrying about the cook. As they entered the light, I could see that the limp weight Eye Natalia's partner was dragging across the icy cement was a woman. A petite, young-looking woman with wavy, flyaway brown hair, most of which was drenched in blood from a head wound.

My stomach began to ice over, but I forced myself to keep watching as the man stopped in front of Caldswell and yanked the bloody woman to her knees. This close, I could now see that the bloody rags she was wearing were actually the shredded remains of a suit of Paradoxian underarmor. The woman had clearly put up a fight before being brought here, because her knuckles were bloody, too. That was to be expected, though, because when the big man yanked the woman's head up, it was my face that appeared, teeth bared in fury and vengeance despite the blood that trickled from my split temple.

By this point, my brain was moving at a snail's pace. I could see the whole scene frozen like a picture in front of me, Natalia standing hand in hand with her Ren across the room, watching dispassionately while the huge man held the bloody Devi, me, on her knees in front of the cook with Caldswell standing slightly to the side, the captain's hand resting on his own daughter's shoulder. I could see every detail in sharp relief, the blood running down her, *my* legs to pool on the icy ground, the frantic, terrified jerk of my chest as it rose and fell beneath the shredded suit of underarmor, but no matter how hard I tried, I couldn't make sense of it. All I knew was that this was a very bad dream indeed, and I needed to get out, now, before it got any worse.

But when I turned to go, Ren's fingers tightened on my hand. I looked down to see her staring at me, her eyes dark and deep as space itself. *Watch*, her voice whispered in my mind.

The word was a command, and I had no choice. I watched.

When the bloody Devi was more or less steady, Caldswell reached under his coat and drew out a huge pearl-handled pistol. I'd never seen this particular gun before, but I recognized the type immediately. It was the old-fashioned gun Rashid carried to kill xith'cal, a disrupter pistol. Caldswell's was clearly a trusted old gun, personal favorite, I'd bet, which was why I was surprised when he turned the weapon around and held it out to the cook.

The cook hadn't moved a muscle the whole time. He was staring at the woman on the ground, my bloody self, like he'd seen a ghost, and the longer he stared, the more his perennially icy gaze melted. By the time he spoke, he looked almost human, and almost broken.

"Not this," he whispered, voice shaking. "I did it for her, Brian. Don't make me do this."

The captain's answer was cold and dry and terrible. "If you'd followed orders in the first place, we wouldn't be in this situation."

"No," the cook said, his breaths coming quicker and quicker. "I was careful. I combed her mind and took everything that could possibly lead back to us. She's clean, I swear it."

"She's nothing of the kind," Caldswell replied. "Come on, Charkov, don't be a fool. You know scrubs don't stick on strong emotions or traumatic memories."

"They can if you get the victim out," the cook hissed, looking at the captain for the first time since this began. "If you'd gotten her off the ship when I asked—"

He broke off as the Devi on the floor whispered, "Rupert…"

The cook winced like the name was a blow, and Caldswell's eyes narrowed. "The mission comes first," the captain said, pushing the gun at him. "Follow your orders, Eye Charkov."

The next few moments seemed to take forever. The bunker was utterly silent except for the howl of the snow outside and the soft drip of blood on cement. And then, slowly, the cook's hand reached out. The moment his shaking fingers curled around the pistol's pearl grip, the Devi on the floor began to thrash.

"No!" she shrieked, and I winced at the sound. I cannot begin to describe how unsettling it is to hear your own voice screaming in desperate terror. The bloody Devi was throwing her weight around now, trying to wrench herself out of the other man's hold. It was a good effort, but she was too badly injured, and the man was so much bigger. He held her down easily, and all her thrashing managed to do was lose her more blood. When it was clear she wasn't getting out that way, she turned back to the cook. Her tanned face was nearly white from blood loss now. I wasn't sure actually how she hadn't passed out yet, but she was still up, and she was staring up at the cook with such desperate hope that my heart nearly broke.

"Rupert!" she cried. "Don't do it! Get me out, we can take them!"

Her words were frantic, and they did no good. Above her, Rupert lifted the gun. His hand was shaking so badly the barrel trembled in the air, but it stilled as he pressed it against her bloody forehead.

"*No!*" she cried, or she tried to. The Devi on the floor was too weak to shout now, but her brown eyes were wide and bright with tears and pain. "I love you, Rupert, don't do this. *Please*, Rupert!"

Her voice broke after that, collapsing into a pleading gibberish of Universal and King's Tongue that made me want to weep. I didn't know how the cook could bear it. Maybe he couldn't, because though the pistol was pressed into Devi's forehead, his finger still hadn't moved on the trigger, and with each second that ticked by, Caldswell's scowl deepened.

And then, just when the captain's patience seemed to be running out, an explosion split the air.

Devi's pleading, *my* pleading, cut off like a switch. For one breathless moment, she seemed to hang, and then her body toppled over. She hit the bloody cement with a dull thud, a thin line of smoke rising from the perfectly circular blackened hole the disrupter pistol's blast had burned through her head. Through *my* head.

Then, like a mirage, the body flickered and vanished. The blood vanished as well, just disappeared like it had never been. In the blink of an eye, all signs of my other self were gone completely, leaving nothing but a fist-sized smoking crater in the bunker's cement floor.

For one long moment, I thought Rupert was going to fall, too. He was staring at the place where my body had been like the world no longer made sense. Finally, his eyes went to the two Rens he could see, flicking between Caldswell's and the one clutching Natalia's hand. He swallowed once, then again, and in a small, throaty voice, he whispered, "An illusion?"

"Your punishment," Caldswell replied, plucking the gun from Rupert's limp fingers. "And your test. After your disobedience on Falcon Thirty-Four, we had to be sure we could count on you to do the right thing when the time came, and you did. You passed." He put his hand on Rupert's shoulder as he said this. The move was probably supposed to be congratulatory, but as the captain's fingers tightened, all I could think was this was the closest to an apology Caldswell would ever come. "Welcome back to the fold, Eye Charkov."

Natalia and her partner stepped forward to offer their congratulations as well. Rupert stood cold and straight, accepting their words with murmured thanks, but his blue eyes were still fixed on the crater his shot had blasted in the floor, and his jaw was clenching tighter and tighter, like he was about to shatter. I didn't wait around to see if he would. I was already marching out of the building.

I fully expected Ren to stop me as she had every other time, but to my surprise, the girl followed meekly, her fingers soft on mine as we walked right through the bunker's wall and into the snow outside. It was only when we'd gotten far enough away that the blizzard hid the mountain completely that I turned around. *"Why did you show me this?"*

I screamed the words so hard my throat ached, but even as they left my mouth, I knew it was pointless. This was a dream. Yelling at Ren was about as useful as yelling into the void, but I couldn't help it. I was confused, scared, and terrifyingly angry. So angry my body would burst if something didn't come out.

"Why did you do this?" I demanded, dragging up the hand Ren was still clutching until I was shaking it in her face. "Why am I here?"

"To see the truth," Ren whispered.

My rage sputtered to a stop. Ren's voice sounded just like before, but now the sound came from her lips. She was staring up at me, and for the first time ever, her face was not a blank mask. She was looking at me in earnest, her eyes fever bright and her cheeks wet with tears. "I know what you've become," she said over the wind. "Maat is sending help. When you get it, come and find me."

"Find you?" I snapped. "You're Caldswell's daughter, we live on the same ship."

"I am Ren," Ren said, shaking her head. "But Ren is not me. None of them are. You have to find *me*, Deviana Morris. It's the only way to set us free."

"Free from what?" I cried. "What does any of that even mean? And why me?"

Ren released my hand only to grab my face. She was a small girl, but she wrenched me down with no problem, putting us nose to nose. This close, I could see my face reflected in her wild too-bright eyes, and what I saw made me recoil in horror. There was something on my skin, crawling up my neck and over my cheeks.

Black soot. Black soot just like the stuff that had been on my fingers at Caldswell's door was spreading over my face like an ink stain spreading through cloth. It was so horrible I couldn't do anything but stare for several seconds, but when the scream finally rose in my throat, Ren's hand covered my mouth, locking it in.

"It must be you," she whispered as the black stuff started seeping from my skin into her fingers. "Because you are the only one who can."

I screamed against her hand, a wordless demand for understanding, for answers. But as she finished speaking, Ren shoved me away, and I slammed back into my body so hard it knocked my breath out.

"Miss Morris!"

I blinked as the world spun and settled into a familiar setting. I was back in the cargo bay, standing in my suit with the mop still in my hands and Rashid and Hyrek in my face.

"Miss Morris!" Rashid shouted again, waving his hand back and forth in front of my face.

I dropped the mop and yanked my helmet off, making Rashid jump away with a startled yelp. I ignored him, turning my helmet around. But when I looked in my mirrored visor, all I saw was my own panicked reflection staring back at me.

If I hadn't been wearing my suit, I would have collapsed. There was no black stuff on my skin, no spreading darkness. It *had* been a dream. My relief was so intense I actually started to laugh. I was trying to stifle my giggles when Hyrek shoved his handset into my face.

What is going on?

"A dream," I panted.

I knew from Hyrek's scowl that was not the right answer, but my brain was too scrambled to lie. The fear of the dream was still clinging to me, so much so that I still wasn't sure if I was really awake yet. I looked away from the xith'cal doctor and bent over, resting my hands on my knees as I tried to clear my head. "What happened?"

I'd asked Hyrek, but Rashid answered. "I asked you a question over the com and you didn't respond. After several tries, I came down and found you standing still as a statue. You didn't react to words or touch, so I called for the doctor. He'd just arrived when you woke up."

I blanched. It sounded pretty bad when he put it that way. Hyrek saw my reaction, and his claws flew over his handset. *Medbay*, it read when he turned it back to me. *Now.*

The order sparked a mini panic. Thanks to my earlier mistake, letting him know I could see the glowing bugs, Hyrek thought I was half insane already. If I wanted to finish out my tour on the *Fool*, I couldn't give him more ammunition.

That thought was enough to kick the last of the dream away, and I straightened up immediately, snapping back into professional merc mode. "No need for that," I said with a smile. "I'm perfectly..."

My voice trailed off as my eyes caught sight of the soft blue-white glow behind Hyrek's head. I'd been so wrapped up in the dream and fending off my shipmates, I hadn't even noticed the creatures.

The cargo bay was resplendent with tiny glowing bugs. They carpeted the floor and walls, dangled from the ceiling and floated in the air. There must have been thousands of them, and their combined blue-white radiance was so bright it hurt my eyes. But though the glowing creatures had crowded themselves into every nook and cranny in the cargo bay, the space around me was clear. The glowing carpet stopped three feet from my boots, and not a single one of the floating bugs was within arm's reach. It was like I was standing in a bubble, surrounded by some kind of invisible boundary the creatures would not cross.

Before I could think better of it, I took a step to test the theory. The movement nearly caused a stampede as all the bugs skittered frantically to keep away from me. It was pretty funny to watch, actually. Grinning, I lifted my boot to send them scrambling again, but before I could take a step, I realized that Hyrek and Rashid were looking at me like I'd lost my mind.

For one long second, we stared at one another, and then Hyrek's hand shot out, his claws hooking into the open neck of my suit. *Medbay*, his handset read. *Or you're relieved from duty.*

There was no point in fighting after that little display. I let the lizard drag me away, calling for Rashid to take care of things until I got back. He promised he would, waving at me with the weak half smile used for appeasing crazy people. Behind him, the glowing bugs began to drift away, scattering like blown snow through the *Fool*'s hull and out into the blizzard beyond.

———

I had to do a lot more pleading to get Hyrek to let me out of the medbay this time.

"For the love of the Sacred King, Hyrek," I moaned after the fifth round of inconclusive tests. "Just let me go."

The doctor snapped his fangs at me and clicked his claws furiously across his handset. *No. There's something wrong with you, and until I figure out what that is, you go nowhere.*

"You didn't find anything the last four times you checked," I pointed out. Again. "You're not going to now. I just fell asleep."

On your feet, in the cargo bay, in midmop, Hyrek typed with a snort. *You want to try a new one?*

"No, because that's what happened," I said, keeping my voice calm and reasonable. "The stress of living with a xith'cal has given me narcolepsy."

Narcolepsy is genetic, Hyrek wrote. *And I don't think you get stressed. Stress implies an instinct against danger. You have no such thing.*

I sighed and flopped back on the medical bunk that was starting to feel like home. "Well, poke away, then," I said. "But you can't keep me here forever."

Hyrek responded by jabbing the needle back into my arm with a vindictiveness that was not medically necessary.

It would probably have been easier to convince him to let me go if the floating bug things weren't still hanging around. I was no longer seeing huge hordes of them like back in the cargo bay, but ever since Hyrek had dragged me away, they seemed to be staying close. Sometimes it was just one dancing along the ceiling. Other times there were dozens floating lazily in the air like tiny glowing jellyfish. No matter how many there were, though, none of them ever got closer to me than arm's length. For my part, I was trying my best to ignore them, but it's *really* hard not to look at things that glow and move.

Every time my eyes darted to something that wasn't there, Hyrek would glare at me like I'd just proved him right, but he was overruled in the end. The captain had wrapped up his business in Io5, which meant we were back in flight, and since our only other security guard had been on the job for less than a day, there was no choice but to put me back to work, though not before Caldswell himself came down to look me over.

He talked with Hyrek while I got back into my armor. The little glowing bugs must have liked the captain, because he'd gathered a fine swarm of them by the time he sent the lizard away. Once

Hyrek was out of the room, the captain took a seat on the examining table and leaned back, resting his weight on his palms. "You're not cracking on us, are you, Morris?"

I'd been so busy watching what looked like a little glowing puffball float back and forth through the captain's chest that I almost missed the question. "No sir," I said, putting my helmet on with less grace than usual. When my cameras kicked on, the glowing bugs vanished, and I breathed a silent sigh of relief.

"No sir," I said again. "I am perfectly capable of doing my job."

The captain leaned forward again, rubbing his hands over his face. Now that the bugs were gone, or at least hidden by my cameras, I could look at the captain without distraction. What I saw was disconcerting. I was the one who'd fallen asleep randomly, but Caldswell seemed like he needed to be in the medbay more than I did. The man looked ready to fall over from exhaustion.

"There's no shame in admitting you have a problem," Caldswell said quietly when he finally dropped his hands. "If you want to tell me anything off the record, now would be the time."

I went ramrod straight. "I do not have a problem," I lied.

Caldswell looked at me for a long time after that. I was used to being under officer scrutiny, but the strange dream was still with me, and I found myself cringing under his gaze. Fortunately, the captain couldn't see enough of my face through my visor to tell. Or, if he could, he didn't comment. All he did was shake his head and slide off the table. "Have it your way," he said. "But I want you to take better care of yourself. Get your full cycle of sleep and be sure to eat. I hear you've been off your food."

That wasn't strictly true. I'd been eating, just not in the lounge, because I couldn't look at the cook without feeling ill. But that was one of the problems I was not discussing with the captain, so all I said was, "Yes sir."

Caldswell nodded and started for the door. "We hit the gate at IoThree in four hours. After that, we have a twelve-hour jump to the Sevalis. I want you to spend it resting. Understood?"

"Yes sir," I said again, falling into step beside him as we walked back to the bridge.

Rashid was there when we arrived, talking scanners with Nova. They were both so happy to see me out of the medbay that I felt a little guilty. Rashid offered to take over until we jumped so I could get some rest, but I told him if I didn't get back to work I really would go crazy. It was supposed to be a joke, but Rashid didn't seem to think it was funny, and I made a mental note to act as normally as I could around him from now on.

Despite its lonely appearance, Io5 was actually the last planet in what was otherwise a reasonably developed solar system. Its neighbor, the far more temperate Io3, was a major farming center for the Terran core worlds, and the four-hour flight to reach it was every bit as safe and uneventful as you would imagine. I spent the time going over patrol patterns with Rashid, but it was hardly necessary. The old man was a better ship guard than I was.

We made the jump without incident. Caldswell must have wanted everyone to get some sleep, because as soon as the stars outside were replaced by the dull purple-gray blankness of hyperspace, the *Fool*'s lights switched to night cycle, plunging the ship into darkness.

Even though I'd fallen asleep in my armor earlier, I didn't actually feel that tired. I wasn't about to disobey the captain, though, so I dutifully went to my bunk. I was half hoping I could convince Nova to play cards with me for a bit, but when I stepped into our room, I found a note from her on my pillow informing me that she would be spending the jump with Mabel so as to "ensure no disturbance to the solemnity of my needed rest time."

My shoulders slumped. It was a sweet sentiment, but I almost went downstairs to ask her to come back. I didn't want to be alone tonight, especially since now that my helmet was off, the glowing creatures were back.

There were three of them in the room currently, all smaller than my thumb. Two were just sitting on the ceiling, the third was crawling across the closed door. Since they didn't show up on cameras, I wasn't sure if they'd been here the whole time or if they'd followed me in, though considering the little critters were afraid of me, or at least unwilling to come close, following seemed out.

I finished putting my suit away and changed into my nightshirt, cutting out the light as I crawled into bed. In the dark, the glowing bugs were much brighter, shining like little ghostly lanterns. If it wasn't for the part where seeing them probably meant I was insane, they would have been beautiful.

I closed my eyes and rolled over, burying my face in my pillow. *This* was why I hadn't wanted to be alone. Losing my memories was bad enough, but at least that was explainable as the result of a head wound. Now, between my weird reactions to the cook, the dream, and the bugs, it was getting harder to convince myself that I wasn't going batty. I didn't feel insane, though. Confused, sure, and sick of things I couldn't explain, but not *crazy*. But then, didn't all crazy people think they were sane?

I groaned and burrowed deeper under the covers. This was going nowhere. The responsible thing would be to go back to Caldswell and take him up on his offer. He played the hardass act to a T, but I was reasonably certain the captain would work with me. He couldn't trade to save his life, but otherwise Caldswell was a practical man. He didn't want to replace another security officer. I knew I should just get up and go talk to him, but when I thought about walking downstairs and knocking on his door, all I could picture was him standing in that dark bunker, handing his gun to the cook while I bled to death on the floor at their feet.

It was *really* insane to be afraid of someone for a thing they'd done in a dream, but I just couldn't seem to get over it. It didn't help that the stupid nightmare wasn't fading. A normal dream would have been long gone by now, but I could still remember every second of what I'd seen in the bunker like it had really happened. Just thinking about it was enough to make my fingers ache where Ren had squeezed them.

I balled my throbbing hand into a fist. This was getting ridiculous. I had enough to be afraid of in the real world, like hell was I going to lie here and be scared of a dream. That stupid thing had already messed up my life enough, making me look like an idiot in front of Rashid and Hyrek. I was not going to let it keep me awake when my captain had ordered me to sleep.

Forcing the whole mess out of my brain, I put my pillow over my head to block out the bugs' light and shut my eyes tight, focusing on my breaths. It was an old merc trick, and it worked like a charm. One lungful at a time, I breathed slower and slower until my body was still and my mind was empty. And finally, in the emptiness, I fell asleep.

Not surprisingly, I had bad dreams.

In most of them, I saw Cotter. He was back in his stupid yellow armor, firing his gun at something that looked like a human but was armored like a xith'cal. Sometimes I was firing too, but whoever was doing the shooting, it did no good. No matter how many bullets we put in it, the black thing wouldn't go down.

Cotter always died in those dreams. Sometimes I did, too. Once the black monster bit me through the shoulder, an impressive feat considering it had no mouth. Another time it ripped my head off while I was pinned on my back. My least favorite was when it stuck its hand in my stomach and I could feel its black claws closing inside my gut. But it wasn't the pain that made the dreams so awful, it was the confusion, because the black monster wasn't always my enemy. Sometimes he was dear to me. Sometimes, the worst times, he was both at once, stabbing me in the stomach even as he whispered my name in a soft, accented voice that made me want to cry.

I woke up in a blind panic, scrambling out of bed and into a crouch before I knew what I was doing. My body was soaked in sweat and charged to attack, but there was nothing to fight. I was alone in my dark bunk with only my fear and a single glowing bug for company.

I slumped to the floor, panting as I tried to calm my thundering heart back down to a reasonable pace. According to the clock on the dresser, I'd only been asleep for five hours, but there was no way I was going back to bed. Not with my whole body stuck in fight or flight.

When my pulse still hadn't calmed down after a minute of sitting still, I decided it was time to take a walk. Something repetitive and nonstrenuous would drive off the panic, and if I was quick, I could get another couple hours of rest in before the jump ended. That sounded good enough to me, so I heaved myself off the floor and slipped into the hall.

The *Fool* was dark and silent. Since there was nothing to do in hyperspace, it was one of the only times everyone on the ship could be asleep at once. I crept past the other bunks, my bare feet silent on the rubber mats. My idea was to go down to the cargo bay and run some laps where I wouldn't bother anyone, but when I reached the lounge, I was surprised to see a light shining under the closed door. Apparently, I wasn't the only one who couldn't sleep.

I opened the door and stuck my head in, but I didn't see anyone. The lounge was dark except for the runner lights and the lamp over the kitchen counter, the light I'd seen. Hopes for company dashed, I walked into the kitchen to cut the light off. But as my fingers landed on the switch, I caught something out of the corner of my eye.

Normally, it takes a bit more than a glimpse to send me into battle mode, but I was already jacked up, and I whirled around, hand going for the pistol that wasn't there. Good thing, too, because it wasn't the black-scaled creature from my nightmares waiting for me in the dark. It was the cook.

He was sitting on the couch in the corner, which was why I hadn't seen him from the door. He was hunched over with a glass cupped between his hands like an offering, and there was a freshly opened bottle of whiskey on the low table in front of him that, even in the dark, I could see was mostly empty. It was that more than anything that made me pause, because for some reason, I had the very distinct impression that the cook did not drink.

The memory of the weird immunity I'd had in my dream must have stuck with me, because I looked straight at him without thinking. But I was back in the real world now, and the revulsion hit me with a vengeance. I spun away at once, pushing my hands into my stomach. I was still fighting the nausea when I heard the soft whisper of movement behind me as the cook started to get up.

"Don't," I said. "I mean, don't leave on my account. I'm just passing through."

The movement stilled, and then I heard the couch creak as the cook sat back down. I let out the breath I'd been holding and started for the cargo bay stairs, eager to get out of this awkward situation. But after the first step, my feet stopped.

I couldn't begin to explain why. The cook was the last man in the universe I wanted to spend time with. Not only was I apparently allergic to his face, my brain had picked him out of everyone to be my dream executioner back in the bunker. That had to mean something, but I just couldn't make myself leave. The image of the nearly empty whiskey bottle was stuck in my head like a hook, and I just couldn't shake the feeling that the cook drinking alone was wrong. Very wrong. And I needed to do something about it.

"Need" was too light a word, actually. This was more like a compulsion. Maybe it was just another sign that I was going nuts, but whatever the reason, I was too tired to fight it.

Feeling like a complete moron, I turned and walked into the kitchen to grab a tumbler off the rack. Glass in hand, I crossed the lounge again and sat down on the couch beside the cook. When I was settled, I leaned over and snatched the bottle off the table.

"What are you doing?"

His voice was a whisper, but the words were remarkably crisp for a man who'd consumed most of a fifth of whiskey.

"Taking a shot for you," I answered, emptying the last of the liquor into my cup. "King's health."

I tossed the drink back before he could reply. It was a pretty big slug, even for me. There'd been enough whiskey left in the bottle to fill my glass almost to the brim, and it took me four swallows to get the whole thing down. The whiskey burned my throat as it went, and by the time I'd drunk the glass dry, I could feel the fire all the way to my toes.

I lowered my empty glass with a deep breath, blinking against the sudden spinning feeling that always followed a serious shot. I was still recovering when I heard the cook's sigh very close, and then his hand reached out to take the empty glass from me. "What was that about?"

The sound of his accented voice speaking softly in the dark sent my whole body rigid. "Solidarity," I choked out at last. "Now you're not drinking alone."

His hand stilled on the rim of the glass. I held my breath, terrified he was about to try and make me explain something I didn't understand myself. How did you explain to a man whose name you couldn't even keep in your head that the idea of him drinking alone was so awful you felt morally compelled to butt in? Fortunately, I didn't have to, because the cook didn't say anything else. He just sat there with his hand resting on the edge of my empty tumbler. And then, slowly, his fingers slid down the glass to touch mine.

It was such a small thing. His fingertips couldn't have been brushing more than a square inch of my skin, but we might have been tangled naked considering the effect it had on me. All at once, my heart was pounding, putting my whole body right back on edge, but not for a fight this time. What his touch brought was lust, pure and strong and completely inexplicable. How I could want a man I couldn't even look at without feeling sick I had no idea, but my body didn't care about the details. All it cared about was touching more of him.

The full cup of whiskey must have been hitting my brain right then, because I flipped my hand over to grab his without a thought, dropping the glass in the process. He caught it instantly, snatching the glass out of the air with his free hand. It was the most amazing catch I'd ever seen. Any other time I'd have made him do it again.

Now, though, I barely noticed. My entire focus was locked on the place where our skin touched.

Maybe it was the drink, but his fingers were noticeably warmer than mine. His whole body was. I could actually feel the heat of him radiating across the few inches that separated us, and I desperately wanted to get closer, to wrap myself around that warmth. But I wasn't that far gone just yet, so I settled for pulling his hand toward me so I could study his fingers, the only part of his body it seemed I could look at directly without feeling nauseous.

The cook took a sharp breath as I pulled him closer, but he didn't resist, just let me move him as I liked until his hand was sitting in my lap. It was a pretty tame touch, but by the time I'd gotten him where I wanted him, my own breaths had shrunk to pants. I kept expecting the cook to ask me what I was doing, which would have been a good question, because I didn't know myself. My body was moving on autopilot, touching his with a familiarity I couldn't begin to explain. But though I was acting like a total freak show, taking his booze uninvited and grabbing his hand like it was my property, the cook wasn't trying to escape. He was actually leaning closer, his body inching toward mine until I felt his forehead land on my shoulder.

I went completely still. My nightshirt was thin enough that I could feel the heat of the cook's skin where he rested against me and the soft pressure of his breath as he inhaled deeply, like he was trying to breathe me in. At the same time, the hand I was holding tightened on mine, his long, elegant fingers closing over my palm and gripping until I could have sworn I felt him begin to shake. Drunks are usually relaxed, but the cook was so close now I could feel the tension in his body, almost like he was straining against something even as he leaned a little farther into me.

By this point, I he was vaguely aware that I should be furious over such a massive invasion of my personal space. But I'd grabbed him first, and anyway, his weight felt good against me. Right, like it should always be there. The strange madness that had made me touch him was only fanned hotter by his nearness, and with his head right next to mine, I couldn't help thinking how easy it would be to turn and press a kiss against his hair. It would feel lovely, I bet, soft as silk and warm against my lips.

I'd already started to move when I caught myself. I jerked to a stop and closed my eyes with a silent curse. Drunk or no, this was getting out of hand. I needed to leave, now, before I did something really stupid, but the insane part of me wasn't ready to let go yet.

Since I couldn't make peace between the half of me that wanted to flee and the half that wanted to climb on top of the cook and put the lounge couch to the test, I settled for touching his hand, running my finger down his palm to the thin black tattoo that peeked out from under the edge of his shirt's old-fashioned button cuff. That surprised me, actually. The cook didn't seem like the tattoo type. But when I started nudging his sleeve up to see the black mark in full, a sentence appeared in my mind.

"This life for Tanya," I read, tilting my head to get a better look at the black markings. They were no language I'd ever seen, but that didn't seem to matter. I knew what they said. I was trying to figure out how that could be when I realized the cook had gone stone still.

Quick as he'd caught the glass, the cook stood up, pulling away from me so deftly I didn't even feel him moving until he was gone. I jerked up in surprise to see him stepping over the short coffee table, pulling down his sleeve as he went. The revulsion struck as soon as I looked, but I couldn't tear my eyes away as he deposited my glass in the kitchen and walked to the hall door. He paused when he reached it, but he didn't look back. Just lowered his head.

"I am sorry to have bothered you, Miss Morris," he said, his voice polite and distant. "Have a good evening."

Before I could answer, he was gone, leaving me alone in the dark. I stared at the closed lounge door for almost a minute before I stood and followed.

It was hard going. The whiskey had me now, and I stumbled

into the hall, using the wall to keep me up as I trudged back to my bunk. The glowing bug was right where I'd left it, but I didn't spare it another glance as I fell face-first into bed.

There were no nightmares this time. No black monster, no deaths. Instead, I dreamed I was lying on a narrow bunk in a small room while the cook made love to me with a thoroughness that took my breath away. And when I woke up flushed and panting to the hyperspace exit alarm, I was hard-pressed to say which dream was worse.

CHAPTER
4

"You do not look well," Rashid said when I walked into the lounge thirty minutes later. "Did you not sleep?"

"I slept great."

It was embarrassing to lie about something so petty, but I'd spent my whole shower putting what had happened last night out of my head, and I wasn't about to even brush that topic now. Rashid was still looking at me funny, though, so I hid behind my helmet, sliding it on so quickly the neuronet connectors snagged in my freshly braided hair. "Where are we?"

I'd meant the question for Rashid, but my com was on, and it was Basil who answered. "It's"—the aeon made a deep whistling sound that vibrated my speakers—"but since your throat can't handle that, most humans use the rough translation 'Ample.'"

It was a fitting name. The planet we were orbiting was huge and green, its sprawling landmasses covered in a grid of verdant fields so large their boundaries were visible from space. "Lot of traffic for a farming planet," I said, eying the dense swarm of ships around us and the even larger clump waiting to use the jump gate floating in orbit around Ample's moon.

"There's always traffic in the Sevalis," Caldswell said, his dry voice buzzing over my com. "This is actually light. You should see the pileups around the Seval itself."

I wrinkled my nose. "Aren't we already in the Seval?"

"We're in the *Sevalis*," Basil snapped. "The *Seval* is the name of the aeon home planet. Honestly, don't they teach you anything besides how to kill each other in Paradoxian schools?"

I probably had learned about the Seval at some point, but that was a long time ago, and anyway, I wasn't about to pass up an opening like that. "Oh sure," I said. "We also studied poultry butchering. I can demonstrate it for you sometime if you like."

I could almost hear Basil's feathers poofing up at that, but before the bird could retaliate, Caldswell cut him off. "Prepare for landing. We're on a schedule, people."

Despite being a farming planet, Ample had several cities. Huge ones, actually, with blocks of high-rises so big and tall they looked like mountains. Unlike Wuxia, though, or any other heavily populated planet I'd ever seen, including Paradox, there was no urban sprawl. The huge, vertical cities just ended, skyscrapers giving way to lush fields with nothing but a road between them. We landed in an empty field a few miles away from one such transition, but even though we were close enough to walk into town if we wanted, there was nothing around us. Just the dusty landing field sitting like a brown island in a vast green sea of farmland.

After the traffic we'd seen coming in, the emptiness was jarring. I didn't spot so much as a single aeon out in the fields. In fact, from the line of combine harvesters I could see moving on the horizon, it looked like everything here was automated, which was a letdown. Being so far from the Sevalis, Paradox had almost nothing to do with the aeons. Consequently, I'd never been on an aeon world before. Colonies were all well and good, but this was my first time on an honest to god alien planet. I'd run down to open the cargo door like a kid on King's Day the moment Basil cut the thrusters, so you can imagine my disappointment when, instead of a mysterious world full of gloriously colored alien birds, I got automated farm equipment and a bunch of plants.

"Where is everyone?" I asked, putting my hands on my hips.

"In the cities," said a cheerful voice behind me. "Aeons can't relax unless they're packed in like fish in a can."

I glanced at my rear camera to see Mabel coming out of the engine room with her cat in her arms. The captain's sister-in-law had traded her mechanic's coveralls for a colorful shirt, shorts, and a huge straw hat. She looked like a tourist, and because I'm the helpful sort, I told her so.

"And you look like an invasion force," Mabel said, setting Pickers gently on the floor before reaching up to touch the brim of her hat. "It keeps the sun out. It's bright here."

It was. Ample's sun was surprisingly strong, but the air was just warm, not hot. Perfect growing weather. "What are we here for again?"

"Ground nuts," Mabel said. "Assuming my order got through."

I made a face. "We're shipping nuts?"

"We've been doing *that* for years," Mabel said with a laugh. "And for your information, Ample's ground nuts are excellent profit per pound. Out here the price is low, but when we get closer to the Seval we can charge through the nose for them."

That perked me up. "We're going to the Seval?" Maybe I would get to see some birds after all.

"With an aeon for a pilot?" Mabel snorted. "Can't avoid it. It's the pull."

I frowned. "Pull?"

"The homing instinct."

I gave her a blank look, and Mabel tried again. "Aeons feel a constant pull toward their home planet. That's why they're the best navigators in the galaxy, because no matter where they are in the universe, they always know which direction home is, no equipment needed. And the farther away from the Seval they are, the stronger the pull gets. That's why the Sevalis controls such a relatively small area of space even though aeons outnumber humans two to one. They're trying to stay close to home." She paused, thinking. "Being near other aeons helps too, I'm told. That's why you'll never find an aeon city that doesn't look like they're all trying to stack on top of one another. Comfort in numbers."

"I guess that explains why Basil is always in such a bad mood," I said. "He's all alone."

Mabel's eyebrows shot up. "What are you talking about? Basil's a doll for an aeon."

I grimaced, suddenly glad that our section of Ample was so empty. If *Basil* was a doll, I never wanted to meet another aeon.

"Though I imagine he'll be a pill for the next few weeks," Mabel went on with a sigh. "The flock mentality can make him as pecky as the rest."

I was about to ask what she meant by that when the heavy sound of boots cut me off. We both looked up to see Caldswell coming down the cargo bay steps. Rashid was there too, suited up and serene as always. Next to him, the captain looked downright sour. "You ready to get this over with?"

"Just waiting on you," Mabel said.

Caldswell nodded and turned to me. "We should be back before dark. Keep up normal patrols and don't slack just because there's nothing around but plants and tractors."

I straightened up with a scowl. "With all due respect, sir, I don't slack."

To my surprise, Caldswell smiled at that. "I know, Morris, I know," he said, trotting down the ramp after Mabel. "Keep an eye on the new kid."

Rashid was fifty if he was a day, but he didn't seem bothered in the slightest by the captain's comment. He was dressed for business, too, with his sniper and assault rifle strapped over his back. He'd moved both pistols to thigh holsters to make room at his waist for an ammo belt that put my spare clips to shame, and there was a broad tactical knife at the small of his back that, judging from the wear on its handle, had seen a lot of use.

I looked him over with an appreciative whistle. "Ready for a war?"

He shrugged. "Considering the reputation of this ship, it seemed wise."

I couldn't help laughing at that. "If you knew what you were getting into, I'm surprised you took the job at all."

"A man must eat," Rashid replied, resting his hands on his pistol grips as he watched Mabel and Caldswell get into the nicer of the ship's two atmospheric skimmers and set off for the city. "And I am good at staying alive."

Looking at his arsenal, I believed it. "How do you want to work this?"

"It should be simple, I think," Rashid said, pulling his handset out of one of his chest pockets. He flipped it open, hit a few buttons, and then turned it around for me to see.

My eyes widened. His handset screen was divided up into ten small squares, each showing a different scene, but it still took me a few moments to realize that I was looking at a grid of the *Fool*'s security camera feeds. All of them.

"Holy shit," I said, grabbing the handset from him. "How did you get this?"

Rashid shrugged. "I asked Miss Starchild to patch me into the ship's security system." He gave me a look that, were it any less polite, would have been insultingly smug. "We are paid to be watchers. It seems absurd, then, not to watch with all the eyes available."

I could have punched myself in the face. I'd been on this ship for over three months now and it had never even *occurred* to me that I could ask for such a thing. Before I could get really pissed, though, Rashid took his handset back with a self-deprecating smile.

"Do not think I am so clever, Miss Morris. It is just experience. I've been told you were a Blackbird mercenary before this, used to far bigger worries. I, on the other hand, have been doing security work for many years, and I am well acquainted with all the little shortcuts." His smile widened. "Old dogs pick up many tricks in time."

I shook my head with a grin of my own. "I am *so* glad we hired you."

"I am delighted to hear it," Rashid said. "Now, as I was saying, I think I will set up on the roof and keep an eye on the cameras."

"And I'll take the ground," I said with a nod. "Guns up top, armor on bottom." Smooth and professional.

Just the thought made me feel better. I try not to indulge in self-pity, but things had been rough for me lately. After making such an idiot of myself in front of the cook last night, executing a smooth, professional job with a man who knew what he was doing sounded like heaven.

Since the hatch hadn't been part of our tour, I took Rashid up to the *Fool*'s roof myself. It was a good position for a sniper. There were no other ships on the landing field, and the terrain here was so flat you could see for miles in all directions. Still, I made sure he had everything he needed before hopping off the ship.

I might have been showing off a little, but after Rashid had shown me up so badly with the cameras, I was in the mood to prove something. My suit handled the eight-story drop from the *Fool*'s highest point with barely a twinge. I landed perfectly, rolling to my feet to the sound of Rashid's polite praise over our com.

And that was the height of excitement for the day. The fine weather lured everyone out of the ship. Even Hyrek went outside. When I asked him only half jokingly if his leaving the ship voluntarily was a sign of the apocalypse, he'd given me a superior look and told me he wasn't afraid of aeons.

"Why not?" I asked. "They can shoot, too."

But they usually don't, Hyrek typed, his sharp teeth gleaming in the sunlight. *Though they are now far removed from their roots, humans were originally predators. Aeons, however, are prey through and through. Most humans will react with violence if startled or threatened. Birds always run.* His toothy smile widened. *It's very entertaining.*

"Well," I said. "Try to keep the stampede away from the ship."

I'll see what I can manage, Hyrek replied, strolling out across the grass in long, ground-eating strides.

In the end, the only person who didn't go out was Basil. At first, I thought he was just being a grump like normal, but when he wouldn't even come down for lunch, I began to suspect that he was hiding. Other than my curiosity, though, our bird's behavior wasn't inconveniencing me, and I didn't give it much thought until just before sunset when three trucks drove into the field and parked beside the *Fool*'s ramp.

Not surprising considering where we were, the drivers were aeons. Beautiful ones, too, with electric blue and green feathers that looked much too fine for farmwork. The vehicles were aeon designed with the cab on top, which put the drivers nearly eleven feet off the ground. Still, the birds made the jump down with casual grace, flapping to a delicate landing at the foot of the *Fool*'s ramp.

There were six aeons in all, two for each truck. Once they were out, they grouped up in a tight knot and strolled into the cargo bay like they owned it. As they got closer, I saw that their talons had been painted to match their feathers, and several of them wore gold rings on their necks, almost like necklaces. It was a very striking look, and I smiled as I walked out to greet them.

"Can I help you?"

The largest of the birds, a huge, beautiful creature with a dazzling crest of aquamarine feathers, whistled at me, a long series of notes followed by a chirp that sounded like a question. I asked again, but all I got was more whistling, and that was when I realized these birds didn't understand Universal.

It had been so long since I'd met anyone who didn't speak the universe's second language that I wasn't sure what to do, and then I remembered I had a bird of my own. Basil was extremely put out about being asked to play translator, but I didn't have an aeon language program in my suit and I wasn't about to make these birds run everything they said through the ship's computer when I had a perfectly good aeon on board. I won in the end, and Basil came down, though from the way he trudged into the cargo bay, you'd have thought I was sending him to face a firing squad.

All the birds perked up when Basil appeared, their heads swiveling as one to watch him walk down the steps. A few of them even raised their wings a little, making them look larger. By contrast,

Basil looked shrunken, so much so that I didn't realize he was actually slightly taller than all but the largest of the new birds until he was standing next to me.

The aeon's leader began to whistle at once. Basil whistled back and turned to me. "They're here to deliver our shipment."

"I guessed that much," I said, glancing at the packed trucks. "Tell them to go ahead and load it into the bay."

Basil began to whistle again, but the other bird cut him off with a sharp whistle that sank to a delicate trill accompanied by a shake of its feathers, almost like a girl tossing her hair. Basil's eyes went wide at the motion, and he took a step back. The bird followed him, trilling again as it gracefully spread its wings to reveal the beautiful splash of orange across the inside.

Basil shivered like he'd been dunked in ice water, but I was grinning wide behind my visor. I might not know squat about aeon culture, but it didn't take a genius to guess what was going on. The beautiful feathers, the painted talons, the jewelry, the soft trilling... clearly, our little Basil had caught the eyes of some lovely local lady birds on the prowl for some fun.

When the first bird spread her wings wider and ducked her head, looking up at Basil through her short, spiky lashes, I decided it was time to stop being a buzz kill and leave Basil to his admirers. Who knew? Maybe getting lucky would chill him out a bit. I nodded politely at the birds and started down the ramp toward the trucks to get a look at the cargo, but before I'd taken two steps, Basil said, "Don't go, Morris."

I froze. It was hard to identify emotions other than scorn in the aeon's chirping voice, but I could have sworn Basil sounded afraid. The other aeons must have heard it too, because suddenly they were all moving forward with their wings spread, their beautiful whistles turning to angry squawks. Basil squawked back, pulling himself up straight for the first time since he'd entered the cargo bay.

I've never wished I'd sprung for a translation program as much as I did at that moment. I would have paid a month's wage to know what Basil had just said, because it hit the other birds like a match to a firecracker. All at once, the aeons were right in Basil's face, pushing him with their large wings. He stumbled back under the onslaught, tripping over his normally graceful legs. The others closed the distance in a flash, their painted claws lashing out to slash Basil's wings, only to hit my suit as I stepped into the fray.

"That'll be enough of that," I said, hand dropping to Sasha.

The aeons glared at me, and then the shortest one said, in perfect Universal, "This is none of your affair, monkey."

Rage shot through me. These damn chickens had been faking the whole time. But I knew better than to let my anger show. I rested my hands casually on my hips instead, thumb moving easily over my gun. "I'm afraid it is," I said, letting my Paradoxian drawl through nice and thick, just to make sure they knew exactly what kind of monkey they were dealing with. "Now, are you going to move along, or am I going to have myself a turkey shoot?"

And then, just for effect, I popped Sasha's safety.

The birds shrank back at the metallic click, and the biggest of them shot me a nasty look. I responded with a nice, predatory smile, and like the prey Hyrek claimed they were, the birds turned and ran, their painted claws clicking on the metal as they trucked double time down the ramp. I could see Basil getting back on his feet through my rear cam, but he didn't move an inch from my shadow until all the aeons were back at their trucks.

"Unload it neatly," I warned.

The aeons squawked at me, but they were already pulling hover platforms around to get the crates. I watched until I was sure the birds weren't going to screw us over before clicking Sasha's safety back into place. "You mind telling me what that was all about?"

"Yes," Basil answered.

I arched an eyebrow as I turned to face him. "What did you say to those girls, anyway?"

"I told them what I thought of their display," Basil said, resettling his feathers with a shake. "And they aren't girls. Those are males."

I blinked. "But," I said stupidly, "they're so pretty."

Basil rolled his huge yellow eyes. "I know it is difficult to lift your mind out of the rut of your humancentric expectations, but what you call *pretty* aeons call *macho*. The brighter the plumage, the more macho the male, and as you could see from that incredibly garish display, those are very aggressive males. Thugs, you might say." He turned up his beak. "Painted claws and *jewelry*, ugh. How much tackier can you get?"

While he was talking, I was looking over Basil's chocolate feathers with a new eye. "So," I said. "If aeon males are brightly colored, what's your story? Did your feathers never grow in or something?"

Basil puffed up into an angry ball. "*Of course my feathers grew in!* What kind of idiot are you?"

"The kind who just saved your drumsticks," I said, giving him a flat look.

Basil snapped his beak closed, and for the first time since I'd met him, our bird looked almost ashamed. "It's dye," he said at last, swiveling his head so that his rust-red crest bobbed. "I dye my feathers to a female shade every molt."

My face must have been a sight, because Basil got even poofier. "It's not like I go around cross-dressing or anything!" he snapped. "I don't pretend to be female, it's just a personal choice. There are certain expectations put on males that I'm uncomfortable meeting."

"You mean like being an aggressive, macho asshole?" I said, glancing back at the aeons, who were still whistling insults at me as they worked. "But you're yourself, aren't you? Can't you just, I don't know, not be a jerk?"

Basil heaved an enormous sigh. "You are *so* human."

"Thanks," I said. "You don't mean that as a compliment, do you?"

"No," Basil said.

I rolled my eyes, and Basil gave a long, whistling sigh.

"Look," he said with uncharacteristic patience. "You've heard how all aeons can feel the Seval, right?"

I nodded.

"Well, it's more than just knowing where the planet is," Basil said. " 'Seval' is a human transliteration of—" He chirped sharply, and he was right, it did sound like he was saying *seval.*

"There's no actual corresponding word in Universal," he went on. "But 'flock' is close enough. And the nearer I am to the aeon homeworld, the stronger the seval, the flocking urge, is. You're human, so it's easy for you to say 'just don't be that way,' but I don't have a choice. When we're around other aeons, it becomes harder and harder to be an individual, to make your own decisions. The flock pulls at you until you become what the majority expects, whether you want to or not."

I cringed. That did sound pretty horrible. "So you dye your feathers to get out of what's expected of you?"

"I dye my feathers because I don't want to look like a tacky, over-sexed moron," Basil snapped. "I get *out* by working a job that keeps me well away from the Sevalis. Most of the time, anyway." He shot a death glare at the other aeons.

"Well," I said with a grin. "At least that explains why you're on the *Fool.* After dealing with a flock full of jerks, even Caldswell's madhouse would be a step up."

Basil turned on me so fast I almost fell over. "Listen, simian," he said, the words whistling with anger. "I don't know where you think you get off talking like that about the captain, but Brian Caldswell is a *good man.* I realize you Paradoxians have a hard time appreciating that idea since it doesn't have anything to do with shooting, stabbing, or drinking, but try to get it through your thick helmet. I owe the captain my life and I will not tolerate you slandering him any further, do you understand?"

"God and king, Basil. It was just a joke."

"Do you understand?"

"Yes sir," I said, putting up my hands.

Basil nodded and whirled around, his claws clicking on the metal as he climbed the stairs two at a time. "I want to be informed the moment the captain or Nova gets back," he announced. "In the meanwhile, make sure those idiots don't eat the nuts they're supposed to be loading."

"Yes sir," I said again, but the bird had already vanished into the lounge. I sighed at the empty stairs then turned back to the cargo ramp, yelling at the aeons to get a move on.

———

Despite the rocky ending of our escapade in the cargo bay, Basil was actually much nicer to me than usual when we prepped the ship for takeoff that evening. We had everything packed in and secured by the time the crew got back. Rashid kept me posted on arrivals, but I took care to stay on patrol and out of the way. I'd successfully avoided the cook since our incident last night, and I wasn't about to break that streak now. Fortunately, he seemed to be tied to Ren. The two of them vanished into the captain's quarters as soon as they got back, much to my delight.

It was full dark by the time Mabel and Caldswell returned. We had the ship warmed up and ready to fly when they got on, but we never actually made it into the air. When Basil called the tower for final departure clearance, the flight control office informed him that all flights were restricted due to a magnetic storm in the upper atmosphere. The sky was perfectly clear and full of stars, so I didn't see what the fuss was about. Neither did Basil.

"There's less interference here than there was on Wuxia," he was shouting when I poked my head into the bridge to see what was going on. "What are they waiting for, a bribe?"

"Maybe," Caldswell said. The captain was lounging in his worn chair with his feet up on the new instrument board in front of him. "Relax, Basil. So long as we get moving by dawn, we're still on schedule. There's nothing wrong with a peaceful night every now and then."

Basil folded his wings in a huff, but he didn't argue. Considering how he'd been acting all day, I'd expected a full-blown tantrum, but Basil's demands about respecting the captain apparently went for himself as well. That, or he knew it was pointless to try to push Caldswell around. The man was about as movable as a mountain range.

It was kind of nice to have a peaceful night, and, other than our run-in with the thug birds, Ample certainly was peaceful. Even the automated harvesters had shut down for the night, leaving nothing but dark and the sound of the wind in the fields. We'd already locked the doors for liftoff, so I just left them sealed. With Rashid on the roof, there was no point in patrolling outside anyway. Anything hostile that got within a hundred feet of the ship would be shot before I could reach it.

Since I was avoiding the cook like the plague, I asked Nova to bring me up two plates from the lounge. She was confused by the request but did as I asked, bringing me two plates loaded down with delicious-looking food. I thanked her profusely and ate mine in a rush before taking the second up to Rashid.

My new partner didn't look like he'd moved all day. He was lying exactly where I'd left him, flat on his stomach with his rifle ready. I'd have felt a little bad about that if not for the fact that he'd just earned a day's wage for lying in the sun.

He took his dinner with effusive thanks and a fawning note to the cook over the com. Since he couldn't shoot and eat at the same time, I sat beside him, enjoying the night air while I kept an eye on the rest of the ship through Rashid's open handset. It was amazingly handy to be able to watch things inside even while I was on the roof, and I was making plans to see about patching my suit into the security system as well when I realized Rashid had gone still beside me.

He held up his hand before I could say anything, motioning me down. I obeyed, flattening myself on my stomach next to Rashid's discarded plate. With the moon overhead and the *Fool*'s exterior floodlights, the night was actually pretty bright, but it still took me almost a minute to catch what had put Rashid on edge.

The tall crops in the field across the road from the landing area were moving. That wouldn't have been weird except that there was no wind at the moment, and the crops were rustling in a straight line. Far too straight for a wild animal.

Cursing under my breath, I flipped on my density sensor and cranked the sensitivity as high as it would go. The field was at the very edge of my suit's range, but the Terran armor pushing through it was big enough that I saw it no problem.

"There are two behind us as well," Rashid said.

I looked over at him. The voice had come through my com, not my outside speakers, but I didn't see a mic on his suit. Even stranger, my side camera had been pointed right at his face when he'd spoken, and his lips hadn't moved at all.

Rashid's eyes slid to me, and his mouth curled up in a tight smile. "Implanted throat mic," he said without moving his mouth, lifting his head a little so I could see the tiny scar on his neck.

My eyes widened. Implants like that were expensive as hell. What kind of merc had Rashid been, anyway?

But this wasn't the time for that. I turned my attention back to the shapes my density sensor had drawn against the plants. "I see four in front," I said, swirling my cameras. "You said two behind us?"

Rashid nodded, pulling on a pair of extremely nice goggles I hadn't even noticed hanging around his neck. "And two more on the left flank as well," he added, tilting his head. "Might be too far for you, though."

"But not for you?"

Rashid smiled. "I am usually a sniper, Miss Morris. If I can't see far, I'm rather useless, am I not?"

He had me there. "Can you show me?"

He nodded, and a video feed patched into my suit instantaneously. Suddenly, I had a new set of eyes to look through. Very, very good ones. Whatever sensors Rashid had in those goggles, they were phenomenal. My suit counted ten enemies in total, all armored, in a ring around the field where the *Fool* was sitting, closing at a steady pace. That was threat enough for me, and I beeped Caldswell.

The captain answered immediately. "What is it, Morris?"

"Sir, we've got ten bogeys closing in. Terran armor. You expecting someone?"

"Not tonight," Caldswell said with a sigh.

I glanced at Rashid. "You want us to try talking first?"

"You're sure they're coming for us?" Caldswell asked.

I looked around at the empty field. "We're kind of the only target, sir."

"Fair enough," he conceded. "Is the ship locked up?"

"Yes sir," I answered, pulling Sasha from her holster.

"Then do it," Caldswell said, and the com clicked off.

"You heard the captain," I said to Rashid with a wide grin. "Pop 'em."

"Yes ma'am," he answered, easing his finger onto the trigger of his long, sleek rifle.

As a close-quarters fighter, I didn't normally get a chance to watch snipers at work, but even I wasn't ignorant enough to think that what Rashid did was standard practice. There was no hesitation while he lined up his sights, no careful aiming. I didn't even hear the shot. He simply squeezed the trigger, and four hundred feet away, the plants stopped rustling.

Rashid was already moving to the next target. He pivoted his rifle slightly to the left and squeezed again. I was listening hard this time, but all I heard was a click and a soft whistle of air before another target went down. He'd dropped a third man before the enemy finally realized what was happening and started to charge.

As soon as Rashid squeezed off his second shot, I'd known that if I didn't get in soon, there'd be nothing left. By the time the third shot fired, I was jumping off the *Fool*'s edge. No show-off maneuvers this time, though. I fell fast and landed hard, letting my suit roll me back onto my feet. Sasha was ready when I came up, and I hit the first man who broke cover square in the head from across the field.

I watched the bullet hit with visceral satisfaction. Even for me, that was a nice shot, and it just felt so damn good to be back in action after days of worry and bullshit. But as I looked for my next target, I realized something was wrong. Sasha had hit the first man dead-on in the helmet for a clean head shot, but he wasn't going down.

That happened sometimes with the cheaper suits. Their response system kept them running forward even when the man inside was dead, but I didn't think that was the case now. The armor's helmet was dented and its visor cracked, but the enemy was still coming. My shot hadn't gotten through.

I bit back a curse and fired again, hitting him at the knee joint where armor is always weakest. This time, the shot got through, and the heavy suit went down with a crash. My confusion had cost me, though. The enemy was clear of the crop cover now and close enough that I no longer needed to look at them through my density sensor. In the glare of the *Fool*'s floodlights, I could see that this was no bandit team in secondhand suits. These men were dressed head to toe in Terran High Velocity Full Plate, which meant we were in trouble.

"HVFP team!" I yelled. "Military grade, you won't get through on the normal spots." I pulled up my gun and jumped back, using the shadows at the ship's base for cover while I lined up my next shot carefully. "Aim for the joints, they're the hardest to armor."

"Yes ma'am." Rashid's voice was calm in my ear. As he spoke, I saw the man whose leg I'd shot jerk as a sniper shot finished him off.

I shot the next man at the same time, but the enemy was as well trained as they were well armored. Their suits seemed to fly across the field, weaving in a pattern so erratic my targeting computer couldn't keep up with it. Even with a wide-open field and the light at my back, I only managed to take out two more before they reached me. After that, I holstered Sasha and prepared for hand to hand.

As always, the Lady Gray was looking out for me. My suit had been keeping a running tally on our enemy since I'd first picked them up. Of the ten we'd seen at the start, three were down to Sasha and four were down to Rashid's deadly silent rifle. That left three to go, the first of which was almost on top of me.

Like all Terran armor, my enemy was huge. His suit was black, sleek, and even larger than Cotter's had been. But for all the expensive polish, he was still just a Terran tin can, and I let him get in close before I punched him in the side.

The second my fist connected, I let Elsie fly. She shot out of her sheath on the side of my wrist, her thermite edge firing as it touched the air. Phoebe never could have handled a kidney shot like this. She'd been a slashing blade, not a thrusting one. But with Elsie's steel core attached to my armor, I was able to throw my full weight into the blow, and with the thermite going, the combined effect was breathtaking. The burning tip of Elsie's tungsten blade lit up like the sun as it melted through the overlapping plates of the heavy suit's articulated side, melting the blade-catch like a welding torch through a spiderweb to stab deep just below my enemy's rib cage.

The Terran had braced for a punch, though not too hard. He'd clearly assumed, like most Terrans did, that my smaller suit couldn't hurt his. If I'd only been punching, he might have been right, but it's always a bad idea to let your enemy get close before you know her weapons. Unfortunately for him, people who make that mistake with me don't usually survive to put the knowledge to use.

I could see the Terran's surprise on his face through his tinted visor as he staggered. Then his breach foam fired, filling his suit with quick-hardening goo as his systems tried to plug the hole I'd made. But breach foam doesn't mean jack to a thermite blade. I shifted my weight and pushed up, yanking Elsie through his ribs to finish the kill. The gutted man went down with a stagger, dropping his own weapon, a type of gun I'd never seen before, at my feet.

I didn't have time to examine it. My next enemy was already rounding the *Fool*'s port side fifteen feet away. He must have been using a density sensor too, because he fired the second his arm was clear, shooting blind around the corner. My shield flipped up to catch the bullet automatically as soon as my camera saw the gun pointed my direction, but it wasn't a bullet that hit me. It was a lightning bolt.

Electricity arced from the man's gun, blasting through my shield and hitting my suit hard enough to blow me backward. For a moment, my systems flickered, but my Lady doesn't go down that easy. She was back on line before I hit, flipping me over to land on my feet. Sasha was in my hand when I came up, and I fired a three-shot spread before I could think.

The man had made it around the *Fool*'s corner by this point, and all three bullets hit him dead in the face, but not before he fired a second time. The lightning shot out again, and this time I recognized it. He was using a charge thrower, the clunky, extremely expensive guns used to subdue armored combatants without injury. I'd never even seen one outside of the arenas, where they were used to take down blood-mad gladiators. Definitely not the kind of gun a pirate would carry, but then I'd known these assholes weren't pirates from the second I'd seen the HVFP.

The bullets I'd shot into the man's face threw off his aim, and the lightning missed me. Thanks to the damn HVFP, though, he was still moving. He jerked his gun up again, but I didn't give him another chance. I jumped on him like a tiger, slicing through the neck of his suit with Elsie's burning blade.

It was a beautiful piece of work. Elsie's white fire was burning full tilt now, and the thermite's heat combined with the hard strength of her tungsten core ripped through the superheavy armor like paper. But as I pushed up to finish the slice, I realized I probably shouldn't be doing this. We needed to know who was attacking us, and it was hard to question a man without a head. I was finding it hard to care, though. The battle fury was singing loud and lovely in my head. For the first time in days, I didn't feel sick, crazy, or confused. I felt powerful, and I took my enemy's head in a clean, masterful stroke.

I was just finishing the follow-through when my suit's proximity alarm went off. I looked up from my defeated enemy to see the final man standing directly behind me. I spun as soon I saw him, smoke trailing behind my blade as Elsie burned off the last of his teammate's blood, but it was too late. The man's charge gun was already pressed against my back, and my whole suit jerked as he pulled the trigger.

Charge throwers are short-range weapons. The first bolt I'd eaten had lost some of its potency over the fifteen feet of air it had passed through to reach me. This time there was no such problem. The lightning blasted my suit full force, throwing me twenty feet down the *Fool*'s hull. Or that was what I assumed happened. I couldn't actually see, because the moment the charge hit, my suit had gone dark.

I landed facedown hard enough to knock my teeth, bouncing across the dirt like a skipping stone. I was sending frantic signals to my cameras, but my suit was overloaded and nothing was coming up. But as I lay panicking in the dark, trying to get my dead systems up and under control so I could see my enemy before he killed me, I had the weirdest sense of déjà vu.

I had no time to worry about it, though. I rolled myself over, thanking the king that I wore a suit light enough to move in when its motor was dead. I pushed my visor up with clumsy fingers just in time to see the man running toward me, charge gun sparking and ready. Elsie was still burning blindingly white on my arm, but a fat lot of good that did. In an unforeseen consequence, the combined weight of my new blade and Sasha made my right arm too heavy to lift without my motor, effectively pinning me to the ground. I could still tilt my wrist, though, so that was what I did.

The man must not have expected me to still be kicking, because he didn't even try to dodge when I swiveled Sasha toward him. Or maybe he just didn't think I could do it. Considering the weird angle my hand was pinned at, I didn't blame him. It would take a miracle for me to land a shot. But when you practice enough, miracles happen more often than you might think.

My first shot whizzed over his shoulder, but the second hit him in the chest hard enough to make his huge suit stagger. By the third shot, I'd gotten the hang of the weird angle, and I got him square in the neck. This close, even his HVFP wasn't thick enough to save him from a pistol built to shred armor. Sasha's bullet ripped through the articulated joints at his neck, and the man went down on top of me like a falling tree.

Thank the Sainted King he was the last one, because with my suit dark and the enormous weight on top of me, I was trapped. Even without power, the Lady protected me from most of his bulk, but I didn't have the strength to push the dead man off. Fortunately, I wasn't stuck long. As soon as the last man went down, the cargo bay door opened, and Rashid ran out with the captain.

"You all right, Morris?" Caldswell yelled.

"I will be once you get this tank off me," I yelled back, shoving the huge suit as hard as I could.

Even with the captain and Rashid there to help, I didn't see how we were going to move a suit of HVFP without a crane. Somehow, though, Caldswell got the body rolling enough that I was able to pop my armor and scramble free.

"What the hell was that?" I asked, gasping for air.

"I don't know," Caldswell said, looking out at the fields around us. "But I mean to—"

He cut off abruptly, and I shot to my feet, whirling around with Sasha ready in my bare hands. It was a stupid thing to do. Firing my anti-armor pistol outside my armor was a ticket to a broken arm, but I was still stuck in the battle fury. My body was primed for another attack, but when I saw what had made Caldswell go quiet, all of that drained away.

The monster from my dream was standing at the edge of the *Fool*'s floodlights. Even this far away, there was no mistaking those glossy black scales. Just like in my nightmare, it was human shaped but covered in black scales like a xith'cal. It had claws like a xith'cal too, only larger, more deadly, and as soon as I saw them, the old wound in my stomach seized up. I was too distracted to wonder about that, though, because the monster wasn't looking at us. It was looking at *me*, its black eyes glittering with alien intelligence, and though the creature had no mouth at all, I could have sworn it was smiling.

The whole thing was too surreal to be believed. I was trying to figure out if I was dreaming again when the captain grabbed my arm so hard I yelped.

"Get in the ship," Caldswell said.

The command was absolute, and I was moving before I thought to argue, scrambling to gather the Lady's pieces. Rashid moved to help me a few seconds later, and we soon had my suit together. The captain didn't move the whole time.

Only when we were both safe inside the cargo bay did Caldswell follow us, which meant I didn't see his huge pearl-handled disrupter pistol until he was at the top of the ramp. For the second time in as many minutes, I felt like someone had punched me in the gut. The gun in the captain's hand was the same gun he'd given the cook in the bunker. The gun from my *dream*.

I was still staring dumbfounded when the sound of someone pulling a gun snapped me back to the fight. Rashid had his anti-armor pistol out and was aiming it at the thing across the field to cover the captain's retreat. I was pretty sure there was no way he could hit the thing from this distance with a sidearm, but before he could even try, the black monster vanished into the dark.

Without my suit, I didn't have sensors, so I looked at Rashid. My new partner already had his goggles up. He swept across the field, then pushed them down again with a shake of his head. "Gone," he said quietly. "Like a ghost."

We both looked at Caldswell then, but the captain was already mashing the button to close up the cargo bay with the butt of his gun. As the door slid down, Caldswell yanked out his com and started for the stairs. "Basil," he barked. "Get us out of here."

"Yes, captain," Basil said, his whistling voice all business.

I wasn't so calm. "What about them?" I shouted, pointing at the downed HVFP suits as I ran after the captain. "We need to search the bodies at least. Find out why—"

"We're not investigators," Caldswell snapped, holstering his gun. "We're taking our cargo and getting out of here. You each get your combat bonus, and that's the last I want to hear on the subject. Understood?"

I opened my mouth to say like hell that was the end of this, but Rashid beat me to the punch.

"It will be hard to just let go of being attacked by such a high-grade military team," he said smoothly. "But my memory is easily addled by large numbers. If the combat bonus was increased, doubled perhaps, it might be enough to put all of this out of my mind."

I turned on him, horrified. "Are you seriously trying to extort—"

"Done," Caldswell, pausing at the lounge door just long enough to point his glare at me. "Morris?"

I shrank under the captain's gaze. If looks could kill, I'd have been sliced to ribbons by this point. But I wasn't dead yet, and a meek nod made sure I stayed that way.

"Good," Caldswell said. "Take care of your suit and meet me downstairs in five minutes. As for you," he turned back to Rashid, "your memory better stay addled."

Rashid's smile was cool as ever. "It is already forgotten, sir."

I was too flabbergasted to do more than stare as Caldswell nodded and marched into the lounge. But while I was dumbly watching the captain walk around the corner, I noticed the cook standing just inside the lounge door. He didn't look at me, just stepped into place behind Caldswell like he'd been waiting for the captain to come up. But as he turned, I saw that he also had a gun in his lowered hand. A huge pearl-handled disrupter pistol that was almost a twin of Caldswell's.

"Miss Morris?"

I looked over to see Rashid holding the pieces of my Lady in his arms. "Shall we go? The captain sounds impatient."

I didn't honor that with a reply, just turned on my heel and stomped up the stairs.

CHAPTER
5

I had Rashid put the Lady's pieces on my bunk before sending him off to lash in for launch. It was a bit late—Basil was already pushing the engines—but he did as I said without complaint. I held on to my bunk for the worst of the initial thrust, but the second the gravity evened out, I was on the floor fitting my suit into her case.

Thankfully, it looked like the Lady was only shorted out. I ran a full diagnostic anyway, checking each system before I sealed my suit into her case to let the nano-repair do its work. Once I'd finished everything that could safely be called taking care of my suit, I headed down the hall to meet my fate.

Basil must have lit a fire under someone, because the jump flash washed over the ship before I'd reached the spiral stair to the *Fool*'s lower deck. There was no destination announcement, not even a notice of how long we'd be in. But while the quick jump meant whoever had attacked us wouldn't be able to follow, it made me feel worse rather than better. There was nowhere to escape in hyperspace, and I was suddenly feeling very trapped.

I wasn't ready to face Caldswell. I needed more time—time to figure out what that monster I'd seen across the field really was, time to figure out where I could have seen the captain's gun other than in my dream. Most of all, I needed time to sort out what was real and what wasn't, because with the glowing bugs floating ahead of me down the hall, I was no longer sure of anything. But needing gets you nothing, and though I hadn't felt like much of one lately, I was still a merc and this was still my job. My captain had ordered me to appear, so I squared my shoulders and marched up to his door.

It opened on the first knock, and I stepped inside to see Caldswell waiting at the little table by his window just like before. This time, though, there was a tiny glowing bug crawling up the arm of his jacket. I did my best not to look at it as I stopped at parade rest like I was back in the army.

Caldswell gave me a long look and waved at the couch across from him. "Sit down, Morris."

I obeyed. The little glowing bug scurried away when I got close, hopping off the captain's arm to land on the wall behind him. The sudden movement caught my eye, which was why I didn't see the cook until I was trapped.

He was leaning on the frame of Ren's bedroom door, not looking at me as pointedly as I had avoided the bug. For an irrational moment, that actually pissed me off. He'd been the one who'd put his head on my shoulder, and now he didn't want to look at me? Fortunately, the revulsion picked that moment to kick in, knocking some sense back into me, and I jerked my eyes away, looking at the captain's daughter instead.

Ren was sitting on her bed, staring blankly down at her feet. For a moment, seeing her sparked a swell of panic, and I grit my teeth. Was there nowhere safe to put my eyes? Fortunately, the panic eased when I realized that this Ren hadn't even noticed me. That, at least, was normal.

"Morris."

I turned back to the captain with a silent curse. Caldswell was glaring daggers at me, and justifiably so. Spacing out when you were supposed to be reporting in was not a wise career move. "Sorry, sir," I said, giving him my full attention.

Caldswell waved my apology away. "Do you know why I called you here?"

I could think of a lot of reasons, but only one seemed safe. "Because of Rashid?"

Caldswell's laugh surprised me. "Hardly," the captain said. "I've been employing mercenaries longer than you've been alive. If I balked every time I had to bribe one into keeping his mouth shut, I wouldn't be in business. I actually like him better now that I've seen him acting like the usual money-grubbing merc."

I took a deep breath. So much for safe. "With all due respect, sir," I said cautiously, "if you're not mad about that, why am I here?"

Caldswell grabbed something off the couch beside him and put it on the table. It landed with a plastic clack, and when he moved his hand, I saw it was one of the HVFP team's lightning guns. "Do you know what that is?"

"It's a charge thrower," I replied. "Nonlethal anti-armor weapon."

"And why do you think a military team would attack my ship with nonlethal anti-armor weapons?"

I opened my mouth, then closed it almost immediately. I'd been so caught up in the black-scaled monster and Caldswell's disrupter pistol, I hadn't actually gotten a chance to think through the attack itself yet. But when he put it like that, the answer seemed pretty obvious.

"They were after me," I said, far more calmly than I felt.

The captain nodded. "You were the only target those guns would be effective against, and they must have wanted you alive. Otherwise, it would have been much easier to just shoot you and be done with it."

I disagreed. The fact that I was still alive after so many combat tours was a testament to exactly how hard it is to "just shoot me and be done with it." Ego aside, though, I understood what the captain was saying; what I didn't get was why.

"Why me?" I asked. "I mean, it makes sense to take down the most dangerous target first, but why attack the *Fool* at all? If they wanted ground nuts, there's a warehouse just down the road that doesn't have two mercenaries guarding it."

Caldswell leaned forward to rest his elbows on the table. "Have you remembered anything from the attack on Falcon Thirty-Four yet?"

I wanted to ask him why the hell that mattered, but all I said was, "No sir."

The captain sighed. "I don't know exactly what happened tonight," he said. "But I'm going to make some calls and see if I can't find out. In the meanwhile, I'm confining you to the ship."

"What?" I said, horrified.

"Just until I get some leads in," Caldswell assured me. "You'll still get on-planet pay, but shore leave and other excursions are out of the question until…"

The captain was still talking, but I wasn't listening anymore. My upset at being put under house arrest had been momentarily derailed by the sight I'd just caught out of the corner of my eye.

Behind the captain, I could see through the open door into Ren's room. She hadn't moved the entire time I'd been here, so when she did, it caught my attention, but it was what she was doing that kept it. While Caldswell and I had been discussing the attack, the little glowing bug had made its way over to Ren's bed. It had been gracefully bobbing on the sheet beside her when Ren's hand shot out and grabbed the bug midhop.

She hadn't even taken her eyes off the floor. Her hand had snatched the bug out of the air blind, crushing it so fast my breath caught before I remembered that the glowing bugs moved through bodies as easily as they moved through walls. But as I was waiting for the bug to drift out of her clenched hand, a flash of light went off like a spark inside her fist. It was so faint and fast I never would have caught it if I hadn't been staring straight at her. But I was, and now that I'd seen it, I couldn't help cringing, especially when Ren's eyes slid over to look at me. With a small smile that cut me to the bone, she opened her fist to show me the empty space where the little bug had—

"Morris!"

I jumped and looked over to see Caldswell staring at me like I'd lost my mind. The cook had pushed off the wall as well, and though I didn't dare look at his face, I could feel his eyes boring into me. Behind him, Ren was staring at her feet again like nothing had happened.

Caldswell snapped his fingers in front of my face, and I looked back to him at once, blushing furiously. "Sorry, sir," I said quickly. "I'll stay on the ship."

The captain sat back and fixed me with a searching look, and I started scrambling to come up with an excuse for my distracted behavior that didn't involve glowing bugs. In the end, though, it wasn't necessary, because Caldswell just picked up where he'd left off.

"As I was saying, we'll be doing a series of short jumps to be sure we weren't followed. After that, I'm putting us in at one of the aeon commerce stations so I can try getting to the bottom of what happened on Ample. I won't need you back on duty for another three hours, so go get some rest. That's an order."

"Yes sir," I said, standing in a rush. "Thank you, sir."

Caldswell nodded and shooed me toward the door, but as I turned to go, keeping my eyes firmly away from the cook or Ren or the newest little glowing bug that had just drifted through the ceiling right in front of me, the captain said, "And Morris?"

I stopped.

"The offer to talk is still open."

I closed my eyes with a long, silent breath. "I'll keep that in mind, sir."

"Dismissed."

I was out the door before the final syllable was out of his mouth. It was an appalling breach of decorum to run out while your officer was still talking, but I couldn't stay in that room another second. I jogged down the hall, picking up speed, but I didn't go up the spiral stair to my bunk. Instead I swung through engineering and entered the cargo bay from the back.

Caldswell had told me to get some rest. Considering I'd just come off a fight and a full day's worth of work, you'd think that would be an easy command to follow, but I knew if I tried to go to sleep now, I'd only have more nightmares. What I really wanted was to get drunk and forget about this shit for a while, but I couldn't do that either, not so long as the cook was also the bartender. So I did the next best thing. I ran.

The aeons had stacked the crates of ground nuts almost to the ceiling, but there was still a clear pathway around the outside of the cargo bay. I ran it as fast as I could, my bare feet slapping on the metal as I whirled around the corners. I ran until my legs burned and my lungs felt like they would explode, pushing harder and harder until my pounding heart drowned out all the fear and uncertainty.

But sweet as it was, it couldn't last. As much as I wanted to, I couldn't run forever. Eventually, I stumbled to a stop, flopping down on the stairs to catch my breath and finally face what I'd been running from.

Funny enough, it wasn't the HVFP team. Terrifying as it was to think there was someone out there who wanted me badly enough to send that kind of hardware, I understood armor. I could shoot up Terran tin cans all day and thank them for the exercise. What I couldn't understand was everything else.

I dug my hands into my sweaty hair. If Rashid and the captain hadn't clearly seen the black monster across the field, I would have chalked it up to another hallucination. Honestly, I almost wished it had been. At least a hallucination would have fit in with the rest of my weird shit, but I didn't have a category for the real thing. I didn't know where to put any of this—the guns from my dream, the floating bugs, Ren. I knew it was ruining my life and my chances of reaching goals, but I didn't know how to beat it. I didn't know what to do at all.

I knew what I *wanted* to do. I wanted to shoot something, just kill whatever it was that was causing this and retake control, but there was nothing to shoot. I didn't know where to find the black monster or what it was, and I *couldn't* shoot the bugs. I couldn't even touch them. I couldn't do *anything*, and that made me angriest of all.

Shaking with rage that had no outlet, I slammed my hands down and heaved myself to my feet. I would run some more, I decided. Run until I was too tired to care about any of this bullshit. It was a coward's escape, but anything was better than sitting here being furious over things I had no control over. But just as I was about to get going, I noticed that my hands were dirty.

At first I thought the black gunk must have come from the cargo bay stairs. They were high traffic and metal, prone to grime, and I hadn't been looking when I'd flopped down on them. But the backs of my hands were dirty as well as my palms, and none of it rubbed off on my clothes. It was almost like they were stained, like I'd dipped them to the wrist in ink. Also, now that I was paying attention, I realized my hands were tingling with pins and needles, like they'd fallen asleep.

A cold trickle of fear ran down my spine, but I kept my breathing steady. I couldn't panic. My senses hadn't exactly been trustworthy recently. Just because I saw a black stain on my hands that happened to match the one I'd seen in the bunker dream from Io5 didn't mean it was really there. This could be just another hallucination. It could also be something perfectly explainable, like an allergic reaction. A really, *really* bad one. Still, there was no need to panic. None. I almost had myself convinced of that when I saw the stain move.

It wasn't nearly as dramatic as it had been in the dream when I'd watched the blackness sweep over my skin in the reflection of Ren's eyes. This was just a twitch, like watching the last bit of water slowly seep into paper. Only this wasn't paper and water. It was *my arm* and an *unknown black substance*, and before my brain could even finish processing that, I was running up the stairs as fast as my legs could go.

Considering all the running I'd been doing, I shouldn't have been able to go faster than a jog, but fear gave me wings. I shot into the lounge like a bullet, vaulting over the kitchen counter and throwing myself at the sink. My hands were shaking so badly it took me two tries to get the faucet going. Once I had the water pouring, I shoved both my hands under the stream, willing the black to wash away.

It didn't. The blast of hot water made the pins and needles ten times worse, but the stain didn't budge. Heart pounding faster than ever, I knocked a soap pad off the sink's edge with my elbow and began scrubbing my hands like I was trying to flay off my skin. But no matter how hard I washed, the black stayed put.

I was now closer to true panic than I'd been in years. I had no idea what this shit was, but after my dream, the animal part of my brain was absolutely convinced it would kill me if I let it. I was still scrubbing frantically when I heard a voice behind me.

"What are you doing?"

It's a sign of how upset I was that I didn't whirl around. Instead, I jumped with a yelp, banging my head sharply on the cabinet over the sink. I cursed and grabbed my smarting forehead, which of course got soap all over my hair, but at least the pain knocked a little sense into me. I took a deep breath and snatched my hands down, grabbing the kitchen towel off the sink as I went. My sopping wet hands soaked the thin cloth through at once, but that didn't matter. I wrapped the towel around my stained hands like a muffler before looking over my shoulder at the cook, who was standing in the door to the kitchen.

I was so far gone, I didn't remember not to look straight at him until it was way too late. I got a good dose of revulsion for my trouble, but I was so upset already that the nausea actually had a hard time getting through. I wasn't even angry at the cook for sneaking up on me. I just wanted him to go away, and not for the usual reasons. Something deep inside me was screaming that I shouldn't let anyone get close to the thing on my hands. I had to make him leave.

"Nothing to see here," I said, turning back to the sink. "I'm just washing up."

I heard the cook sigh. "Devi, what's going on?"

My whole body cringed. Something about hearing him say my name that way, like he actually cared, twisted me up like a spring. "Nothing," I snapped. "Cool your jets. I'll be out of your kitchen in a minute."

I'd tried to be sharp, controlled, but my voice sounded panicked even to me. That would never do. Black stuff aside, the cook already wanted me off the ship, and acting like a terrified nut job was just giving him more ammunition. I had to get a grip, so I slammed my eyes shut and focused on being still . . . being calm . . .

I was still working on it when I felt the cook right beside me.

My eyes popped open, but before I could react, I felt something soft brush my forehead. The cook had gotten a clean towel out of one of the cabinets and was using it to wipe the suds from my hair. He didn't say anything while he worked, and I didn't either. I couldn't. I was spellbound by the gentle pressure of his strokes and the warmth of the hand he'd placed on the crown of my head to keep me still.

I usually hate it when people try to take care of me, especially men. I hate the sense of obligation it creates, the imbalance of power, but I didn't hate this. For some reason I had this deep certainty that the cook wanted nothing except to make me feel better. The feeling was as intense and inexplicable as my need to drink with him last night, and I had about as much chance of fighting it now as I'd had then.

Also, not that I would ever admit it, but it was kind of nice to have someone touch me. After the panic over my hands and running myself half dead, my body was desperate for comfort, and though I knew it was the absolute wrong thing to do, I started to relax. With every stroke of his fingers, my terrified need to get away faded, and as the fear retreated, so did the pins and needles crawling over my hands. By the time the cook finished wiping the last of the suds away, the tingling feeling was gone completely, and I was so relieved I slumped sideways into his chest before I could think the better of it.

The cook went still as my weight landed. For a long moment, we stood, frozen, and then the hand on top of my head slid down to grip my shoulder as the cook pulled me into him.

I'm pretty strong even without my suit, but it didn't matter. The cook moved me like I was a doll, crushing me against his chest so fast I gasped. My hands were still tangled in the towel I was clutching against my stomach, but even if I had dared risk showing him the black stuff, I don't think I could have pushed him away. Worse, I wasn't sure I wanted to.

I've never been a nostalgic person—I prefer looking forward—but as the cook folded his body around me, I was overwhelmed by an intense pang of loss. Even though I couldn't remember touching the cook other than during the madness last night, I knew, *knew* I'd been in his arms before, and it had been good. Something worth fighting to keep, but I couldn't remember. Not that not remembering was anything new for me, but this was bigger. It was like the small pit of missing time I'd grown accustomed to stepping around had suddenly opened into a yawning chasm, and I was teetering on the edge. I was still trying not to fall in when the cook stepped back.

I didn't dare look up at him. The horrible feeling of forgetting was bad enough. If I had to deal with the nausea too, something might break. Instead, I focused on the wet spot on his shirt where my head had rested. But even though I wasn't looking, I knew he was getting ready to speak, and from the tension in his body, I knew it was going to be big.

I almost did raise my head then, because for a crazy moment, I had the feeling that whatever the cook was about to tell me would explain everything. But he didn't say a word. He just stood there, his hands gripping my shoulders tighter and tighter. And then, without warning, he let go, practically shoved me away, and walked out of the kitchen without a word.

I looked up just in time to see him vanish around the corner, too shocked even to be angry. I'd thrown my hand up without thinking, like I could stop him, make him tell me whatever it was he kept himself from saying. But when my fingers came into view, I got another shock, because my hand was clean.

They both were. My skin was bright red from all the scrubbing, but there was no sign of black. The pins and needles were gone as well, leaving my hands feeling normal, like the whole terrifying experience had never happened. I was still staring down at them when I saw a little glowing bug drift up through the floor by the kitchen door.

It bobbed there for a second, twitching its cloud of feelers at me. I stared back, and then, because I had to say it or I would explode, I whispered, "What is going on?"

The bug jumped at my voice and scuttled away, vanishing back through the floor in a flurry of tiny kicking legs, leaving me alone in the kitchen.

After that, I decided it was time to go see Hyrek.

This was a very big deal for me. I have a deep-running distrust of doctors. But between the hallucinations, the black gunk on my hands, and the fact that I was clearly missing way more memories than my bump on Falcon 34 accounted for, even I could no longer deny that something was seriously wrong.

Unfortunately, I didn't get a chance. True to his word, Caldswell had taken us through a series of short hyperspace jumps followed by a long stopover at Sevalis Station Seven, an enormous dual-gate station in orbit above a planet so built-up you could barely see the ground. But station docks followed the same rules as planetary layovers, which meant Rashid and I were on duty from the moment the *Fool* latched in.

Honestly, I was relieved work kept me from going straight to the doctor. Admitting to yourself that you're not well is nothing compared to a doctor officially pronouncing you bonkers. After all, a bad mental evaluation could ruin my chances with the Devastators forever. I knew I'd have to face the music eventually, but for now, I was more than happy to procrastinate. Especially since I was procrastinating in such an interesting place.

Sevalis Station Seven was the biggest space station I'd ever seen, and it was packed floor to rafters with birds. I'd never even realized so many creatures could live in one space, but just as Mabel said, the aeons seemed perfectly happy living packed in together. They came in every sort, too: big, beautiful males like the ones Basil and I had had our run-in with on Ample, rust-colored females who stayed together like their lives depended on it, even aeon chicks. The latter moved through the station in huge groups of peeping yellow puffballs shepherded by sharp-looking gray females, and they were probably the cutest things I'd ever seen. If it wouldn't have caused an international incident, I would have grabbed one and hugged it.

But interesting as the packed station was, the planet below was even crazier. I'd thought Wuxia was dense, but the Terran core world was nothing compared to what the aeons had built here. Every bit of land on the planet had been taken over by huge cities. They'd even built out into the oceans, creating huge floating complexes that bobbed on the tides. It was so overbuilt, I thought for sure this must be one of the aeon core worlds, but when I asked Basil about it, he'd laughed in my face and told me this was just a fishing colony.

"A fishing colony?" I cried, staring down at the cities that were so large and vertical they acted like mountain ranges, creating rain shadows behind them as they turned back the clouds. "How is *that* a fishing colony?"

"This is nothing," Basil replied. "I mean, you can still see the water in places, and the icecaps haven't been utilized at all. The colonies closer to the Seval are much bigger."

I didn't see how that was possible, but the captain agreed with Basil.

"Aeons like to nest in piles," he said drolly, leaning back in his chair. "Ample was open because they needed the space to farm. Most other aeon colony worlds are like this."

I shook my head in wonder. I simply could not fathom living like this when there was a whole universe out there to expand to. I was about to ask Caldswell how much longer he was planning on docking when I heard the bridge door open.

I glanced back through my camera, expecting to see Rashid. But it wasn't my fellow security officer. It was Ren.

The cook was right behind her, but I ignored him. Actually, I'd been ignoring him since his stunt last night, but even if I hadn't, Ren would have won. The captain's daughter *never* came to the bridge. She was here now, though, walking with more purpose than I'd ever seen in her as she strode down the steps to whisper something in her father's ear.

Caldswell's face had gone suspiciously blank when his daughter entered the room. That didn't change as she talked, but I could see his fingers tightening on the worn arms of his chair. Whatever she had to say didn't take long, and the moment she was done, Caldswell burst into action.

"Basil," he ordered, swinging his chair around to the console in front of him. "Get me the gate commander, emergency channel. Then call over to the dock office and tell them I want immediate takeoff clearance."

Basil stared at the captain for a second, which was a second too long for Caldswell. "Now!" the captain snapped.

The aeon jumped and grabbed his headset, whistling into it frantically. But the captain wasn't done. "Nova," he said, hitting the com. "Have these coordinates ready for the gate when it patches in for the jump: 34H-3848-A998-22K7-8801."

Nova wasn't even on the bridge. Last I'd checked, she'd been meditating in our room. But when the captain finished reciting the string of coordinates, all Nova said over the com was, "Yes, captain."

By this point, I'd already started for the door, signaling Rashid to meet me in the cargo bay. You never went anywhere good when your captain changed course this quickly, and I wanted us ready to roll out. The cook and Ren were already gone, thank the king, so we didn't have to worry about noncombatants. I was messaging Mabel to seal up engineering when Caldswell called my name.

"I want you and Rashid to scramble," he said, looking at me over his shoulder. "This won't be a long jump."

"Way ahead of you, sir," I replied.

Caldswell actually grinned at me. "That's my Morris."

I wasn't above giving him a superior smile as I jogged out into the hall, passing a running Nova on the way.

———

I have no idea what massive handful of strings the captain pulled, but despite the posted four-hour line for the gate, we jumped ten minutes later.

I spent them in the lounge, prowling back and forth in front of the windows like a caged animal. Rashid waited with me, fully loaded out just as I'd ordered, but as soon as he'd secured the jump, Caldswell had inexplicably left the bridge and gone downstairs. I had no idea why the captain would terrify his crew and then go down to his room, but I could hear the building freakout in Basil's voice over the com, so I sent Rashid up to the bridge to keep order. It was a cruel thing to do to my fellow security officer, but other than the times he'd snapped at the captain about Ren, Rashid was calm as a placid lake, and if anyone needed placid right now, it was Basil.

Tactically, I should have waited in the cargo bay, but I wanted to see myself what we were in for, so I stayed in the lounge by the windows. It wasn't like I was going to go crashing out the door the moment we left hyperspace anyway, and besides, I still had no idea what all this was about. I couldn't begin to think what Ren could tell her father that would precipitate this kind of scramble, but as the minutes ticked by, my feeling of impending doom got worse and worse. It was like that moment when you step on a rotten board. You haven't started falling yet, but you know it's coming, just as you know there's nothing you can do to stop it. All you can do is brace.

I was braced so hard my muscles ached. I stalked back and forth in front of the lounge windows, glaring at the blank gray-purple wall of hyperspace outside as I waited to see just how hard this fall would hit me. I was working on wearing a rut in the floor when the cook walked into the lounge.

As always, he entered silently, his footsteps like shadows. I kept my eyes off him out of habit, though I would have loved to glare at him when I said, "Why are you here? Get back downstairs."

"The captain is watching his daughter," he replied. "He ordered me to come and work instead."

I didn't believe that for a second. The cook hadn't even glanced at the kitchen. Instead, he walked to the cargo bay stairs and leaned on the door like he wanted to be first in line to get out when we landed.

I couldn't argue with a direct order from the captain, though, so I decided to ignore him. I put my back to the cook and stared out the window, double- and triple-checking my equipment. But hard as I tried to focus on not looking, I kept catching glimpses of him through my rear camera. I was this close to ordering him out anyway when the jump flash rolled over the ship, signaling our exit from hyperspace.

I was glued to the window the second the jump finished, my suit checking in with the *Fool*'s computer to look up where we were. *Unity* was the answer that came back, another overpopulated aeon colony world much like the one we'd just left. There was even a picture of a built-up planet so covered in city I couldn't see the oceans.

But something wasn't right. Even though my suit was insisting there should be a colony stuffed with birds right in front of us, I didn't see anything out the window, not a planet or a moon or a gate station, not even any other ships. All I saw through the lounge windows was a bunch of floating rocks and dust glittering in the light of the system's sun.

"Did the jump team mess up the coordinates?" I asked over the com. "This isn't a planet." It looked more like an asteroid belt.

My only answer was dead silence. And then, very quietly, Basil replied. "There's no mistake. This is Unity."

"This is nothing," I protested.

"You're both right," Nova said. "These are Unity's coordinates, but there's nothing here. The jump gate, the traffic control, the moon, the planet—they're all *gone*. I can't even get a signal."

Her voice became higher pitched with every word, and cold began to sink into my bones. It was a dark day when Nova panicked.

"It can't be gone," I said in my most authoritative voice. "Planets don't just—"

The ship lurched under my feet, cutting me off. My stabilizer took the bump nicely, but I braced on the window anyway, craning my neck in an attempt to see what had hit us. With so many rocks around, that should have been an easy call, but I hadn't heard anything hit the hull. I hadn't felt a crash either. It was more like we'd bumped into something. I was about to ask Basil what that could be when the aeon's voice whistled over the com.

"Oh, what *now*?"

The words were barely out before the channel collapsed into static. At the same time, my cameras began to short out, the picture obscured behind a rain of thin white lines that crackled as they fell. I shook my head hard, smacking my helmet on the side that held my receiver, but that didn't clear the interference, which was so bad now I couldn't even see my diagnostic screen to figure out what was wrong.

I ripped my helmet off with a curse and turned it over, running my finger over the neuronet feeds just to make double sure the problem wasn't on my end. It was only by chance that I glanced back up at the window. When I did, what I saw hit me so hard I dropped my helmet on the floor.

There was something outside the ship. Something *huge*.

In my shock, all I could think was that it looked like a squid. A gigantic squid glowing like the moon with its own blue-white light. It was so big I couldn't even see all of it from the *Fool*'s window, so big that the asteroids that dwarfed our ship looked like grains of sand floating around it. It had no eyes I could make out, no mouth or nostrils or any other opening. Just two huge clusters of tentacles, one at either end of its tubelike body, waving slowly through space like the thing was treading water.

There were so many tentacles I couldn't begin to count them. They started out enormous where they attached to the creature, but then they tapered off, finally ending in a delicate point that was still twice as big around as the *Fool.* I knew that last bit for a fact, because there was one right next to the ship. The thing we'd bumped into earlier.

"Devi!"

I jumped. I'd been so wrapped up in the monster outside, I'd actually forgotten about the cook until he yanked me away from the window.

"The coms are down," he said, his voice calm and serious as he turned me toward the hall door. "I realize this is frightening, but I need you to go to the bridge and tell them to prepare for another jump. The system should be coming back up in just—"

"What the hell are you talking about?" I shouted. I was too freaked out to care that the cook was trying to give me orders. I tore away from him and ran back to the window, stabbing my finger at the glass. "Don't you see that thing?"

Without my rear cameras, I couldn't see him behind me, but I knew the cook had turned to look. Instead of the horrified gasp I expected, though, he just sounded bewildered. "What thing?"

And that was when I got the sinking feeling in my stomach again, the one I was becoming way too familiar with, because that was when I realized the cook didn't see anything outside the window. I was hallucinating again.

But fast as it had come, the sinking feeling vanished. I *couldn't* be hallucinating. He'd felt that bump earlier just as I had. Whatever that thing was, we'd *hit* it, and you sure as hell didn't hit hallucinations.

I reached back and grabbed the cook, yanking him up to the window. "Shut up and look," I said, pointing at the tentacle floating beside the rear of the ship. The one that had bumped us. The one it was impossible to miss. "Do you see that?"

To his credit, the cook looked hard. In the end, though, he shook his head. "I don't see anything," he said softly. "Just rocks."

I swore and let him go, staring hard at the monster while I tried to think of something that could explain why I saw it and he didn't. This turned out to be a good move, because my staring was the only reason I saw the blow coming.

With astonishing speed for something so huge, the monster flicked its tentacle like a whip. As the undulation ran down the huge appendage, I saw for the first time that the monster's flesh wasn't just glowing, it was semitranslucent. This thing had the same frosted-glass look as the tiny bugs, though my little bugs were to this monster what specks of dust were to a mountain. I felt a bit like a speck myself as I watched the huge tentacle swing through the expanse of space, growing brighter and more solid as it raced toward the ship.

"Oh shit," I whispered, bracing against the glass, the only thing I had time to grab. "Here it comes."

The cook looked at me in alarm. "Here what com—"

The tentacle landed before he could finish, sending the ship tumbling. All the alarms began going off at once as the *Fool* spun like a whirligig. The centrifugal force crashed me into the window, banging my unprotected head against the glass hard enough to make me see spots. The artificial gravity had cut out on the second spin, so at least I didn't have to deal with that, but I still felt like I was going to throw up by the time the emergency thrusters finally kicked in to stop the spinning.

I was back up before the gravity reestablished, using my suit's magnets to keep my feet on the ground as I wobbled toward the door. It was much harder than it should have been. Without my helmet, I couldn't see any of my readings, but I didn't need them to know something was seriously wrong with my Lady. She was moving like she'd been dunked in cement, fighting me for every step.

My Lady wasn't the only one struggling. The *Fool* was going nuts. I don't know if it was the impact or something else, but the whole ship seemed to be going haywire. The emergency lights were flicking on and off, the alarm changing pitch like something was messing with the speakers, and the gravity was swinging wildly. We also had a pressure leak somewhere—I could hear it hissing—but the breach alarm seemed to be the only one not going off.

But while my suit was on the fritz, there was nothing wrong with my battle instincts. Despite the confusion around me, I knew exactly what I had to do. Whatever that thing outside was, it wasn't a hallucination, and if I was the only one who could see it, that meant it was up to me to shoot it.

With that goal to guide me, I took a huge breath and popped the lock on my malfunctioning suit. The Lady released me with a relieved hiss, falling off my body like a shed shell. The second I was free, I sprinted for the cargo bay stairs. I was plotting the fastest way through the toppled piles of nut crates to the gunner controls in engineering when the ship bucked again, sending me flat on my face.

I landed on my chin, knocking my teeth together so hard I tasted blood, but I couldn't even feel the pain. I was in the battle now, and I heaved myself up instantly, charging the door. Considering how the last hit had sent us spinning, I probably should have stayed down, but luck was with me this time. This new blow only rocked the ship instead of sending it hurling like before, and I took my chance to run. But before I could reach the first stair, an iron arm wrapped around my waist, stopping me cold.

"No!" I shrieked, digging my fingers into the cook's arm. "*Let me go!* I have to shoot it!"

"Devi, calm down," he hissed in my ear, yanking me off my feet. "There's nothing you can do."

Bullshit. There was always something you could do, but I didn't waste my breath telling him that. Instead I craned my neck back, looking over my shoulder to try to catch a glimpse of when the next hit would land, but the tentacle wasn't there anymore. All I saw through the window now was flat blue-white fog, almost like we were in some kind of weird hyperspace. It was so unexpected, it took me a moment to realize that the reason I couldn't see was because the creature's tentacle was wrapped around the ship. That was why the last bump hadn't sent us flying; the thing had *caught us*.

And like it had been waiting for me to notice, the monster chose that moment to start squeezing.

The *Fool*'s hull began to groan, and then the lights died completely, leaving only the soft blue-white glow of the monster itself. The alarms died next, sputtering out with choked squeals. The engines cut out a second later, and I suddenly felt like a fool for taking off my suit. If I got thrown into space with nothing but my skin, I'd have only myself to blame.

Suit or not, though, I wasn't done yet. If I could just get to the ship's cannon, maybe Mabel could get me enough power to use it. I couldn't aim with the cameras out, but with the tentacle wrapped all the way around us, it wasn't like I could miss. I just had to get there, which meant I needed to get away from the cook.

He might not be able to see the monster, but he'd certainly heard the crunching as it began to squeeze the ship, because his grip was growing slacker, giving me the opening I needed. I hurled my weight forward, slipping out of his arms. But as I was starting my charge down the stairs, light blossomed over the ship.

For a moment, I thought someone had conjured a miracle and gotten the hyperdrive back on line, but then I realized the light was the wrong color. Jump flashes are pure, harsh white. This light was softer, like moonlight, and it rose up from the center of the ship like water from a welling spring. When it passed over me, my skin tingled, but when it reached the monster wrapped around our hull, a scream hit my mind like a switchblade.

I fell to my knees on the stairs, hands clapped over my ears. It did no good; there was no blocking this sound. Behind me, the cook was on his knees too, but I didn't have time for him. All I could do was sit and try to keep myself together as the scream ripped through me. Then, just as it started to get really unbearable, the tentacle outside the window began to dissolve.

Everywhere the soft light touched, the tentacle vanished. It was like the light was melting it, evaporating the translucent, glowing flesh as I watched. As the glowing mass dissolved, I could see the monster behind it again. It was thrashing wildly, flinging its countless arms through the floating rocks that were supposed to be a thriving aeon colony world. But though other tentacles were flying by, the tentacle around us was nearly gone. In a few seconds, it had faded altogether, and the *Fool*'s engine sputtered back to life.

The hyperdrive came on a moment later, spinning up so fast I could almost see Basil mashing the button. By the time I realized what we were about to do—an ungated jump with no prep in the middle of a debris field—the flash was already washing over the ship. I had one final glimpse of the thrashing monster as it started to edge away from us before the universe vanished, replaced again by the dull gray-purple bleakness of hyperspace.

I flopped over as the sudden stillness landed, collapsing on the stairs in a heap. But my relief was short-lived. Almost as soon as I relaxed, a pair of merciless hands grabbed me under the shoulders and yanked me up again.

Before I could even think about fighting, the cook had tossed me over his shoulder. I yelped in surprise and pain, but it was too late. He had me pinned, carrying me down the stairs toward the cargo bay like a sack of flour. I wasn't about to let this pass, though. My arms were trapped beneath me, but I could still kick my legs, and I did, slamming my bare feet into his chest as hard as I could.

I might as well have been kicking a cement wall. The cook was freakishly strong and seemingly impervious to pain. I think my kicking hurt my foot more than his ribs, but I didn't stop, especially since he was now walking me through the door to engineering.

Mabel was there, elbow deep in some critical system. She looked up when the door opened, and I took my chance.

"Mabel!" I shrieked. "Help me!"

The captain's sister-in-law glanced at the cook, then at me, and then went back to work without a word, her face grim. The cook hadn't even stopped. He marched straight through engineering, but it was only when we passed the base of the spiral stair that I realized where he was taking me.

"Caldswell?" I shouted, kicking harder than ever. "You did this to get me to *Caldswell*?"

The cook didn't answer, just tightened his hold and walked into the captain's rooms without knocking. Caldswell's sitting area was in disarray from the earlier spinning, the table knocked over and the couch upside down. The captain himself was nowhere to be seen, and I realized he must be on the bridge. I was about to tell the cook that his little stunt was all for nothing when he turned us around and I spotted the captain at last.

Caldswell was in his daughter's room, standing over the bed where Ren was lying curled on her side with her face hidden in her hands. Caldswell's head snapped up when the cook entered, eyes flicking to me. I opened my mouth to yell at him to help me, but the cook beat me to it.

"Sleep her," he said.

Caldswell didn't even blink, he just looked from me to the cook, and then he was on the move, striding past us into the little sitting room. "Can't," he said. "Ren just gave everything she had to get us out. Hold her down; we'll do this the old-fashioned way."

I should have tried to reason with them then, should have told them I'd be good and the old-fashioned way was definitely not necessary, but I couldn't. The moment the captain had spoken, I was back in the bunker under the mountain on Io5, watching my body fall, the hole still smoking in my head. The vision lasted only a moment, but the horror of it was like a claw in my stomach, and before I could recover, the cook had slid me off his shoulder onto the couch. I'd barely landed before Caldswell's hand grabbed my neck, turning my head away.

"Sorry, Morris."

That was the last thing I heard before something hard, sharp, and metal slammed into the back of my skull.

CHAPTER
6

I woke up to the feeling of someone gently slapping my cheek. I made a frustrated noise in my throat and turned away, but the slapping didn't stop. Eventually I opened my eyes out of self-defense to see Caldswell standing over me.

"Sorry about that, Morris," he said, dropping his hand from my cheek. Unfortunately, his next move was to pry my cracked eyes wide open to check my pupils. He checked the back of my head too, and I winced as his fingers brushed the painfully tender spot right below my crown.

"What happened?" I muttered when he finally stopped tormenting me.

"I knocked you out."

My eyes went wide. As he said the words, the memory of how I'd ended up here came back in a flash, and I lurched forward. "You hit me!"

Caldswell dodged easily. "Didn't I just say that?"

I tried to go after him again, but I couldn't move any further. I was tied to a heavy chair with my arms behind my back. I must have been out for some time, because my hands were both asleep. I couldn't even wiggle my fingers. I could yell, though, so that was what I did. "What the hell is this about?"

"You," Caldswell answered. "And what you claim to have seen in hyperspace."

"I'm not *claiming* I saw it," I shouted. "I *did* see it!"

"Like you've been seeing other things?" Caldswell said.

The question was so quick, I almost slipped up and said yes. Caldswell hadn't knocked all the sense out of my head, though, and I caught myself just in time.

"No point being tight-lipped, Morris," Caldswell chided. "Hyrek tells me everything."

I looked him straight in the eyes and said nothing, but my bravado was all bluff, and Caldswell wasn't buying it.

"I've known you were having problems for a while now," he said, giving me a flat look. "I was trying to give you a chance to come forward on your own. Now, though, I think it's time you told us exactly what you've been seeing."

"You'll think I'm crazy," I warned.

Caldswell shrugged. "I have a pretty high threshold for crazy. Just try me."

I took a deep breath. Considering how I'd come to be sitting here, I didn't want to tell this man a thing, but like it or not, Caldswell was still my captain. This was his ship, and as Mabel had proven earlier, my opinion meant exactly zip compared to the captain's business. If I wanted to get out of this at all, I was going to have to give him what he wanted. I just hoped the truth was it.

So, with a deep breath, I told him. I told him everything I could remember about the first time I'd seen the glowing bugs, both the one out on the hull and the one in the medbay. I didn't tell him about the one Ren and I had both seen, mostly because I didn't want to get any more involved with the captain's creepy daughter than I had to. I didn't tell him about the dream on Io5 for the same reason, though the fact that omitting this also meant I wouldn't have to explain what I'd seen in the bunker didn't hurt. I did tell him about the bugs I'd seen filling the cargo bay when I'd woken up, though, and the bugs I'd seen almost constantly since then, excepting the one I'd seen Ren squash earlier today.

By the time I was finished, I felt like a complete lunatic. To his credit, though, Caldswell had listened to everything with a straight face. He didn't even look concerned until I got to the part about the monster that had attacked the ship.

"You're sure about the size?" he said, cutting me off before I could get to the part where his cook had scooped me up like an unruly toddler.

"As sure as I can be," I said. "There wasn't much outside I could use for reference, but as I said, the end tip of each of those tentacles was still twice as thick as the *Fool*. I'd say the creature's body must have been several thousand times that." *Or larger*, I thought with a swallow.

Caldswell leaned back on the couch with a sigh. "All right, Morris," he said. "Thank you for being honest."

I smiled before I could stop myself. "So you don't think I'm insane?"

"No," Caldswell said. "Unfortunately for you, I believe every word."

I did not like the way he said that at all. "How is my being sane unfortunate?"

"Because if you were crazy, we could let you go," Caldswell said. "But since you're not, this situation is now officially too large for me to ignore anymore. We need to know what you've forgotten."

My blood ran cold. "My memories," I whispered. "I didn't lose them from a bump to the head, did I?"

"No," Caldswell said. "They were taken to protect you."

I glared at him hard. "Protect me from what?"

"Us," said an accented voice behind me.

I jumped. I hadn't even realized the cook was here until he spoke. I turned as far as I could to see him leaning against the door to Ren's room, just as he had been yesterday. Behind him, Ren was no longer curled in a ball. Instead, she was lying on top of her bed staring wide-eyed and vacant at the ceiling, which was almost worse.

Looking at him brought the revulsion back strong as ever, but I didn't drop my eyes as the cook walked over to the bed. Ren stirred when he touched her hand, and then sat up slowly, her movement clunky and stiff, like an old, old woman's. The cook waited patiently for her to stand before leading her over to take Caldswell's place in front of me.

"Undo it, Charkov," Caldswell ordered, moving to guard the door. "All of it."

I didn't know what that meant, but the cook's scowl deepened. "We talked about this, sir," he said. "A full return is dangerous. If I give it all back—"

"All of it," Caldswell repeated, his voice cold and sharp as a hard winter. "That's an order, Eye Charkov."

My eyes went wide in horror. It was the title from my dream. The cook flinched too, but it was over so quickly I almost missed it, and he didn't try to argue with the captain again. Instead, he reached down and gently grabbed the top of my head. The position of his fingers was just as they'd been last night in the kitchen, but there was no tender gentleness now. He grabbed my head hard, forcing me to look up until I couldn't see anything but him. But though his grip was as harsh as the revulsion curdling my stomach, the cook's face was set in an expression of regret so deep it took my breath away.

"I tried, Devi," he whispered, fingers pressing harder into my hair. "I tried."

"Tried what?" I whispered back, my voice trembling.

He gave me the saddest smile I'd ever seen. "To save you."

Before I could demand to know what he meant by that, Ren's hand shot out, grabbing my shoulder in a vise, and as she touched me, her voice spoke in my head.

Remember.

The word had barely formed before everything I'd lost came roaring back.

———

Memories are unruly things by nature. Some come when called, but most do exactly as they please, vanishing when you need them and popping up when you'd much rather they didn't. Mine had always had a bad habit of surfacing at the worst moments, but even the biggest fit of unwanted nostalgia couldn't have prepared me for what Ren did to my head.

I hadn't even realized how much I'd lost until it was all back. The past flooded into my brain like a storm surge, and every single memory was clamoring for me to relive it, thrusting itself to the front of my mind to tease me with a flash before being pushed away by the next one. I was still conscious, still aware, I could even hear Caldswell talking, but I couldn't make sense of anything. My memories took up every bit of me, leaving no room for anything else. But then, just before the flood of memories could pull me under, Ren's touch on my mind gave way to a new hand. A strong, familiar, masculine one.

To this day, I could not tell you what Rupert did, but he did it well. Everywhere his touch landed, the chaos retreated. The jumbled memories rearranged themselves into an orderly timeline, connecting as they fell into place until I could no longer tell which ones were new and which had always been there.

Naturally, the first thing I looked for was what had happened on Falcon 34. Every time I'd reached for it before I'd gotten nothing. Now, though, the memories came as soon as I called them, and the whole bloody night—the symbionts, Cotter's defeat, my capture, Brenton, my own near death—unrolled in my mind. Every event was as fresh and vivid as though it had just happened. I could feel the pain in my stomach where I'd been stabbed, the shock of Cotter's death. He *had* died bravely, I knew it.

Mostly though, I remembered Rupert. I remembered the haunted look in his eyes when he'd changed from human to symbiont. I remembered his fury as he'd tried to kill Brenton on the lounge floor and his speed as he'd thrown the symbiont off me, abandoning his enemy to save my life.

That memory brought others. I remembered him touching my hair the night he put me to bed when I was drunk, and again when

I'd lain stretched out against him the one night we'd slept together. I remembered the way he used to smile at me, the gentle brush of his kiss against my knee in the medbay, the quiet desperation in his voice as he promised he'd never hurt me.

He'd kept that promise at first. He'd saved me twice, on Mycant and on the tribe ship. God and king, how could I have forgotten my escape from the tribe ship? I remembered it all with perfect clarity now, Rupert in his scales killing his way through the horde to save me. He'd been the one who'd picked me up when the battle drugs wore off, and then, when I was lost in the seizures, he'd been the one who held me down. He'd saved me, just as he always did. Even that horrible time in the rain, he'd been trying to protect me, to keep me safe from what he was. And then he'd told me he loved me and taken my memories, making me hate him without even asking.

I sucked in a furious breath. It was all coming together now. My inability to remember the cook's name, the revulsion I felt every time he walked into my line of sight, it was all *Rupert*. He'd rewritten my mind, changed me, reordered my life as he saw fit . . .

Rage washed over me, clean and hot, and I threw myself into it. The bastard had actually had me believing I was nuts. I'd probably never even had a hallucination. The thing I'd seen outside the ship had certainly been real, and now that I had my memories back, I knew I'd killed a woman with the black stuff on my hands, so that was real, too. *Everything* was, and though I still didn't understand what it all meant, I was sure as hell going to find out. My mind was back in order at last, bringing back all the old questions, only I was done being silent. This time, I was going to get some answers. And with that determination to pull me forward, I finally managed to wake up.

When I opened my eyes, I was alone in the captain's sitting room. I must have been out for a long time, because we weren't in space any longer. The gravity was heavier and the reentry shutters on

Caldswell's windows were down, which meant we were on a planet. What planet, I had no idea, but it didn't seem immediately important, so I moved on to more pressing concerns.

They'd moved me from the chair to the couch while I'd been stuck in the memories, and though my hands were still bound behind me, I was no longer tied down. There was something on my feet, though.

I leaned over, wiggling my toes experimentally, but I couldn't move them more than a quarter inch in any direction through the thick, invisible mass they were buried under. Inert plasma. Goddamn Caldswell had put a plasma weight on my feet.

"You can't break it, so don't try. We use that stuff to lock down symbionts."

My head snapped up as Caldswell emerged from his room. Since he hadn't bothered with a hello, I didn't either. "Not even going to play at secrets anymore?"

"Doesn't seem to be much point now," the captain said, sitting down in the sturdy chair they'd tied me to before.

I leaned over to peer into Ren's room, but it was empty. "Where's Rupert?" I demanded.

"I sent him away," Caldswell said. "I thought this might go smoother without Charkov. He tends to lose his head around you."

I glowered. That wasn't all he was going to lose the next time I got my hands on him. "What did he do to me?"

Caldswell sighed. "That's a complicated question. The simple answer is that he returned the memories he took on Falcon Thirty-Four."

"You mean Ren returned them."

"Charkov guided her," Caldswell said, meeting my scowl with one of his own. "He did it for you, you know."

"To save me from *you*," I snarled, lurching forward as far as the weight on my feet would allow.

"Yes," Caldswell said matter-of-factly.

I rolled my eyes. "So why aren't I dead?"

The captain sighed again, deeper this time. "I've known Charkov for a long time," he said at last. "In all those years, I've never seen him be anything but exemplary, a model soldier in every way. So the one time he went soft and messed up, I wanted to honor his sacrifice." Caldswell flashed me a sad smile. "I must be getting romantic in my old age."

I didn't believe that for a second. "A model soldier for what?" I asked. "What are you really? And *don't* say a trader captain."

Caldswell sat up a bit straighter in his chair. "I wasn't going to," he said. "Unfortunately, Morris, any chance of keeping you out of this is long gone, so I'm just going to lay it out straight. Rupert and I belong to an organization called the Joint Investigatory Spatial Anomaly Task Force, though no one besides government bean counters actually calls it that. We're more commonly referred to as the Eyes, and we're supported by every major government, including the Terran Republic, the Aeon Sevalis, and the kingdom of Paradox. Our job is to track down and destroy phantoms."

I'd guessed most of that from Brenton's rambling back on Falcon 34. Hearing Paradox was in on this too was a bit of a shock, though it did explain Caldswell's Royal Warrant nicely. "What are phantoms?"

Caldswell shrugged. "No one knows for sure. The current theory is that they're creatures from another dimension. Our first recorded encounter with one happened a little over seventy years ago, though since phantoms cannot be detected, tracked, or seen, we really have no idea how long they've been here."

"Wait," I said. "If you don't know how long they've been here, how do you know they're from another dimension? Wouldn't it make more sense if they were just another kind of alien?"

"No," Caldswell said. "Even the strangest life-forms in our galaxy share certain traits. But phantoms don't exist in the same way everything else in our universe does. They move through space without a thought for gravity, energy, even time. So far as we can tell, they are creatures of pure plasmex. They can't even interact with the physical world until they've reached a certain size. Once they can, though, they start destroying it."

"You mean like what happened on Mycant," I said, remembering the quakes and the invisible monster's effects on my clock. "The phantom was destroying the planet."

Caldswell gave me a sharp look. "You figure that out on your own, or did Brenton tell you?"

"Both," I replied, lifting my chin.

The captain shook his head. "What else did he say?"

"That phantoms break down the rules of the universe, and that the two of you used to hunt them together." I looked the captain up and down. "Must have been one hell of a breakup. Brenton hates your guts."

Caldswell actually chuckled at that. "John and I have differences of opinion on many things. Though when it comes to you, I'm afraid he might be in the right." The captain's face grew serious as he leaned forward. "It's starting to look like letting you live was the best mistake I've ever made. But before we jump to too many conclusions, I need you to tell me what Brenton wanted from you back on Falcon Thirty-Four."

I set my jaw stubbornly. Oh hell no. Caldswell might act like I was his soldier, but I was still a merc, and mercs didn't give shit up for free. "You want info?" I asked, lifting my eyebrows. "Fine, but I'm not talking without a little reciprocation."

"I suppose you are due an explanation," the captain admitted. "Where would you like to start?"

That threw me. I hadn't expected him just to give in. "How about the beginning?" I said when I'd recovered. "You're an Eye, that means your job is to fly all over the universe killing phantoms, right?"

"Mostly," Caldswell said.

"So why the big secret?" I asked, shrugging my shoulders as much as I could with the restraints. "I mean, you were willing to kill me back on Falcon Thirty-Four just for knowing about Rupert, but you guys are the ones protecting the universe from invaders. Seems to me that would make you heroes. Why hide it?"

That was a leading question, but I wanted to give Caldswell a chance to tell me the truth on his own. On the surface, the Eyes sounded more like glorified pest control than a secret government organization, but now that I had my memories back, I remembered how Rupert had trembled against me when he spoke of the terrible things he'd done, and I was willing to bet that being an Eye was a lot dirtier than simple phantom killing. Unfortunately, Caldswell didn't go for the bait.

"We can't tell the universe about phantoms," he said, incredulous. "Can you imagine what would happen if we told people that there were giant invisible space monsters that couldn't be detected on any sensor who could destroy their planet just by sitting on it? Oh, and they can't be killed by any known conventional means, including orbital nukes."

"Are you sure about that?" Because enough orbital nukes could do just about anything.

"Positive," Caldswell said. "We've tried. They can't be killed, can't be seen, and can't be stopped. Can you imagine how the average person would react to something like that?" He shook his head. "Panic doesn't even begin to cover it."

"But they wouldn't panic forever," I said. "I mean, phantoms have been around for seventy years, right? I've been all over the galaxy, and I've never heard about them, so you guys must have things pretty well under control. If you put it that way, not even Terrans could be worried about..." My voice trailed off. Caldswell's face had changed while I spoke, becoming almost frighteningly blank.

"Morris," he said quietly. "What the hell do you think you just saw?"

I gasped like he'd kicked the couch out from under me. I'd been so lost in the past I'd just gotten back, I'd completely forgotten about the disaster that had landed me here. Now, though, my mind was flying back to the monster I'd seen through the lounge window. I recognized its stabbing scream now, too. It was the same one I'd heard on Mycant, only so much bigger my mind had trouble comprehending it.

"We call them emperor phantoms," Caldswell said when I didn't speak. "Unity is, *was* a class-four habitable planet, roughly the same size as Paradox. We can't tell for sure since we can't sense them, but we think the emperor was there for less than five hours before the planet reached critical destabilization and flung itself apart."

He leaned forward, bearing down on me. "Five hours, Morris. Unity was a colony of nearly twenty billion aeons, and that phantom destroyed it like a giant stomping an anthill. They never even had a chance to run."

For several moments, I had no idea what to say. I couldn't even imagine twenty billion aeons. The number was simply too huge, too abstract. But while I was trying to get my brain around it, a memory flashed in front of my eyes. It was a glimpse from a window of a ship, staring out at the ruins of a planet just as I'd done from the *Fool*'s lounge, but in this memory, there was no monster.

I paused, confused. The memory felt...odd was the only way to describe it, like trying to walk around in a shoe that's slightly the wrong size. It was disconcerting to say the least, and infuriating, because I'd thought I was done with all this déjà vu crap. But apparently I wasn't, because the more I tried to push the memory away, the harder it pushed back, making me see.

I was standing in the bay of an old-fashioned Terran-style cargo ship much, much larger than the *Fool*. There were strangers crowded all around me, and we were staring together out the window at the remains of a planet. I didn't know which planet; the memory didn't come with anything useful like names. Just a view of broken rocks where a home had once been and anger. So much anger and pain and grief that I thought I would choke. Suddenly, I wanted to scream, to lash out and take back what I'd lost, but I couldn't. They were all gone, and all I could do was stand there and stare at where they'd been.

That was it. Just an image, almost like a picture, and an intense knot of feelings so tangled I could barely pick them apart. But strongest of all was the overwhelming sense that I was alone. Truly alone in a way I had never comprehended before, and that feeling was the one that brought the tears to my eyes.

Horrified, I ducked my head before Caldswell could see, scrubbing my face on my shoulders. To my relief, Caldswell didn't comment. He just waited patiently until I spoke again.

"How do you fight something like that?" I asked when I had my voice under control.

"We can't," Caldswell replied. "But remember how I told you the Eyes were supported by every major government? Well, in this case, that includes the lelgis."

I blinked in confusion. "The squids?" I didn't even know they had a government.

"We've given them huge concessions in return for their aid," Caldswell said bitterly. "But we have no choice. Their queens are the only things in the universe that can kill the really big ones. Fortunately, planet-sized phantoms are extremely rare."

The idea that anyone could bargain with the lelgis was still blowing my mind, but something about this wasn't sitting right. "Wait," I said. "If it's the lelgis' job to stop the big phantoms, how did that one get to Unity?"

Caldswell's expression darkened. "That's something I intend to find out. But done is done. All we can do now is invent a plausible story for what happened and work with the Sevalis to cover up the damage."

My eyes went wide. "You can't just cover up the destruction of an entire planet!"

"Of course we can," Caldswell said. "We've done it before."

I shot him a dirty look. "You're lying."

Caldswell arched an eyebrow. "You've heard of Svenya?"

"Svenya was pulled off its orbit by a gravitational anomaly," I said. "It's got a Remembrance Day and everything. What do..." I trailed off, eyes going wide. "You *can't* be serious."

"As a gun to the head," Caldswell said calmly. "Svenya was one of the oldest Republic core worlds, an established planet of thirteen billion with almost twice the mass of Unity, and yet it took an emperor phantom less than twelve hours to reduce it to rubble. We actually found out about it much faster than we heard about Unity, but this was in the early days before we'd worked out our agreement with the lelgis. There was nothing we could do except help with evacuations and watch the planet fall apart."

I stared at him, dumbstruck. Just as with Unity, the number was simply too huge for me to comprehend. Thirteen billion souls, gone. "How did the Eyes hide something like that?" I sputtered. "We're talking about a planet. A major colony."

"We didn't," Caldswell said. "The Terran Republic hid it all by themselves. They declared the area unsafe and restricted all access. Even now, no one gets in. That's how serious this is, Morris," he said, his voice going sharp. "Unity and Svenya are outliers, but phantoms attacks are always happening. Situations like Mycant occur constantly all over the universe, and the only reason planets aren't shaking themselves apart every day is because we save them."

"Right, I get it, you're heroes," I said. "But I still don't see why you need to keep it under wraps. It's not like anyone could blame you for the loss of Svenya."

"It's not about blame," the captain said sharply. "It's about keeping the universe ticking over. It's about managing fear. Even if we outed the truth, there would be nothing people could do that we're not doing already, and all the fear and attention would make our jobs even harder. The only reason I'm telling *you* is because you need to understand how much is at stake."

The captain leaned forward, getting right in my face. "We're not playing around here, Morris," he said quietly. "I've answered your questions honestly. Now, what did Brenton want with you?"

I didn't like the captain's tone one bit, but he had a point. He'd answered my questions, and fair was fair. Also, I was pretty curious myself at this point.

"He wanted to know about the xith'cal ghost ship," I said, meeting Caldswell's stare head-on. "I didn't tell him anything, but then his mercs hacked the medical records and found out I'd been bitten. After that, he got a little crazy and said I was the one who was going to save the universe."

The words sounded just as pretentious and stupid coming out of my mouth as they had coming out of Brenton's, but Caldswell was suddenly looking at me like he'd never seen me before. "Interesting," he said after a long silence.

"Interesting?" I cried. "That's *it*? That's all you have to say?" I slammed myself back into the soft couch with a furious snarl. "Why the hell am I here, then?" I demanded. "What do you want from me?"

"To be perfectly honest, I'm not sure," Caldswell said, returning to his chair. "Did Brenton tell you about the daughters?"

"He had a girl with him," I said cautiously. "She looked exactly like Ren, but thinner, like she was sick. He called her Enna."

It might have been my imagination, but I thought Caldswell winced when I said the girl's name. Whatever it was, though, it was gone in a flash. "I wasn't entirely accurate, earlier," he said. "We Eyes help to hunt and subdue phantoms, but we don't kill them. The daughters do. So far as we know, they're the only ones other than the lelgis who can actually kill the things."

I took a breath, remembering the flash of light when Ren had touched the downed phantom back on Mycant. "They're plasmex users."

"They're much more than that," Caldswell said. "They're some of the most powerful plasmex users humanity has ever produced, created from *the* most powerful plasmex user, a woman named Maat."

That name sent a cold shiver through me. I was sure I'd heard it before, but I couldn't place it before Caldswell went on.

"Our job is to protect and guide them," he said. "The daughters pay a great price for their power, and we do whatever we can to honor their sacrifice. But killing the phantoms isn't all the daughters can do. They're also the only ones who can see the damn things. Or they were, until you."

"Don't be stupid," I said with a nervous laugh. "I'm not a plasmex user."

"No, you're not," Caldswell admitted. "Frankly, Morris, I have no idea what you are. Because of their centuries of isolation from the rest of humanity, Paradoxians have the lowest plasmex sensitivity of all humans. But according to Hyrek, your numbers are even lower than the Paradoxian average. You have about as much natural plasmex talent as a piece of plastic, and yet somehow you can see what no one except the most powerful plasmex users can."

"That's ridiculous," I said. "I've only seen one phantom, and it was really really big. I didn't see the one on Mycant at all."

"But you've seen every one since," Caldswell said.

I was about to ask what he was talking about when I figured it out. "The bugs," I groaned.

Caldswell nodded. "Phantoms come in all shapes and sizes. The little ones are everywhere. Fortunately they don't get dangerous until they're bigger than a person or we'd all be long dead. Considering the number of 'bugs' you told me about earlier, though, it also seems that you're attracting them. If you were actually plasmex sensitive, this would be normal. Phantoms are drawn to plasmex use. But since your numbers are in the gutter every time we run them, you can see my confusion. If Brenton hadn't tried to make another grab for you on Ample, I would have written you off as a freak anomaly."

"Hold on—Brenton?" I said. "That HVFP team was *Brenton's*?"

Caldswell rolled his eyes. "Nonlethal anti-armor pistols and a symbiont? Who else could it be?"

I hadn't actually thought about the fight on Ample through the lens of my returned memories yet. Now that Caldswell said it, though, I had to admit he was probably right. "You think that's why Brenton wants me, then?" I asked. "Because of the seeing phantoms thing?"

"No," Caldswell said. "He'd never risk so much for something that small. Whatever he thinks you are, it's big enough for him to gamble everything. I'd actually meant to go over what you've been seeing in more detail to see if we couldn't figure it out, but you took longer to wake up from the memory return than we expected, and we're almost out of time."

The cold dread began to creep back into my stomach. "Out of time for what?"

"Talking," Caldswell said. "I had Ren send for a pickup as soon as we got away from Unity."

"A pickup?" I repeated dumbly.

"We'd already be in hyperspace if we could jump ourselves," Caldswell said. "But the phantom wrecked our air system when it squeezed us. Fortunately, our emergency jump protocol dumps out in a pretty dense area of space, so Basil was able to limp us over to the closest planet to wait for reinforcements. That was five hours ago. The pickup team should be here any minute to take you to headquarters."

The creeping dread in my stomach went colder still. "Why would I go to headquarters?"

Caldswell looked at me, and what was left of his amiable captain mask vanished. "We lost a planet today, Morris," he said quietly. "Tomorrow, we could lose another. I don't know what the hell is going on with you, but if you can see phantoms like the daughters do, there's a chance you might be able to learn to kill them as well."

"But you just said I can't use plasmex!" I protested. "I can't do anything like Ren can do, I can't even do stuff Nova can do."

"Maybe I haven't made our situation clear," Caldswell snapped, pinning me with a glare. "Other than the lelgis, who, as you've seen, only help when they feel like it, the daughters are our only weapons against the phantoms. Right now, we have sixty-two of them in active service. Sixty-two weapons to cover a front of nearly three hundred thousand inhabited planets across the known galaxy. You're a soldier, you can see exactly how bad that situation is.

We're holding the line by the skin of our teeth. I might not understand what's going on with you, but I know John Brenton. If he was willing to risk as much as he did to get you, it's worth investigating. I don't have the tools to do that here, so I'm sending you to the people who do."

"And what about me?" I cried. My voice was shaking openly now, but I didn't care. I was just starting to realize what all this meant. Caldswell was giving me to his secret phantom killing organization. Giving me over to be made into a weapon, like Ren. A shudder went through me at the memory of her blank eyes, the tears on her face back on Io5 when she'd begged me to free her. I didn't want that. I wouldn't let them do that to me. "I'm not going."

I expected Caldswell to tell me I had no choice, but he didn't. Instead, the captain looked me over like I was a troublemaking cadet. "I've always liked you, Morris," he said. "Even when you were being a pain, you were always a good soldier. You did your duty and fought with honor as a Paradoxian should. This is just the next step."

"Disappearing into some secret organization isn't my idea of honor," I snapped.

"But serving your king is," Caldswell calmly replied. "The Eyes protect Paradox and her colonies just like we do every other planet. Are you saying you would not lay down your life for your homeland?"

I closed my eyes, cursing him for bringing the Sacred King into this. When he put it like that, he made me a traitor and a blasphemer if I denied him, but I could not accept what he was saying. If I did what Caldswell asked, my future was finished. My dreams of being a Devastator, everything I'd fought for, my whole *life* would be gone. I couldn't do it. I would not throw myself away just so Caldswell could have the *possibility* of a new weapon in his war, and I was about to tell him so when I felt a hand on my knee.

I jumped, my whole body going rigid as my eyes snapped back open, but Caldswell didn't let go. He grabbed my knee and held it, his fingers strong as steel and surprisingly warm through the soft fabric of the thin pants I wore under my armor. "This isn't the end, Morris," he said quietly. "Whatever you might think of us, we're not monsters. You'll be well taken care of."

"Like a lab rat," I muttered.

"Like a resource," he corrected. "A valuable one."

His words rang hollow. "I didn't fight for a decade to become someone's *resource*."

"Better than being dead," Caldswell said, giving my knee a final squeeze before standing up. "I'm going to go back into my room so you can have a few minutes alone before the retrieval team gets here. It might be your last time to yourself for a while, so I suggest you make the most of it. And if you have anything to say to Rupert, I'll pass it on."

I lifted my eyes. The captain's face was all concern, but I knew now that it was a mask, just like Rupert's. "Go to hell," I snarled.

Caldswell sighed deeply, but then, as he'd promised, he left, retreating to his room and shutting the door to just a crack.

The moment he was out of sight, I started trying to break free. I bent my body into shapes I'd never known I could make as I yanked with everything I had on the plasma binding my feet and the metal cuffs that kept my wrists locked behind me. But all my struggling earned me were strained muscles, and after a few moments I flopped defeated back onto the couch. Fighting was useless, it seemed. Everything was useless.

Since it didn't matter anymore, I threw back my head with a string of curses that would have made my mother faint. In a matter of minutes, my whole life had unraveled. Even if I did turn out to be nothing more than an anomaly who could see floating bugs, they'd never let me go after everything Caldswell had told me. Not alive, anyway.

I shut my eyes tight, but it didn't help. All the things I'd lost were pounding on me one after another. Nine years of armored combat, all my honors, my illustrious record, gone. I'd never go home to Paradox again. I'd never be a Devastator.

I felt the moisture welling behind my eyelids, but I kept them shut tight. I felt more hopeless right now than I'd ever felt in my life, but I was determined not to cry. Caldswell had taken everything from me—my future, my past, all of it—like hell was I giving him my tears as well.

To distract myself, I turned to the window. The heavy reentry shutters were down, but I could see bright daylight shining through the cracks. I could tell from the color that the light came from a yellow-star sun, probably somewhere in the Sevalis. If I'd had my computer, that information might have been enough to narrow down my location, but my suit was almost certainly locked up in some cabinet by now. They probably wouldn't even take my equipment when they came for me, I realized with a pang. I might never wear my beautiful Lady again. She'd rot on the ship until Caldswell sold her, and then we'd both be victims of the *Glorious Fool.*

That thought brought me closer to crying than anything else had yet, and I doubled over, pressing my forehead against my knees. I would *not* cry. My will was the only weapon I had left. I would not let it crack now before the fight had even begun.

I was still swearing oaths to myself when I felt something touch my cheek. It was a tiny brush, little more than a breeze, but my head shot up anyway, teeth bared for a fight. But fast as the anger had risen, it fled, because it wasn't Caldswell standing in front of me. It was Ren.

The moment I saw her, I knew it couldn't *really* be Ren. First, she was alone, which the real Ren never was. Second, she wasn't wearing the simple shirt, loose pants, and flats Caldswell dressed his daughter in. This Ren was barefoot, wearing the same side-tied white medical gown she'd worn in the snow on Io5, and her brown eyes were looking straight at me with an intensity I'd never seen on Ren's face, not even when she was playing chess.

Don't cry, her voice whispered in my mind.

"Wasn't planning on it," I said bitterly.

She raised a finger to her lips, tilting her head toward Caldswell's door.

I got the point and dropped my voice to a whisper. "Why are you here? Your father's already given me the speech about your noble war."

The girl who looked like Ren narrowed her eyes. *Brian is not my father.*

I winced. I hadn't known a whisper could be so full of hate. "Okay," I said more slowly. "Who are you?"

The girl smiled at my question, a too-wide grin that was somehow more upsetting than her hateful glare. *You've already guessed who I am, Deviana.*

That cold creeping feeling that had been crawling through my stomach for so long it was starting to feel normal suddenly got even stronger. I glanced at Caldswell's door, but it was still closed, and it wasn't like I had anything left to lose at this point if he caught me talking to things that weren't actually there. "You're the one who makes the daughters," I said. "You're Maat."

The girl's face fell. *Maat doesn't make her daughters,* she said. *They're made from Maat. I don't want their lives, their pain.* She covered her mouth with her fingers, eyes suddenly wide, vacant, and terrified. *Don't want. Don't want.*

I pushed myself even farther back into the couch. It was unnerving to see so many emotions pass over Ren's usually blank face. But then, from what I'd gathered, Caldswell's daughter was some kind of copy. Maat was the original, and while I'd always suspected Ren was crazy, I knew for certain that the girl in front of me was several shots shy of a full clip.

"Why are you here?" I asked. "*How* are you here? What do you want from me?"

The girl blinked like she'd just remembered she wasn't alone. *Maat is wherever her daughters are,* she said. *But that's not important now. Maat came to Deviana because I can see through you. Listen.* Her hands shot out, grabbing my knees hard. **Listen!**

I had to bite my tongue to keep from crying out. Though I knew she couldn't actually be here in the room with me, Maat's hands certainly felt solid as they dug into my skin. It was just like the dream, vision, whatever I'd had on Io5, only worse, because now I knew it was real, and if Maat didn't stop squeezing my knees, she was going to break something.

"I am listening," I gasped, fighting against the weight on my feet as I tried in vain to pull my legs away from her hands. "You can see through me, okay? Now what the hell does that mean?"

Maat eased her grip but didn't let go. Instead, she leaned down until our noses touched, her too-bright eyes fixed on mine like stickpins. *I know what you are.*

Her words doused my anger faster than a bucket of ice water. "What am I?"

Maat smiled and stepped back. I blinked at her sudden retreat, but when I looked up to see why she'd moved, my breath caught.

The room was full of phantoms. They hung behind Maat like a glowing mist made of tiny legs and transparent bodies. But though they seemed drawn to her like flies to honey, not a single one of them came within arm's reach of me.

They told me, Maat said, reaching out her arm so the glowing bugs could crawl over her skin. *They speak in little voices, but Maat hears. Maat has learned to listen, because it is Maat who keeps them prisoner.*

My hopes faded with every word she spoke. I'd really believed she was just going to tell me what was going on, but Maat wasn't even looking in my direction anymore. She was staring down her arm at the phantoms that had clustered on the palm of her hand, and the longer she looked, the angrier she got.

They will not leave me alone, she hissed, closing her fist around the crawling phantoms. I flinched, waiting for the flash of light, but it never came. Instead, the phantoms drifted through her hand unscathed, and Maat pulled her arms back to bury her face in her palms.

I tell them again and again that Maat cannot help them, she whispered. *Maat cannot free them because Maat is also a prisoner. Maat was the first prisoner, and her daughters are slaves. Nothing sets me free, not even the madness. Not anymore. Maat can kill millions, but she can't even die.* She looked up at me in panic, biting her lip so hard I thought she'd bite it off. *Why can't I die?*

I couldn't begin to think of an answer to that. Fortunately, Maat didn't seem to need one. She stepped forward, leaving the phantoms behind as she leaned over until she was right in my face again. *The phantoms know you,* she whispered as the mad smile crept back over her face. *They tell Maat, Go and find her. She can set you free. So I did, and you can, can't you? You can free us all.*

I pushed back to get some distance. "I don't know anything about—"

She leaned in again, taking over the space I'd just put between us. *Maat will make you a trade, yes?*

I blinked. "A trade?"

Maat nodded frantically. *You are a prisoner, too. Right now you are safe because Brian does not know, but when he gives you to the others, they will find out the truth. They will find out what you are, and when that happens, they will make you like me.*

I jerked back against the couch. I'd already braced for imprisonment and death, torture at the worst, but the idea of becoming like this madwoman in front of me turned my blood to snowmelt. My fear must have been plain in my eyes, because Maat's smile went even wider.

Brian's war is not so simple as he makes out, she continued. *There are others, you've already seen them. I sent them to help you before, but you fought them.* She scowled. *That was very stupid of you,* she scolded. *This time you will not fight, though. Maat has friends who will help you escape. Whatever happens, though, you must not go with the Eyes. If you trust them even for an instant, they will make you a slave like Maat, and then no one will be free.*

As she spoke, an image of a woman appeared in my head. She was strapped upright to some kind of padded wall, tied with so many restraints she almost looked mummified. But worst of all was her head. Her entire skull was enclosed in a thick metal helmet. There were no eye holes, no ventilation breaks, nowhere at all that light could creep through.

140

That was it, just an image, a flash, but it was enough to drive a spike of claustrophobic, horrified dread deep into my guts. That was Maat, my brain whispered. That was what was in store for *me*.

I began to shake uncontrollably. The only reason I didn't break down was because I couldn't. I had to avoid that future at any cost, which meant I had to act fast. So I sucked in a breath and got myself together, looking Maat square in the eyes. "What do I do?"

Maat will help you, she said eagerly. *I can get you away from here, but you must promise to find Maat and free her in return.*

I'd already opened my mouth to say yes, but I stopped just before the word came out. Terrified or not, that was a high price. I didn't even know where Maat, the real, physical Maat, was, but it was sure to be one of the most secret and high-security facilities in the universe. How could I possibly get into a place like that and set her free when I would be on the run myself?

Like she could read my thoughts—and for all I knew she could—Maat grabbed my face between her hands and yanked me forward. *It has to be you*, she snarled. *Promise!*

"Okay okay, I promise," I said, wrenching my head out of her grasp. "Help me escape and I promise I'll do everything I can to set you free."

It was a rash thing to swear, but I was past desperate. I could hear people walking around on the *Fool*'s upper deck above my head. For all I knew, Caldswell's retrieval team was already here. I didn't even know if this crazy girl really could help me escape, but if she was going to do something, it had to be *now*.

But the moment I'd told her I'd help, Maat's urgency seemed to drain out of her. The intensity in her eyes had faded to something distant, almost like she was dreaming while awake, and I felt a stab of fear, followed by a burst of anger. I'd already lost everything once today. If this crazy lady had gotten my hopes up just to space out on me when it mattered, I was going to explode.

"Maat!" I hissed, eyes flicking between her and Caldswell's door. I could see him moving inside. We were running out of time. "*Maat!*"

She blinked at her name, and her eyes drifted back down to me. I gave her my most encouraging smile and lifted my bound hands, but she just tilted her head, her lips pressing together into a severe line. *She will betray you*, she muttered, staring through me rather than at me. *But it matters not. She cannot help being what she is. It's already done, isn't it? I can wait a little longer. And when she succumbs at last, Maat will be free.*

"I won't betray you," I said, leaning forward so fast I sent the phantoms hovering around Maat skittering to the other side of the room. "I swear it by the Sainted King. On my honor as a Paradoxian, I'll do everything in my power to set you free, but if you don't get me out of here soon, it's gonna be a moot point."

My voice sounded so desperate I was almost embarrassed, but Maat didn't seem to notice. She just looked over at the phantoms I'd sent running, head lolling on her shoulders. *Free, free, free*, her voice sang in my mind. *If the rabbit wants to be free, it must run.* She looked at me again like something had just occurred to her. *Are you the rabbit, Deviana Morris?*

"Sure," I said, eying Caldswell's cracked door. I was leaning over to try for a better look when Maat grabbed my jaw and wrenched my head back to her.

"Then *run!*" she screamed.

The command was still ringing in my ears when the shuttered window beside me exploded.

CHAPTER
7

The blast threw me off the couch.

I hit the floor hard, ears ringing and eyes blinded from the bright light that was now flooding the room. The explosion had blown the captain's window clean off, landing shutters and all. Outside, the sunlight was white and harsh, but the air that blew into my face was cool and woodsy smelling. I blinked hard a few times, letting my eyes adjust until I could make out a line of shadows moving at the edge of the sunlight. Trees.

Something brushed against my wrists, and I heard the steel manacles pop open. The weight on my legs was already gone, the plasma melted into a puddle at my feet, leaving me free. Across the room, I could see Caldswell crawling out from under his blown-out door. Time to go.

I shot to my feet, pushing off the wreckage of the couch as I bolted out the newly made hole in the *Fool*'s side into a rocky clearing. Overhead, sunlight beat down from the yellow star riding high in the powder-blue sky, while in front of me wooded mountains stretched out in all directions like a leafy green sea. I was sure they stretched out behind me as well, but I was only looking one way, directly ahead toward the line of trees I'd spotted earlier.

I ran as hard as I could, bare feet pounding against the sun-warmed stone. Rashid would be on the roof already. Once he recovered from the surprise of the blast, the shot would come from behind, in my back. Getting to the tree cover was my only hope.

"Morris!"

Caldswell's bellow was so furious I stumbled. I caught myself at once and kept running, legs pumping faster than ever. I didn't dare look back, but I didn't have to. I could hear the captain chasing me, his boots slamming against the stone at double my pace. He was right behind me now, so close I could feel the wind as his hand grabbed for my shoulder and missed. And then, just when I knew he was about to try again, Maat's voice whispered in my head.

Duck.

I obeyed before I could think. The second my head was down, a shot cracked through the air.

I grabbed my chest instinctively, but the explosion of pain never came. Instead, I heard a crash behind me. Still running forward, I risked a look back.

I almost wished I hadn't. Caldswell was lying facedown on the stone. His jacket and chest were splattered with blood from a gaping bullet wound just above his heart. Even so, he was struggling to get up, his face furious as he screamed my name.

He deserved that and more, Maat said, her hatred ringing through my mind. *I told you Maat had allies.*

As though to prove her right, another shot rang out. The bullet pegged Caldswell in the leg, and I held my breath, waiting for him to go down again. But he didn't. The stubborn bastard was still after me. Seeing him trying to move with those horrible wounds was so insane, I actually stopped to stare. As soon as my feet stopped moving, a sharp pain spiked through my head.

No stopping, rabbit, Maat chided. *Your burrow's in the woods.*

The words brought an image with them this time. A wooded hollow beneath a steep stone ridge hidden by a fallen log.

Run rabbit run, Maat whispered. *I'll see you soon, yes?*

I didn't bother with an answer. I was already running again, charging across the last of the open ground and into the woods.

The shade hit me like a slap in the face. The sunlight in the clearing had been cool, but it was almost cold here in the tree shadow. The scattered leaves and moss were soft under my bare feet, though, and I was able to run silently down the slope from the high ridge where the *Fool* had landed. I'd just reached the bottom when I spotted the sheltered place Maat had shown me.

I dove for the cover as soon as I saw it, rolling under the fallen log to lie still, ears straining, but I heard nothing but the wind in the trees. Heart pounding, I turned around to see why Maat had sent me here, praying to the king it wasn't something crazy, like an actual rabbit den. But all my fears vanished when my eyes landed on a familiar silver box with the Verdemont crest hidden at the base of the rotting tree.

I'm not ashamed to admit the sight of my armor almost made me cry. The only reason I didn't was because I didn't have time. I was already throwing my armor on.

I didn't beat my nineteen-second record, but it was close. My guns were here too, both neatly packed into their cases like I'd put them up myself, and I said a prayer of thanks for whatever miracle had brought this about. I'd already locked Mia on my back and was just sliding Sasha into her holster when I caught a flash of movement in the woods behind me.

I spun, gun ready, but it did no good. The thing hit me before I could fire, slamming me into the soft ground. I weigh almost four hundred pounds in my armor, but the man threw me down like I was nothing. His arms were impossibly strong as he pinned me to the ground, and I looked up in fury to see Rupert on top of me.

By this point, my gun was already wedged into his ribs to shoot him off me, but as I dug the barrel in, my finger hesitated. Rupert was staring down at me, and his cold mask was gone like it had never been. Instead, his face was a haggard mix of anger, fear, guilt, and love. So much love it made me pause, and in that moment, Rupert flicked up my visor and kissed me.

It should have been awkward to kiss through the opening of

my helmet, but Rupert kissed me with such desperate passion he made it work. He was still on top of me, his body pinning down my suit with impossible strength, his shoulders hunched as his hands gripped my shoulders, caging me in. It was a familiar position, and it sent a memory rushing up so fast I couldn't do anything but let it come.

It was another odd one. A strange, unfitting memory like the one I'd had before. This time, though, I'd guessed why. The memory felt weird because it wasn't mine. It was Rupert's. I knew this because there was simply no other way I could have a memory of seeing myself naked and asleep on his chest.

In the memory, I was looking down at myself lying on top of him with the sheets bunched up over our hips. I was facedown with one arm thrown across his chest like I was afraid he'd run away. My cheek was pressed flat over his heart, but my sleeping face was tilted up toward his, and my lips were curved in a smile so beautiful I could actually feel the ache of it in my bones.

If circumstances had been different, I would have burst out laughing. I have never looked that good in my life, and there was certainly no way I looked that good passed out with my sweaty hair clinging to my back. But I wasn't seeing the truth, only Rupert's perspective of it, and in his eyes, I was beautiful. The most beautiful, beloved, wondrous thing he had ever seen.

The memory vanished as fast as it had come, leaving me reeling. For a second, I couldn't imagine how this could be, but then I remembered the feel of Rupert's hand in my mind putting the memories Ren had dumped into my head back in order. He must have left some of himself behind in the process, because there was no question the image I'd seen was Rupert's memory of our time together.

I could still feel his love for me like a hook in my stomach, and I knew here, at last, was the truth. This was no crush or infatuation. Rupert loved me with the same intensity he did everything else, loved me so much that the echo stayed with me even after the memory had sunk back into my unconscious, and now that I'd felt it, the red of my rage was all I could see.

Rupert was a symbiont, stronger than my suit. Anthony's letter had warned me they were stronger than any armor, even the King-class suits, but raw strength wasn't everything. Unlike a symbiont, the Lady Gray's power could shift, and that was exactly what I did. Rupert was still on top of me, his lips on mine like a plea, but I didn't even do him the courtesy of breaking the kiss before I swung all of my suit's power to her legs and kicked him as hard as I could.

The blow sent him flying through the felled tree that had hidden my armor. I rolled to my feet the second I was free, coming up with Sasha trained on Rupert's head as he crashed through the rotten wood. He landed in a crouch, but his blue eyes weren't even looking at my gun. They were focused on my face, and the sad look in them made me want to scream.

"Devi…"

"*Shut up!*" I shouted. "Don't say a word."

He closed his mouth and started forward, but I shot the moss at his feet. He froze, looking at the little crater Sasha's bullet had made, and he then sighed. "Devi," he said sadly. "Stop this. I don't want to hurt you."

I went stiff. I'm no stranger to rage, I could even admit that I had a bit of an anger problem, but sometimes things got out of hand. Sometimes, my rage burned so hot that it went full circle, leaving me cold. I'd only hit the cold rage a few times in my life, but every time it happened, I did something I came to regret. I didn't see how there was anything I could regret now, though, so I didn't bother fighting the cold fury as I lowered my gun.

"You loved me."

I didn't realize how awful my voice sounded until Rupert winced. "I still love—"

"You reordered my memories," I snarled. "Made me sick whenever I looked at you. You rewrote my life!"

"To save you," Rupert snapped, his hands closing into fists.

"To save me," I repeated, my voice so cold I was surprised the words didn't come out with little puffs of frost. "Until you shot me in the head."

If I'd had any lingering doubts that what I'd seen in the bunker hadn't been a dream, the look on Rupert's face would have done them in. He didn't argue, didn't deny it. He just stopped, his pale skin going even paler. "What?"

I formed my free hand into a gun and tapped my finger against my forehead through my still-open visor. "Pow," I said. "Good job. Welcome back to the fold, Eye Charkov."

As long as I live, I will never forget the look Rupert gave me then. If I hadn't been trapped in the cold anger, it would have made me cry. I didn't even know there was an expression for abject guilt and horror until it was staring me in the face. "How do you know about that?" he whispered.

"Doesn't matter," I said. "It happened. But for the record, I would *never* grovel like that."

Rupert closed his eyes and dropped his head. When he spoke again, his words were calm, soft, and so sad I almost lost the cold rage. "I would apologize," he whispered. "But I know there's no excuse. I did something in that place that cannot be forgiven, and I regret it more than anything I've ever done."

"And yet you keep doing it!" I shouted. Cold rage or not, I was so mad I was shaking, and I stepped forward so hard my boot sank three inches into the leaf litter. "You stand there saying you love me, that you did all this crap to save me, but you gave me to *Caldswell* to hand over to the Eyes! And now you're going to do it again! You're here to grab me for Caldswell so he can shove me in a lab for the rest of my *life*!"

"I have no choice!" Rupert shouted. He was breathing heavy too, his icy calm shattering before my eyes. "You know what I am, what we do. You know what's at stake. If it were up to me, I'd never have given you a reason to run in the first place, but it's *not*. It doesn't matter how much I love you, I'm an Eye, just like Caldswell.

I have a duty I cannot betray. You saw the wreckage of that planet, you saw what the phantoms do."

"And what would you have done against that?"

"Nothing," Rupert admitted. "We could not have saved Unity, but we have saved thousands of other planets, Devi. Every day, all of the known universe, the Republic, the Sevalis, even Paradox is in danger. It's only because of our work that planets aren't lost all the time."

"Save it," I sneered. "Caldswell already fed me the hero bullshit."

Rupert's lips pulled back in a snarl. "It's not *bullshit*," he growled. "We can't even count the lives we've saved."

"How about the lives you've ruined?" I countered.

"It's not like that," Rupert said, his voice furious and frustrated. "We don't know what's going on with you, but something is wrong. We have to run tests to be sure, and the only place to do that is back at headquarters. This isn't a death sentence, Devi!"

"You of all people should know by now that my life isn't what I value most," I snapped. "I go with you, and everything I've ever fought for, risked my life for, is gone. They're going to lock me up until I'm crazy as Maat, aren't they?"

He shot me a confused look. "How do you know about—"

"*Aren't they?*" I shouted.

Rupert sighed. "I don't know what plans are being made for your testing," he hedged. "But it is likely you will never leave the Eyes' custody again."

"Right," I said. "But you're still not going to let me go, are you?"

Rupert's eyes went cold and hard as blue ice. "No."

"Well," I whispered, reaching up to flip my visor back into place. "I guess that's that."

Rupert looked away with a word that sounded like a curse. "I tried, Devi," he said bitterly. "If there was any other way, I'd find it, but there isn't. It doesn't matter how much I love you, no single life can outweigh the greater good of the Eyes' mission. But you have to know I tried to save you. I tried everything I knew."

His words were pleading, but I was already stepping back, kicking my suit into battle mode as I planted my feet. "Save it," I said, giving Elsie the command to start heating up. "I must have been some kind of idiot, Charkov, because for a while there, I loved you, too. That's why I'm going to give you a chance to change before we do this."

My voice was crisp and cold, and it must have scared Rupert. He put his hands up, his voice going gentle, like he was trying to talk down an enraged animal. "It doesn't have to be this way."

I shrugged. "You want to put me in a lab, I disagree. Sounds like we're at an impasse."

"I'm not your enemy, Devi," Rupert said, staring me down. "I never was and I never will be."

That claim almost made me laugh, because now that I had my memories back, I knew that Rupert had always been my worst enemy. From the very beginning he'd gotten under my skin. Even when I knew he'd lied to me, I'd still trusted him, loved him. I knew he loved me even without seeing his memory, but it didn't matter. When the line had been drawn, Rupert had made his choice, and it wasn't me. If that didn't make us enemies, I didn't know what did.

With that thought, the cold rage blossomed in me clear and crisp as a battle drug, pushing all the conflicted feelings away. Oddly, it also sent my fingers tingling, the tips prickling with the pins and needles I'd come to associate with the black stuff, but I was too angry to care. I had only one focus. Rupert the man tied me in knots, but an enemy I knew how to handle, and when I looked at Rupert now, that was what I saw: a clever, dangerous enemy who wanted to take away everything I'd worked for.

He was still watching me with those pleading eyes, and he must have seen the decision on my face, because his mouth opened. Whatever he was going to say, though, he never got the chance. I was already in the air.

I'd put all my suit's power into the jump, and I flew at him so fast even Rupert was surprised. I was just cold enough to savor the look of fear on his face as Elsie ejected on my wrist, her thermite firing like a shot of sunlight as I brought her down on Rupert's arm.

For one moment, I thought he was actually going to let me cut him. I should have known better. Just before I hit, Rupert moved, flicking away like a shadow. But he must have forgotten who he was dealing with. I'd seen him fight several times now, and fought him myself. I couldn't match his speed, but I knew how he moved, and the second he dodged, I spun, slamming Elsie's glowing blade deep into his side.

It was like trying to cut through a reinforced cement pillar. Even with my new tungsten blade and the thermite going full burn, there was enough resistance that I couldn't finish the slice before Rupert jumped back. To his credit, he didn't cry out, though when I spun around to gauge the damage, I didn't see how.

I'd cut him clean across the side. The thermite had burned his dark jacket and shirt away like they were tissue, so there was nothing to hide the gaping hole I'd put in the smooth skin just below his ribs. Anti-armor bullets might not work on symbionts, but like the xith'cal they resembled, thermite sliced them open just fine. I couldn't get too cocky yet, though, because Rupert was still standing.

Elsie's intense heat had cauterized the wound, so there wasn't as much blood as there should have been, but Rupert's hands were still crimson where they held the wound closed. I expected him to change into his scales and charge me then, but he didn't. He just stood there, staring at me with that brokenhearted look, like this was all my fault.

"Change," I ordered, swinging Elsie's blade at him, letting the thermite hiss through the air. "Now."

"No," Rupert said solemnly. "I don't want you to see me like that."

"Are you kidding?" I shouted. "That cat's been out of the bag."

Rupert set his jaw. "I won't be a monster for you, Devi."

"If you think I'll hold back just because I can see your puppy dog eyes, you've got another think coming," I snarled. "You don't take me seriously and I will take your damn head, scales or no."

Rupert said nothing, just pulled himself a little straighter. I was about to give him a final warning when I saw his eyes flick toward my thermite blade. I glanced at my timer and cursed myself for an idiot. I'd thought Rupert was playing on my sympathies. I'd even thought he didn't want to fight me because he loved me. What a joke. Rupert wasn't holding back out of love, he was wasting my thermite. I'd just lost twenty of my eighty-five seconds of burn time *talking*.

With that, the cold rage fell on me like fresh snow, and I charged. I had just enough time to see Rupert's eyes widen before I crashed into him, blade going deep into his stomach. Or that was the plan. He spun at the last second, grabbing my shoulder and using my own momentum to send me falling past him.

On anyone else, that move would have sent them to the ground, but I'm not anyone else. I'm a Paradoxian armored merc, and the second he threw me, my suit caught me. I spun on a pin, flipping around with my blade up to catch him on the back step, only to grind to a halt.

There was no dodge this time; I hadn't missed. Elsie's glowing edge was less than an inch from Rupert's side, but I couldn't move her forward because the shining blade was caught on a black claw. I was so close to Rupert now I couldn't see his face on account of our height difference, but I saw the change all the same. Black scales bloomed across his body, starting with the hand that had caught my thermite blade and spreading up his arm, shredding his already ruined clothes. As before, the transformation took less than three heartbeats, and it was on the second one that I struck.

I wrenched my arm up, twisting my blade. Those black claws of his were hard, but they weren't indestructible, and with the extra torque, Elsie's blade sliced through them like wooden pegs. I heard Rupert hiss as the sharp ends of his claws were cut free, and then something grabbed my shoulder. Rupert was going for a submission hold.

I ripped out of his grip and spun away, my left hand reaching for

Mia. I swung the plasma shotgun off my back, dialing the charge to max as I whirled to face him again. Rupert's other form was just as I remembered, all sleek black scales, speed, and power. A few scraps of his shredded suit still clung to him, but the symbiont had covered the wound in his side without leaving so much as a bloodstain.

He was looking at me as well, those black, alien eyes watching my feet as Mia's whine filled the forest, but I didn't give him a chance to figure out which way to dodge. I didn't even give myself a chance to finish turning. The moment Mia's charge was primed, I fired.

He dodged the first blast by a hair, but the second one hit him across the shoulder. He staggered as Mia's sticky white fire splattered over his body, clinging to his scales. I was actually a little amazed it wasn't eating through him, but I'd learned the hard way to take nothing for granted with symbionts.

But though it didn't consume him, the fire slowed him down enough for me to shoot him three more times before dropping Mia in the grass. I had one more shot in the charge but no time to take it. Mia's fire only crippled him anyway, and I had less than twelve seconds left on Elsic's burn. It was now or never.

I closed the distance between us in a heartbeat. Rupert had fallen to his knees in an attempt to get the burning plasma off him, and he saw me too late. My shining blade was already falling toward his neck, the thermite smoking through the air as I bore down, throwing all my power into the stroke that would take his head. But then, just before I hit, my hand twisted.

It wasn't even a conscious decision. I'd committed to the strike fully, or I thought I had. But something inside me must have gone soft, because the blow veered at the last second, and instead of cutting through Rupert's neck, Elsie's shining blade lodged in his shoulder.

I kept pushing anyway, hoping against hope to get something useful out of it, but I was down to seconds on my thermite, and cutting through Rupert's symbiont body was like cutting through bedrock. Before I'd even made it to his collarbone, Elsie's light snuffed out.

Elsie wasn't brittle like Phoebe had been, and her blade didn't snap when her fire died. But hard as Elsie's tungsten core was, Rupert was harder, and my blade stuck fast inside him, trapping me. For almost a full three seconds, I couldn't do anything but stand there and pull. Finally, I managed to yank Elsie free by retracting her back into her sheath, and not a second too soon. She was barely clear before Rupert punched up with his uninjured arm.

I dodged the punch by a fraction, but no amount of fancy footwork could stop me from falling. I stumbled backward, my suit rolling automatically when I hit. This time, though, even the Lady's speed wasn't enough.

Rupert was on me in an instant. He landed on my stomach with his full weight, slamming me into the ground so hard even my stabilizer couldn't save me from the neck snap. He was burned and bleeding freely from his shoulder, but the damage barely seemed to slow him down as he grabbed my right arm and squeezed, crushing the little motor that ejected Elsie from her sheath.

I cried out in dismay. Elsie might not be burning anymore, but she could still stab, and I'd been ready to shove her straight into his damned lungs. But it seemed like my moment of idiotic softheartedness was about to be my undoing, because with Elsie locked in her sheath and Mia lying on the ground a dozen feet away, I was running low on weapons. I still had Sasha, but I knew from experience that she wasn't the best weapon against symbionts. I couldn't reach her anyway, not with Rupert pinning my arms.

I tried another kick instead, but Rupert had learned from his previous mistake. He'd already shifted his weight to pin my joints, ruining my angle so that I couldn't get the leverage to land a hit. All I could do was lie there and thrash while Rupert sat on top of me like a victorious gladiator toying with his kill.

"Stop this," Rupert said softly. "It's over, Devi."

The hell it was. I still had my grenade string. My low-ordnance explosives weren't strong enough to actually hurt Rupert, but I could blow him off me. I was about to drop the whole string in his face when my proximity alarm began to beep. That was all the warning I got before a gunshot exploded through the woods.

Rupert and I jumped at the same time, and then Rupert rolled off me, falling slack on the ground. I lurched to my feet at once, but Rupert didn't move. A second later, I saw why. There was a huge blast wound in his back, turning his scales into a burned, bloody mess, and not three feet behind him was Rashid, dressed in his tactical armor with his disrupter pistol in his hand.

Rashid looked at me briefly, like he was just checking to make sure I was alive, then he walked over Rupert's fallen body and dropped his arm, aiming his disrupter pistol at the back of Rupert's head.

"Don't!"

Rashid looked up, finger paused on the trigger. I stared back at him, panting. I hadn't even realized I'd spoken until he looked at me, but I didn't take the word back.

"He is one of them," Rashid said, his voice as cold as mine had been earlier. "He does not deserve your pity."

My eyes went back to Rupert as I tried to work up the courage to tell Rashid to go ahead, to end it, but I couldn't. Despite everything that had happened, I hadn't been able to kill Rupert even in my cold rage, and I couldn't let Rashid kill him now. "Just don't," I said quietly. "Please."

The anger was draining out of me so fast I felt like I was going to faint. I didn't even know if I had it in me to stop Rashid if he tried to fire. Fortunately, I didn't have to. Rashid sighed and holstered his pistol, kicking Rupert in his injured side before turning away.

"Come on, then," he said, walking into the woods.

I stared at his retreating back for several seconds before bursting into motion. I ran across the ground Rupert and I had torn up in our fight and grabbed my armor case. I snatched up my gun boxes as well, strapping them to the Lady's case before hefting the whole lot onto my shoulders. When everything was secure, I ran after Rashid, scooping Mia off the ground where I'd dropped her as I passed. I didn't look at Rupert as I left, but I watched his still body through my cameras until the trees hid him from sight.

Rashid was waiting for me a few dozen feet away. He looked me over, then nodded at my armor case. "You should leave that. It will slow us down."

"Nothing doing," I said. "My case charges my suit. Without it, the Lady's only got five days of power and no nano-repair. Besides"—I glared at his tactical armor, which didn't even have a motor, much less anything that could help him run at even a quarter of the Lady's encumbered speed—"I don't think you should be worrying about *me* slowing us down."

Rashid held up his hands in peace. "You are correct, I meant no offense. Shall we go?"

I motioned for him to lead the way, but rather than jog into the woods as I'd expected, Rashid walked over to a place where the trees were thick and held out his hand. I was about to ask him what the hell he was doing when I saw a slender, small hand reach out to wrap around his as Ren stepped out of the undergrowth.

"Holy hell, Rashid," I breathed. "Is that the real Ren?"

"The very same," Rashid said quietly, grabbing the girl's hand tight as he set off down the hill. "Hurry, please. They will be here soon."

Ren followed him into the forest without a sound, her brown eyes wide and vacant as a doll's. I looked back up to where Rupert was lying before jogging after them, my stomach sinking further with every step. "Caldswell is going to murder us."

"He's going to do that no matter what," Rashid replied.

I started to say there was a difference of degree but swallowed the words again just as fast. Now was not the time. Rupert was down, but I had my memories now to tell me just how fast symbionts could heal, so I kept my mouth shut as we jogged into the woods.

The direction Rashid chose led straight down the dell and then up into the mountains. The up and down landscape made me doubly glad of my suit's help, but Rashid handled the steep slopes on his own without complaint. He kept Ren going as well, carrying her when things got too rough. We made good time, and when we were thirty minutes and five miles of rough country away from where I'd fought Rupert with no sign of pursuit, I decided it was time to get a few things straight.

"So," I said. "Did you sell Caldswell out, or were you a plant from the start?" When Rashid didn't answer, I went on. "I'm betting you were in on this from the beginning. Why else would all of my applicants not show up for their job interview?"

"Not showing up for an interview on the *Glorious Fool* sounds like an excellent act of self-preservation," Rashid said, glancing at his handset.

"Why did you do it?" I asked, jerking my head at Ren, who was following Rashid like a toy dog on a string. "Was it for her?"

"Yes," Rashid said, sliding his handset back into his pocket. "But the daughter was a target of opportunity. My primary mission was to infiltrate the *Glorious Fool* and protect Deviana Morris until we had a chance at a successful extraction."

"Guard *me*?" I scoffed. "Why?"

"Because I heard you were the one who was going to save the universe."

I stopped cold. "Dear Sacred King, you work for Brenton."

Rashid just smiled.

I looked away with a groan, but I looked back just as quickly when I realized how little sense that made. "If you work for Brenton, why did you fight his merc team on Ample? You killed more of his people than I did."

"It was a calculated move," Rashid said with a shrug. "We needed Caldswell to trust me."

My look turned into a glare. "So you killed your own men?"

"They were told they'd be facing a sniper and a Paradoxian armor user," Rashid replied. "It wasn't like they were sent in unprepared."

"And what if they'd gotten me?"

"Then you'd be safe, the mission would be accomplished, and we wouldn't be here," Rashid said, completely unruffled. "As it was, we won, and Caldswell trusted me enough not to bother watching me when he landed here, allowing me to seize the daughter while the Eyes were busy as well as cover your own escape. So you see, both outcomes were in our favor." His smile widened. "John Brenton does not waste his moves."

I rolled my eyes. "And I suppose extorting the captain for double hazard pay was just more character acting?"

"Indeed," Rashid said. "Caldswell understands money-hungry mercenaries very well, and we tend to overlook that which we think we understand."

I sighed. He had a point. "Okay," I said. "Excellent inside job. Bravo and well done. What happens now?"

Rashid took Ren's hand and started walking again. "We hide from the Eyes until the others arrive. I've already sent the signal, but it could be hours before we get a pickup, so we're going to use that time to put as much distance between ourselves and the *Fool* as possible. Without their daughter, the Eyes will be at a temporary disadvantage. She is what allows them to communicate instantly between teams. But they are still a great threat, especially since you refused to let me eliminate Caldswell's most dangerous weapon."

He said this last bit with a glare over his shoulder that I ignored. "So that's your plan?" I said, walking after him. "Run and hide?"

"I think I did quite well considering the circumstances," Rashid said. "We did rescue you right out from under Caldswell's nose on minimal notice. With your armor, I might add. Certainly that is worth a little hiding in the woods?"

"We?" I asked. "Who's we?"

Rashid smiled down at Ren. "The daughter helped me. She spoke in my mind and turned off the security on your armor case, which was the only way I was able to get your suit to where you could find it without being shocked to death."

That was not the answer I'd been expecting, but it made sense.

No one else on the *Fool* would betray Caldswell. Maat had been busy, apparently. "Is she speaking now?"

"No," Rashid said. "She has been silent since the explosion."

"Well," I said. "Thanks for saving my bacon, then. That was a nice shot you got on Caldswell, by the way."

Rashid chuckled. "I missed, actually."

"Missed?" I said. "You blew a hole in his chest."

"But I was aiming for his head."

I had to laugh at that. "So," I said. "Disrupter pistols take down symbionts?"

"They're the only handheld weapon that can," Rashid said bitterly. "And only if you get it in the head."

That explained why Caldswell had scowled so hard at Rashid's weapon choice when we'd first hired him, and why the captain and Rupert both carried the things. "I guess this means you're against the Eyes, then."

"Utterly and completely," Rashid replied.

"Why?" I asked. "I mean, do you think nothing should be done against the phantoms, or do you just disapprove of their methods?"

It felt more than a little awkward asking Rashid why he was against the people I'd just thrown everything away to escape, but I had my own reasons for fighting the Eyes, and if I was going to have Rashid at my side, I needed to know his. Considering how quickly he'd claimed to be against them, I thought it would be a simple question, but Rashid gave my words careful consideration before he answered.

"On the surface, the life of the Eyes is admirably self-sacrificing," he admitted. "The brave heroes who give their lives fighting a shadow war for the good of the universe. It's a heroic tale that the Eyes love to sell, and I think many of them believe it."

I thought of Rupert standing across from me with his fists clenched as he talked about all the lives he saved. Though I wasn't feeling very kindly toward him at the moment, I knew Rupert was fundamentally a noble, self-sacrificing kind of guy. A perfect soldier, just like Caldswell had said. And if Rupert hadn't been so ready to sacrifice me, too, I could almost have admired him for it.

"But you don't buy the hero act," I said. "You and Brenton."

Rashid shook his head.

"Why?"

He stopped and looked at me. "What would you do if you knew the end of all was upon you?"

I frowned. "Is that a rhetorical question?"

"Unfortunately not," Rashid said. "What if I told you right now that we were under attack by a powerful enemy who could not be fought or detected."

I saw where this was going. "You mean the phantoms."

"The word 'phantom' is insufficient," Rashid said with a wave of his hand. "How do you contain a natural force responsible for the meaningless death of billions in a single word? It is impossible. Everything with phantoms is impossible. They are like the earthquakes they cause: unpredictable, unpreventable, and invariably deadly, leaving none to blame but fate. Now, imagine that you are tasked with defending the universe against earthquakes. Impossible, right?"

I nodded.

"Ahh," Rashid said. "But now, imagine that while you're waiting helpless for that impossible horror, that unseen death, you stumble over a miracle that could save everyone. Would you take it?"

"Of course," I said cautiously, feeling around for the trap that was always buried in questions like these.

"Of course," Rashid repeated, his voice growing more heated. "But what if that miracle came with a price? What if, in order to save your life, you had to sacrifice someone else, someone innocent and completely unconnected to you? A child, say. What if by torturing, enslaving, and eventually sacrificing a child, you could build the weapon that saved the universe? Would you take the miracle then? Would you call it a miracle at all?"

I didn't have to ask what he was talking about. The memory

of Maat's voice was stuck like a barb in my mind, repeating over and over that Maat was a prisoner and her daughters were slaves. I thought of Ren lying curled in a ball on her bed after the phantom attack, her eyes wide and dead. I remembered Enna clinging to Brenton with her skeletal arms as she cried in great, soundless heaves. I looked at Ren now, who was staring up at the sky like we didn't exist, and a chill went through me.

"Maat is the only plasmex user humanity has ever produced who is powerful enough to stop a phantom," Rashid said, his voice tight and angry. "She was the first. But she is only one woman, and she went mad decades ago from handling more plasmex than any human should. So, to keep fighting, the Eyes made copies. Clones at first, but they all died as children. After that failure, they sought a more reliable solution and found the daughters."

He looked at me, his face pained. "They test every human girl born in the Terran Republic and Paradox. Those found to be compatible are invited to attend a private school when their plasmex starts to mature at puberty, but it is a lie. The ones who go are taken, and the ones who refuse are stolen from their homes." As he spoke, the hand he'd wrapped around Ren's began to shake. "They are taken from their families, taken from their fathers, taken even from their own minds. And where they were, only Maat remains.

"This is the Eyes' *miracle*, Miss Morris," he said, his dark eyes flashing. "This is their solution to the phantom problem, these girls they wield like weapons, girls who succumb to Maat's madness and must be put down after only a few years. The Eyes do not care. They replace the broken ones like spare parts, leaving the children who die for their cause without so much as a look back. And those who would care, the mothers and fathers, all they can do is stare at the sky and wonder which star shines on their child's grave."

Strangely enough, the first thing that popped into my head as he told this horrible story was that now I finally understood why Caldswell was so ruthless about keeping phantoms a secret. Even at the time, the panic excuse he'd given me on the ship had rung hollow, especially considering how unbelievable phantoms would sound to anyone who hadn't bumped into one personally. But the systematic abuse, enslavement, and eventual murder of little girls? That was definitely a secret I could see a man like Caldswell killing to keep. But even so, the real surprise for me in all of this was Rashid.

Despite his expert double-cross, I'd still pinned Rashid as a mercenary. Even when he'd talked about Brenton, he'd only spoken of orders and plans, nothing fanatic. But when Rashid talked about the daughters, he didn't sound like a hired gun. His voice was bitter as ash, and the more he talked, the more I knew that this wasn't about Brenton's mission at all. This was personal.

"Back on Wuxia, you told me about your daughter," I said quietly. "She was taken, wasn't she?"

Rashid nodded, and I tilted my head at Ren. "Is that her?"

"I do not know," Rashid said, reaching out to gently push some of the hair out of Ren's face. "She looks nothing like my Yasmina, but that's how the change works. Maat takes everything from them, even remaking their bodies into copies of hers so that she may ride in them more comfortably." He slid his fingers down Ren's cheek as he spoke, but the daughter didn't even seem to notice. She wasn't even blinking anymore.

"I've searched for my little girl for three years now," Rashid whispered. "I've freed several daughters in the process, and every time, I looked for some sign. A gesture, a familiar turn, something to show me that here, at last, was my little flower. But I see nothing. Even now, when I am standing right beside her, I do not know."

"But that's why you saved her," I said. "Because there's a chance."

Rashid dropped his hand. "I saved her because she is someone's daughter. Whether or not she is my Yasmina, she has a father, a mother, a family."

I winced at the anger in his voice, but that was nothing compared to the look he fixed on me when he turned to face me again.

"I am a father, Miss Morris," he said. "One among many. Our

children were taken to be fodder for a salvation that was a miracle for everyone except those it destroyed. But the true villainy of the Eyes isn't that they made a hard choice, but that they never sought to find another. I have been a soldier all my life. I understand that sacrifices must be made. But we've known about the phantoms for seventy years now. In that time, the Eyes have become experts at keeping the secret, experts in hiding, in responding quickly to signs of a phantom attack. They even learned to manage the lelgis. But the one thing they have never improved, never *sought* to improve, were the lives of Maat and her daughters. They had their miracle, their *weapon*, and they have never sought to find another."

"Is there another?" I asked.

"I do not know," Rashid admitted. "But I know we'll never find it if we do not take the time to look. The Eyes have the support of every government in the universe. They have virtually unlimited resources, and yet the only research they do is for new ways to stabilize the daughters so they can use them longer. They do not care about the innocents they crush, and so they do not care about finding a new path. But we care. That is why we fight the Eyes, because we believe we can find another way, one that does not kill children, if we only have the courage to look."

"And that's what you think I am?" I said. "An alternative?"

"Nothing is certain," Rashid said, shaking his head. "But Mr. Brenton believes you are important. That is enough for me."

I stopped walking and took a long breath. Rashid stopped too, waiting patiently while I figured out how best to put this. "Look," I said at last. "I'm very grateful to you for saving me from the Eyes. If it weren't for you, I'd probably be drugged up and on my way to a secret lab right now. But just because I'm thankful doesn't mean I'm ready to throw all in with you guys yet. I like you, Rashid, and I get why you're doing this, but I *don't* like Brenton."

"Understandable," Rashid said. "The last time you met, I believe he was very impolite."

I arched an eyebrow. Brenton had raided my ship, killed my

partner, and threatened to kill me. "Impolite" wasn't the word I'd use. But that wasn't why I didn't like him. "Brenton is the kind of man who uses the greater good to justify being ruthless."

"So is Caldswell," Rashid pointed out.

"And I don't like him either," I snapped. "What I'm trying to say is I'm sympathetic to your plight. I understand how dangerous phantoms are, okay? And I sure as hell don't like what was done to your daughter. I'm perfectly willing to listen to what your people have to say, especially considering they're on the non-child-abusing side of this setup, but I Don't. Like. Brenton. I don't trust him, and quite frankly I'm feeling a little backed against the wall right now."

That was the understatement of the century. Now that the adrenaline from my fight with Rupert had faded, I felt like I was cornered against a wall of spikes by five Terran tanks. But trapped wasn't beaten. No matter how much I needed an out, I was not about to give in to Brenton without setting some ground rules.

"I'm not going to vanish into some lab," I announced, lifting my chin. "I'm willing to submit to testing, but on my terms and with my informed consent. I also want to keep my suit and my weapons."

"We are not the Eyes," Rashid said scornfully. "Of course you will keep your freedom."

My skepticism must have been clear on my face even through my visor, because Rashid sighed. "Miss Morris, if I wanted to take you against your will, I could have disabled you and dragged you off during your fight with Charkov. But those are the Eyes' tactics, not ours, and we will not stoop to their level. If you wish to leave right now, I will not stop you. All I can do is beg you as a father, and as someone who has saved your life several times now, to please come and hear us out."

"That's it?" I said. "Just listen?"

"I would explain it myself," Rashid said. "But I do not know all of the particulars, and we've lost a great deal of time already."

He looked at the woods as he spoke. I did too, scanning the dense trees for any sign of pursuit. I didn't see anything, but then, I wouldn't, would I? Those damn symbionts were ghosts.

I sighed and leaned back into my suit, letting the Lady hold me up while I tried my best to think through all the angles. I *really* didn't want to team up with Brenton. Even forgetting how Falcon 34 had ended, his assault on Ample had only reinforced my opinion that he was the sort of man who never hesitated to throw a life away in the pursuit of his goals. Not exactly a person I pictured fighting the Eyes to find a way to stop them from abusing children. But if I left now, I'd be stranded in the woods on a planet I didn't even recognize.

That made my decision. Even if Rashid was about to screw me over, I was much more comfortable with my odds against him and Brenton than I was with the idea of wilderness survival. My Lady was made for fighting, not camping, and out here in the woods with no power source or chance to resupply, I'd be a sitting duck when Caldswell's pickup team came for me.

"Okay," I said at last. "I'm in. Lead on."

Rashid grinned and slapped me on the shoulder. "Welcome to the good guys," he said with a wide grin.

I grimaced in reply, but Rashid had already started up the hill again, pulling Ren gently behind him.

CHAPTER
8

The hill ended at a steep cliff. Rashid climbed onto the ledge first, pulling Ren up after him. I tossed my armor case over as soon as they were clear before jumping onto the ledge myself. I landed on the flat rock neatly, but when I glanced around to see where we'd ended up, all I could do was gasp.

Whatever this planet was now, it must have been a mining colony originally, because Rashid and I were standing on the edge of a quarry pit the size of a small gorge. The side of the mountain in front of us had been scooped out to form a huge bowl that had to be half a mile from end to end. Big as it was, though, the mine was clearly no longer in use. The steep cliffs were riddled with tunnel entrances cut into the light gray stone of the mountain like cavities in a tooth, but more than half had already caved in, and the bottom of the quarry had been allowed to fill with murky black water, forming a small, disgusting lake at the ruined mountain's base.

The ledge we were standing on ended in a vertical cliff that fell straight down into what looked to be the lake's deepest part, though it was hard to tell for sure. The water was so dirty I couldn't see the bottom even around the shallower edges. Rusted cranes still stuck up out of the water like broken reeds, but other than a few ashy campfire pits along the lake's edge, there was no sign that anyone had been here in years. Only the lonely moaning of the wind as it blew past the empty tunnels.

"Where are we?" I asked, leaning over the edge to peer down at the black water far below.

"One of the mining planets the Sevalis sold to Confederated Industries," Rashid said, dropping his pack on the ground. "CI-Twelve, I think."

I blew out a long breath, thanking the king that I hadn't tried to run. Even if the other mines weren't dead like this one, corp planets were famously empty. I could have wandered for months without seeing a soul.

A clatter interrupted my gloomy thoughts, and I looked over to see Rashid setting up something that looked like a wire clothes rack attached to a battery. "What's that?"

"Signal beacon," Rashid replied, extending the antenna. "Encrypted, of course. But we have to make sure our rescue can find us."

I glanced at the beacon, which had started making a low humming noise. Apparently, Rashid's professionalism extended to more than pretending to be an excellent ship guard. That was nice to know. But while I was sure the flat ledge made for a good beacon site, our position was much too open for my liking. I was about to suggest that we find somewhere more sheltered to wait when I heard a soft sound behind me.

It was so faint it could have been a distortion in my speakers, but I'd heard enough symbiont claws by now to recognize the distinct click. I spun before I could think, pistol coming up just as Rupert finished landing on the ledge behind us.

I could tell from the way he stood that he was still injured. That was something, though considering the hole Rashid had put in his back, I'd hoped for more time. But as I lowered Sasha's barrel to plug him in the chest wound I knew was hidden under his scales, my camera picked up another black shape coming in from the side.

"Rashid!" I shouted.

Rashid spun so fast I would never have believed he wasn't wearing real armor. One moment he was drawing his disrupter pistol to shoot Rupert, the next he was leveling his gun at the head of the symbiont behind him, the one Rupert had been playing decoy for. The one going for Ren.

What happened next happened all at once. I fired, Rashid fired, but neither of us hit. My yell had alerted Rashid, but it had also tipped off our enemy, and fast as we were, the symbionts were faster. Rupert dodged my shot easily, turning sideways to let Sasha's bullet fly by. I should have seen it coming and shot again, but I was too caught up in Rashid's fight to pay proper attention to my own.

The new symbiont had flattened to the ground before my partner's shot went off, ducking under the disrupter blast only to jump up again when the air was clear. But when its claws struck out, they weren't going for Rashid. The symbiont was reaching for Ren, who hadn't even flinched at the shots flying past her head.

This time, though, Rashid had the advantage, because he already had a hold on the daughter's hand. But as he pulled Ren behind him, the symbiont changed its trajectory, straightening out its hand. I didn't even have time for another shout before the long black claws flew through the air where Ren had been to stab deep into Rashid's side.

By this point, I was already swinging my gun around. I fired as Rashid screamed, but my shot went crooked. While I'd been focused on the new symbiont, Rupert had stepped in to grab my arm. But though he'd ruined my shot, I wasn't done yet. Quick as a thought, I loosened my grip, letting Sasha slide in my hand until her barrel was pointed down at Rupert's shoulder.

This close, even a symbiont couldn't dodge. The force of Sasha's bullet ripped Rupert off me, pounding him into the ground at my feet. Now that my arm was free, I recovered my grip and dropped my arm to shoot him again, but all I hit was rock as Rupert rolled away.

But even though I wasn't fast enough, my suit had followed his trajectory. I let my Lady guide me, trusting my targeting computer to line up a head shot that would blast Rupert back into the woods.

But as the lock beeped on and my gun came up, I heard a sharp, unmistakable crunch.

I was focused on my targeting system, so I didn't see what happened, but I'd heard enough bones crack to know what that sound meant. Forgetting Rupert for a second, I glanced back at Rashid. He was standing where he'd been when I'd looked away a second before, and the second symbiont was standing beside him with Rashid's head gripped in its sharp-clawed hands, his neck broken clean through.

The symbiont let go as I watched, its black claw shooting out to grab Ren as Rashid's body crumpled to the ground. It was a suicidally stupid thing to do in a fight, but for an endless second, all I could do was stare. It had all gone so wrong so quickly, and now I was alone, facing two symbionts and a daughter back under the Eyes' control.

It took the sound of Rupert rolling back his feet to snap me out of my daze. I turned on my heel at once, putting my back to the ledge as I commanded my targeting computer to keep track of both symbionts now that I was outnumbered. Up until this point, I hadn't paid much attention to the new symbiont. Now, I saw that it was shorter than Rupert by several inches and, I realized with surprise, female. That was all I got before the woman released her grip on Ren and charged me.

I fired on reflex, plugging three shots at the female symbiont's chest. The woman dodged each bullet, getting right in my face. As soon as she was there, she kicked up, her foot slamming into Sasha as she tried to knock my pistol out of my hand.

She almost got it, too. But I love Sasha the best of all my guns, and I clenched down at the last second, hammering the woman's toes with my pistol butt instead. I'd hoped that would be enough to throw the symbiont off balance at least, but the woman simply stopped her kick midswing, hanging for a moment before lowering her foot as gracefully as a dancer.

I leveled my gun for another shot, but the symbiont held up her hands in surrender. I should have fired anyway, but the armor on her face was sliding away before my eyes, and the sight it revealed was better than a stun gun.

When the new symbiont had first appeared, I'd thought for sure it was one of Caldswell's pickup team, but the woman behind the scales wasn't a stranger. It was Mabel, and she was smiling the same sunny smile she'd given me back on the Fishermarch when I'd first seen her walking up to the *Fool* with her cat crate tucked under her arm.

"Drop the gun, Morris," the captain's sister-in-law said.

As she spoke, Rupert stepped behind her to take command of Ren. He'd dropped the scales from his face as well, but it wasn't actually an improvement. He was back in his cold mask now, and ice would have been friendlier than the closed-off look in his eyes as he stepped in front of the daughter.

To say I was in a bad spot would be a criminal understatement. Rupert's new position formed a V with the two symbionts at the tips, me at the point, and the cliff at my back. I was cornered tight and proper, and from the smug smile on her face, Mabel knew it.

"We don't want to hurt you," she said, her voice easy and cajoling, like she was trying to get me to drink one last beer. "Just put the gun down, sweetheart. Nice and easy."

That "sweetheart" was the last straw. I snapped Sasha up as my computer painted a fat red target on Rupert's wounded shoulder. My gun might not be able to really hurt him, but her force would still blow him back. If I could just make a hole, I could run for it. But as I squeezed the trigger, I felt something prickle across my mind.

The sensation stopped me cold. It was like something slimy had touched my consciousness, and I wasn't the only one. Rupert and Mabel had both stopped with a shudder and were now looking back at where Ren was standing over Rashid's crumpled body.

For the first time ever, the daughter's eyes weren't blank or hyper-focused, and that wasn't a good thing. I'd have taken the empty doll stare in a heartbeat over the expression of horrified comprehension she wore now. Rupert recovered first, reaching out to grab her, but Ren didn't even twitch as his claws circled her wrist. She just kept staring at Rashid's broken body, and then, in a tiny, raspy voice, she whispered, "Papa?"

The word was barely louder than the wind, but the silence that came after it hit me like a phantom's scream.

Pressure filled my mind so fast I thought I was going to pop. My cameras went snowy at the same time, the white lines filling my vision until they were all I could see. If I hadn't been so used to my suit, I might well have toppled backward off the cliff, but I managed to fall forward instead, going to my knees as Ren's silent scream dug into my brain.

I couldn't see squat by this point, so I took a chance and popped my visor. As my eyes took over from my cameras, I saw Ren lying over Rashid's body with her head pressed against his bloody chest. Her shoulders were shaking violently, but it took me several seconds to realize she was crying. Ren was sobbing without making a sound, and with each heave, the pressure in my head grew worse and worse. And then, just before it crushed me, the pressure stopped.

The pain in my head evaporated, the white lines clearing off my side cameras like someone had cut a switch. In the space of seconds, my suit was back to normal, and I looked up to see Rupert standing next to Ren. The two of them side by side was such a normal sight, it took me a few moments to realize Ren's feet were dangling off the ground, her body suspended from Rupert's black claw wrapped around her neck.

Silence fell over the cliff like snow. My suit was perfectly functional; *I* was the one who couldn't move as Rupert gently lowered Ren's still body to lie next to Rashid's. Next to her father.

My vision started to go blurry, and I blinked rapidly, snapping my visor back down as I shot to my feet. I had no time to be weak. Mabel was back on her feet already, stalking toward me like a hunting wolf. I backed away instinctively, almost stepping off the cliff in the process. The near miss sent a few rocks clattering over the edge, and Rupert looked up at the sound. His face was closed and cold as ever, but I could see a hint of fear in his eyes as he glanced at the ledge, and then back to me.

"Step away from the edge, Devi," he said softly. "It's over."

I ignored him and peered down the cliff through my rear camera instead. The fall to the black water below was so far it made me dizzy, but I forced myself to get past that and *really* look. What I saw wasn't encouraging, but it was enough, and I looked back at the symbionts with a new eye.

Other than that first tiny flash of fear, I couldn't read Rupert's blank expression at all. Mabel on the other hand looked insufferably smug as she stalked closer, and with good reason. The symbionts were stronger, tougher, and faster than my suit would ever be. My allies were dead, leaving me cornered and outnumbered. That was a winning combination in any game, but I had one card left. There were still a few things my Lady could do that symbionts couldn't, and that was the hope I clung to as I lowered my gun.

"Good girl," Mabel said, giving me a warm smile as I returned Sasha to her holster. "See how easy that was? Now—"

She never got to finish. The moment my gun was locked in, I jumped.

———

I flipped backward off the cliff in a beautiful arc. At first, all I could hear was the wind whistling through my speakers, and then my velocity alarm started screaming. I silenced it with a thought and rotated in the air until I was feet down, straightening my body to a plank in the process.

When I was certain my position was right, I locked my suit and turned off all my cameras except the one looking at my feet. The sight of the cliff hurtling by did nothing but terrify me anyway. If I was going to survive this fall, I had to hit the water at exactly the right angle. For that, all I needed was my gyroscope and my ground cam, so those were all I left on as I plummeted through the empty air.

I've fallen longer distances in my suit, but never without a parachute, and as the seconds ticked by, I began to wonder if I'd ever hit. Finally, after what felt like years, my proximity alarm began to blare. The water was close. I turned off the beeping and closed my eyes, putting my faith in the Lady Gray as we fell the final dozen feet.

Even knowing it was coming, hitting the water caught me by surprise. I crashed into it so hard I was knocked breathless despite my stabilizers. Every alarm I had was blaring in my face, and for a horrible moment, I thought I'd broken my suit for good. But though I couldn't feel anything but adrenaline, my vitals told me I was alive and unharmed. More importantly, I didn't feel anything cold or wet on my skin. A quick scan confirmed it; there were no breaches. My suit had held, and we were now sinking into the black water like a stone.

As the rush of survival began to ebb, another set of instincts took over, the sweet, efficient energy of my battle sense. Like a weapon switching firing modes, I flipped from shock to action, unlocking my suit and flicking my cameras back on to get a good look at the water around me.

The disgusting lake that filled up the mine's base was black as tar and about as thick. Even my floodlights couldn't penetrate more than a few inches, so I cut them and switched everything to my density sensors. I was setting up a scan to see how far I was from lake's bottom when my speakers picked up the crash of something hitting the water above me.

I looked up before I remembered I couldn't see anything. A quick thought switched my cameras to thermographics, and a huge smile spread across my face. Density sensors were for big things—walls, armor, rocks, and so forth. They didn't pick up symbionts for squat, but I knew from experience that Rupert ran warm. Down here in the cold water, he glowed like a beacon. I could see him swimming above me, looking around in vain, and my smile grew wider.

Symbionts might be stronger and faster than I was, they might be unkillable monsters tough enough to cross the vacuum of space in only their scales, but Rupert was swimming through the black muck with nothing but the air in his lungs and his eyes to see by. My suit, on the other hand, had a crush depth of two thousand feet, a full suite of sensors, and a sixteen-hour air supply. I wasn't sure how long symbionts could hold their breath, but I was pretty sure I'd won this round.

I watched Rupert's heat signature all the way down. My suit landed neatly on the silted floor of the flooded mine pit, and I sank into a crouch. Rupert had actually made it almost all the way down as well by this point. He was only a few feet above me, one of his hands grabbing blindly just above my head.

Looking at that reaching hand, it occurred to me that I could drown him. Blind and underwater, his superior strength wouldn't matter. I was heavier, and I didn't need to go up for air. I could finish what I'd been too soft to end in the woods. But I didn't reach up to grab his hand. I didn't move at all, not even when his clawed fingers came within a half inch of my visor.

But as his grasping fingers missed me yet again, a memory bubbled up in my mind, pushing its way to the front of my thoughts. I shoved it back ruthlessly, because I knew now what sudden bubbling meant. This was another of the memories Rupert had left in me, and I wanted nothing to do with it. I might have decided not to drown him, but that didn't mean I wanted any more of his life story. But like the others he'd left, this memory completely ignored my wishes and shoved itself forward until it was all I could see.

I was inside a crowded starport. All around me, people were screaming and panicking while a line of uniformed soldiers tried to hold the mob back. The crowd was terrifying and I wanted to leave, but I couldn't. A pale teenage girl with long black hair and blue eyes had a death grip on my arms, and she was shoving me at a soldier, yelling at the top of her lungs, "Take him! Take him!"

In the din of the panic, her voice was clear and commanding, and it worked. The soldier grabbed me around the waist and turned away, hoisting me onto his shoulder like a sack of flour.

"No!" a voice cried, but it took me a second to realize it was my voice. Not mine, but mine in the memory. A little boy's frantic scream. "*Tanya!*"

But the teenage girl scowled at me sternly. "*Go!*" she shouted. "We'll be on the next ship! Go with them, we'll find you!"

I screamed, my hand reaching out frantically, straining as far as I could, but it was too late. The crowd had swallowed her, leaving me alone with the guard as he ran me toward the battered cargo ship that was already full of children.

The memory vanished with a rush that left me breathless. I'd been out for less time than it took to blink. Rupert was still right above me in the black water, his hand reaching out for me just as it once had for Tanya, and my hand went up to meet it of its own accord.

I caught myself just in time. Above me, Rupert snatched his arm back as well. He must have pushed himself to the absolute limit, because he flipped and swam straight for the surface at a speed that astonished me, even though I'd seen enough symbionts to know better. I watched his bright shape on my thermographics until he surfaced, but he didn't dive again. Instead, he turned and started swimming for the shore. When he'd shrunk to a bright dot against the black wall of the water, I turned and started walking in the opposite direction.

My density sensors had been scanning the lake the whole time Rupert and I had been doing our little dance in the dark, and they'd built me a pretty good map of this part of the flooded mine pit. Good enough to guide me to one of the still intact tunnels. Even looking at it in outline through my density sensors, the dark hole was forbidding. Crush depth and air supply aside, I wasn't exactly thrilled at the idea of going into an underwater mineshaft, but I didn't have much choice. Down here I had the advantage, but if I surfaced, it was over.

I took one last look at the flooded tunnel. Then, with a deep breath of my precious air, I stepped inside and started walking, trusting my suit to draw a map that I hoped would keep me from dying an ignominious death lost underwater on a planet whose name I'd already forgotten.

————

I've done a lot of scary shit in my life. I've fought my way out of a xith'cal ambush with nothing but a recruit's suit and an army standard sidearm, had a drug-crazed pirate get the drop on me from above with a thermite knife, and been stuck under a trauma shell without being able to pass out. All of those had been horrible in their own special ways, but I would have taken any of them in a heartbeat to get out of that damn flooded mineshaft.

The first hundred feet were fine. The tunnel was a little silted up, but the way was large enough that I could walk upright without feeling too claustrophobic. But then, at the hundred and fifty foot mark, the mineshaft had started to get narrower. Soon I didn't have enough room to turn around, but that was still bearable until the ceiling started getting lower, too. I made it a bit farther by hunching over, but soon enough I was crawling on my hands and knees without enough room to double back, or even lift my head.

The floor was the icing on the cake, though. As you'd expect in a flooded tunnel, the ground was squishy and silted over. The mud was like tar, grabbing my hands and knees with sticky suction. Sometimes the tunnel was blocked completely, forcing me to stop and dig my way through, scratching at the mud with my fingers like a drowning mole.

Even when the path was clear, though, I moved at a snail's pace. My suit can take being underwater, but it's not made for it, and the Lady was dragging like never before. The dirty water was starting to work its way into her cracks, and after an hour of horrible crawling, I swore I could feel her motor slowing. If I didn't get out and flush the Lady's system soon, there was a real danger something would jam and I'd be stranded down here in the dark, unable to turn around, unable to move forward, unable to do anything except watch my air meter run down as I slowly suffocated.

Given all that, you'd think the silt would be my biggest worry, since it was the variable most likely to kill me. But stupid as it was, what really made me panicky was the fact that I couldn't *see*. True, my density sensor mapped things for me, drawing little colored lines across my screen to show the edge of the wall, the floor, the ceiling, and the tunnel ahead, but colored lines aren't much comfort when you're crawling underwater with your head scraping the roof of the tunnel and you can't even see where you're putting your hands. Colored lines were what I had, though, so colored lines were what I clung to, following the glowing edge of the walls like the Paradoxian princess who followed her magical ball of yarn out of the labyrinth.

In a way, it was actually good that the tunnel was so narrow I couldn't turn around. I'd never thought of myself as claustrophobic, but crawling on my knees through the dark with the walls scraping on all sides was bringing me closer to a breakdown than I'd ever been. If there'd been any chance of going back, I would have jumped on it and ended up right back in the lake where I'd started. But the only thing that scared me more than crawling in the dark through a tiny, flooded tunnel was the idea of doing it backward, so I kept going, making my way at a painfully slow pace until, at last, my density sensor picked up a wall in front of me.

I started crawling faster. When I was ten feet from the wall, the low ceiling vanished, and I shot to my feet, craning my head back as far as it would go, even though I still couldn't see a damn thing. My sensors told me there was nothing overhead for at least fifty feet, but it was my groping fingers that figured out the truth when they found the rails set into the walls on either side. I was standing at the bottom of an empty elevator shaft.

You'd have thought I'd found heaven's gate from the way I started jumping around and singing praises to the king. I knew I was making an idiot of myself, but with no one around to see, I didn't care. I grabbed the rails next, putting all my weight on one, then the other. Both held, and I gave another whoop as I started pulling myself hand over hand up the wall.

It was a slow climb, but after spending the last hour at a literal crawl, I felt like I was flying. The water pressure lessened with each hand up, and fifteen minutes and almost a hundred feet later, I broke the surface at last.

The sight of normal darkness instead of ink-thick water made me want to shout for joy all over again, but I kept my mouth shut, turning my speakers as high as they would go. I didn't hear anything except the water splashing against the rough stone walls, but I still didn't dare turn on my lights to have a look around. Instead, I checked the air. It came up stale, but breathable, and I took a few moments to refresh my supply. While my suit was running the mine air through its filters, extracting and compressing the oxygen, I turned my mind to other problems.

The tunnel had been horrible, but at least it had kept me too busy to think about just how screwed I was. It felt petty and selfish after what had happened on the cliff, but while I was sad as hell about the pointless, bitter deaths I'd witnessed, my worries at the moment were purely practical. With Rashid gone, I'd lost my contact with the people who could get me off this rock. Even supposing I could find some way to get in touch with Brenton while dodging Caldswell's people, I was still screwed, because when I'd jumped to get away from Rupert and Mabel, I'd left my armor case up on the ledge. Without my case, I couldn't repair the motor Rupert had crushed when he'd grabbed Elsie's sheath, and I couldn't recharge my suit when her batteries started running low. More immediately, though, I couldn't replenish any of my chemicals.

Most of my critical supplies like breach foam and the cocktail needle weren't the sort of things I used regularly, but the stuff that kept my less glamorous systems going, like the purifiers for my water system and the liquid filter that scrubbed the excess CO_2 out of my air, were going to start getting low soon. I had enough silicate flush left in my tank to clear the dirt out of the Lady's joints when I got out of the water, but after that I was empty. I was also only carrying two spare clips for Sasha. I had plenty of thermite gel, but that was a moot point since I couldn't get Elsie out of her sheath.

I popped my visor and stared up into the dark, breathing in the dank reek of the mine. Behind me, my compressor whirred softly, the little sound bouncing up the elevator shaft. I focused on the noise, slowing my breathing until it was as soft as the little motor's purr. There was no use worrying about things I couldn't change. I'd deal with those problems when they became problems. Right now, I had to keep moving before Rupert and Mabel found me.

Mission firmly in mind, I locked my visor and resumed my climb, stopping just above the water line to flush the silt out of my suit. Once she'd drained, my Lady was almost back to normal, and I shimmied up the final two hundred feet of elevator wall like a spider.

When my density sensor told me I was nearing the top, I slowed. The shaft was still black as pitch, but it was no longer silent. In addition to the soft splash of water below, I could now hear the distant moan of wind. Somewhere up there was an exit, and I was going to find it. Before that, though, I had a more immediate problem. The elevator shaft I'd been climbing was no longer empty. There was a mine elevator parked at the very top, and it was blocking my way.

Considering it had been made to haul up giant carts of unprocessed ore, the metal platform was surprisingly shoddy. Unfortunately, even a shoddy mine elevator was still thicker than I could punch through without Elsie's help. Worse still, the corp's lack of safety consideration didn't extend to gaps between the elevator and the wall. The damn thing was set flush against the stone, leaving me nothing I could grab to pry it down.

I could have shot through it with Sasha, but it would have taken all the ammo I had just to make a hole big enough for my head. Likewise, I could have used Mia, but my plasma shotgun only had one shot left before she'd have to recharge, and I didn't have the power to spare. Plus, Mia was *loud*. I wasn't sure where Rupert and Mabel were, but there was no way they'd miss something as distinct as a plasma shotgun blast, not to mention the inherent danger of shooting an elevator while you were crouched beneath it.

I bit my lip. No shooting, then, but what did that leave? I could pry Elsie out of her broken sheath and slice a hole, but then I'd be stuck with my blade out instead of in. That would limit me severely if I had to crawl again, assuming I didn't accidentally break my new blade in the process.

I was about to try it anyway when I had another idea. A fantastic one. I ran it through my head several times, looking for weaknesses, but after three times through it was still fantastic, and I decided to roll with it.

I reached into the nook under my arm where Phoebe used to sit and pulled out my block of thermite gel. Thermite clay would be a better name, because that's what the stuff felt like as I rolled it between my fingers. When I'd worked it into a putty, I reached up and pressed it against the elevator's underside, smearing it over an area slightly larger than the width of my shoulders. It took almost my entire block to get enough coverage, but thermite gel is cheap and it wasn't like I'd be using my blade until I could repair the motor anyway. When I'd made a good, thick coat of the stuff, I pulled open the little panel hidden beneath my suit's wrist, revealing my sparker.

My fellow Blackbirds had laughed themselves sick when they heard I'd ordered a sparker put into my state-of-the-art custom armor. Sparkers were exactly what they sounded like, a little fork that sparked electricity on command. Back in the old days they were used for starting fires, jumping batteries, and lighting smokes if you were crazy. They were so notoriously dangerous I'd had to sign a waiver before Verdemont would agree to install one in my suit. I'd signed it gladly, because by the time I'd been able to afford my Lady, I'd been in the killing business long enough to develop a deep appreciation for the simple effectiveness of thermite, and while the safer modern heating coils would work eventually, nothing fired the stuff as quickly and reliably as a good old-fashioned zap.

Pressing my body against the wall, I stretched out my arm until my sparker touched the edge of the smeared thermite. The little lightning bolt of electricity from the sparker's fork was blinding after so long in the dark, but it was nothing compared to the thermite's glare. The moment the charge hit, the rough circle I'd made lit up like the sun.

Since this was just mashed-up thermite gel smeared over metal rather than a measured ration fit into a specialized blade, it burned unevenly, dropping huge glowing globs down into the dark, where they continued to burn even after hitting the water. But inefficient as my work-around was, it got the job done. The thermite burned through the heavy steel like it was paper, and by the time the last embers winked out ten seconds later, there was a nice Devi-sized hole in the elevator's floor.

The heat had left the metal brittle, though, and the hole's edge broke the first time I grabbed it, forcing me to scramble to keep from falling two hundred feet back into the water. Fortunately, my suit is faster than I am, and the Lady found a handhold before we tumbled. I flipped myself up after that, rolling off the dangerously brittle elevator platform into the tunnel beyond.

Thank the king, the new tunnel was much larger than the one below. The ceiling wasn't towering, but I could stand without hitting my head. Better still, it wasn't pitch black. I could actually see the gray edge of the tunnel's curve in my night vision, and a faint breeze was whistling over my speakers, showing me the way out.

For one giddy second, I almost ran forward. Fortunately, my soldier's sense kicked in before I could, and I fell into a crouch instead, listening. Burning through the elevator had been much quieter than a plasma shotgun, but it had still made a lot of noise, and the flash from the thermite would have been a signal flare to anyone looking for me. But even with my speakers turned to max and my sensors sweeping every inch of the tunnel ahead of me, I didn't spot so much as a nesting bird. I did another sweep anyway, just in case, and only when that came back negative too did I pull Sasha off my hip and follow the breeze down the tunnel.

I'd thought it would be a long trip, but all the crawling must have skewed my perception of distance, because I reached the end of the tunnel after only ten minutes. I passed several branches off the main path on the way, other shafts going down into the dark. My suit added each one to my growing map, but I was focused only on getting to the light. The exit turned out to be much wider than I'd expected, a truck-sized hole leading out to a sunny ledge that dropped off into nothing. I'd guessed from the wind that I was high up, but it wasn't until I crept to the edge that I realized just how far I'd come.

The tunnel was one of the holes I'd seen in the mountain across the quarry from the cliff where I'd jumped. I was even higher now than I'd been then, and I had a bird's eye view of the whole pit, including the other tunnels and the lake below. Unfortunately, what I saw wasn't good.

The abandoned mine was crawling with soldiers, all humans, dressed in security uniforms with the Confederated Industries logo splashed across their backs. They had dredgers working the black lake and patrols checking the tunnels at the water's edge, and the air was full of security drones. One actually buzzed my tunnel while I was looking, forcing me to dive back into the dark. I hit the ground hard and lay still, taking shelter in the dust. When the hum of the little flier was gone, I grabbed Mia, the only gun I had that was big enough to take down aircraft, and crawled back to the ledge for another look.

A quick count from my suit confirmed my fears. There were almost five hundred corp guns down there. Even though I was staring right at it, the size of the response seemed crazy to me. I'd only been in the tunnels for an hour and a half. Even assuming Mabel had put in the call the second I'd jumped, how the hell did you get this sort of muscle to an abandoned mine in the middle of nowhere on such short notice?

I spotted my answer down by the filthy lake's edge. Three men in corp suits with expensive-looking ledgers were standing on a rocky outcropping not far from where I'd hit the water, and beside them, looking out over the black lake like it was his own private sea, was

Caldswell. The captain looked pretty good for a man who'd taken two sniper shots today, I thought bitterly. But then, after what I'd learned about Mabel, that wasn't surprising. If the *Fool*'s engineer was a symbiont, there was no question that Caldswell was one, too.

When I zoomed in for a better look, I saw that Caldswell was talking to the men in suits, sweeping his hands out at the water like he was giving orders. The corp suits didn't look happy about that, but they didn't argue. From what I knew of Caldswell, they couldn't. All he had to do was flash his Royal Warrant or whatever the Terran equivalent was and even a corp planet fell at his feet to do his bidding, and from the huge search going on below, it didn't take a genius to see that his bidding was to find *me*. The only question left was how the hell was I going to escape?

I could hear another air patrol coming, so I ducked back into the tunnel to consider my options. I hadn't seen Rupert or Mabel down there, but that only made me warier. A battalion of corporate cannon fodder was annoying, but even on low ammo, I could take a lot of rent-a-soldiers before I got overwhelmed. Symbionts were a different story. If I was going to survive this, I had to get away. Fast.

I looked back down the tunnel with a long sigh. I really, really, *really* did not want to go back into the mine, and I thought I might die if I had to go underwater again, but there was nothing for it. With that army outside, it was tunnel or nothing, so I pushed myself back to my feet and walked into the dark, using my map to pick the shaft that looked most likely to go in the opposite direction from Caldswell.

———

The next dozen hours were some of the most stressful of my life. The abandoned mines were huge, pitch black, and endlessly complicated. I tried to stick to a pattern, using my map, compass, and sensors to plot a course west from the lake. Even so, I ran into countless dead ends, cave-ins, and tight squeezes. I went back underwater two more times, both for mercifully brief periods. Mostly, though, I walked through absolute blackness, blind except for the map my suit drew of where I'd been and the fifty feet my density meter could pick up ahead of me.

I stopped listening for pursuers after the first two hours, not because I thought I was safe, but because the paranoid ear I kept out for footsteps also picked up the groan of the tens of millions of tons of rock above me. Every collapsed tunnel I passed reminded me I was only one vibration away from being entombed myself, and the more I listened, the worse it got. I caught myself jumping at imaginary rumbles, and every now and then I'd see things in the dark. This combined with my blindness and the constant fear of pursuit was quickly mounting up to be more than I could handle, so, three hours in, I set my speakers back to normal, flipped all my lights on, turned my music up loud, and just focused on walking in the right direction.

Around the ten-hour mark, my luck finally changed. I'd been hitting dead end after dead end for hours when the little tunnel I was following intersected what I'd come to recognize as a main branch shaft. A main branch shaft that was going *up*.

With a prayer of thanks, I turned and started jogging up the incline. The big tunnel got wider the farther I went, which I took as another good sign, and when my lights picked up a line of dusty trucks, I almost cheered. Despite how I'd spent the day, I didn't actually know much about mines, but it didn't take an expert to guess that trucks were parked near exits. I hadn't spotted any outside light yet, but I could hear a breeze whistling over my speakers. Still, it wasn't until I rounded a wide corner and nearly ran into a lowered steel door that I realized just how close to freedom I was.

The door was huge and heavy, an enormous trundling blockade to protect the truck depot I'd been jogging through. There was no power to run the motor that moved it, but the door was set on a rolling track, and after a little shoving I was able to push it open wide enough for my suit to get through. When I cracked the door, I realized why I hadn't seen any light from this exit as I had from the first one. Night had fallen while I'd been underground. But even the darkest night is nothing compared to the blackness of the mines, and my suit's night vision kicked in like clockwork.

I cut my lights and wiggled through the gap I'd made into what must have once been a loading zone. The trees had been cleared for hundreds of feet to allow hauler ships to set down, but the clearing hadn't been tended in years, and the forest was taking it back. I walked out of the mountain into a field of saplings, tilting my head back to get a good look at the sliver of large blue moon overhead. And then, because it was so nice to be out in the open air again, I fell backward, flopping into the overgrown weeds for the sheer joy of it.

But my happiness was short-lived. I wasn't trapped underground anymore, but I was still stranded in enemy territory with no way out, no way to repair or replenish my armor, and no food. Even if I did find a town, Caldswell undoubtedly had control of this planet by now. If I showed my face, I'd be turned in before I could buy dinner.

I was getting good and depressed over this when my suit beeped a warning in my ear. I sat up at once, rolling into a crouch as I scanned the tree line for what had triggered my suit's early warning system, but all I saw was the normal movements of the woods at night. I was about to dismiss it as a false alarm when my body stopped.

I'd only been frozen in place with plasmex once before in my life, but it wasn't a feeling you forgot. The moment the heavy pressure landed on me, I knew I was hosed. I was already braced for the hand to land on my spine and yank me around to face my doom when I heard a familiar voice.

"Hello again, Miss Morris."

Never in my life would I have thought that I'd be happy to hear that voice again, but I was almost ready to sing when I glanced at my rear cam to see John Brenton step out of the forest. He looked just as he had back on Falcon 34—same smug look, same leather pilot's jacket, though I knew it had to be a different one since I'd seen him shred the first when he'd brought out his symbiont. I looked around for his backup next—mercs, more symbionts, even another HVFP team—but I didn't see anyone except the pale young man who'd been with him last time. The plasmex user who'd locked me down, Nic.

"Turn her around," Brenton said.

Nic nodded and turned his fingers, lifting and spinning me like a puppet. I didn't fight it, just slumped against the pressure, letting it carry me. The wall of force wobbled when I put my weight on it, and I saw sweat spring up on Nic's brow. That hadn't happened before, but then, Nic hadn't been the one moving me before. That had been the girl, Evelyn. Until I'd killed her, anyway.

That thought put me on guard. I didn't feel the pins and needles that I'd come to recognize as the sign the black stuff was spreading, but after what I'd done to Evelyn, I didn't want to risk killing another plasmex user. At least not by accident.

"No need for the invisible lock," I said, putting my weight back on my feet. "I'm not going to run."

Nic glanced at Brenton, who nodded slowly. "Sorry," Brenton said as the pressure melted off me like snow. "Old habits die hard."

I shrugged. I might not think much of Brenton, but I couldn't fault anyone for healthy paranoia. Especially considering I'd shot him in the head the last time we were together.

"Where's Rashid?" Brenton said, looking around. "He was supposed to be with you."

"He's dead," I replied. The words were harder to say than I'd expected. I'd liked Rashid. I hadn't known him well, but what I'd seen had been good. Even if I hadn't liked him, though, no one deserved to die like that. Not him, and not Ren.

Brenton's smile fell into a grief-stricken grimace. "He knew the dangers," he said quietly. "But Rashid was a good man. I am very sorry to hear that he is dead."

"He found his daughter," I said.

Brenton's head snapped up. "Is she still with them?"

"No," I said. "She's with him."

Brenton caught my meaning and heaved a deep sigh. "Another daughter would have been useful, but I'm glad she's free. Maybe their next lives will be a little happier."

I frowned. I didn't like that his first thought had been disappointment that he wouldn't get to use Ren, but then, I couldn't talk. My first thoughts had been of survival, too.

"Well, done's done," Brenton said, holding out his hand. "Can I see his handset?"

I blinked. "I don't have his handset."

"Of course you do," Brenton said. "How do you think we found you?"

Now that I thought about it, how *had* they found me? I'd come out of the mine miles away from where I'd gone under. Glowering, I pulled up my suit's security monitor. I don't normally use my bug sniffer because I'm not normally worried about being tailed, and I hadn't actually done a full sweep in months. I did one now, though, and sure enough, the reading came back an angry red.

I swore and began feeling over my armor. Finally, my hands found a small lump on the back of my right shoulder, right where Rashid had slapped me. I dug in and pulled, ripping off a small black tracker.

Brenton started laughing the second he saw what was in my hand. "God rest the sly old fox," he said. "Any other bugs I should know about?"

I did another sweep, but everything came up green. I'd cut my suit's connection to the *Fool* when I'd put it on, and so far as I could tell, I was now flying solo. I did a manual bug check anyway, going over my suit inch by inch with my hands, but all I found was dirt. Brenton had stopped laughing by the time I finished. He was staring at me, leaning back on his heels with his thumbs looped through his belt. "You ready to get out of here?"

I fixed him with a no-nonsense look. "No," I said. "Not until I get some assurances. Is the deal you offered me on Falcon Thirty-Four still valid?"

Brenton tilted his head. "It is. I'll answer all your questions if you'll answer mine. Tit for tat, and when we're done, you can go. Assuming you still want to, of course. We had to dodge some pretty serious security to get over here. It seems your life has gotten a bit more dangerous these days."

I folded my arms. "We'll see. You answer my questions truthfully and fully, I'll do the same. Then, when I know exactly what is going on, we'll work it out from there."

Brenton looked hard at me, searching my face through my visor for the trap, but there wasn't one. I was being completely honest. I had no idea what was wrong with me, but whatever it was, it was clearly dangerous, and no one ever did herself a favor by staying ignorant. Of course, that didn't mean I was just going to roll over either.

"I'm not going to be a lab rat or a prisoner," I announced. "This is a two-way street. I keep my autonomy, weapons, and armor, and you keep your willing participant. You corner me at any point and I will die without telling you shit."

That was not a bluff, and Brenton knew it. "There's no need to make ultimatums."

I just stared at him.

"Fine," he said with a sigh. "You have a deal."

"Good," I replied. "Now let's get out of here. If you could find me, it won't be too much longer before Caldswell figures it out."

Brenton nodded and motioned for me to follow him into the woods.

CHAPTER
9

The forest here was denser than the high woods Rashid and I had walked through. I couldn't see more than few feet through the trees, but I scanned the undergrowth with every sensor I had. Other than the usual wildlife, though, the forest was empty, and that made me more nervous than finding a whole battalion of the king's armored corps.

"Okay," I said at last. "I give up. Where are your goons?"

"Why would I bother hiring mercenaries if I was just coming to talk to you?" Brenton said.

I glowered at his back. "That's not what I was talking about. Where are your other symbionts?"

"I didn't bring them," he said casually. "Didn't have time. Rashid's message said Caldswell had already called in a retrieval team."

"So it's just the two of you?" I was almost insulted.

"We expected to have Rashid as well," Brenton said with a shrug. "He's no slouch. And it was the Eyes we were worried about fighting, not you." He glared at me over his shoulder. "I've learned my lesson, Miss Morris. If I want to take you on again, I'm going to hire a tank."

"Don't count on it," I said proudly. "I've beaten a tank." Barely, with help, but his words still made me happy. It was a foolish, idiot kind of happy. Brenton was blatantly buttering me up, but after hours of crawling through the dark trying not to get caught by monsters who could hand me my ass without blinking, I was ready to take any reminder that I was actually someone to be feared. The last twenty hours had not been kind to my ego.

The undergrowth was so thick I didn't see Brenton's ship until I nearly walked into it. It was a sleek little planet jumper with a long aerodynamic shape that looked brand new and seriously expensive. The heavy guns on its nose and the sound dampeners over its thrusters showed it was all business, too, and I gave an appreciative whistle.

"Damn, Brenton," I said, reaching up to run my gloved hand over the smooth muzzle of the plasma cannon. "What army did you steal this beauty from?"

"I prefer to say we requisitioned it," Brenton replied as the door slid soundlessly open.

The ship's interior was just as nice as the exterior. It was small, just a cockpit directly attached to a crew cabin with two bunks that were currently folded over to form padded benches, but everything had that slick, professional feel you only find in top of the line equipment. Brenton went straight to the pilot's seat, poking things on the projected display as the engines hummed to life.

"Better strap in," he said as Nic sank into the navigator's chair. "Going to be a quick takeoff."

I dutifully grabbed the wall harness, bracing for a rough ride. But despite Brenton's warning, the sleek ship lifted off the ground light as a butterfly. Maybe I'd spent too long on the *Fool*, with its deafening roars and constant shaking, but I barely even felt the thrust as we shot into the night sky. That was actually kind of a bad thing, because without the shaking to keep me busy, I spent all my time scanning the air for missiles.

Considering the force he'd mustered to get me out of a lake, I had no doubt that Caldswell had air traffic on lockdown, and I didn't see how we'd be getting out of the atmosphere without a fight. Not unless Brenton could bribe better than Caldswell could threaten.

But while I could see the blips of the patrol ships on the navigation screen, none of them seemed to see us, not even when Brenton turned out of the planet's orbit and punched the engines, sending us darting into open space.

"Don't look so surprised, Miss Morris," Brenton said, grinning at my disbelief as he reached up to set the autopilot. "This is a stealth ship. Even Caldswell can't see everything."

"Well, that would have been nice to know earlier," I grumbled, pulling my arms out of the harness.

Brenton laughed and turned his chair around. "We've got a few hours before we reach the gate. Are you hungry?"

"We're jumping?" I said, instantly wary. "Where?"

"NJM0921," Brenton answered, getting up and walking past me toward the little galley at the back of the ship. "It's an asteroid. We've got a base there where we won't have to worry about the Eyes."

I did not like the idea of jumping to some random asteroid with Brenton, but it was a little late to complain now. "How long will the jump take?" I asked as I sat down on the portside padded bench, taking care not to get mud on the pristine wall behind me.

"Four hours, give or take," Brenton said, unlocking one of the cabinets and pulling out a military-style supply crate. "Now, do you want to talk first or eat first?"

My questions were burning a hole in my tongue, but I'd been a merc too long to turn down food. "Can't we do both?"

Brenton shrugged and pulled down two handfuls of prepackaged rations. "Sorry it's the plastic stuff," he said, handing one package to me before dropping the rest on a little table he folded down from the bulkhead. "Unlike Caldswell, I don't have the luxury of keeping a cook."

I ignored the barb and focused on the food. "Picky mercs are hungry mercs," I said as I peeled back the shrink-wrap. "Do you want to start or should I?"

Brenton sat down on the bench across from mine. "Why don't

you start by telling me why Caldswell decided to wipe your memory after our attack rather than kill you."

"How do you know about that?" I asked as I removed my helmet so I could eat without getting crumbs in my suit.

Brenton shrugged. "When Rashid's report came in that you were not only alive, but moving freely, as head of security no less, a memory wipe seemed the only rational explanation." He paused, frowning at me. "That's what confuses me the most, actually," he confessed. "No offense to you, but it's not like Brian to take that sort of risk."

I took a bite of my ration to stall while I decided just how honest I wanted to be with this man. I was feeling decidedly less loyal toward Caldswell than the last time Brenton and I talked, but even though we were playing nice right now, I wasn't stupid enough to think this Brenton was different from the one who'd killed Cotter and a crash team just to corner me. If I hadn't just spent twelve hours lost in the dark, I probably would have been more cautious, or at least a little more clever about what information I gave him, but I was exhausted, starving, and more than a little overwhelmed by everything that had happened. Finally, I decided just to spit it out. All my bridges were good and burned at this point anyway, I figured. Might as well try to make something out of the ashes.

"It wasn't Caldswell," I said at last. "It was Rupert."

"Charkov?" Brenton asked. "What does he have to do with anything?"

"He wiped my memory so Caldswell wouldn't kill me." Just saying it made me feel guilty, but I squashed the sentiment ruthlessly. Rupert had betrayed me in every possible way; I owed him nothing. "We were lovers," I finished, swallowing against the tightness in my throat.

Brenton's eyes went wide. "Let me see if I have this right," he said. "You slept with Rupert *Charkov*? The iceberg? Mr. Cold Killer?"

"I never heard him called that," I snapped. Things might be

over between us, but that didn't mean I was going to sit here and listen to Brenton talk shit about Rupert.

Brenton didn't even seem to hear me, though. He was leaning back on his bench, scratching his chin thoughtfully. "Why would Charkov sleep with you?"

"Gee, I don't know," I said, glowering. "Maybe because he's got good taste?"

Brenton's head shot up at my sharp tone, and he held up his hands. "No offense meant, Miss Morris. You're an attractive girl, but you have to understand, if Charkov slept with you, he did it for a reason. Oh, he can be charming when it suits him, but the man is a machine, calm and controlled at all times, and he never does anything without evaluating risk and reward. That's what makes him such a good Eye."

"He's not a machine!" I couldn't believe I was defending Rupert, but this was just unfair. It was also untrue. I knew for a fact that the night we'd slept together, Rupert had been just as out of control as I was. "He can be cold," I admitted. "But he's not heartless."

Brenton gave me a scornful look. "You don't know the first thing about cold," he said. "Rashid told you what the Eyes do?"

"Caldswell told me the propaganda," I replied. "But Rashid filled in the ugly parts."

"It's all ugly parts," Brenton said, his voice as hot and bitter as banked ashes. "Eyes are monsters, murderers. I know, because I used to be one."

I'd guessed as much already, but hearing the truth from his own mouth made me fidget. I was trying to figure out how best to respond to his confession when Brenton suddenly changed the subject. "Do you know why the Eyes use symbionts?"

"Because phantoms break powered armor," I replied.

Brenton smirked. "Phantoms break anything electronic, but that's not the whole reason. If we just wanted something that would keep working around phantoms, there are other less dangerous options. The *real* reason every Eye is required to have a symbiont is because they make us highly resistant to plasmex."

"To resist the phantoms?"

"To resist the daughters," Brenton said. "Every daughter breaks free of her conditioning eventually, and when she does, the first person she attacks is her Eye."

I shrugged. "That makes sense. The Eyes are her guards."

Brenton shook his head. "You don't understand. This isn't like a prisoner escaping. There's no rational thought to it, no planning. When a daughter is made, Maat takes her over completely. Everything she was before is wiped out and replaced by Maat herself, and Maat hates the Eyes with a madness that cannot be calmed. Rightly so—they deserve nothing less for what they've done to her—but the point I'm trying to make, Miss Morris, is that the only way an Eye survives past his first assignment is by shooting his daughter before she cracks."

Brenton leaned forward, his eyes bright with the same fanatical gleam I'd seen back on Falcon 34. "Rupert has been a perfect Eye for a long time now," he said. "When I left, he had an unblemished record, and he must have kept it up because they put him on Caldswell's ship."

I arched an eyebrow. "Why is that special?"

"Because Brian Caldswell is the Eyes' field commander," Brenton explained. "He's number two in the entire organization, and his partner, Mabel Cobb, is widely considered to be one of the best covert ops combat symbionts ever made."

I sighed. That explained a lot. You didn't get to be as overbearing as Caldswell without some real power behind you.

"Caldswell's team handles the most difficult and dangerous daughters," Brenton continued. "The ones Maat has the most control over, the ones who break the sharpest and have to be killed most decisively." He smiled at me. "The *Glorious Fool* is a death sentence for more than just security officers. The only Eyes who sign up to fly with Caldswell are the ambitious ones willing to risk their lives to learn from the best. So, what does that tell you about our dear Rupert?"

He was looking at me like he expected an answer, but I was barely listening anymore. My mind was back on the *Fool*. The night I nearly broke my leg on him, I'd told Rupert all about growing up on Paradox and my ambitions to be a Devastator, but the only thing I'd learned about him was that he considered it an honor to serve under Caldswell. At the time, I couldn't see how. Now, thanks to Brenton, I understood.

That thought was still finishing when a memory rushed into my mind like a flood. I had enough experience now to recognize it immediately as one of Rupert's. Even if I hadn't, though, I would have known soon enough, because in this memory, I was looking in a mirror, and it was Rupert's face that was staring back.

It must have been a while ago, because his hair was cut military short. Otherwise, he looked just like he always did: same black suit, same intense blue stare, but his reflection was blurred by the blood that was sprayed over half the mirror. There was blood on him, too, splattering his pale face and hands, one of which held his pearl-handled disrupter pistol. It must have just fired, because I could feel the intense heat against Rupert's hand, but his attention wasn't on the burning metal pressed against his palm. It was on the body lying at his feet.

The corpse looked far too small and thin to be the source of so much blood. Its head had been completely blown off by the disrupter pistol blast, but even so, I knew it was a daughter. Curious, I poked the memory, trying to pick out why this daughter was special, but all I got was horror, regret, and a sadness so deep it brought tears to my eyes as the Rupert in the memory fell to his knees. With slow, jerky motions, he took off his coat and tucked it around the girl's body, whispering something again and again in a language I didn't know. The words didn't matter, though; I understood. He was saying he was sorry, repeating it over and over until the syllables ran together.

The regret was still throbbing in my skull when the memory

vanished, and it was all I could do to turn away before Brenton saw the tears. I wiped them away in a quick, furious motion, but they just kept coming back. I didn't know if what I'd seen was the first time Rupert had killed a daughter or just the one that got to him the worst, but the damn misery wouldn't fade. Worse still, Rupert's memory was triggering others. My own this time.

I was freshly out of the trauma dampener after the fight on Falcon 34, lying helpless and weak as Rupert leaned over me. The newly returned memory was so vivid I could almost feel the brush of his hair on my cheek as he leaned down to whisper about the horrible things he'd done, still did, could not undo. How he did not deserve me, how he could not be forgiven, and how he had no right to love me. Like the others, the memory was just a flash, fading as quickly as it came, but it left a dead, bitter taste behind in my mouth, and suddenly I didn't want to talk about Rupert anymore.

"My turn," I said, turning to Brenton. "Back on Falcon Thirty-Four, you said I was the one who could save the universe. Why? What am I? Does it have anything to do with my ability to see phantoms?"

Brenton jerked. "You can see phantoms?"

I nodded, and he whistled. "No wonder Brian was after you so hard. Did he tell you what he thought you were?"

"No," I said. "He claimed to be stumped, but the seeing phantoms thing was special enough that he was ready to stick me in a lab for the rest of my life on the off chance I might be a useful weapon in his war."

"Better than being shot," Brenton said with a shrug.

The glare I gave Brenton snapped his mouth shut. "I would shoot myself in the head before I let them take me," I growled. "I've seen how they treat their weapons, and I'd rather be dead five times over than end up like Maat."

Brenton eyed me with new respect. "Fair enough," he said. "But your escape tonight might be luckier than you know. For you and the universe. Do you remember what I told you back on Falcon Thirty-Four about Stoneclaw's virus?"

I had to hunt through my newly returned memories before I found what he was talking about. "You said she was making a biological weapon," I said. "And that was why the lelgis destroyed her ship."

"She was making more than that," Brenton said. "Given the vast differences between species, even between the various xith'cal clans, viral weapons have limited effectiveness. But Stoneclaw wasn't just engineering a virus, she was making a *plasmex* virus, which is another thing altogether."

Brenton held up his hands and spread them slowly, like he was stretching something invisible between them. "Plasmex flows through every living thing. Certain races can feel it more than others, but the same plasmex that flows through the xith'cal flows through aeons and humans. What Stoneclaw figured out was a way to corrupt plasmex itself, creating a one hundred percent lethal virus capable of infecting any living thing regardless of genetic difference."

"Well, if that was the idea, she messed up," I said. "That ship was full of downed xith'cal, but they weren't dead." I didn't even have a word for what they were, other than wrong. I could still remember the horrible stench of them, the terrible white film over their eyes. Dead but not dead.

"My sources believe the virus that killed off that tribe ship was not yet complete," Brenton admitted. "Now, of course, it never will be."

I frowned. "What do you mean?"

"I mean there is no more Stoneclaw," Brenton replied. "The lelgis have spent the last few weeks hunting down her tribe ships and destroying them one by one. If there's so much as a scout ship left bearing her mark, I'd be very surprised."

I sucked in a sharp breath. It seemed impossible that one of the three xith'cal clans, the monsters of my childhood, could just *vanish*. But even as I tried to work my brain around it, a part of me could only think that at least this explained why the lelgis hadn't caught the emperor phantom that had destroyed Unity as they were supposed to. They'd been off killing lizards.

"Unlike the rest of us, the lelgis are nearly pure plasmex," Brenton continued. "Though she didn't make it to fight them, they had more to fear from Stoneclaw's virus than anyone else, and they burned her entire clan to a cinder just to be sure it was destroyed. They did a good job, too. So far as we know, all records and samples of the virus are now gone. All, that is, except one."

I didn't need his pointed look to get where this was going. "You mean me," I said. "You think I have the virus?"

"I don't think," Brenton said, reaching into his pocket to pull out a handset. "I know. Take a look at this."

I took the offered handset gingerly, but it took me a moment to recognize the black shape on the screen as a woman's body. It was Evelyn, Brenton's other plasmex user, the one I'd killed. Her corpse was covered head to toe in the black stuff that had come off my finger when I'd touched her, and as I stared at it, I could feel my blood running colder and colder.

"Now tell me, Miss Morris," Brenton said. "Does that look anything like the xith'cal you saw on Stoneclaw's tribe ship?"

I closed my eyes. Part of me wanted to throw the handset back at him and scream that he was wrong. That I couldn't have this virus. But it all lined up so nicely—the rotting xith'cal biting me across the shoulder, the black stuff that appeared on my skin with its pins and needles, the weird smell Hyrek claimed I had. But even if I accepted Brenton's explanation, it still didn't make sense, because that would mean I had the virus that was made to kill everything, and I was still alive.

"Okay," I said slowly. "Let's assume for the moment that I do have this virus. Why aren't I dead? Why haven't I killed everyone around me?"

"That's a very good question," Brenton said. "One I don't have a definitive answer for, actually. That's why I'm taking you to see some experts."

"But I've already been tested up and down!" I cried. "Caldswell's doctor ran more of my blood than I knew I had in me through his machines, and he still found nothing."

"He wouldn't," Brenton said. "Because this sickness isn't in your blood. It's in your plasmex, and even the Eyes have never figured out a way to test plasmex properly."

"But your 'experts' have?"

"Yes," Brenton said simply.

I dropped his handset on the table and flopped back against the bench with a curse. I suppose I should have been relieved to finally have a name for what was wrong with me, but finding out my mystery illness was a xith'cal supervirus wasn't something I could be happy about. Worse, my xith'cal supervirus was apparently malfunctioning, which meant I couldn't even predict what was going to happen. It felt ungrateful to be miserable about something that was the only reason I was still alive, but I hated working with unknowns. What if my virus suddenly kicked in and I started a plague?

But all this doom and gloom brought another question to my mind, and though it was technically Brenton's turn to ask something, I jumped in anyway. "If I do have this virus, what are you going to do with it?"

Brenton leaned back. "Let me put it this way," he said. "The reason the Eyes used daughters to kill phantoms in the first place is because phantoms are pure plasmex, even more so than the lelgis. You can blast their physical manifestations into soup, but unless you destroy their plasmex, they always come back. Now, here you come with a virus that corrupts plasmex and spreads exponentially. What do you think I'm going to do with it?"

"God and king," I whispered. "You're going to kill all the phantoms."

Brenton smiled. "Bingo."

I blinked. When I'd decided to throw my lot in with Brenton, I hadn't given much thought to what he was after beyond fighting the Eyes. But this? This was *huge*. "How many phantoms are we talking about?"

"No one knows for sure," Brenton said. "But that doesn't matter to the virus. We know the little ones follow the big ones. All we have to do is spread the virus to a large enough group and let nature do the rest."

"It's too reckless," I said, holding up my hands, which, though currently clean, had been black and dirty and deadly several times before. "You said yourself that plasmex is everywhere. If you just put this out in the wild, you could kill *everything*, not just phantoms."

"That's why I'm taking you to the experts," Brenton said. "As I said, the virus is incomplete. Stoneclaw's tribe was destroyed before they could finish it, but that doesn't mean we can't. If we can make it so it only infects phantoms, which shouldn't be hard since they have more plasmex than anything else, we'll have the miracle the Eyes should have been searching for for the last seven decades."

Brenton leaned forward, grabbing my hand before I could move. "Don't you see, Deviana?" he said, clutching my fingers. "You're *it*. If we make this work, if we kill all the phantoms, there will be no more need for Maat and her daughters. You can set them free. You can set things *right*."

He didn't have to tell me that. My mind was already racing. If this virus really did what Brenton said, the tragedy I'd witness with Rashid and Ren would never happen again. I'd be able to keep my promise to Maat *and* put an end to disasters like Unity. I took a deep breath. Rupert would never have to shoot another daughter.

But even as I started to get excited, I realized it couldn't work. I didn't know how big Brenton's organization was, but there was no way he had the facilities necessary to safely complete a virus that an entire xith'cal clan hadn't been able to control. "I hate to say this, but I think we might need to go back to the Eyes."

The joy on Brenton's face vanished like a snuffed candle. "What?"

"This is huge," I said. "Government huge. The Eyes have enormous resources on their side, and once they hear what this virus can do, I'm sure they'll work with us." I knew Caldswell would. He might be an overbearing ass, but I knew the old captain had a heart. If he didn't, he would have killed me back on Falcon 34, memory wipe or no. Mostly, though, I knew Caldswell was a practical man, and I was sure he would jump on a chance, any chance, to end the wasteful, dangerous, destructive cycle of the daughters.

But while I was certain, Brenton clearly wasn't. The words had barely left my mouth before his lip drew up in disgust. "You're *sure*, are you?" he snarled. "Well, let me tell you what *I'm* sure of, Miss Morris. *I'm* sure that even if I could banish every phantom in the universe with a wave of my hand, the Eyes would never release Maat or her daughters. They would never set them free. Because to the Eyes, Maat and the girls they feed her are weapons, and I've worked for governments long enough to know that people in power never, ever, *ever* give up weapons on their own accord."

I believed that, but—

Brenton held up his hand, cutting me off before I could speak. "I'm not a young man," he said softly. "And I've been fighting phantoms for the vast majority of my life. Over the years, I've lost track of how many girls I've taken from their families, how many children I've shot because Maat's madness took them completely and they could no longer be controlled. I've killed fathers like Rashid whose only crime was trying to learn where their babies had gone. For decades I was able to pretend that the blood on my hands was shed in a good cause. That I was winning the war. That I was a hero."

He broke off with a sigh and ran his hands over his face. "We all believed that dream at one point," he whispered. "But some of us, the best of us, woke up. The truth is that there are no heroes. We're all villains excusing our actions by hiding behind a greater good."

He dropped his hand then and stared at me, his eyes sharp and too bright in a way that reminded me of Maat's. "I don't care about the war with the phantoms anymore," he said. "I left the Eyes for one reason: to free Maat. If we gave your virus to the Eyes, the phantoms would die, but the madness wouldn't stop. Maat and her daughters would still be prisoners, and nothing would change. But what you fail to see, Miss Morris, is that by keeping the virus away from the Eyes, we create an opportunity like never before. For the first time, *we* will have the weapon that kills the phantoms, and if the Eyes want it, they'll have to play by *our* rules."

When he finished, Brenton looked pretty crazy, but for the first time since I'd nearly run into him on the boardwalk back on Seni Major, I felt a trickle of respect for the man.

"You're going to hold it hostage," I said. "You're going to use the virus as leverage against the Eyes, to make them free Maat and her daughters in return for a final solution to the phantom problem." It was a ruthless plan that put the salvation of everyone on the line for an ideal, just the sort of thing I'd come to expect from Brenton, but for once I couldn't fault him. If it worked, it would be a coup indeed, and I started smiling despite myself.

"You're crazy as hell," I said, shaking my head. "But I have to admit, I like it."

Brenton's face broke into a wide smile. "So does this mean you're going to join us?"

I frowned, working it through one last time, but my conclusion was the same. If I had a virus inside me that could stop the monsters that killed entire planets, then I would be the worst person possible if I didn't at least make an effort to use it. But even that reasoning was still too abstract, too clean and rational. The truth was, I'd already made the decision in my gut to stop this when I'd heard Mabel break Rashid's neck.

For all that he'd been a Terran, I'd liked and respected Rashid, both as a man and as a professional, and the way he'd died bugged the shit out of me. To fight and suffer so much for so long and then die like an afterthought, achieving nothing—it was intolerable. He'd deserved better. So had Ren. They all deserved better, and if the king in his grace had given me the means to make things right, then I would. To do otherwise would be shameful cowardice and bring eternal disgrace.

But even as these grand notions circled like a royal parade through my head, I had to admit that my motives weren't *entirely* selfless. The ambitious corner of my mind had already worked out what it could mean to be the weapon who killed the phantoms. They might be secret from the universe at large, but Caldswell had a Royal Warrant, which meant someone powerful on Paradox had to know about the Eyes and their mission. Fixing that problem for good was exactly the sort of huge, heroic, universe-changing service to the king that got peasants like me royal knighthoods.

That thought was enough to make me grin. Back in Caldswell's quarters, I'd been sure my dreams were dead. Even if I escaped, there was no way I could become a Devastator with the Eyes after me, but Royal Knights were the king's own weapons answerable only to his own sacred word. If Brenton was right, this horrible curse I'd picked up could turn out to be the very ticket I'd been looking for when I'd first signed on with the *Fool*. It was a long shot to be sure, but considering how hopeless I'd been when Maat found me, the return of any hope, no matter how far-fetched, was enough to fill me to bursting.

"All right," I said, lifting my head to look at Brenton dead-on. "I'm in."

Brenton shot me a wide, blindingly white smile. "Welcome to the good guys, Deviana."

The way he said that still made me wince, but Brenton was already walking back toward the cockpit. "Finish your food and get some sleep," he said as he dropped into the pilot's chair. "You look like death warmed over."

I *felt* like death warmed over, but I couldn't rest yet. Not with my suit in this condition.

After my fight with Rupert and my adventures in the mines, my Lady was in desperate need of repair. Despite the flush I'd done earlier, I could still feel the grit in her joints, and Elsie was still jammed in her sheath from where Rupert had broken it. My gear needed serious work if it was going to be any use at all, and though I'd never admit it aloud, I needed work, too.

A life of fighting had made me pretty good at putting off stress, but even I couldn't go forever. I'd been able to hold things together in the mines by focusing only on the present, but now that I was still, it was all starting to catch up with me. Add to that the way my life had just been turned on its ear *again* and it was no wonder I was well past my limit. Already my hands were shaking so badly I could barely hold my ration, and I knew from experience it would only get worse. If I was going to be in any sort of fighting shape when we reached wherever we were going, I needed some serious down time, and since sleep was impossible on a small ship with two strangers I didn't trust, that left mechanical therapy.

Shoving the last of the ration bar into my mouth, I popped the pressure lock on my suit and peeled the Lady off piece by piece. When she was completely disassembled, I grabbed her chest piece and pried off the hidden panel that stored my emergency tools. They weren't a patch on my case's nano-repair of course, but they'd do. Power was a larger issue. I had only four days left in my battery before I'd need to find a way of charging my suit without my armor case, but that was a worry for later. Right now, I'd focus on what I could fix.

Using my fingernails, I plucked my little file out of its niche and then reached over to grab the arm piece that Elsie was bolted on to. Moving the piece to my lap, I pulled my legs up until I was sitting cross-legged on the bench and put on my helmet. Then, with my music blasting and my camera acting as a magnifier, I let myself become completely absorbed in the painstaking process of repairing the motor Rupert had crushed.

———

Hours later, we were in hyperspace, and Elsie's blade was working again. I couldn't do anything about the dent in her sheath, so she deployed a little crooked, but it was good enough. I'd just started scraping the mud out of the Lady's seams when I spotted Nic walking toward me from the cockpit.

I stopped my music with a thought and pulled off my helmet. "Do you need something?"

"All my immediate needs are met," Nic said calmly, sitting down on the bench across from me. "We made our jump to hyperspace successfully. More than that I could not ask at this moment."

He smiled wide as he finished, and I couldn't help smiling back. The way he talked reminded me of Nova. I was about to get back to work when Nic nodded at the Lady's scattered pieces. "Cleaning your suit?"

"Cleaning and repairing," I said, tapping a line of dried silt from my boot into the plastic cup I was using as a dirt catch.

Nic nodded. "You're very good at it."

I snorted. "I should be. Been doing this long enough. Anyway, I like working on my armor. It's soothing. Gives me a sense of control when the universe feels a bit too big."

"Oh, you shouldn't worry about that," Nic said cheerfully. "Any sense of control is merely illusion. We are all just tiny specks in a cosmic system larger than we can possibly comprehend. You are no more out of control now than you have ever been."

He clearly meant the words to be comforting, but the thought of being a speck didn't exactly do it for me. Still, the ridiculous reply was enough to send me into a giggle fit. Nic tilted his head at my laughter, and I shook my head. "Sorry, sorry," I said, returning to my boot. "I swear I'm not laughing at you. It's just that you just remind me of my old roommate."

"I could only hope so," Nic said humbly. "Novascape always had a more innate understanding of the truths than I. To hear that I remind you of her is praise indeed."

My head snapped back up. "How do you know Nova?"

Nic raised his pale eyebrows. "Can't you see the resemblance? Novascape is my sister."

"*You're* Copernicus?" I said, louder than I'd meant to.

He smiled. "Only my family calls me that. Everyone else calls me Nic."

"What the hell are you doing with Brenton?" I said, speaking right over him.

"Helping him," Nic replied.

Suddenly, several things made a lot more sense. "God and king," I muttered, rubbing my temple. "That's how Rashid ended up the only good candidate on Wuxia. Nova told you everything over dinner."

"Actually, Basil told me about the hiring," Nic said with a smile. "He had a great deal to say about you."

I bet he did.

"We suspected Caldswell would go to Wuxia," Nic admitted. "He tries to keep his movements unpredictable, but the years have left him with certain habitual ruts, and Wuxia has long been his favorite repair port. I merely arranged to be in town when he arrived. After that, the setup was fairly simple." He paused. "You're not angry, I hope?"

I had to think about that one. "No," I said at last. "I mean, I don't like feeling like a chump, but Caldswell was the one who got played, not me. Still, how the hell did you end up on Brenton's side? Nova said your dad put her on the *Fool* because he believed in Caldswell's work. That puts you on the wrong end of things, doesn't it?"

Nic's face went suddenly serious. "My father's beliefs do not always align with my own," he said. "But he does not allow his will to impede the flow of his children's. I believe in what Mr. Brenton is trying to do, and father believes in following one's own path."

Wish someone would have told my dad about that. He'd only believed in yelling. "So who is your father?" I asked. "How does he know about all this?" Because Mr. Starchild was now involved with two of the primary players in this supposedly secret game, and I was curious.

"Our father has a...complicated past," Nic said quietly. "But such things mean nothing in a universe where time only flows forward. Wherever we were before, we are all now exactly where we are meant to be."

"Right," I muttered, fighting the urge to roll my eyes. "So does Nova know what you do?"

"No," Nic admitted. "I thought it best for her safety if I kept my involvement with Mr Brenton to myself. Novascape does not possess a duplicitous soul."

That was true. Nova kept secrets pretty well, but the girl couldn't lie to save her life. But man, what a pair. Between Nova's permanent position on the *Glorious Fool* and Nic acting as Brenton's private plasmex factory, it was a miracle there were any Starchilds left. "Your family sure likes dangerous work."

"Living is dangerous work," Nic said serenely. "And invariably deadly."

I chuckled at that, and Nic flashed me a warm smile. "I am pleased to share space in harmony with you at last, Deviana. My sister spoke so highly of you, it pained me to be seen as your enemy. I hope our future orbits will continue to be equilibrious."

I couldn't help chuckling at that one. "You really are her brother."

"I would not be false with you," Nic said, affronted.

"No, I mean you talk just like her."

"We are children of the stars," he said, like that explained everything—which it kind of did.

Nic glanced up at the cockpit, where Brenton was sitting in the pilot's chair. "You really should try to get some rest," he said softly, his face growing serious again. "We'll be coming out of hyperspace in another few hours. Once we arrive, I do not know when you'll get another chance."

I still had the rest of my suit to clean, but I promised Nic I'd try. He smiled and returned to his seat, pulling up a star map on the projection around him that was almost as complicated as one of Basil's. Meanwhile, I put my helmet back on and got back to scraping.

An hour later, I called it quits. My Lady was still dirtier than I liked, but without real tools, there was nothing else I could do. My guns weren't much better. Sasha still had a clip and a half left, but Mia was down to one shot. I could have charged her off my suit, but it would have cost me a day of power and I wasn't willing to risk it. One shot would have to be enough.

Once all my equipment was sorted out to my satisfaction, I put my armor back on and stretched out on the bench. I still didn't trust Nic or Brenton enough to actually sleep, but I did doze. I must have been more tired than I thought, because I didn't notice Brenton until his hand touched my shoulder.

"Showtime," he said when I jerked away, flashing me a smile that didn't touch his eyes. He walked back to the cockpit as I sat up, and since I was already suited, I stood and strolled after him to see what I'd gotten myself into.

A lot of nothing seemed to be the answer. Though we'd dropped out of hyperspace, which should have meant we were reasonably close to our destination, I didn't see so much as a blip marking the asteroid we were supposedly headed for. I didn't see any asteroids, actually, which was weird. In my experience, space rocks traveled in packs.

"Did we come out in the wrong place?"

"This is it," Brenton said, easing the throttle forward, though with nothing outside, it didn't feel like we were moving at all. "Patience, Miss Morris."

I'm not patient on a good day, and I hadn't had any of those for a while. Fortunately, I didn't have to wait long. About ten minutes after our departure from hyperspace, I felt a cold chill run up my spine, like someone was walking on my grave. When it passed, the space in front of us, which a second ago had been nothing but empty blackness, was now taken up by a large asteroid with no less than three xith'cal battle cruisers sitting in space around it.

I'm not ashamed to say I gasped. I've never actually seen a non-junked xith'cal battleship up close. You usually didn't want to, not unless you were also in a battleship. I'd heard they dwarfed even the Royal Cruisers, but even that didn't prepare me for the sheer mass of the huge dark-green ships hulking above us like ugly giants looking for something to step on.

I expected Brenton to whip our little ship around and hit the thrusters, but he just kept flying forward, matching the asteroid's slow spin as he piloted us toward the huge floodlit cave in the space rock's side. This trajectory took us directly under the battle fleet, and as the xith'cal's lights hit us, I felt the need to say something.

"Brenton," I said with a calm I was not feeling. "Why is your asteroid surrounded by lizards?"

"Because it's not my asteroid," Brenton replied. "It's theirs. They're the experts I was talking about."

And this was where even the appearance of calm went out the window. "*What?*" I shrieked. "*This* is who you're taking me to see? The goddamn *xith'cal?*"

"I don't know why you're so surprised," he said. "Haven't you heard that the enemy of my enemy is my friend?"

"I don't care how many enemies away they are!" I cried. "Have you forgotten the part where the lizards want to enslave and eat our species?"

"No more than I've forgotten who made the virus that's the only reason you're still alive right now," Brenton said, glaring up at me. "Where did you think I learned all that stuff about Stoneclaw from anyway?" He looked back at the rapidly approaching asteroid. "Relax, Deviana. This is a long-running arrangement. I have everything well in hand."

I didn't believe that for a second, and I was feeling decidedly less happy about the new alliance that Brenton and I had struck, but I kept my mouth shut as he navigated our little ship into the asteroid's entrance as delicately as a tailor threading a needle.

The floodlit cave was too straight to be a natural formation. It ran a good three hundred feet into the black space rock before ending abruptly at a huge steel door that had started rolling open as soon as our ship passed the cave's mouth. Inside, I could see a huge, brightly lit cavern, though the details were obscured by the blurry lens of the shield that kept the atmosphere from escaping.

Brenton cut the engines at the fifty-foot mark, and we floated the rest of the way, sliding through the thick shield like a slow-motion dive into a clear pond. The artificial gravity snagged us the second we were in, and Brenton hit the thrusters, jumping us up several feet before the ship's fancy autopilot took over and set us down light as a falling leaf.

The cavern was just as artificial as the tunnel leading into it, an enormous carved-out hangar packed to the brim with ships, mostly smaller xith'cal fighters and what looked like civilian vessels, if the lizards could be said to have anything so civilized as civilian craft. But though the lizard ships took up most of the room, a small area toward the front corner seemed to have been designated for human ships. There were two at the moment, a small trade freighter not too dissimilar from Caldswell's *Fool* and what looked like a six-man version of our little stealth ship. The human vessels were separated from the xith'cal ships by a wide stretch of empty pavement, and it was in this empty space that Brenton set us down.

As we landed, I took note of the lizards' positions. Fortunately, most were well away from us, clustered on the hangar's far side. None of them had suits on, which meant the air was breathable, though undoubtedly full of arsenic like the xith'cal preferred. It wouldn't hurt me unless I sat around breathing it for days, but I sealed my Lady anyway. A virus was bad enough. No way was I adding poison on top of that so long as I had a viable clean air supply.

Nic lowered the walkway as soon as we were stable, but I waited to let Brenton go out first. After my experiences with Hyrek, I'd revised my shoot-all-xith'cal policy. Slightly. But I was not about to be the first one into the lion's den when I wasn't even getting paid for it. And despite Brenton's claims that everything was under control, I put my suit in battle mode and kept it there as I followed him down the ramp to where a trio of the strangest-looking xith'cal I'd ever seen were waiting to greet us.

My best guess was that I was seeing living, healthy female xith'cal for the first time. Like the sick females I'd seen on the ghost ship, they were shockingly short, not much taller than I was in my suit. They were also bright green, greener even than Hyrek, and they wore what looked like long chains of delicate silver metal that jingled when they moved looped around their necks, arms, and over their stubby horns.

They watched us descend through slitted yellow eyes. When we reached the end of the ramp, the female at the front of the pack pulled on the largest of the chains wrapped around her wrist. A second later, a small shape shuffled out from behind her. It was so stooped and dirty I thought it must be some kind of alien dog at first, but then the female xith'cal jerked the chain again, and the thing straightened up, turning a small, frightened face in our direction.

It's one thing to hear that the xith'cal keep human slaves, but it's another altogether to actually see one. The cowering creature on the end of the xith'cal's chain was a woman about my age. She was shorter than me with skin that might have been coppery if it wasn't so dried out. Her cheeks were sunken, her dark eyes made darker by the deep circles below them, but the fear in her face wasn't for the lizards behind her. It was directed at us. More specifically, the girl was looking at me like I was her death. For a second, I couldn't figure out why, then I saw her eyes roving up and down my suit, and I realized that this woman had never seen powered armor before.

When her human was in position, the xith'cal spoke. Her voice was higher than any of the xith'cal I'd killed. Higher even than Hyrek's, but it had that same tearing metal resonance that all xith'cal shared. When she was finished, the slave woman lifted her head and put on what she probably meant to be a haughty expression. "Highest Guide Krisek, chosen flesh of Reaper, welcomes John Brenton," she announced in Universal. "She wishes to know if this is the specimen you promised her."

The woman's accent was the strangest I'd ever heard, thick and too sharp all at once. I was so busy trying to place it that I missed the Reaper part of her greeting entirely until Brenton answered.

"Thank you, Highest Guide, and thanks be to Reaper, long may he guide the flesh of his flesh. This is the one I spoke of."

He put his hand on my shoulder, and the three xith'cal backed away with a hiss. The human girl looked like she was about to try climbing up onto her lizard's shoulders to get away, but she didn't get a chance. The lead xith'cal—Highest Guide Krisek, I guessed—was speaking again.

"It must be tested," the girl translated when the Guide was finished. "We must know the extent of its contagion. Will it be safe in its containment suit?"

"It should be," Brenton said. "Are you ready now?"

All three xith'cal started speaking at this, and the sound of them talking to one another was like listening to a garbage compactor eat a wind chime. The translator girl cowered back against her lizard masters, staring at me like *I* was the one who might eat her, but I didn't care about her anymore. I was glaring at Brenton. "What test?" I asked in King's Tongue, since I was pretty sure the girl didn't speak it but I knew damn well that Brenton did. "And what's this about my suit? And why are they calling me an *it*?"

"Xith'cal have a hard time telling human genders apart," Brenton answered with a shrug. "And I messaged them on our way in that your suit was a containment unit so they wouldn't try to make you take it off. It's not like you're contagious, right?"

"I could be!" I hissed, eying the arguing females. Apart from the three who'd come to greet us, there had to be at least fifty other lizards in the hangar. If I set off an outbreak, things could get very bad very fast.

"Relax," Brenton said. "I don't like working with lizards any more than you do, but they're the only ones who can work on the virus. Just play along, and if they try anything that jeopardizes our goals, we'll deal with it."

"Deal with it how?" I snapped. "We're kind of outnumbered."

"Not so much as you would think."

His eyes slid past me as he said this, and I followed them to the two other human ships. What I saw lifted my spirits a bit. There were ten people standing a little too casually between the hauler and the larger version of the ship we'd flown in on. They were evenly mixed between men and women, and though none of them wore armor and only one had a gun, all of them were in the fantastic shape I'd learned to associate with symbionts. That cheered me up enormously until I caught sight of a small figure at the very back.

In the door of the freighter, a girl was slumped in a woman's lap. She was skeletally thin, her face hidden behind the fall of her limp, brittle hair. That didn't matter, though; I already knew what she looked like.

"That's your daughter, isn't it?" I whispered. "Enna."

"She's actually Mettou's daughter," Brenton said. "I shot my last daughter years ago when she'd degenerated to the point where she was killing people in her sleep. But it makes no difference, they're all Enna to me."

"Aren't you worried the Eyes will use her to find you?" I asked. "I mean, the daughters are all connected, right?"

"They are," Brenton said. "But you forget, Maat is the one who connects them, and she's on our side."

Trusting a crazy woman to keep our secret didn't sit well with me, but then, if there was anyone who hated the Eyes more than Brenton, it was Maat. That made me feel a little more secure, but something Brenton had said was still bugging me. "Who was Enna?" I asked. "The real one, I mean."

"A little girl who loved me very much," Brenton replied. "If you ever get the chance, you should ask Caldswell about her. He loves that story."

I winced at the naked hate in Brenton's words. I was debating whether or not it was worth trying to get more information when the human slave spoke again.

"Highest Guide has agreed that we are ready to test the human carrier," she said, standing as far away from me as possible. "You will follow us."

The female xith'cal nodded and patted her clawed hand on the human's head like a master praising a dog. The woman leaned into the caress, her eyes closing in happiness, and I had to turn away before I gagged. The other xith'cal were already walking toward the far end of the hangar. Brenton sent Nic over to the rest of the humans before falling into step behind them.

At the back of the giant cavern was a surprisingly small tunnel with a low ceiling and a rail set into the floor. Perched on the rail was what looked like a converted mining train with seats instead of ore carts. I sat gingerly on the metal bar that served as a bench, and Brenton sat down next to me. As soon as we were settled, the lizard called Highest Guide said something that sounded like a gunshot, and the train shuddered to life, rolling down the rail into the tunnel.

Once we left the hangar, the lights were few and far between. There was a light on the front of the train, but it was pathetically dim, probably because xith'cal didn't need much light to see. I did, though, so I turned on my suit's floodlight. It might have been over-kill, but this was the path to *my* test. I wasn't about to miss anything, especially since I might have to leave in a hurry.

We traveled for what felt like miles at a slight downward curve, or at least down according to the artificial gravity. I knew it couldn't *actually* be miles since the asteroid wasn't that big, but by the time we finally rolled to a stop, I was more than ready to get off.

I hopped down and looked around to see where the train had brought us, but all I saw was more tunnel. The xith'cal were getting off, though, and the one in front was saying something.

"Highest Guide commands you to follow her," the slave translated, pointing down the tunnel. "This way."

We didn't have to walk long. A few dozen feet from where the tracks ended, the tunnel curved sharply and opened into a cave the size of a small house. The xith'cal stopped at the place where the ceiling began to rise and turned to look at me. Brenton was looking at me too, and I got a sinking feeling in my stomach. Was this the test? Was I failing it? I was trying to think of some way to ask what they wanted without giving myself away when I saw a white line drop down through my cameras.

My hand shot up, popping my visor. Cold, thin air rushed in as my suit's seal broke, letting in the bitter smell of the xith'cal's atmosphere and the dusty metal reek of the asteroid itself. My front camera feeds vanished as soon as my visor was up, and as my eyes took over, the empty cave filled with the most beautiful light I'd ever seen.

CHAPTER

10

Phantoms crawled over everything. There were even more here than there'd been in the cargo bay back on Io5. They came in all shapes and sizes, from tiny pinpricks to glowing worms almost as long as my hand. Some looked like little more than bundles of legs crawling across the ground, others were rolling blobs with no legs at all, and still others floated in the air like jellyfish, their glowing tendrils filling the room with light. Their combined brilliance was so bright it was actually hard to look at. But crowded as the cave was, I had a buffer.

Not a single phantom was within three feet of my body. This clear zone stayed with me when I took a step forward so the xith'cal could enter, sending the creatures scrambling over one another to get out of my way. They ignored everyone else, floating through the lizards, the human slave, and Brenton like they weren't even there. But when I moved, the whole room moved with me, all the tiny glow bugs running as one to stay clear of my path.

If I hadn't known what their aversion meant, their desperate scrabbling would have been funny. Part of me wanted to run forward and scatter them anyway like a kid with a flock of pigeons, but I kept pace with the xith'cal and Brenton as we walked toward the center of the cave.

There were so many tiny phantoms, I didn't actually see what we were walking toward until we were almost there. In the middle of the cave was a phantom that was much bigger than the others. Its body was about the size of a large dog, though it was closer to a horse once you added in all the legs. This phantom alone stayed put as I approached, though not because it wanted to. It was trying to run, its spindly legs kicking frantically, but it was held fast by a long, glowing spike that had been driven through its middle.

That description didn't make a lot of sense even to me, and I was looking at it. But that's what I saw: a big, glowing bar stabbed right through the phantom's center like a spear, pinning it to the stone floor. As I got closer, I realized I could actually see the phantom's blood around where the bar bit in, running down its side like a soft, wet shadow against its frosted-glass body. The sight sent a shiver through me. The blood would be slippery to the touch, I bet. Slippery and icy cold.

When I was close enough that the circle of empty space around me brushed the pinned phantom, its struggles went from terrified to frantic, sending a snow of white lines across my remaining cameras. I stopped immediately, but it was too late. The phantom's screech dug into my head like a claw hammer. It wasn't anywhere near as loud as the emperor phantom's had been, or the one on Mycant, or Ren's for that matter, but it still hurt like a bitch. My only consolation was that everyone else heard it, too.

Brenton and the xith'cal, even the slave girl, winced at the sound, and then one of the xith'cal threw out her hand. When her claws were fully extended, a barrier appeared around the phantom. It looked no thicker than a soap bubble—it even had the same rainbow sheen—but it cut off the thing's screaming like a switch, and I sighed in relief. Of course the xith'cal dealing with this would be plasmex users, I realized. Nova had said the xith'cal were more sensitive to plasmex than humans. At the time, I hadn't wanted to give them the credit. Now, I was glad of it.

"Nice bubble," I said.

The Highest Guide made a soft sound, almost like a trill, and the human slave said, "You saw?"

"Of course." I pointed to the other xith'cal, the one who'd thrown out her hand. "She put a bubble around the phantom to stop the scream, and…"

My voice trailed off. You'd think I'd be used to people staring at me like I was crazy by now, but getting the stink eye from xith'cal was a whole new level of uncomfortable. Brenton, on the other hand, looked like a kid who's just spotted his birthday present.

"You *can* see it!" he cried, grabbing my shoulders and spinning my armored body around with his bare hands, something I would never get used to even if I lived the rest of my life with symbionts.

I shoved out of his grip. "Of course I can see—"

A xith'cal screech cut me off, and the human slave stomped forward. "Describe it," she demanded. "You see the invisible as well as the eater. Describe."

I looked at Brenton. "You saw plasmex and the phantom," he clarified. "They weren't expecting that. Just tell them what you see."

I looked back at the cave. How did you describe a room full of glowing bugs to a lizard? I didn't even know if xith'cal ships had insects.

"Well," I started. "There are a lot of little phantoms and the big one, which is about this big." I spread my arms to show width, then height. "That one has a spike pinning it down through its back, and now there's a bubble about it." And thank the king for that. On the other side of the bubble, the speared phantom was still throwing ten kinds of a fit. If not for the shield, the screams would have fried my suit for sure.

I'd tried to keep my description as simple and accurate as possible, but as soon as I finished, all the xith'cal began hissing and screeching so fast the slave was having trouble keeping up. "How many, how little, and what do you mean by spike?" she said at last.

"I couldn't even begin to count," I said. "The whole cave is swarming with them. As for size, except for the big one, they range from pinprick to a little smaller than my hand. Oh, and they glow blue white, like moonlight." I smiled as I looked around. "It's pretty."

The xith'cal fell into a heated conversation. Before their hissing could get too intense, though, Brenton grabbed my arm. "We need to get on with the test," he said. "You'll have plenty of time to identify her other abilities later."

Interrupting three clearly powerful xith'cal plasmex users seemed kind of dumb to me, but to my surprise, the lizards settled down. As usual, it was the Highest Guide who addressed us, speaking in a haughty metallic staccato. "No eyes see the invisible," the human slave translated. "Stoneclaw's weapon is strange indeed in a lesser race. But John Brenton is right, the time for full testing comes later. First, we must see if the weapon can be used."

As the human finished, the xith'cal pointed at the phantom. I scowled, but the xith'cal just pointed again, hissing this time.

"What does she want me to do?" I whispered to Brenton.

He looked at me like I was stupid. "Prove the weapon works," he said. "Kill it."

My eyes went wide as I looked back at the phantom. It was still thrashing against the spike that pinned it, clearly terrified out of its mind, if phantoms even had minds. I took a deep breath and thought about all the damage these little menaces could do. I remembered the broken ruins of the aeon planet and the invisible monster that had nearly taken me out on Mycant. But as I watched the phantom thrash silently behind the barrier, all I could think was that it looked pathetic, like a dog with its leg caught in a trap.

But everyone was staring at me now, so I walked forward until I was standing right beside the phantom. Its thrashing got wilder as I got closer, and though I couldn't hear its screaming through the bubble, the other phantoms must have, because they'd begun to flee, slipping out through the walls like ghosts until the cavern was empty except for the big one, who couldn't get away. I walked up to the edge of the bubble and glanced over my shoulder at the lead xith'cal. I didn't expect her to understand, but my meaning must have been clear enough, because the bubble vanished. The second it was gone, the phantom's scream hit me like a boulder, sending my suit black.

I cursed and staggered as the Lady's unsupported weight landed on me. Fortunately, my suit flickered back on almost immediately. As soon as my systems were up again, I started turning them off just like I had on Mycant until I was down to the most basic movement controls and my clock, which I could still see clearly at the edge of my vision, thanks to my neuronet. Already, the seconds seemed to be ticking over more slowly, but I didn't really believe what I was seeing until I took another step and the numbers stopped moving altogether.

At this point, I was practically standing on top of the phantom. It was howling at my feet, its spindly spider legs bumping against my suit like it was trying to push me away. I drew my gun and aimed at the squirming mass of whisker-like feelers I could only guess was its head. I don't know if that was right, but I must have been close enough, because the phantom's screaming stopped on the second bullet of Sasha's three-shot burst. I sighed in relief as the pressure in my head faded and holstered my gun while I figured out what to do next.

The phantom on the ground was clearly not dead. It wasn't screaming anymore, but it was still wiggling. I didn't actually know why my bullets hurt the thing. The little ones didn't seem to care about physical objects at all, but the bigger ones clearly felt them. Maybe it was a side effect of the big phantom's ability to distort time and space?

I dropped to a squat, peering carefully at the wounded phantom. Now that I could see the thing, I could actually watch the bullet's damage mending. Sasha's burst had ripped three holes in the phantom's frosted-glass body, but the wounds were repairing before my eyes. No, not repairing. It was like the damaged phantom was turning into jelly and reforming, and as it rebuilt itself, I felt the pressure of the scream begin to rise again.

"Anytime, Miss Morris."

I ignored the threat in Brenton's voice and kept my focus on the phantom. Then, reluctantly, I removed my glove. I'd killed Evelyn with a touch, so it made sense I'd need a touch to kill a phantom. Screwing up my courage, I reached down, brushing my fingers over the semitransparent body. Its flesh was just as cold and slick as I remembered from Mycant, only now I could see the thing's slimy blood on my skin like a shimmering stain. I suppressed my shudder and pushed down harder, digging my fingers into its freezing, squishy, glowing bulk.

I don't know what I expected from my efforts. A plague of blackness, maybe. What I got was pain, intense, terrified pain shooting up my arm.

I snatched my hand back with a yelp, staring at my fingers, but I didn't see any black stuff, just the fading glow of the phantom's freezing blood. But even as my eyes told me I wasn't wounded, I could feel the pain echoing through my body, bringing with it a terrible fear. Fear of the death bringer.

I stopped, eyes widening as the realization hit me. The pain and fear wasn't mine at all, it was the phantom's. To be sure, I touched it again, just a tiny brush, but even that was enough to send the pain shooting up my arm before I could snatch my hand away.

By this point, I was getting pretty damn sick of things moving into my mind without my permission. For once, though, even my anger couldn't beat out the heavy feeling of pity, because though I was now certain the pain I'd felt was coming from the phantom, I was just as sure the thing wasn't doing it on purpose. If anything, the phantom was desperately trying *not* to touch me, wiggling weakly against the spike that pinned it in a desperate attempt to get away from my hand. It probably couldn't help projecting, I realized. The phantom was a creature of pure plasmex; it probably just sent things out. It certainly didn't seem intelligent. In fact, the more I watched it struggle, the more I was sure that the phantom really was like the wounded dog it had reminded me of when I'd first seen it.

Suddenly, I felt sick. I'm a soldier for hire, I kill things, that's my job, but this was different. This wasn't some inimical space monster plotting the death of mankind. It wasn't even another soldier. This was an animal in pain that didn't even understand why it was here. All it knew was that I was its death. Me, the death bringer who had shot it and now stood watching as it nearly ripped itself in two trying to get off the spike that trapped it beside the thing it feared most in the universe.

I took a deep breath and fell to my knees, plunging my fingers into the phantom's back again. The pain shot up my arm the second I made contact, but I ignored it, pressing harder as I willed the virus to work. Not because I wanted to prove something to Brenton or his xith'cal, but because there was no other way besides a daughter to put this creature out of its misery, and I was not going to make them bring poor, broken Enna in here to do what I could not. I had no idea how to reach for plasmex, no idea how to trigger what I'd done when I'd killed Evelyn, but I still tried with all my might, digging my fingers into the phantom's soft, freezing flesh until it whimpered.

The sound cut right to my core. I could feel its pain like the fingers were digging into my own back, but that wasn't what made me bare my teeth. My eyes were locked on my fingertips, which I could see through the phantom's translucent flesh. Fingertips that were still clean without a trace of black soot.

I punched down harder, suddenly furious. After being such a pain in my ass, coming and going whenever it saw fit, I couldn't call the black stuff up when I actually needed it? The phantom was crying below me, its pain sawing on my brain, and I couldn't even put the damn thing out of its misery.

But while virus failure was enough to make me want to punch something, what really made me angry was the thought that this, *this* was why daughters were taken from their parents and sacrificed to Maat. To kill these poor, stupid animals when they blundered into planets. This phantom was less of a threat to humanity than the xith'cal standing behind me, and yet it was the root of so much suffering: Maat's, Ren's, Rashid's, even Rupert's. So much goddamn tragedy over a stupid invisible animal who probably didn't even realize it was doing harm.

But as I sat there getting madder and madder, I realized the pain shooting up my arm was fading. I blinked in confusion, snapping my attention back to my fingers, but what I saw stopped me cold.

The hand I'd dug into the phantom's back was completely black. I'd been so angry, I hadn't even noticed the pins and needles replacing the phantom's pain. Now I could actually see the black stuff inching up my wrist, but the real sight was the phantom itself.

It was frozen midstruggle, its light shining painfully bright in every place but one. On its back, where my hand dug in, a black stain was spreading through its frosted-glass body like ink dripped in water, seeping down the phantom's legs, through its tentacles, and up to the nearly healed place where I'd shot it. The blackness spread so quickly, I couldn't do anything except watch. I didn't even try to pull my hand out until I realized the stain was starting to creep up the spike that held the phantom down.

I jumped to my feet, bracing as I tried to tug my hand out of the phantom, but the thing's freezing flesh was locked around my fingers. I set my suit and pulled with all the Lady's might, but it did no good. I was stuck fast. I was just about to try ejecting Elsie to cut myself free when the blackness finished its spread through the phantom.

The moment the last tentacle blackened, the world cut out like a switch.

It happened so suddenly, I thought I'd passed out. The fact that I could think that proved I hadn't, though. I was clearly still conscious, I just couldn't see anything. Or move. I was trying to work out why that was when the pain hit.

Back when I was a stupid teenager, I'd hurt my back messing up a flip I never should have attempted. The injury was long healed, but every now and then I still got twinges in the weirdest places, like some muscle I'd never known I had was cramping. That was how this felt, only it was in my brain.

At the center of my mind, in the space I envisioned as being behind my eyes, something seized up. The pain was intense at first, like snapping a joint, but it faded just as fast, leaving not the blinding headache you'd expect, but a strange feeling of emptiness. I felt hollow, not like something was missing, but like I'd been widened. Suddenly, I had this enormous sense of space, like the first time you get back under the open sky after spending months crammed into a tiny ship, and my whole body was twitching to uncurl.

Caught up in the exhilaration, I let it, pushing out into the emptiness. It was the strangest feeling I'd ever experienced, like moving an arm I hadn't known I'd had until that moment. Encouraged, I pushed further, reaching out until the strange new feeling began to ache. But even that was a good ache, like stretching after a workout. I was savoring the sensation when I realized I was not alone in the dark.

I don't know how I knew. I couldn't see anything, couldn't feel anything except emptiness, but I knew they were there just as I knew I still had all my toes. Something was waiting out in that vast emptiness, and as I became aware of them, they became aware of me. I could actually feel their attention sliding over my mind, a cold, dry brush, like a stranger's hair brushing your shoulder on a crowded street. For a second, the touch was soothing, almost friendly, and then it snatched back in alarm as a new pain hit me hard.

If the first pain had felt like a joint snapping, this was like being hit head-on by a sonic train. It landed with a slug, whacking me out of the emptiness like a flyswatter. But even while it was happening, my momentum felt trivial. Unimportant. Because as I flew, I heard it.

"Heard" is the wrong word, actually. The thing I caught wasn't a sound. It wasn't even an image. It was an impression, almost like when Rupert's memories popped up, but with none of the familiarity. In it, I got the strangely distinct sense of a crowd turning in unison to look at me in alarm. The great threat had resurfaced, the death of us, only *us* didn't include me, because I was the threat.

That was the last thing I got before I left the emptiness like a shot and slammed back into my body, my eyes popping open to see Brenton right in my face.

"Deviana!"

He had me by the shoulders, his face red and panicked. He'd clearly been shouting for a while, but I hadn't heard a thing. Now that the emptiness was gone, though, the world came rushing back. Suddenly, I could hear alarms blaring everywhere. Behind me, the three xith'cal females were flat on the ground with the human slave curled up beside them. The woman was so still, it took me a second to realize her dull skin was now black as soot.

I jumped back with a curse, head whipping down to look at my feet. What I saw was not what I'd expected, though. I'd thought to find a carcass, some black, desecrated mass of dissolved phantom, but there was nothing. No body, no ooze, not even a lingering feeling of cold. The phantom was just gone. They all were, leaving the cavern dark and empty except for the flashing orange emergency lights.

But while the phantom was gone, the legacy of what I'd done was not. My hand was as black as the dead slave girl's flesh. I couldn't see how far up the black stain went because of my suit, but I could feel the pins and needles all the way up to my elbow on both sides. Trembling, I lifted my hand to my open visor, holding my black fingertips under my nose.

I was expecting it, but that didn't make the smell of rotten meat any less horrifying. It was very faint, not nearly as strong as the stench I remembered from the ghost ship, but it was there, and now that I knew what it meant, I couldn't stop shaking. I was still standing there quivering when Brenton grabbed my shoulder.

"Come on," he said, turning me around and shoving my glove, which I didn't realize I'd dropped, back onto my hand. "We have to go."

Too numb to protest, I nodded, pulling on my glove as I followed him back to the train. We had to step over the three dead xith'cal to get out of the cave, and as I edged past them, I realized the blackened bodies were already twitching. I went for my gun with a yelp, plugging a shot into each of their heads before I could think better of it. That stopped the twitching all right, but I swore their glazed eyes still followed me as I scrambled onto the train. "What the hell just happened?"

"I was hoping you could tell me," Brenton said, hitting the switch that started the train's engine. "From what I could see, it looked like you stood around waving your hand back and forth through the air until your fingers turned black. The xith'cal died right after that. Just keeled over and started convulsing. The slave went down a few seconds later. That was when I grabbed you, but you didn't wake up until just now."

I looked down at my hands. With my glove back on, I couldn't see whether or not my skin was still black, but I didn't feel the pins and needles anymore. I ripped my glove off, hands shaking, but when my fingers appeared, they were clean.

"I saw the blackness spread up their plasmex spike," I said, putting my glove back on again as the train began to move. "I tried to pull out, but then the phantom died, and everything went..." I trailed off. How could I explain that endless emptiness? Or the things inside it? "Black," I said at last. "Everything went black."

"I saw that much," Brenton said as the train raced us backward down the tunnel. "Get ready, we've got a hot exit."

His warning broke the emptiness's spell. All at once, I remembered that I was on a xith'cal asteroid with alarms going off all around me. I slammed my visor back into place and sealed my suit, searching the com channels at the same time for something I could use. All I got was a lot of lizard squawking, but it didn't take a genius to guess the alert might have something to do with the three xith'cal leaders I'd just killed.

"What do you think we're in for?" I asked, grabbing Mia off my back. My plasma shotgun had only one shot left, but that would be enough to blow a hole if there were warriors waiting at the tunnel's end.

"Actually, I don't think that's for us," Brenton said, nodding at the blinking lights.

I scowled. "Then why—"

I was cut off by an enormous blast as something struck the asteroid. The impact knocked the train off the rails, throwing me into the stone wall. Brenton was thrown too, though he landed on his feet. I was up a second later, flipping on all the functions I'd turned off when I was dealing with the phantom so I wouldn't be caught unprepared again. I'd just gotten everything back on line when the next blast hit.

This time I was ready. My suit rolled with the shock, adjusting between one step and the next as Brenton and I started running full tilt down the tunnel. For once, I thanked the king the man was a symbiont. I didn't have to slow down for him at all. Instead, I was the one struggling to keep up as we raced toward the hangar.

"What's the plan?" I yelled, keeping Mia close.

"Get you out," Brenton yelled back as another, softer blast rocked the stone beneath our feet. We'd barely gotten steady again before Brenton turned to grin at me. "You did it, Deviana!" he cried. "You've got the virus!"

Considering what had just happened, I didn't see how that was anything to be happy about. "And killed the lizards who were supposed to know how to control it!" I shouted.

"Doesn't matter," Brenton said. "We've *won*. Now all we have to do is get you to the ships and we're going straight to the Dark Star."

I slammed to a halt, my boots grinding on the stone. "*What?*"

Brenton stopped more gracefully. "Dark Star Station. It's the Eyes' secret headquarters and the place where they keep Maat prisoner."

"Why the hell would you want to go there?" I said. "Did you not see what just happened?"

"I saw you killed a phantom," Brenton said.

"Are you crazy?" I cried. "We can't use something this unstable for leverage! I don't even know what I did! If we go to the Eyes like this, I'll probably kill Maat just trying to show them what the virus does."

Brenton nodded excitedly. "Exactly!"

You know that moment when you go to take a step and the floor isn't there? The terrifying second when it feels like the whole world is falling? That was what I felt now. The asteroid was still shaking, but I couldn't even manage to feel worried over the fact that we were under attack. All I could do was stare at Brenton's grinning face as the cold realization slowly condensed in my gut.

"You *want* to kill Maat," I whispered.

"Of course," Brenton said. "I told you before, I don't care about killing phantoms. I just want to end her suffering."

"End her suffering?" I repeated, my voice rising to a squeak. "We're supposed to be in this to save Maat, save the daughters, and end this cycle of infinite bullshit. We're supposed to be finding a new solution, not…" My voice trailed off as I took a deep breath, pulling myself in and straightening up until I was looking Brenton dead in the face. "The Eyes kill daughters, not us," I said coldly. "You said you wanted to free them. That's the *whole reason* I came with you."

"Death is the only freedom left for Maat," Brenton said, his face going hard. "She's been their prisoner since she was a child, suffering for decades. Even when she went mad from it, they didn't let her rest. Instead, they hooked her to machines. They even put a symbiont in her to help keep her alive." He was speaking faster now, his voice shaking. "All she wants to do is get away, but they've filled her up with too many voices, too many dead girls' lives. She can't even escape in her own head."

He stepped toward me, clenching his fists. "I swore, Deviana," he whispered. "When I left the Eyes, I swore to her that I would not stop until she was free. And I won't, not until I've found a way to kill her so they can never use her again."

Fear and disgust had closed my throat so tightly by this point I could barely breathe, but I got the words out somehow. "And you found me."

"Yes," Brenton said with a relieved smile. "You're the salvation she's been waiting for, and with the virus this unstable, we might not even have to get you inside the Dark Star for it to work. Maat is stronger than the Eyes realize, and she's been waiting for this for so long. If you can do whatever you just did near her, even in space, I'm sure she'll reach you. Even the Eyes' security can't stop a plasmex virus. With your help, she'll be free at last, just like you promised her."

I shut my eyes tight. Part of me agreed with Brenton. Being trapped and used like that without even the ability to kill yourself sounded like a special kind of hell. If I was in Maat's place, I'd probably welcome the virus with open arms, too. But this wasn't just about Maat.

"What about the daughters?" I asked, looking at Brenton once more. "If Maat dies, what happens to them?"

Brenton's face fell. "Haven't you been listening? The daughters *are* Maat. She eats them, taking their lives, their memories, everything and replacing it with herself. She even changes their bodies to look like hers. The daughters are dead already, we can't save them, but we can stop them from making any more. If we kill Maat, it all ends. The Eyes will have no choice but to find another way to kill phantoms. Maybe they'll use your virus, maybe they'll find something better. But Maat will be free, and our job will be over."

"*Your* job," I snarled. "But the daughters aren't dead, Brenton." They couldn't be. I'd seen Ren break. Seen her horror with my own eyes as she looked down at her father's dead body. I could even still hear her thin, broken voice whisper, *Papa?* Whatever had been taken from her, she'd known her father and mourned his death, and that was enough for me. "I'm not going to the Dark Star."

Brenton's jaw tightened, but before he could start arguing with me, something hit the asteroid hard enough to send it spinning. Brenton and I were thrown off our feet, landing together in a heap against the wall as the asteroid rocked like a toy boat on the ocean. The xith'cal must have installed stabilizing thrusters, though, because the asteroid righted itself almost immediately, and Brenton and I jumped back up. We stared at each other for a long second, and then, by silent agreement, we both turned and started running for the hangar.

I knew this wasn't over. The moment I set foot on his ship, Brenton would try to take me to Maat. But I'd fight that battle when it came. Right now, we both had to focus and work together if we were going to get off this rock alive.

We had a lot of tunnel left to go, but a symbiont and a suit of Verdemont armor can cover a lot of ground in a very short amount of time. Not three minutes after we started, I spotted the end of the tunnel in the distance. I raised Mia, ready to blast us a path through whatever the hell was going on outside, but there was no need. When we burst out of the dark tunnel into the brightly lit hangar, all the xith'cal were too busy to spare us a glance.

The hangar was swarmed with lizards running around like ants on a kicked-over hill. The males were scrambling the heavy fighters docked against the hangar's far wall, while the females were frantically loading equipment crates into the smaller civilian craft. Several ships must have already launched, because the huge cavern was much emptier than it had been when we'd landed, but though the hangar door was wide open, I couldn't see who was attacking through the heavy shield.

"What's going on?" I shouted at Brenton as I holstered Mia.

"Don't know, don't care," he shouted back, raising his voice over the xith'cal screeching that was blaring through the hangar speakers. "All that matters is getting you out."

I wasn't going to argue. Across the hangar, all three of Brenton's ships were fired and ready. He was already running full tilt toward the largest one, and for a few glorious moments, it looked like we might actually make it. But then, when we were fifty feet away, something exploded through the shield that covered the hangar door.

It was not a xith'cal ship. It wasn't a human ship either. I wasn't even sure it *was* a ship at first. The thing had no windows, no hard edges, and its deep blue hull looked almost spongy. It was so big its nose was the only part that fit through the door, but though it was hanging half in and half out of the gravity, the ship didn't seem to mind. It didn't list forward or even put down landing gear. It simply settled onto the hangar's stone floor and opened its prow like a mouth.

"Lelgis!" Brenton shouted, skidding to a stop in front of me. I slammed into him a split second later, but the man didn't even budge. He was already changing, his scales slicing through his clothes. By the time I'd backed off, he was fully transformed, and his symbiont was screaming at me. "*Get to the ship!*"

You'd have thought I was back in the army from how fast I obeyed. I leaped forward, running full speed toward the freighter, the largest of Brenton's ships. Another transformed symbiont was waiting on the ramp for us. His clawed hand ready to grab me the moment I was in range, but I never got there. Twenty feet from safety, my path was blocked.

If Brenton hadn't shouted, I never would have connected the thing that jumped in front of me with the dead lelgis Cotter and I had seen back on the tribe ship. Those had looked like popped balloons. This creature was beautiful.

It stood nearly eight feet tall. Its huge purple head floating weightlessly over a dozen spindly white legs with feathery edges that tiptoed along the ground. The effect reminded me a bit of a jellyfish, especially when the lelgis moved like it did now. Seconds after landing just in front of me, the lelgis jumped again, rising into the air like gravity didn't touch it. I raised my gun to shoot, but it wasn't coming for me. Instead, the lelgis jumped backward, landing on top of the symbiont on the ramp.

The man started convulsing before the lelgis even touched him. It was like watching someone have a seizure, but the symbiont wasn't going down. Instead, he reached for the lelgis as it landed, one hand shooting out to claw his attacker while the other flew sideways, pointing at the ship beside his as he shouted something at the top of his lungs.

I couldn't hear him over the blaring alarms, but I didn't need to. The message was clear, and I obeyed, turning midstep toward the other ship. The little stealth two-seater we'd arrived in was up and running. I could see Nic in the pilot's seat through the glass, watching me run, his pale face pinched in fear. For a second, I couldn't understand why, and then another lelgis landed right in front of me.

My suit reacted before I could. Before my mind could even take in the yards of delicate legs or the huge, featureless mountain of its bulbous body, the Lady launched me into the air.

For five seconds, I was flying. My suit had jumped me over the alien in a graceful arc. As soon as I realized what had happened, I adjusted, flipping in midair a dozen feet above the alien's head. But as I started to fall, my feet angled perfectly to land right on the ramp of Nic's ship, something grabbed my ankle.

It was a light touch, like a feather had brushed over my foot, but the second it connected, a presence exploded into my mind. It reminded me of the hand Ren wrapped around my spine when she wanted to drag me around, but that at least had felt like a hand. This felt like nothing I could describe. It was feathery and dry and wiggling, gnawing into my mind almost like a caterpillar eating a leaf, but faster and directed. It shuffled through my brain methodically, like it was looking for something, and I had a pretty good idea what.

The lelgis had exterminated Stoneclaw's tribe to destroy the plasmex virus, the virus I'd just used, opening me into that weird emptiness where I'd felt the other presence looking at me. The one that had called me the threat. Now, the squids were here on a tiny rock in the middle of nowhere with what sounded like a battle fleet, and it didn't take a genius to guess what had drawn them. They were here to eliminate the threat, my threat, and if I didn't want to be exterminated, I had to act *now*.

My first thought was to use the virus. After all, that was what the lelgis feared. But I dismissed the idea just as quickly. First, I couldn't actually use the black stuff on command yet, and second, even if I did manage to get the plague going, there was a good chance it would kill everyone else in the process. So, with the virus not being an option, I decided to do the thing I *was* good at.

I bent over, tucking my legs as I swung my right arm down toward the feathery tentacle wrapped around my ankle. Elsie shot out of her sheath when I was an inch away, but I didn't even need to fire my thermite. My tungsten blade sliced through the tentacle like a knife through a noodle, and the presence in my mind vanished.

Given how I'd just whacked off a piece of it, I expected a scream like the phantom's, but the lelgis made no sound at all, mental or otherwise. It just shot another tentacle at me, this time for my neck. But I was in the fight now, and the tentacle had barely made it off the ground before I had Mia in my hand.

Normally, shooting backward while falling is a stretch even for me, but the nice part about plasma shotguns is that you don't have to be too accurate. I swung Mia over my shoulder, pausing just long enough to make sure her barrel was pointed at the lelgis' bulbous head before I pulled the trigger. I saw the white-hot plasma slug hit the thing dead-on in my rear cam, and then my feed whited out as the sun-bright clinging fire consumed the alien's soft flesh.

My suit landed me neatly on my feet a second later. As soon as my boots touched the ground, I started running, keeping one eye on the burning lelgis in my rear cam. Considering its head was now a mass of white fire, I was pretty sure the fight was over, but experience had taught me never to take my eyes off an enemy before I was certain it was dead. But though the lelgis was now smoldering merrily, it still wasn't making a sound, and it was still coming for me, its wispy tentacles reaching out even as the fire consumed them.

I didn't even have time to swear as I clicked Mia, now empty, back into place and grabbed Sasha. I spun round, shooting the first burning tentacle off at the base just before it landed on my shoulder. I shot the others off as well, letting my targeting system line up the shots until, at last, the huge thing fell.

The lelgis has been burning all this time, Mia's fire eating through its head as I shot off its tentacles. But even lying on the ground burned and shot to pieces, the alien was still twitching toward me. I fired one final shot for good measure before I gave up and ran, barreling full tilt toward the waiting ship.

Nic had the ramp down for me, and I charged it full speed, yelling through the com at him to go ahead and get off the ground, I'd jump in. He obeyed, and the thrusters came on with a roar. But as the ship began to rise, something landed on the open ramp, slamming the ship back down.

I skidded to a stop. The thing blocking my path was nothing like the jellyfish alien I'd just shot to pieces. That one had been little more than air and feathery tentacles, but this one had weight, and its tentacles weren't feathery, but thick and barbed with wicked hooks. It was definitely a lelgis, though, and it was in my way.

Quick as a thought, I whipped Sasha up and plugged a three-shot spread straight at the new alien's dark, pointed head. The shots struck true, hitting in a tight triangle, but they didn't split the alien's skull. Instead, they stuck in the air, caught by something thick and shimmery. A shield, I realized belatedly. But as I was processing this, the bullets flipped in midair, turning around to point back at me, and my eyes went wide. A *plasmex* shield.

I dove as the lelgis sent my own armor-piercing rounds flying right back at me. I managed to dodge the first two, but the third caught me in the leg. I gritted my teeth as my own expensive ammunition bored through the Lady's ballistic steel just like it was supposed to and dug into my calf. The pain came a second later, a stabbing blast that made my whole body seize before the soothing cold of the breach foam filled my suit.

I landed on my side, skidding across the hangar's stone floor for a moment before I slammed my hands down. My fingers dug deep grooves in the compacted landing bed for nearly a foot before I finally jerked to a stop. The moment I was still, I checked my leg.

The shot had chewed a two-inch hole in the plate over my calf.

Through it, I could see the puffy white wall of my breach foam. The quick-hardening antiseptic goo had plugged the hole in me as well, soothing the pain and stopping the bleeding, but I was still in a bad spot.

Back on the ship's ramp, the lelgis was reaching for me, its huge, hooked tentacles stretching out a surprising distance, and I shot on instinct before I remembered not to. Fortunately, it seemed that only the lelgis' head was shielded, because my bullet blew the barb off the first tentacle's end. Before I could get a second shot off, though, something big and black barreled into the lelgis from the side.

After bouncing Sasha's bullet, I half expected the lelgis to bounce this too, but apparently even a plasmex shield wasn't strong enough to take a pile drive from a symbiont. Brenton hit the thing hard enough to knock it off the ramp, and the two of them slammed to the ground in a tangle of black claws and barbed tentacles. Through it all, though, the lelgis made no sound. It didn't even seem to feel pain. It just flipped its barbs around and dug them into the new attacker.

The thick spikes went right through Brenton's scales, drawing blood before I could shoot another one off. I was about to shoot again when Brenton bellowed at me. "What the hell are you waiting for?" he screamed, digging his claws into the lelgis below him. *"Get on the ship!"*

I was scrambling up to do just that when my suit's proximity alarm began to beep. When I looked away from Brenton's fight to see why, I nearly dropped my gun. The huge hangar was filling with lelgis. Aliens of all kinds were pouring out of the mouth of the ship that had breached the plasma shield, big spindly giants like the one I'd burned, barbed ones like what Brenton was fighting, and others, huge ones and small ones, flying ones and ones I couldn't even make sense of. There were so many even my suit couldn't count them, and though none had eyes so far as I could make out, every single one of them was clearly searching for something. Searching for *me*.

"*Go, Deviana!*" Brenton screamed, slamming the lelgis into the floor. "*Go now!*"

He didn't have to say it again. I ran, kicking my suit into high gear as I jumped over Brenton's fight. I landed on the ramp of the little stealth ship and used my momentum to roll inside. The door closed the second I was through, and the ship jumped as Nic hit the thrusters hard.

I scrambled off the ground and up to the cockpit, but as I dropped into the copilot's seat, I saw we were flying the wrong way, toward the rear of the big hangar cavern rather than the front where the door was. Not that we could have escaped through the hangar door when the lelgis' ship had it completely blocked, but I didn't see a way out the direction Nic was flying either.

"Please tell me you have a plan," I said.

"We had several," Nic replied, gripping the flight stick like he was holding on for dear life. "Though this is the one I was least hoping to use." He reached over and hit the live fire button on the gunnery console. "You should fasten in, Miss Morris."

I grabbed my harness as the ship's main cannon whistled to life right under my feet. Nic was flying us straight at the top of the cave. I couldn't even see the other ships or the lelgis anymore, just the curved wall of the hangar's ceiling thirty feet away. Twenty feet.

When we were ten feet from crashing, the cannon fired. A pulse of white light exploded in front of us, blasting a hole in the asteroid. The rock blew outward, sent flying both from the cannon blast and the force of the cave's atmosphere as it was sucked into the vacuum of space.

Through the ship's tail camera, I saw the lelgis begin to scramble as the air vanished through the hole, and I grinned wide. A phantom would have just kept floating along, but it seemed the squids needed atmosphere, or at least they couldn't take the vacuum. I couldn't see any of the symbionts anymore, but I didn't have time to worry about them. We had bigger problems.

Our impromptu exit had taken us out on the far side of the largest, weirdest space battle I'd ever seen. The xith'cal battleships were clustered tight around the asteroid, and the xith'cal fighters, little ships with fast engines and huge cannons that all fleet officers cursed, were swarming around them like gnats. Between the battleships' own fighters and the ones from the hangar, there had to be a thousand xith'cal ships at least, enough to give even the Royal fleet serious trouble, but the lelgis barely seemed to notice.

There were five lelgis ships in total, not counting the one currently wedged into the asteroid's hangar. They were the same huge, graceful, beautifully colored vessels I'd seen on the monitor in the medbay destroying the xith'cal ghost ship, and they were attacking like they had then, shooting lines of beautiful blue fire that cut through the xith'cal ships like hot wire through snow.

The lizards were still putting up a hell of a fight, pounding the lelgis ships with cannon fire, but they were clearly outgunned. The battle couldn't have been going on for more than ten minutes, but already two of the xith'cal battleships were listing. That was bad for us. If the lelgis ships had a chance to take their eyes off the lizards long enough to spot our little ship, we were done for.

I turned to tell Nic as much only to find him punching in coordinates into the hyperspace terminal as fast as his fingers could go.

"We're jumping?" I cried as the coil began to spin up. "With no gate? Are you *insane?*"

"If we do not jump, we will be shot down," Nic said calmly, entering the last numbers before going back to check the first ones.

He had a point, but... "What about Brenton?"

"He is the one who planned this," Nic said. "His orders were that you must survive at all costs. Lelgis enter and exit hyperspace at will. We cannot outrun them on normal engines, and there is nowhere to run to out here anyway. Our only chance is to jump while they are distracted."

I didn't like the sound of that at all, but we didn't seem to have a choice. "Let's do it, then," I said, getting a death grip on my seat. "I just hope to the king you're as good at math as your sister."

Nic smiled as he plugged in the last variables. "Not quite," he said, punching the commit button. "Hold on."

The words were barely out of his mouth before the jump flash washed over us.

CHAPTER
11

I braced for a jolt, but the little ship eased into hyperspace as smoothly as a fish slipping back into the water. All at once, the battle vanished. So did the asteroid and the lelgis, leaving us floating perfectly still in the purple-gray blankness.

Nic let out a breath, leaning back in his chair. I followed suit, giving him a sideways look. "That was some fast calculating."

"I cannot claim undue credit," Nic said. "Mr. Brenton knew it might come to this, so we actually had everything preprogrammed. All I did was put in the final variables."

"You mean he planned on an ungated jump?" I asked, horrified.

Nic shrugged. "He had reason to believe we would be leaving quickly."

All I could do was shake my head. Before Caldswell's jump away from the emperor phantom at Unity, I'd only done one other ungated jump in my entire life. Now I'd done two in two days, which struck me as courting disaster. If Nic had messed up even a single number, we could come out of hyperspace a hundred years later than we'd planned, if we came out at all. But done was done, and we had more immediate problems, first and foremost of which was the hole in my leg.

Now that my adrenaline was fading, my calf was throbbing like a bitch. Gritting my teeth, I hauled myself out of the copilot's seat and hobbled back to the bench where I'd cleaned my armor to take a look at the damage. The breach foam had set up into a hard cast, allowing me to remove my boot and leg plate without too much pain, but the moment I cracked the foam around my calf, things were going to get bloody.

I glanced at Nic. "Do you have a first aid kit?"

Nic hopped out of the pilot's chair and hurried to the back of the ship, returning with a large med kit complete with bandages, grafting agents, and prefilled labeled syringes.

"Perfect," I said, setting the kit on the table. But as I was laying out my tools, I realized Nic was still hovering beside me like a brooding hen. "You might want to turn away," I warned.

Nic shook his head. "I would be helpful if possible."

I shrugged. "Suit yourself."

I took the armor off my left arm and gave him the tourniquet, holding out my biceps so he could tie it tight. When the vein at my elbow was good and puckered, I injected a painkiller followed by a clotting agent. The throbbing in my leg dulled as the drugs hit my system, but not nearly as much as it should have. I rolled my eyes as the tourniquet came off, thankful that Hyrek wasn't here to crow over being right. While the drugs finished kicking in, I grabbed a bandage out of the medkit and tied myself a nice fat knot.

"Okay," I said, tapping on the shell of hardened breach foam around my leg with one hand while I wedged the knotted bandage between my teeth with the other. "Pull it."

Nic obeyed, and I bit down hard as he yanked the foam away from my wound. The pain hit me like another shot when the breach foam tore free, and for a second I was afraid I'd black out. I didn't, barely, but there certainly was a lot of blood. Fortunately, Nic was ready with a towel, so I didn't make too much of a mess. I stayed still until I'd gotten the pain, or at least my reaction to it, under control, and then I grabbed the tweezers and started the long, arduous process of digging out the bullet.

Sasha's anti-armor rounds have two phases. The first is designed to drill through ballistic plate, while the second splinters to tear through flesh and electronics. It's a nasty little one-two shot, and I was hating it at the moment. The bullet in my leg had split into three shards. By the king's own miracle, all three of them had missed the bone, but my calf was wrecked.

By the time I finished digging out the final shard, I was ready to pass out. Fortunately, the next bit was easy. I motioned for Nic to hand me the can of grafting solution. I shook it hard and sprayed the mixture of synthetic skin, glue, and anti-infection agents over the wound.

Even with the painkillers, it stung something awful, but by this point I was so happy to be almost done I didn't even hiss. The canned stuff wasn't nearly as good as an actual skin grafter like the one Hyrek used, and I would definitely have a scar from this, but the spray patched me up better than a bandage could. I'd still need to get to an actual doctor at some point, but for now at least I wouldn't bleed to death.

The wound wasn't a terribly large one, but it still took most of the can to cover the area to my satisfaction. When I was done, Nic helped me get my leg up on the bench for the thirty-minute wait while the graft dried. "You're, um, very skilled at that," he said as he propped my heel against the corner.

"Survival skill," I said with a weak smile. "You don't last very long as a merc if you don't get good at patching yourself up."

I expected him to smile back. Instead, Nic's face turned a little gray, and I decided it was time to change the subject. "Where are we going?"

"Montblanc," Nic replied. "That's our base inside the Republic."

I barely hid my relief in time. Apparently, Brenton hadn't worked his decision to go directly to Maat into his emergency plans. I'd never been to Montblanc, but I knew it was one of the bigger Terran colonies. It was also the farthest out of all the major Republic holdings, which explained why Brenton was using it as a base.

"We'll be there in forty-five minutes or so," Nic said, glancing at the ship clock.

"Or a hundred years," I mumbled.

Nic shot me a disapproving look. "Dwelling on unfortunate outcomes only leads to internal disharmony, Deviana."

"I'll keep that in mind," I said, leaning back against the wall. "Now, if you'll excuse me, I'd like to pass out for a bit."

"Of course." He stood up at once. "I'll wake you when we exit."

I nodded and turned away, pressing my face into the cool glass of the little port window. Behind me, I heard Nic settle back into the pilot's seat, but I didn't care about him anymore. I didn't even actually care about passing out, though that would probably have been the smart thing to do. My mind was simply too full.

Before I'd signed on with Caldswell, my life had followed a pattern: obey orders, climb the ladder, keep my eyes on the prize. It was a good gig, dangerous and exciting with glory as my reward. Most of all, though, it was simple. A path of my own choosing where I did what I loved, knew where I fit, and understood where I was going. Now, though, I felt like a dollhouse in a tornado. Over the past thirty hours, my entire life had been uprooted and turned on its head, my hopes and ambitions dashed then reshuffled then dashed again. But now that the storm had quieted, even for a moment, I was determined to pick up the pieces and get myself back on the right track. First, though, I had to figure out what track that was.

I looked down at my bare hands. Beneath the smears of my drying blood, my skin looked normal, but I knew better. The black stuff was still there. Carrying death in my hands was nothing new, but unlike my weapons, which I trusted with my life, I couldn't control the virus at all, and I knew enough now to understand exactly how huge a disaster that could be.

I closed my fists tight. I'd sworn on my honor to Maat that I'd set her free, just as I'd sworn to myself that I'd end the awful system that had killed Ren and her father. I still intended to keep those oaths, but with the lelgis and the xith'cal involved now, this was all getting way too big for one merc to handle on her own.

Hard as it was for me to admit, I needed help—someone with

the knowledge and resources to get this virus out without killing me or the rest of the universe. I'd thought I'd found that person in Brenton, but all he'd cared about in the end was killing Maat, and I just couldn't do that. Anyway, Brenton was almost certainly dead now, and while I was relieved I wouldn't have to fight him over going to the Dark Star, I still needed help, and unless I wanted to go find some more xith'cal, I had no one left to turn to except the Eyes.

Just the thought made me queasy. When I'd first decided to leave the army and look for a private mercenary contract, my grandmother had warned me not to sign with any of the bargain companies. You couldn't trust people who treated life cheaply, she'd said, because they were the ones who'd sell you out for nothing. And while no one would ever call the Eyes a low-cost operation, Rupert and Caldswell had made it abundantly clear that everything was expendable when measured against the threat of the phantoms, and that didn't sit right with me at all.

I'd never thought of myself as a particularly good person. That wasn't the sort of claim you could make when you killed for money and generally had a fun time doing it. But even though I'd probably shot more people throughout my career than all the Eyes put together, my hands were cleaner. I killed, sure, but I killed pirates and xith'cal raiders, armed enemies who fought back. I didn't shoot civilians, I didn't kill children, and I didn't torture animals. I'd known the Eyes did the first two from the very beginning, but after experiencing the phantom's panic myself, I knew now they did the last as well. Worse, they felt it was justified, a sacrifice to keep the universe safe, and that was what bugged me most of all.

I was no stranger to sacrifice. "My life for the Sainted King" was the first oath Paradoxian children learned to say. To die for king and country was the greatest honor a Paradoxian could achieve, but we were soldiers. We chose to die as heroes, but the daughters' choice was made for them. It wasn't that I didn't understand why the Eyes used them, I just didn't agree that all of our survival should be bought with the life of someone who never even got a say. Brenton might have been crazy, but I agreed with him on one thing: what the Eyes did was wrong, and it had to stop.

By keeping the fight against the phantoms a secret, the Eyes made us all complicit in the cowardice that killed children so that everyone else wouldn't have to be bothered. But life wasn't a gift that was given to you. Survival was a prize we all fought for together, not a guarantee bought at the cost of an innocent life. Everyone knew that, which was why the Eyes kept the daughters hidden, because if word of what they were doing got out, it wouldn't be panic over phantoms that tore the universe apart, it would be rage. Rage over what was being done to those poor girls, rage that they had made us murderers, too, without our knowledge. But I knew the truth now, and I refused to dishonor myself any longer.

I looked again at my clean hands, clenching my fingers tight. I hadn't asked for this virus, but it was mine now, and I would be damned if I gave it to those child killers. I didn't know why my king had seen fit to give this burden to me, but I would not let him down. I would use this plague as a weapon to make sure what happened to Ren and Rashid never happened again. I would stop the tragedies, and if I died in the process, at least I'd meet my end as a Paradoxian should, with my honor intact and my head held high. But so long as there was breath in my body, I would do whatever needed to be done to see this through, and I would never, ever go back to the Eyes.

But while all these noble promises made me feel a lot better, they actually made my immediate situation more dire, because now that seeking out the Eyes for help was synonymous with moral defeat, I had no idea where to go. Even if Brenton had miraculously survived the lelgis attack, I didn't want to stay with a bunch of former Eyes who thought Maat's death was the same thing as victory. If I left, though, I'd be on my own with no money, no ammo, and a busted leg. Forget the virus, I couldn't even put my suit back on thanks to the bullet hole. Before I could even think about the long term, I needed a doctor, food, and a Paradoxian armorsmith, but where the hell was I going to find a—

And just like that, the solution came to me.

It was so obvious, I was embarrassed I hadn't thought of it earlier. Clearly, being around Terrans for so long had made me soft in the head. I had it now, though—how to get help for my virus without going to the Eyes, how to avoid the lelgis, even how to get my armor fixed. It was perfect, natural, *beautiful*, and for the first time since I'd jumped off the cliff, I felt like I had my feet under me again.

I sat up at once, leaning over to grab one of the prefilled syringes out of the medkit on the table beside me. I broke the safety cap and palmed the needle, hiding it between the wall and my body. When I was set, I called over my shoulder: "Nic, could you come help me for a second?"

"Of course, Deviana," Nic said, hopping out of his chair. "Are you in pain? We've only got ten minutes of jump left. When we come out, I'll call down to our ground contact to have a medic ready when we land."

He stopped in front of me, all anxious eagerness, but I just pointed at my injured leg. "I need you to take a look at my patch. I think something's wrong."

He looked at me funny for a moment, but I kept my mind perfectly blank. Nova had said Nic could tell when someone was lying, and I'd seen him do as much myself back on Falcon 34. I had no idea if keeping my head empty would actually work, but a few moments later, Nic kneeled to check my leg. The second his head was down, I stabbed the syringe into his neck.

Unlike me, Copernicus Starchild had no built-up resistance to sedatives. I'd barely pushed the plunger down before he was slumping onto the floor. Nova's brother was almost as small as she was, and even on my busted leg, it was no problem to pick him up and hobble him across the ship to the other bench. I laid him out and checked to be sure his breathing was steady, but he seemed to be sleeping soundly. I checked one last time, just to be sure, then I limped back over to my bench and started putting my armor back on.

It took me a few minutes to get my ripped-up leg plate to snap back into place, but eventually everything clicked. Once I was locked in, I adjusted my motors to pick up the weight for my bum leg and walked to the cockpit with only a slight limp, plopping into the pilot's seat just as we came out of hyperspace.

Despite my fears, we came out of the ungated jump only six hours behind where we should have been, dumping out in high orbit above the blinding white expanse of Montblanc's arctic circle. After a long prayer of thanks to my king, I buckled in and grabbed the flight stick. I'm registered to operate most small spacecraft, but that was back in the army, and I was a little rusty. Consequently, I spent the next few minutes remembering how to fly. Fortunately, the basics of space navigation hadn't changed too much in the last few years, and soon enough I was able to merge into the ring of ships orbiting Montblanc's equator while they awaited permission to land.

When the colony tower called, I sent them the faked information Brenton had loaded into the ship and got immediate clearance. Brenton's flight plan called for me to set down at a medium-sized city in Montblanc's northern hemisphere, but I veered off course the moment I got my okay from traffic control, landing in the huge public starport at the colony capital. I locked the ship up tight so no one would rob Nic blind before he woke up, and then, with a bow and a formal thank-you for saving me that he'd never hear, I closed the door on Nic's unconscious body and hopped down onto the tarmac, losing myself instantly in the busy starport.

I didn't have any money, but it didn't matter. Even if I'd had a year's pay in hand, I couldn't have gotten a taxi. Not when I was armed and in full Paradoxian armor without a permit on a major Terran colony. Fortunately, my suit computer had already tapped into the local maps provided by the tourist board, and my destination wasn't far. Two minutes and a four-block jog later, I was standing in front of the heavy steel door of the Paradoxian embassy.

I hit the bell and stepped back, settling into parade rest in front of the camera. A few seconds later, a man with an even thicker accent than mine addressed me from the speaker bank above the door. "Welcome to the Paradoxian Emb—"

The voice cut off abruptly, and I heard the camera whir, focusing on my armor. When the man came back, he was speaking King's Tongue. "My lady, how can we help you?"

I smiled. Verdemont armor came through again. This time, though, I wasn't playing at being a noble lady to scare a mechanic into a timely repair. The other side of that door was the king's land, which meant I was back under the king's law.

"I'm not noble," I said quickly. "My name is Deviana Morris, honorably discharged lieutenant in the Ambermarle First Armored Division. I have important information for the crown and I need to speak with the officer in charge."

There was a long pause, and then the heavy door unlocked with a click. "Welcome, Lieutenant Morris," the voice said. "Blessed be the Sainted King."

"Ever may he reign," I replied as I stepped inside, placing myself, my virus, and all my hopes into the hands of Sainted King Stephen, Holy Ruler of Paradox, and the only power in the universe I could still trust.

Stepping into the Montblanc Paradoxian embassy was like going home.

Unlike Terran buildings with their low ceilings and normal human scale, the embassy was built for armor. Everything was oversized and reinforced, from the marble floors to the steel guard station. It was a lovely, nostalgic sight after so long among Terrans, and I was still appreciating it when a solider in a red suit stepped up to block my way.

I had to tilt my head back to look him in the face. Red suits were for military use only. The infantry model was slightly larger than Cotter's Count-class suit at eight feet tall and plated all to hell. I could empty Sasha's entire clip into the guard's chest and not even tickle him. Just seeing the big lug made me feel a thousand times better, even as he gave me the caustic once-over. "Identification?"

I had my ID up for his scanner before he could finish, and I thought I saw the guard smile behind his thick visor as his suit verified mine. "Glad to be back among civilized folk, Lieutenant?"

"You have no idea," I said. "Who's in charge here?"

"This outpost is run by the noble Baron Kells," the guard replied solemnly. "You said you had important information for the crown?"

"Yes, but I need to tell it to the baron myself," I explained. "Can I see him?"

The guard looked at me like I'd just asked the impossible, which, to be fair, I had. Now that I was back on the king's land, I was a peasant again, and peasants did not demand to speak to barons. But I wasn't about to start talking phantoms and plasmex plagues to a door guard.

"I just need five minutes of his time," I pleaded. "If he doesn't want to hear more after that, I'll take the consequences."

The punishment for wasting a noble's time could be severe if you put them in a bad enough mood. Volunteering to take the heat straight off was a pretty good sign I wasn't messing around. Good enough for the guard, apparently, because after a com conversation I couldn't hear, the red suit turned around and started walking down the hall. I followed, falling into step behind him like I was back in the army.

After the grand marble entry hall, I expected the rest of the embassy to be equally impressive, but the hallway the red suit led me down would have been at home in any Paradoxian bunker. The floor was cement, the lighting was harsh, and my density monitor was going nuts from all the armor in the rooms around us. When we reached the end of the hall, the guard led me into a secure waiting room and told me to stay, locking the door behind me. I'd barely settled onto the reinforced bench when the door opened again, and a woman in Knight's armor just like mine stuck her head through.

"Lieutenant Morris?"

I stood at attention, and she nodded. "The baron will see you."

I was glad my visor hid my surprise as the woman led me back into the hall, or she would have caught me gaping like a fish. With very few exceptions, all high-ranking members of the Paradoxian military were nobly born. I'd served under a dozen barons during my four years in the army, but I'd only ever met two of them personally. Both times had been a giant to-do involving hours of waiting. When the red suit had shown me into the waiting room, I'd fully expected to sit there for the next five hours, not five minutes.

Even though coming to the embassy had been my idea, all the running I'd done recently had made me even more paranoid than usual, and as the woman led me briskly out of the bunker area into a much nicer part of the building, my stomach started to sink. Despite his Royal Warrant, I wasn't sure how far Caldswell's influence extended into the Paradoxian military. If my name was on a watch list, I might have doomed myself by coming home, but it was too late to worry about that now. We were already at the end of a very nice carpeted hall in front of a heavy, expensive-looking wooden door. The woman stopped at the threshold and crisply commanded me to disarm, for I was entering the presence of nobility.

I obeyed, placing Sasha and Mia gently in her hands. Elsie didn't detach, so I held out my arm to let the woman peacebind my blade with metallic tape. She did the same to my grenade cache and then scanned my suit from head to toe to make sure I wasn't hiding anything else. When the scanner beeped green, she opened the wooden door and stood back so I could enter.

The office I walked into was very nice, but it wasn't a patch on the other noble offices I'd seen. There were no expensive ornamentations, no paintings, and no priceless family treasures. The man sitting behind the desk in the middle of the room was just as surprising. He looked to be in his midfifties with short, graying brown hair. He was armored, of course, Baron's armor as befit his rank. Nice stuff, too. Not Verdemont, but definitely custom, though I'd expected nothing less. All nobles had money. What did surprise me was that he was wearing combat armor. Most nobles preferred the flashier racing suits, or dueling models if they were fighters. This man was clearly a fighter, but he looked more ready to storm a Terran battleship than engage in an honor duel. In fact, his suit design was so no-nonsense that I wasn't sure this *was* the baron until he glared at me.

"Been too long among Terrans, girl?"

I jumped and dropped the deepest bow my suit could manage. "Forgive me, my lord. I did not expect to see you so quickly."

Though my face was now parallel with the floor, I saw the baron wave dismissively through my cameras. "Only idiots ignore unexpected urgent messages," he said. "Now, sit down and tell me what's so goddamn important. And it had *better* be important, soldier, or you're going to learn what it means to waste the king's time."

I paled. Threats like that were normal, but I'd never heard a noble curse before. As blood relations of the Sainted King, they were above such vulgarity. But I wasn't about to tell the baron that. I jumped to obey, taking a seat on the heavy armor-scaled chair in front of him. Meanwhile, the baron leaned back in his own chair, watching me through the rainbow of projected screens splashed across his visor.

I fidgeted under his attention, scrambling to think of a place to begin that wouldn't make me sound crazy. When nothing leaped out at me, I decided to just go with the broadest target possible. "Have you heard of phantoms, my lord?"

The baron's face grew grave. "I have."

The words held a clear warning, but all I felt was relief. In those two syllables, Baron Kells had removed a huge weight from my chest. I was no longer alone with my secret, no longer strung up between Caldswell and Brenton. I had my own side now, Paradox, my home, and as the baron listened, my story burst forth of its own accord.

————

It took me nearly two hours to get the whole thing out, plus answer the baron's questions. His grave expression had only deepened as the conversation went on, and by the time I got to the end of the Ielgis attack, he was looking grim as a rainy funeral.

"We're very lucky you decided to come to me," he said when I finished. "Knowledge of the phantoms, even among the nobility, is usually kept to dukes and higher."

I blinked in surprise. "So how do you know about them?"

The baron gave me a murderous look, and my stomach clenched. I *had* been among Terrans too long, because the question had just popped out. I bowed hastily, sputtering apologies, but the baron just rolled his eyes.

"It's none of your business," he said. "But I'm rightly proud of it, so I'll tell you anyway. I wasn't born noble. King Stephen bestowed this office and my title on me last year as a reward for twenty years of service as a Devastator."

I couldn't stifle my startled gasp in time, and the baron's face broke into a wicked smile. "I still keep up with the order, and I've heard your name tossed around a good bit, Deviana Morris. The Blackbird in the Verdemont suit collecting promotions so quickly you'd think they were giving them away. Last thing I'd heard was that you'd signed up with Caldswell's flying coffin, so when you showed up unexpectedly at my door, I knew it would be bad news."

I caught his meaning at once. "You've worked with Caldswell before, my lord?"

"A few times," the baron said. "Enough to know I don't want to do it again." His look turned sour. "Up against the wall or not, you can't trust a man who lets children do his fighting."

"I agree, my lord," I said. "But I hope that won't have to happen anymore."

The baron nodded and stood up, which meant I stood as well. "You were right to come to bring this to me," he said. "If what you're saying is true, and for the record, I believe it is, you've given Paradox a great weapon and an even greater opportunity. I'm going to send a message to the Royal Office right away. Meanwhile, I want you to get that leg to a doctor. Archer?"

The door opened when he said the name, and the woman in Knight's armor who'd been waiting outside stepped in with a bow.

"Take Lieutenant Morris to the medbay," the baron said, looking back at me. "I don't need to tell you to keep your mouth shut about this, do I?"

"Of course not, my lord," I said, bowing low.

The baron nodded and waved me into the hall before returning to his seat. I had just enough time to see him pull a top-security message screen onto his display before his door locked and the woman, Archer, ordered me to follow her.

Under any other circumstances I'd have grumbled at being ordered to the medbay like a first-year recruit who didn't know better, but right then I'd have gladly gone anywhere the baron told me. I was so happy I even let the embassy staff take my armor away to be repaired by the staff armorsmith sight unseen. And as the army doctor numbed my leg in preparation for replacing my emergency patch with a real skin graft, all I could think was that the only mistake I'd made in coming here was not doing it sooner.

The doctor wasn't happy that I'd gone so long on my injured leg. He cleaned the wound and grafted it as best he could, but he warned me I'd have a scar there forever. I had plenty of scars, so I wasn't too worried about that. What really had me in a tizzy was the report from the armorsmith that they'd had to refactor my whole leg piece to repair the damage from Sasha's bullet.

Armor can only be refactored so many times before you have to replace it, and mine had been in the oven a lot lately. Still, my Lady looked good as new when I got her back that evening. I was testing her out in the embassy's gym when I got a message from the baron that my report had been received by the Royal Office and we'd be getting a formal answer by tomorrow.

In the meanwhile, I was put on lockdown, which only made sense. I was dangerous and possibly contagious, after all. Normally this would have chaffed, but this time I couldn't care less. After days of near constant emergency, I was perfectly content to eat familiar foods, sleep until I couldn't sleep anymore, and revel in the fact that I didn't have to crawl through flooded tunnels or worry about monsters—xith'cal, lelgis, or symbiont—grabbing me in the night.

Even the few glowing bugs I saw floating through the embassy walls couldn't bring me down. I was happy as a pig in mud to lie on my bunk in the little room they'd given me, eat my tray of army-style cafeteria food, and watch Paradoxian armor game shows on the delayed feed from Kingston until I fell asleep.

I haven't slept that heavy in years. It took the guard two knocks to wake me up for breakfast late the next morning. I was happily munching my way through the huge platter of fried sausage, fried toast, and fried potatoes he'd brought when Archer came in to announce that the envoy from the Royal Office was here to pick me up.

I almost choked on my breakfast. Montblanc was a major colony, but it was about as far from Paradox as it was possible to get and still be in the Republic. Baron Kells's report must have lit a fire back home to get someone out here so fast.

I abandoned my food and hopped up, reaching for my clean, recharged, repaired armor, but Archer shook her head.

"No armor," she said sternly at my skeptical look. "Orders from the top."

I swallowed. When you were talking about the Royal Office, "from the top" meant someone in the royal family, and as much as I hated the idea of going anywhere without my Lady, I wasn't about to disobey. I locked my armor in the temporary case the armorsmith had dug up for me, lashed my guns to the top, and then followed the baron's officer out into the hall, where four red suits were waiting to walk us out into the formal entry.

That actually made me a little nervous. Four red suits plus Archer's Knight armor was a lot of honor guard for someone wearing no armor, especially since no one was supposed to know what I was. This *was* an envoy from the Royal Office, though. Maybe they'd sent an active duty Devastator to bring me back to Paradox? It could even be a Royal Knight.

That thought cheered me up enormously. I'd never actually met a Royal Knight in person, but they were exactly the sort of completely irreproachable, honorable, nearly fanatic loyalists you'd need to escort a secret alien superweapon back to Paradox. This theory was further supported when we walked into the entry hall to see Baron Kells himself waiting for us in the middle of the lobby. I couldn't see who he was talking to, but with the baron paying such close attention, it could only be the envoy, and my spirits soared a little higher.

But when the baron turned to greet us, my soaring turned to plunging. The man Baron Kells had been talking to wasn't wearing King-class armor as a Devastator should. He wasn't wearing armor at all, actually, just a nice black suit. His back was to me, but that didn't matter. I knew him from any angle, and I froze midstep as Rupert turned away from the smiling baron to lock his icy blue eyes on mine.

The guards around me stopped a second later, looking at me in confusion. Archer even reached out to touch my shoulder. "Lieutenant Morris?"

"Morris!" the baron called, glaring at me through his visor. "Stop gawking and get over here. This is the Royal Knight who will be escorting you to the king."

"But my lord," I whispered. "This man isn't—"

"Lieutenant Morris is confused," Rupert said, and my jaw dropped a second time. His accent was completely gone. Rupert was speaking King's Tongue like he'd grown up in a wealthy Kingston family.

"I have the order right here," he continued, all polite smiles as he pulled out a very official looking ledger marked with the king's own crest. Baron Kells glanced at me curiously one last time, then took the ledger, checking it against his own.

"It bears the king's seal, *and* King Stephen's personal signature," he said, his voice awed. "Yes, sir knight. We've disarmed her as requested. She's all yours."

I heard the baron's words like he was speaking from the bottom of a well. Rupert wasn't looking at me anymore, but I could see his body leaning in my direction, ready to give chase if I bolted. If he'd actually been the Paradoxian he had everyone convinced he was, he'd have known that wasn't necessary. With that order, his status as the voice of the crown was cemented. If I tried to expose him, it would be my word against the king's, which meant my word against the will of heaven. If I fought or ran, if I even tried to argue, I would be committing heresy and treason.

I looked around anyway, but what I saw only sank me lower. Even if I'd had my suit armed and ready with surprise on my side, there was no way I could have taken all the armor in the room. Sasha could have put down the red suits with a little luck, but Baron Kells was a former Devastator. He could probably thrash me solo. Rupert wouldn't even have to move.

By this point, my escort was stepping aside, all the guards bowing to Rupert as he walked up to take my arm. I didn't move a muscle, not even when Rupert's fingers closed like a vise on my wrist. "Come, Lieutenant Morris," he said, his refined Kingston accent chilling the words to puffs of frost. "We've wasted enough time."

I didn't have a choice. I followed where Rupert led, walking past the baron and the bowing guards as Rupert steered me through the embassy's heavy door. He had a car waiting outside, and even this fit the role he was playing. The vehicle was diplomatic issue, brand new and sleek. It was also armored, and as Rupert shut the passenger door behind me, I could hear the layers of steel locking into place like a vault door.

He got in on the driver's side a moment later, landing with his customary grace as the door swung shut, sealing us in. The sound brought a flash of panic with it. The details were different, but this was just like when he'd beaten me back in the woods. Now as then, I was outmaneuvered and trapped, only this time there'd be no Rashid appearing at the last second to shoot Rupert off me.

But just as the panic started to overwhelm me, I forced it down.

This was nothing like the woods, I snarled at myself. Even if she was packed at the moment, I had my suit, my blade, and my guns, all freshly charged. Rupert couldn't do the symbiont thing in such a crowded city. Mia was strapped across the case in my lap; I could use her to blow off the car's armored door and make a run for it. All I had to do was dart down that alley, avoid the cops, and come back around to the starport. I was planning how I could steal a ship and get to Paradox itself when Rupert said my name.

"Devi?"

I went stiff. His voice was gentle and accented just as I remembered it, the refined Kingston lilt gone like it had never been. "Devi," he said again. "Look at me, please."

Looking at him was the last thing I wanted to do. I didn't want anything to do with him at all. I especially didn't want him using that tone of voice on me, saying my name the same way he had when we'd lain tangled together in the dark back before everything fell apart. But even though I'd been planning how to do it when he'd interrupted me, I really didn't want to run. Even if I could have escaped, there was nowhere left for me to go.

That was the only reason I turned, I told myself. It certainly wasn't because I'd been a sucker for Rupert from day one, or because, despite everything, some idiot part of me still wanted to see him. No, I turned because I just wanted to get this over with. But as my head came around, I caught a glimpse of Rupert pulling something out of his jacket pocket just before the handcuff locked around my wrist.

"What the—"

The words faded into sputters as he looped the chain through the security handle between our seats and then caught my other arm, snatching it easily when I tried to get away. "I'm sorry," he said as he deftly lifted my armor case out of my lap and shoved it into the backseat, well out of my now extremely limited reach. "I can't afford to let you run here."

"You son of a bitch!" I shouted, yanking on the chain as I tried in vain to get my leg up to kick him.

Rupert said nothing, and he paid no attention to my struggles. He just started the car and pulled out into the dense morning traffic.

I fought a bit more on principle, but it was hopeless. He'd used a heavy steel cuff, and the car was built like a tank. It wasn't like I could have done anything against him without my suit, anyway. Thanks to that letter, I'd been delivered to him like a shucked oyster.

"So," I snarled, glaring out the window as I flopped defeated back into my seat. "Are you actually a Royal Knight, or was that just a really good fake?"

"I'm not a knight," Rupert said as he pulled us into the starport's main entrance. "But the king's letter wasn't fake. When Baron Kells sent your story to the Royal Office, they called our representative on Paradox. King Stephen formally signed you over to the Eyes four hours ago."

I pressed my eyes shut. Of course. Of *course* the Eyes would have a direct line to the king. Why not? They were everywhere else. I was a bit surprised my king would give away a weapon like me, but then, he had an entire kingdom to watch out for and no reason to distrust the Eyes. They were the heroes, the guardians who kept everything safe from the invisible monsters. I was just a peasant, and now, by my king's hand, I was theirs.

The car eased to a stop, and I opened my eyes again. We were at the gate to the priority docks, the ones used for emergencies only. The guard was already on his way over, and I lifted my cuffed hands, hoping to stall things, but then Rupert took a wallet out of his inside pocket and flashed something that looked like a badge at the window. After that, the man waved us through immediately, no questions asked.

I dropped my hands with a glower. "What was that?"

"Top-level government clearance," Rupert replied, tucking the wallet back into his pocket as he drove us straight onto the dock. "It came with the car."

I rolled my eyes. "Right. Whatever, Mr. Big Shot." I leaned my head against the window as we drove past the lines of emergency vessels. "I guess you know everything, then. About the virus and Brenton and whatnot."

"I read Baron Kells's report," Rupert replied, his face perfectly neutral. "My orders are to return you to Commander Caldswell until we can move you to a proper handling facility."

His cold, calm words slid through me like a knife. A lab. They were sending me to a lab so I could be "properly handled."

Just the idea sent the image Maat had shown me in Caldswell's quarters exploding back into my mind. Suddenly, I could see the girl right in front of me, her body held upright by so many restraining straps she looked like she'd been webbed there by a giant spider. And the mask, that horrible, blank metal mask without holes or light or escape—

I thrust the image away, but the damage was already done. I took a ragged breath, fighting my trembling body. I would *not* break down, especially not in front of Rupert. I refused. But I felt so hopeless. All the grief of the last few days—Rashid's death, Ren's death, the mines, killing that poor phantom, drugging Nic—it had all been for *nothing*. I was right back where I'd started.

A tear slipped down my cheek before I could stop it, and I would have doubled over in shame if it wouldn't have made things worse. The great Devi Morris, crying in her defeat, but I couldn't make myself stop. I *was* defeated. All my promises back on the ship, my grand plans, they'd all come to nothing. I should have let Rupert grab me in the forest, I thought bitterly. I should have just stayed with Caldswell. At least then maybe everyone would still be alive. Rashid and Brenton would still be fighting the Eyes, and there would still be hope for change. Now there was nothing. No glory, no hope. I'd thought I could make things better, but I'd failed. I hadn't changed anything.

The car rolled to a stop, and I heard Rupert's seat shift as he cut the engine and turned to look at me. "Devi..."

"Shut up," I snapped, keeping my head down. It was pointless, there was no hiding the tears, but I tried anyway. "You've won, okay? Take me to Caldswell or whoever actually runs the Eyes. Stick me in a lab. Grind me up and squeeze the virus out, I don't care anymore. Just don't get me near Dark Star or whatever it's called, the place where Maat is, or I'll kill her."

Warning him about that actually made me feel slightly better. At least this way I wouldn't kill every daughter by accident. Assuming Rupert would even listen, of course. I was trying to think of a better way to explain how dangerous I could be when I heard Rupert's door open.

I looked up just in time to see him get out of the car. He opened the back to grab my case and then walked around to my door. As I watched him, I realized for the first time that we were parked in front of a small, nice ship. A *very* nice ship. It was almost the twin of Brenton's little stealther, but even more expensive looking and straight-out-of-the-shipyard new.

"Whose ship is that?" I asked when he opened the door.

"It's mine," Rupert said, reaching across me to undo my cuff.

"Oh, right," I sneered. "Your Eye ship, for when you're not cooking."

"Yes," Rupert replied, straightening up and reaching down to help me.

I smacked his hand away and got out of the car on my own. The ship's ramp was already extended, and since it would be suicidally stupid to do anything else at this point, I stomped up it. Rupert followed with my case, closing the door behind us with a wave of his hand.

The inside of the ship was just as nice as the exterior. It had the same setup as Brenton's, a state-of-the-art cockpit flanked by a tiny cabin with two bunks folded over to act as benches facing each other on the walls. Since there was nowhere else to sit other than with Rupert up front, which I most definitely was not doing, I plopped down on the pilot-side bench as I waited for Rupert to go up to the cockpit, but he didn't. He just stood by the ship's locked door, staring at me.

I glared right back. I might have been beaten, but that didn't mean I was just going to curl up. At this point, defeated, hopes crushed, cast off by my king and bound for a lab, my pride was all I had left. I refused to let him see me break any more than he already had.

But while I was steeling myself for a fight, Rupert still hadn't moved. It was like he'd gotten stuck. I was about to tell him to get the lead out so we could be done with this farce when he walked over and sat down on the opposite bench, placing my armor case on the floor between us.

I froze, eyes darting to my case. My guns were still strapped to the outside with Mia on top, practically in arm's reach. Rupert's eyes followed mine, but he didn't try to move my weapons away. That actually made me angrier than if he'd threatened me. He might be stronger and faster than I was even in my suit, but if he was going to treat me with contempt, I was going to blast his fool head off on principle.

Rupert sighed at the look on my face and leaned over, sliding Sasha out of her holster and holding her out to me handle first.

I snatched my gun out of his grip and flipped it around, pointing Sasha at his head. "If you're counting on me not to shoot because of the kick, you've got another thing coming," I snarled. "I'm not afraid of breaking my arm again if that's what it takes."

"I don't think you're afraid of anything," Rupert said as he returned to his seat on the bunk. "And I'm hoping you won't shoot me, not counting on it."

That seemed like a pretty stupid hope to me, but then, he wasn't risking much, was he? "Doesn't matter, anyway," I said bitterly, tossing my pistol on the bench beside me. "We both know Sasha can't actually hurt you."

The words were barely out of my mouth before Rupert reached into his coat and pulled a gun out of the shoulder holster I hadn't realized he was wearing until that moment. He held it out to me a second later, and my eyes went wide. It was the pearl-handled cannon he'd threatened Caldswell with back on the bridge ages ago, the one I'd seen hanging above his bed when we'd slept together, his disrupter pistol.

When I didn't take it, Rupert leaned over and placed the gun in my hand. It was heavier than it looked, the pearl handle smooth against my palm and warm from his body.

"Actually," he said as he settled back into place, "as you should already know, your Sasha can knock me out just fine in this form. You just have to hit the right spot." He reached up and tapped a long finger against his forehead just above his eyes, right where I'd shot him on the bridge. "A disrupter blast in the same location will kill a symbiont in one shot, even through the scales."

I stared at him, dumbfounded, and then tightened my fingers around the gun he'd placed in my hand. "Why are you doing this?"

"Because I've lied to you since the day we met," Rupert said. "I do not deserve your trust or respect, but I need you to believe me now, and this seemed like the only way." He nodded up at the cockpit. "This ship is stocked with enough supplies to last two weeks. There are emergency clearances for all gates in known space in the navigational computer, and I've loaded the ship's petty cash account with a little over a million in Republic Scrip. You can access the money through the central control panel. The pass code is your birthday."

"How do you know my birthday?"

Rupert's lips curved in the ghost of a smile. "I looked it up."

My arm shot up, pointing the disrupter at his head. "What kind of game are you playing? You sound like you want me to shoot you and take your ship."

"You can if you choose," Rupert said, leaning back. "I've given you all the power, Devi. If you want, you can shoot my head off right now. This ship is fast and stealthy, and I've removed all the tracers from the security panel. Without those, even the Eyes will have trouble finding you."

I held the gun steady, keeping it trained on the spot between

261

his eyes. "Hell of a gamble you're making, Charkov. I've shot you before."

"You have," he agreed, his voice calm and clear, like we were discussing dinner plans and not his possible demise. "But I deserved it. And I couldn't think of any other way to convince you."

"Convince me of what?"

He looked straight at me, heart in his eyes. "That I am not your enemy."

My jaw fell slack. For a moment, I could only sit there staring like an idiot. And then I started to laugh.

CHAPTER
12

I laughed so hard I almost felt sick. I couldn't help it. After all the tension and fear and heartbreak, the idea that he could look at me and say that with a straight face was too much. Rupert watched me crack up with his usual blank hide-everything expression, but I could tell it was getting to him because his jaw was doing that tightening thing it did when he was upset. And that was what stopped my laughter. Not because I cared that he was upset, but because I couldn't believe he had the nerve to try playing this card *now*.

"You're not my enemy, eh?" I said, my lips peeling back in a snarl as I leveled the gun at his head again. "Well, you sure have a screwed-up way of showing it. If you didn't want me to think of you as an enemy, maybe you shouldn't have tried to capture me back in the woods. Or handed me to Caldswell after the phantom. Or forced me off a *cliff*."

"I have done you very wrong," Rupert agreed, raising his hands in surrender. "But you have to understand. At the time, I felt I had no choice. I'm an Eye. Everything I do is in the service of fighting the phantoms. If there was a chance you could be a breakthrough, even a small one, I could not let you go."

"But now you've changed your mind?" I snapped.

Rupert nodded. "Yes."

I stared at him a second longer, and then lowered the gun with a curse. "What the hell, Rupert?" I shouted. "I don't get you at all.

You can't really think all this posturing is going to make me forget what you are, what you *did*. Am I just supposed to buy that you had a change of heart? *Especially* now, when you just read the report about how I'm the phantom killer?"

"The report has nothing to do with it," Rupert said, his voice heating. "And I'm not *posturing*. I gave you that gun precisely because I knew you wouldn't believe me, but I prepared this ship because I wanted to give you a choice."

"*Choice?*" I roared. "Choice between *what*? Running like a coward until the Eyes hunt me down or giving up early and trotting off to the lab like a good little girl?"

For the first time since I'd seen him talking to the baron, Rupert's mask slipped. He lurched forward, eyes flashing with anger. "I'm trying to give you a chance to make your own decisions about your future," he said. "You think I'm not aware of what's at stake? That virus could be the end of the war I've fought my entire life. I should be dragging you back to Caldswell by your hair, but I won't. I *can't*. Because I love you, and I refuse to fight you anymore."

"You love me?" I shrieked. "You loved me when you shot me in the head! You loved me when you drove me off a cliff! If there's anything I've learned about your *love*, Charkov, it's that it only matters when it's convenient for *you*."

"And that's why I'm trying to make it right!" Rupert shouted, slamming his hands down on the bench so hard the steel frame bent.

The sound made us both jump. Rupert snatched his hands back at once, then rubbed them over his face. "I'm not lying to you, Devi," he said, his voice softer but not yet calm. "I know I've hurt you too much to ever make you believe that, but it's the truth." He blew out a long breath. "Can I tell you a story?"

I almost told him no, but that was just my anger talking. I was actually curious to hear what kind of story Rupert thought could make me trust him ever again. I rested the heavy gun on my lap and motioned for him to go ahead, but Rupert didn't start at once.

He'd been the one offering to talk, but now that he was on the spot, Rupert seemed hesitant. That was unusual. He was usually the decisive one, the man with the plan. Now, though, Rupert looked almost afraid, and I slowly realized that whatever story he was trying to tell me wasn't one he told often, or liked to tell at all.

"I've been an Eye for a long time," he said at last. "It was the only thing I ever wanted to be."

His words fell off again after that, so I prompted him. "How do you grow up wanting to be part of a secret organization?"

"I didn't grow up wanting it," he said quickly, squeezing his hands on his knees. "You've heard of what happened to Svenya?"

I nodded. Svenya was the Terran core world whose sudden destruction had alerted the universe to the real danger of phantoms, though the Eyes had covered up the true cause of its disappearance.

"Svenya was my home," Rupert went on. "I grew up there with my parents, my grandmother, and my sister."

"Tanya," I said.

Rupert flinched like her name hurt him. He was staring at the floor now, and with every word he spoke, his voice got tighter. "They came without warning," he said. "Tanya and I were on our way to school when the sirens went off. We thought it was an earthquake, but it went on and on. We tried to go home, but the soldiers stopped us. They said we had to evacuate."

I knew where this was going. I'd seen his memory, the soldiers tearing him away, Tanya screaming at him to go, but I couldn't bring myself to interrupt. Even though there were less than three feet between us, Rupert felt miles away. All I could do was sit and listen.

"There weren't enough ships for everyone," he went on. "The soldiers were keeping people back, trying to get the children out first. There was one spot left. Tanya made them give it to me. She said she was going to get our parents and they'd be on the next ship. She said she'd be right behind me."

"But there was no next ship," I said.

Rupert shook his head. "Five minutes after I got out, the whole planet started to crumble. No one else escaped."

He looked at me then, and I couldn't help flinching. There was no calm in his expression now, just a pain so old and deep it hurt to look at. "Everything I knew died that day," he said. "My family, my friends, my home, even my language, they were all gone. Svenya was a planet of billions. Only ten thousand of us survived."

As he spoke, I could see his memory clearly: young Rupert, standing by the window, looking out at the floating rocks that were all that was left of his home, his family. I could feel it, too, the incomprehension, the anger, the crushing feeling of being utterly alone. "How old were you?"

Rupert dropped his eyes. "Nine," he whispered. "I was nine."

I dropped my eyes as well, because what do you say to that? But as the silence stretched, I realized something was off. "Wait a second," I said. "Wasn't Svenya destroyed seventy years ago?"

Rupert didn't actually move, not that I could see, but I would have sworn his whole body tightened. "Sixty-three."

"So if you were nine…" I paused, doing the math in my head. "That would make you seventy-two."

"Seventy-one," he said, his voice suspiciously sharp. "My birthday isn't until next month."

I gaped at him. Rupert didn't look a day over thirty. "How the hell are you seventy-one years old?"

Rupert shifted his weight, clearly uncomfortable. "It's the symbiont," he explained, running a nervous hand through his hair. "If you survive the implantation, it can extend your life."

The age thing must really bother him, I realized. This was the most flustered I'd ever seen Rupert. If I hadn't been so angry at him, it would have been adorable. "How extended are we talking here?"

"No one knows for certain since we've never had a symbiont die of old age," Rupert said. "But there are some who are well over a hundred."

"So do you age at all?" I asked. "Like Caldswell. Did he get his symbiont late, or is he just really old?"

"Both," Rupert said. "Commander Caldswell had a decorated career before he became an Eye, but he looks exactly the same now as he did when he recruited me."

"So how did he find you?" I said. "Did they comb the survivors looking for likely recruits?" Considering how the Eyes treated the daughters, I wouldn't put it past them to recruit new soldiers from orphaned children with no one else to turn to. It would certainly explain why Rupert was so damn loyal.

Rupert must have suspected what I was getting at, because he glared at me. "Of course not," he said. "I couldn't even apply to the Eyes until I'd served a decade in the army. I knew about them because of the camp."

I frowned. "Camp?"

"After Svenya, they couldn't let us rejoin the Republic," he explained. "The emperor phantom was the one who actually destroyed the planet, but smaller phantoms always follow the larger. Svenya was crawling with the things at the end, and among those who escaped, nearly all of us had run into the invisible monsters at some point during the evacuation. The Eyes couldn't let those stories become public, so they took us to an uninhabited colony world at the very edge of the Republic and ordered us to stay there."

"I'm surprised they let you live," I said bitterly.

"There are those who think they shouldn't have," he admitted. "But even the Eyes didn't have the stomach to kill ten thousand terrified refugees, most of whom were children." He paused. "I guess it wasn't such a bad place, but honestly, I don't remember much from that time. I'd seen enough of the Eyes by then to know what they did, and I'd already decided I'd do whatever it took to become one. Caldswell himself signed the papers to get me out of the camp so I could join the army when I was seventeen. The Eyes didn't contact me again until ten years later, but when they did, I signed on at once. I've worked for them ever since."

I sighed. At least my early suspicions that Rupert had an army background had been on the mark. "So why the rush to be an Eye?" I asked. "Was it revenge?"

Rupert shook his head. "Tanya would hate me if I did what Eyes must do to avenge her death. She never held a grudge, ever. No, I became an Eye to make sure what happened to Tanya, what happened to me, never happened to anyone else ever again."

Now that he'd told me, I could see it. If there was one thing Rupert had a surfeit of, it was responsibility. But there was still one thing I didn't understand. That I'd never understood about Rupert from the moment I'd learned the truth of what the Eyes did. "I get why you wanted to stop the phantoms," I said. "But how could you do that to those poor girls? How could you use and kill the daughters?"

"Because it was worth it," he said. "Maat and her daughters are the only weapons we have against the phantoms, and phantoms destroy worlds. When you look at it that way, what is one girl's life? What is one family's pain weighed against the potential loss of billions?"

He said this quickly and calmly, like he was simply reciting facts, but I knew Rupert's bluffs pretty well at this point. I could see the tightness in his jaw, hear the too-quick clip of his words. I knew the truth.

"You hate it," I said.

Rupert's eyes widened, and then he dropped his head. "Of course I hate it," he whispered. "Do you have any idea what I've done?"

He stopped, running his hands over his face. Then, quickly, he looked up, meeting my eyes like a challenge. "I've killed twenty-two daughters over the course of my career. I've stolen girls from their homes and killed witnesses who were too compromised for a memory wipe. I've shot parents, grandparents, and children. I killed the man who'd been my partner for fifteen years when I caught him trying to run away with a daughter who'd begun to degrade. I shot him in the head while he was begging me to let him save her life, and then I shot the daughter as well. I didn't even hesitate."

When he'd started, he'd clearly been trying to shock me, but as Rupert listed his crimes, his voice grew thinner and thinner. By the time he finished, he wasn't even looking at me anymore. He was staring at his hands, which were fisted so tight I was amazed he hadn't broken something.

"I know it was for the greater good," he whispered. "That I did what had to be done. But when I look in the mirror, all I see is blood. I don't think Tanya would recognize me if she saw me now, and even if she did, she wouldn't call me brother."

He stopped there and took a long, shaky breath. His shoulders straightened as he pulled the air in, and I could almost see him pulling the calm back on as well, wrapping it around him like a protective mantle. When he looked at me again, his eyes were clear and still, like the last minute hadn't happened.

"Someone has to pay the price, Devi," he said solemnly. "The daughters don't get a choice, but I did. I chose to become an Eye knowing full well what it entailed."

"Because you can't change the past," I said.

"Because I can't let the past happen again," Rupert corrected.

I looked down at the disrupter pistol in my lap, thinking of my own family, my parents and sister. They'd driven me crazy every day of my life before I left for the army, especially my mom, but the thought of them vanishing, of Paradox crumbling—I couldn't even imagine it. With that in mind, I could see now why Rupert did what he did. But if the point of Rupert's story was to make our current situation make sense, he'd failed, because I was now more confused than ever.

"I don't understand," I said. "I'm the one who can end all of this."

"You could," Rupert agreed.

"Then what are you doing?" I cried, frustrated. "I'm your solution. If this virus can actually kill all the phantoms, that means you'd never have to shoot anyone ever again, so why would you let me run away?"

Rupert dropped his eyes to his left wrist, the one with the tattoo across it dedicating his life to Tanya. "Because I'm done hurting you."

I stared at him, uncomprehending, and Rupert sighed. "I've lived my whole life looking back at the past," he said softly. "After what happened on Svenya, I thought it didn't matter if I lived or died, didn't matter whom I killed. Even when I knew that what I was doing was unforgivably wrong, so long as I could look back and remember what was at stake, everything was justified. I could do anything, be as terrible as the Eyes needed me to be, and it wouldn't matter. All the good things in my life were safely locked away in those bright years before I lost my home, and without them, I was empty."

A sad smile drifted over his lips. "I liked it," he said. "Being empty, being cold. It made the hard things easier. But then, this year, everything changed."

"What happened?" I asked.

Rupert looked at me like I was crazy. "You did."

I jerked back. "Me? What do you mean me?"

Rupert smiled at me, and I nearly dropped his gun, because it was his real smile, the one I hadn't seen since before that wild kiss in the rain on Seni Major. The one he showed only to me.

"You made quite an impression," he admitted. "After you put Cotter in his place before we'd even left Paradox, I started watching you. I couldn't help it. You were the craziest, bravest, loveliest thing I'd ever seen, and I knew at once that I should keep my distance. I even argued with Caldswell when he ordered me to flirt with you because I knew I wouldn't be acting." His look grew sheepish. "I'd never argued with an officer before."

I couldn't help chuckling at that. "Old man should have listened."

"It wouldn't have changed anything if he had," Rupert said. "I would have done it anyway."

He looked down again, and I swore a blush spread over his face.

"I invented reasons to spend time with you. Before, cooking was just something I did. But when you watched me, when you told me you liked the food I made, I really enjoyed it. It made me happy. Before I met you, I couldn't have said the last time I felt that way about anything."

He blew out a deep breath. "I was appalled by my selfishness. This life, *my* life was supposed to be for Tanya. A life of duty to honor what she'd sacrificed so I could live. Before I met you, that's what I was: an Eye, a soldier. But when we were together, you were what I thought about, and even when you were gone, you stayed with me."

He paused, running his hands through his hair. "At first, I couldn't understand why. You ruined my calm, disrupted me. You even made me lose my temper."

As though on cue, we both looked at the dent where his hand had landed earlier, and Rupert shook his head.

"I told myself I should hate you," he said. "I tried to, actually, but I never could manage it. Even when I was furious at you, you delighted me. I knew I was being unforgivably reckless, that it would be better for everyone if I could just leave you alone, but I kept finding excuses to stay. I wanted to spend more time with you, not less. I wanted—"

He cut off suddenly, scowling like he was trying to find the right words, and even though I knew it was pathetic, I held my breath, waiting.

"You made me want a future," he said at last. "For the first time since I'd lost my family, I started looking forward instead of back. Even after I took your memories and made you hate me, just knowing you were still there, still safe, it made me hopeful. I didn't even realize how much until Caldswell put the gun in my hand and told me to shoot you."

I winced. Even though I'd been there myself, hearing him say it out loud was like a punch in the stomach. But Rupert wasn't finished.

"I've always believed there was nothing I wouldn't do to stop the phantoms," he said. "For sixty-three years, that's been my pride. The heart of my control. When you were on your knees in front of me, I knew it was the ultimate test of my resolve. But it wasn't until I passed that I began to realize just how badly I'd failed."

Rupert looked at me for a moment, and then he slid off the bench, landing on his knees on the floor in front of me. I still had his disrupter pistol, but he seemed to have forgotten the gun entirely as he bowed down and pressed his lips against the back of my free hand.

"I failed," he whispered into my skin. "Failed you, failed the Eyes. I thought I could go back. I thought if I returned to being a good soldier, everything I'd done to you would be justified. A sacrifice to the greater good, just like all my other sins. But I was wrong. There was one thing I couldn't do to stop the phantoms, one person I couldn't sacrifice, and I didn't even realize it until I'd already thrown her away."

With each word, his voice got hoarser, and when he finally looked up, there was no trace of his cold mask left. Only Rupert, staring at me like he was trying to make me believe him through sheer will.

"I can't do it anymore, Devi," he said. "The moment you jumped off that cliff to get away from me, I finally understood. I don't care what that virus of yours can do, I don't care if you're the one who can save the universe, I can't hurt you again. That's why, when the order came down to bring you in, I prepared this ship so you could run instead. I know it's too little, too late, but I wanted you to have the final choice." He bowed his head over my hand. "I wanted to do right by you this last time."

I didn't like the way he said that. "And if I run, what will happen to you?"

Rupert shrugged. "I'm not sure. A court-martial, certainly, though whether or not they kill me after depends on my symbiont. They might decide I'm too expensive to shoot."

His calm tone was giving me the jeebies. No one should be that blasé about their own death. But when I opened my mouth to say so, Rupert cut me off with a sad smile.

"It doesn't matter," he said. "I'd rather die helping you today than live another seventy years knowing I let you down again."

He reached up as he spoke, taking my hand just like I'd taken his the night I'd found him drinking alone. "I'd like to look forward with you, even if it's only for a little while," he whispered. "But I won't ever help them take your freedom away again. I'm sorry I did it the first time. I'm sorry for everything." He closed his eyes, his face stricken. "I am so, so sorry, Devi."

I'm not normally a fan of apologies. I've always believed that you should own your actions, good and bad, but this was different. Rupert wasn't trying to get away with anything. I could hear it in his voice. He truly believed he'd done me wrong. I believed it, too, but I couldn't work up the usual anger. It was impossible to be angry in the face of such sincerity, but I wasn't sure what else to do.

Forgiving him felt like a cheat. I'd loved this man, and he'd betrayed me. He'd also saved my life. He'd fought me, but he'd never tried for a lethal blow. In the end, neither had I. Even when the cold rage had me by the throat, I hadn't gone that far, which was a big deal for me. I'm not exactly known for my mercy or coolheadedness. Even now, after everything that had happened, I didn't hate him. I couldn't, because deep down, I'd never really stopped loving him.

That realization came as a shock, though it really shouldn't have. Love was what had made his betrayal in the woods hurt so bad, and why I hadn't been able to finish the job even in the cold rage. The more I thought about it, the more I suspected I'd already forgiven him, which was even greater proof of how soft love had made me than my inability to shoot him now. But no amount of softness or forgiveness changed the truth of our situation, or the fact that I could never trust Rupert again.

That said, though, I wasn't cruel enough to leave him hanging. Especially not when he looked so damn miserable about it.

"Apology accepted," I said, flipping his disrupter and offering him the grip.

That was clearly not the answer Rupert had been expecting. "But," he said, "I shot you."

"I shot you first," I reminded him, setting his pistol on the bench since he clearly wasn't going to take it. "Actually, if we're keeping score, I'm way ahead. I've got a head shot, a gut wound, and a near beheading on you. Oh, and I chopped off your claws. *And* I was planning on drowning you in that lake. You're only at one head shot, and that wasn't even real."

Rupert stared at me in shock for another few seconds, and then he shook his head. "Only you could make this into a competition."

His exasperation almost made me smile. I liked that I was the only one who could baffle and frustrate him like this. Nice as it was, though, I squashed the warm feeling ruthlessly. Never trusting Rupert again was just common sense, but refusing to let myself like him was a matter of self-preservation.

I'd never been in love before Rupert, but the little taste I'd gotten had been even worse than I'd imagined. The man turned me into an emotional idiot, taking fool risks like that letter to Anthony, or the time I'd nearly gotten myself killed shooting that symbiont off him when he'd been busy fighting Brenton. Back when I'd only had my own life to worry about, the gamble had seemed worth it. Now, though, there was simply too much at stake.

It was funny, but I hadn't actually realized how committed I was to my new course until Rupert had offered me an out. Now, though, I understood. Defeat didn't change anything. My king might have given me away, but that didn't absolve me of my oaths to Maat or Rashid, or to myself. I would never be a Devastator or a Royal Knight, but so long as the virus lurked under my skin, I still had a duty. I still had my honor, and if I wanted to keep it, it didn't matter if Rupert was telling the truth or not, I couldn't let him make me foolish or weak ever again.

I took a deep breath and looked at Rupert, holding his eyes as I pulled my hand firmly out of his. "I appreciate what you tried to do for me," I said, folding my arms over my chest. "But I'm done running. You're supposed to take me back to Caldswell now, right?"

Rupert lowered his empty hands with a sigh. "Yes, but—"

"Take me there."

Rupert paled, and I braced for an argument. In the end, though, he didn't say a word, and that made me deeply suspicious.

"Aren't you going to try to talk me out of it?" I asked, narrowing my eyes. "Or is this what you really wanted all along?"

He actually had the gall to smile at me. "All I want is for you to trust me again. I don't get that by saying something is your choice only to bicker when you don't decide the way I like. Though, if you're asking, I'm just happy you didn't shoot me."

I opened my mouth to say I'd never let him off so easy, but that was a bit too much like flirting for the new distance I was determined to maintain, so I said nothing. But though I was giving him a cold shoulder to rival Io5's blizzards, Rupert's little smile didn't fade as he rose from his knees and walked to the cockpit.

"Caldswell's docked just a bit north of here," he said as he started the ship. "He didn't want to risk alerting Brenton's people by bringing the *Fool* to a major starport. It's not far, though. Once I get us up, we'll be there in five minutes."

That was much less time than I'd expected, but maybe the crunched schedule was a blessing. From the moment I'd decided not to run, a plan had been forming in my mind, one of those dangerous, crazy gambits that I'd talk myself out of if I strewed on it too long. I couldn't afford to chicken out now, though, so I stopped thinking about what was coming and focused on my armor.

The temporary case they'd given me at the embassy wasn't a patch on my real one. That was a state-of-the-art armor-care system; this was a metal box with some foam in it. Still, it had held my suit well enough, and even with the pieces jumbled, I was able to get everything together again in short order.

Thanks to the refactoring job, my armor was cleaner than it had been in weeks. It was also fully charged and repaired, and putting it back on made me feel better than I had in a long time. I locked my reloaded guns in next, checking Sasha especially carefully to make sure she'd be ready the moment I touched her. When I was satisfied, I locked my anti-armor pistol into her holster and joined Rupert in the cockpit.

"I always forget how fast you can do that," he said, glancing at my armor as I dropped into the navigator's chair.

I shrugged off the implied compliment. "Years of practice."

Rupert nodded and returned his gaze to the skyline. "You have a plan."

It wasn't a question, so I didn't answer. Not telling Rupert was actually a large part of my plan. I needed him to be as surprised as Caldswell if I was going to have a prayer. I was about to change the subject when I spotted our destination.

The dock Caldswell had chosen for our rendezvous was a commuter starport in a large, affluent suburb of Montblanc's capital. It was a pretty small operation, though considering the dirt lots and grassy fields the *Fool* usually landed on, I supposed an actual tarmac was a step up. There was only one elevated dock, so I had no problem picking out the *Fool*'s boxy shape. As we got closer, I spotted Caldswell standing at the platform's edge, watching our approach like he meant to glare us out of the sky. I was glaring back when I felt something land on my arm.

I looked down just in time to see Rupert's hand slide over mine. "Remember," he said softly, "I'm on your side now. Whether you believe it or not, nothing changes that."

I didn't trust him enough to believe, but I'd already squeezed his hand back before I'd realized what I was doing. A smile flashed over his face at the pressure, and then it was gone as he removed his hand from mine for the final descent.

Just like Brenton's, Rupert's ship landed softly as a butterfly. Caldswell was already jogging toward us across the landing zone before Rupert cut the thrusters, so I hopped up as well, positioning myself at the exit just in time to savor the sight of the captain's shock when the door slid up to reveal me in full armor, standing ready to greet him.

To his credit, Caldswell recovered in seconds. "Decided to be civil, Morris?"

"Decided not to run, Caldswell," I replied.

My lack of proper address earned me a sharp look. I met it with one of my own. He wasn't my captain anymore; like hell was I calling him sir.

When it was clear I wasn't going to bend, Caldswell switched to Rupert. "I've lined things up with the gate already. We're jumping as soon as we get in range of the scanners. Lock up here and join us when you're done. I'll take the merc."

"Actually," I said, "I've got something I'd like to talk to you about first."

Caldswell shot me a dirty look. "So talk on the way," he said. "You've wasted enough of our time already."

"No," I said, pulling Sasha out of her holster. "We're talking now."

And then I pressed my gun to my head.

Rupert and Caldswell both went still. I could see panic on Rupert's face through my rear cam and fury on Caldswell's through my main, but I didn't move a muscle. Fear is an animal game, and so I stayed perfectly still, giving both men time to process exactly what was at stake.

"This gun is pointed at the last surviving strain of Stoneclaw's phantom killing plasmex virus," I said, tapping Sasha's barrel lightly against the side of my visor. "All the safeties on my suit are turned off. If you try anything, my anti-armor rounds will rip through my helmet, killing me instantly. So, now that you know I'm serious, I'd like to discuss my terms."

"*Devi!*" Rupert's hiss was a mix of anger and fear, but Caldswell put up his hand, cutting him off.

"What did you have in mind?"

I hadn't actually had time to think about how best to put this, but if there was one thing Caldswell and I shared, it was an appreciation for saying things straight, so that was what I did.

"I don't like you," I said. "I don't like how you use Maat, and I don't like how you treat the daughters. I don't like how you operate in general, paying for the safety of everyone with the suffering of a few. And you can save the 'it was the only way' excuse," I added when Caldswell opened his mouth. "I've heard it. I understand why you do what you do, I just don't agree."

Caldswell's face went red, but just when I thought he was about to explode, he took a long breath. "Fine, Morris," he said, leaning on the ship's door. "What *would* you like?"

I smiled. Straight to the chase, that was Caldswell. "Here's my deal," I said. "I'll come along today without a fight. I'll let your people poke and prod and do whatever it is they have to do to get the virus working like it should, but in return, I want you to free the daughters and Maat."

"You know we can't do that," Caldswell said. "Be reasonable, Morris. We don't know if Stoneclaw's virus will ever be stable enough to use safely. We can't free the only weapons we have on the slim hope of maybe getting a new one."

"Can't or won't?" I said, arching an eyebrow. "I'm not asking you to free everyone right now. I'm just saying that when you know the virus works, you let them go."

Caldswell blew out a long breath. "You do realize I'm not actually in charge of the Eyes, right?"

"Brenton said you were second in command."

Caldswell's eyes narrowed at Brenton's name, but he didn't deny it. All he said was, "Second's a long way from first."

I shrugged. "So? You're a stubborn bastard. Are you saying you couldn't make it happen?"

"That's exactly what I'm saying," Caldswell replied. "Even if the phantoms all vanished tomorrow, the daughters couldn't go free. Can you imagine what would happen if someone took one to the press? We get funding from every major government. If people found out their taxes were going to this, it won't matter how many phantoms we've saved them from. There'd be a lynch mob."

Now it was my turn to get mad. "How is that the daughters' fault?" I cried. "They're the victims here, not you or your politicians. So you can save the excuses, unless you don't really care about finding a new solution?" And to make sure my point was perfectly clear, I started squeezing my finger on the trigger.

"Stop," Caldswell said, putting up his hands. I stopped, but I didn't ease my finger back, and Caldswell shoved his hands up to tug them through his graying hair.

"You can demand all you want," he said. "I can't do miracles. I don't know what Brenton told you, but the girls who go to Maat don't come back. Even if we returned them to their parents, there's nothing left of the girls they used to be."

"Then how did Ren remember her father?" I demanded. "There's *something* there, and you know it. All I want is for you to help me get it back."

Caldswell gave me a murderous look, but I just smirked at him. "You can cut the party-line crap," I said. "You play heartless, but I've got you, Brian Caldswell. I've been part of your crew, remember? Basil nearly took my face off when I spoke ill of you, and that kind of loyalty doesn't come for free. You should have killed me five times over, but you didn't. I don't think you like killing anyone. Brenton told me once that you stock your ship with useful pawns you can spend on power, but he was the one who threw people away. You, on the other hand, bend over backward to keep them."

"And *you* are making a lot of assumptions," Caldswell snapped. "Don't get your hopes up, Morris. Just because I didn't kill you doesn't make me a nice man. I've been a loyal Eye for longer than you've been alive, and I've shot a lot more girls than Charkov back there."

I shook my head. "I never said you were nice. In fact, I'm pretty sure I've said you're an overbearing bastard of a captain. But you're also a fair one who was honest with me when it would have been a lot easier not to be. I think you're actually more excited than anyone at the idea of finally finding a real solution to this phantom business. After all, you were the one who was ready to send me to the lab on the slight off chance I could be useful, and you were the one who bounded up to the ship like an overeager dog just now."

Caldswell glared at me a second more, and then he dropped his head with a sound that was halfway between a laugh and a curse.

"You certainly do come in guns blazing," he muttered, crossing his arms over his chest. "Fine, Morris, you want the truth? I hate this bullshit more than Brenton does. But unlike John, I'm a realist. Yes, the system is awful, but it's what we have. For seventy years, that's been the cold, hard truth. But now here you come with your golden ticket, and even though I know it's stupid to get my hopes up, I want to believe you're our miracle so bad it hurts."

He stepped closer, eyes on the gun that was still pressed against my helmet. "You want promises?" he said. "You got 'em. Come with us without trouble, and I'll swear whatever oath you want that the moment your virus proves viable, I'll do everything in my power to free the daughters to your satisfaction. I'll break them out myself if need be. Just please, for pity's sake, stop pointing that cannon at my last hope, would you?"

I didn't move Sasha an inch. "And Maat," I said. "I made her a promise. She goes free as well."

Something went dark behind Caldswell's eyes. "No," he said softly. "Everyone else can go, but not her."

I narrowed my eyes. "Maat too."

"We can't," Caldswell said. "She's mad, and she hates us."

"Maybe if you didn't treat her so badly, she wouldn't hate you so much."

Caldswell didn't budge. "If we let her go free, there's no telling how much damage she could do getting her revenge."

"She doesn't want revenge!" Actually, I wasn't sure about that, but I was reasonably certain that given a choice between freedom and payback, Maat would take the out. "Look, I know she's crazy. I've talked to her, it's kind of hard to miss, but she's not beyond reason. She just wants the pain to stop."

"She wants to kill us all," Caldswell snapped. "You know more about phantoms than most Eyes do by this point, Morris, but you still don't understand just how deep this rabbit hole goes. Even if Maat was sane, we couldn't let her go. I can't say more than that without forcing Charkov back there to shoot me, so you'll have to trust me when I tell you that our current problems are *nothing* compared to what could happen if Maat was allowed to have her way. And don't bother wasting time on more threats. I'd let you blow your brains out and lose the virus forever before I'd even lie about promising to set Maat free."

If I'd thought that was a bluff, I would have tried to call him on it, but Caldswell wasn't nearly as good at faking as Rupert, and I could see plainly that he was deadly serious. Unfortunately, his determination left me in a predicament. This wasn't just a question of right and wrong; I owed Maat for getting me out, and I paid my debts. But I'd played almost all my cards now, and Caldswell clearly wasn't going to be swayed. If I kept pushing, I could end up with nothing, so as much as I hated to do it, I decided it was time to cut my losses.

"The daughters go free," I said. "They get rehabilitated, go back to their families, and no more will ever be made. I also want amnesty for the Eyes if they want to leave, no more lifelong servitude."

I kept my eyes on Caldswell as I said this, but I was watching Rupert through my rear cam. He was too good to let any emotion show on his face, but I saw his breath hitch, and I had to suppress my smile. I wasn't doing this because I liked him, of course. This was just payment for all he'd risked to give me a choice earlier. Now he had an out, too, which made us even. Besides, so long as I was pointing a gun at my head to help others, I might as well grab as many concessions as I could.

"Daughters and Eyes," Caldswell said with a sharp nod. "Anything else?"

"Yes," I said. "I want to avoid destroying all the phantoms if possible."

Caldswell's stern expression collapsed into confusion. "What?"

"They're not monsters," I said firmly. "They don't mean to hurt us, they just blunder into planets because it's their nature."

"So you're going to give us the virus that kills phantoms on the condition we don't kill phantoms?" Caldswell said, putting his fists on his hips. "Are you out of your damn mind?"

"I understand you'll have to kill some of them," I said. "I'm just saying we shouldn't slaughter their entire species. When a wolf comes into your field and kills your sheep, you shoot it. You don't go out and massacre all wolves." Caldswell was still giving me the stink eye, but the poor trapped phantom's plaintive whimpers kept echoing in my head, and I wasn't going to budge. "I don't know what phantoms are," I admitted. "But they're not evil, and they don't deserve to die just for sharing the same space we do."

"A Paradoxian environmentalist," Caldswell muttered, rolling his eyes. "Now I've seen everything. Fine, I'll try to make sure whatever weapon we get out of you only kills bad phantoms. Good enough?"

When I nodded, he held up his hand, counting off on his fingers. "So we've got free the daughters and stop the creation of new ones, amnesty for Eyes who want to leave, and targeted phantom killing. And now I'm afraid to ask, but is there anything else?"

"Yes," I said. "There's the matter of how I can be sure you're going to keep your promises once I lower this gun."

Caldswell looked nonplussed. "I suppose my word as a gentleman doesn't cut it?"

"Not even if you were a gentleman," I said, shaking my head.

"Then we're at an impasse," Caldswell replied. "You can't walk around with that gun to your head forever."

"You're right," I said. "But I don't have to."

I looked Caldswell straight in the eye, and then, slowly, I lowered Sasha. Caldswell watched me like a hunting hawk, but he didn't move a muscle even when I returned my gun to my holster. I let him look. I was about to play my final and biggest card.

Even though I'd told Baron Kells almost everything, I hadn't been able to explain what had happened in the darkness after I killed the phantom. I still couldn't explain it fully, but I'd gotten the general gist. Enough to play the most epic bluff of my life.

"I can call the lelgis," I said. "They're looking for the virus right now. They already killed off an entire xith'cal clan trying to destroy it, and I doubt they'd stop at eliminating you, too, if they thought it would do the trick. Right now I'm safe because they don't know where I am, but I know how to let them find me, and if I ever think you're double-crossing me, that's exactly what I'll do."

I didn't know if any of that was actually true, but I must have been convincing enough, because Caldswell was looking at me like he'd never seen me before. "You don't know what you're messing with," he said angrily. "The lelgis don't operate by our logic. If you bring them into this, you'll start a war that will kill far more than any phantom."

"Then you'd better keep your word," I said, lifting my chin.

The captain stared at me a moment longer, and then his shoulders began to shake. It was so unexpected, it actually took me several seconds to realize Caldswell was laughing. "You are one crazy piece of work, Deviana Morris," he said, breaking into a grin. "I knew there was a reason I liked you. Fine, fine, you win. I don't have the stomach to play in your league."

I smiled back. "Does that mean we have a deal?"

"We do, indeed," Caldswell said, sticking out his hand. I took it and shook hard. If Caldswell had been anything other than a symbiont, I would have crushed his fingers, but he was a tough old bastard, and he just grinned wider.

"Pack up here and meet us on the *Fool*, Charkov," he ordered, motioning for me to go ahead down the ramp. "I'll see you in my office as soon as we enter the jump."

"Yes sir," Rupert said. The reply sounded normal, but when I glanced back at Rupert through my rear cam, his face was defiant.

That seemed to throw Caldswell as well. He stared at Rupert for a moment before shaking his head and turning to follow me down the ramp. "You are a terrible influence on him," he said as we started across the tarmac toward the *Fool*. "Ruined one of my best Eyes."

I could tell he meant that as a joke, but my mouth pressed into a thin line. "If anything ruined Rupert as an Eye, it was you when you made him shoot me."

Caldswell stopped short, and then, to my surprise, the captain's shoulders fell. "Fair point," he muttered, picking up the pace again. I followed a few steps behind, too shocked at hearing Caldswell admit I was right to push any further.

The *Glorious Fool* looked just like always, and no worse for wear for her adventures. The dents the emperor phantom had put in the hull had all been hammered out, and they'd even replaced the captain's window that Maat had blown off to free me. The ramp was down and the cargo bay doors were open, showing the empty hold. Nothing new there, either. I was about to ask Caldswell why he even bothered pretending to ship things when I spotted Mabel leaning against the *Fool*'s ramp.

She also looked unchanged, even had the nerve to flash me her usual carefree grin as the captain and I came closer. "Welcome back," she said, like I'd just been out on shore leave instead of running for my life. "Enjoy your getaway?"

I opened my mouth to say something nasty, but Caldswell cut me off. "Get the engines warmed up," he ordered. "I want off this rock the second Rupert is ready."

"Yes, captain," Mabel said, hopping up onto the ramp as nimbly as a cat.

I watched her go with a scowl. "So is she really your sister-in-law?"

"No," Caldswell said. "But I was good friends with her husband before he died."

I blinked. "Eyes have husbands?"

"Not officially," Caldswell said. "But so long as they keep it inside the organization and it doesn't affect their work, I let it slide."

I shook my head. Caldswell really was a romantic. Before I could call him on it, though, he smacked me on the shoulder. "Mind your mouth," he warned as we walked into the *Fool*. "We're not an open secret yet."

I was about to ask him how much the crew did know when I spotted a pale blur coming down the stairs from the lounge. I turned to face whatever it was just in time for Nova to slam into me.

She was so light I barely felt her hit, but I was happy all the same. "Oh, Deviana!" she cried, hugging me tight. "We were so worried!"

I had no idea what story Caldswell had fed the crew about my disappearance, but I wasn't about to disabuse her of it. The lie was likely keeping her safe, and damned if I was going to mess that up. "I'm fine," I said, carefully hugging her back. "Sorry to worry you."

Nova beamed at me, and I winced. She looked way too much like her brother when she did that, and I didn't want to think about poor Copernicus at the moment. I opened my mouth to ask her how the ship was doing instead, but I never got the words out, because at that moment sirens erupted across the space dock.

The *Fool*'s alarm joined them a few seconds later, as did alarms from all the ships on the docks around us. The racket was so loud I had to cut my speakers before I could concentrate enough to swirl my cameras for the threat that could possibly cause so much noise. Since everything was blaring at once, my money was on natural disaster. Earthquake, tornado, something like that. But the ground was still and the sky was clear. So clear, in fact, that I could see the enormous shadows blinking out of hyperspace into orbit overhead.

There were so many, it took me a second to realize that the huge shapes were xith'cal tribe ships. Dozens of them. That was all I had time to process before the alarms stopped, and in the silence, the deepest xith'cal voice I'd ever heard began to boom from every speaker on the planet.

CHAPTER
13

It sounded like someone was tearing a whole scrap yard full of junk metal in half. The xith'cal's voice was rhythmic and sharp, clearly a command, but since I didn't speak lizard, I had no idea what it said. But the sound wasn't all there was to the message. My suit was beeping at me, dragging my attention to Montblanc's emergency channel, which had popped up when the alarms went off.

I was immediately sorry. The xith'cal's voice had been bad enough, but actually seeing the monster it belonged to made my insides flip-flop. The damn thing was *huge*. Not even normal lizard levels of huge, I mean he was the size of a tank. Even sitting, he towered over the warriors that flanked him on either side. The sight was so imposing that I actually had trouble dragging my eyes away to read the translated text scrolling across the bottom of the screen.

. . . surrounded in a blockade. We have destroyed the pathetic protections you called a defense grid and taken over all your emergency channels. Any ships attempting to flee will be destroyed before they can reach orbit. There is no hope of rescue or escape. You are now the cornered prey of Reaper, mightiest of all the xith'cal tribes, and what Reaper takes, Reaper keeps.

As the huge xith'cal finished, the warriors around him roared, and I began to shake in earnest. I'd never seen a picture of Reaper, but I had no reason to doubt the huge xith'cal was who he claimed to be, or that he was telling the truth. Reaper's name was feared throughout the galaxy for a reason. If he said there was no escape, then there wasn't. But even as my breathing started to speed up, I realized Reaper wasn't finished.

But I have no interest in such weak hunting, the xith'cal said. *There is still a chance to buy your lives back. Bring this female to me, and you may yet be spared.*

My stomach shrank to a tiny ball of ice. No. He couldn't be talking about—

My picture appeared on the screen. I was in my armor, walking through the hangar of the xith'cal asteroid. The shot had been enhanced to show as much of my face as possible through my downed visor. It still wasn't much, but then, seeing my face wasn't really necessary. My custom mist-silver Verdemont armor was a dead giveaway.

You have one hour, Reaper continued, his deep voice grating against my ears. *If the female is not surrendered by then, I will destroy a city every ten minutes until your entire planet is burned to ash. This is the only warning you will receive.*

The transmission cut off with a crack, leaving my picture blown up across the screen. I was still staring dumbly at my own face when Caldswell's hand hit my back, shoving my four hundred pound armored body toward the cargo bay stairs. "*Go!*" he shouted.

I was about to ask him where when I realized he wasn't shouting at me. He was yelling into his com, and Basil, who must have been on the other end, responded by firing the engine so hard the ship bucked. My suit took the lurch in stride. I didn't even have to slow down as I shot up the stairs after Caldswell.

"You can't be serious!" I shouted. "Didn't you hear what Reaper said?"

"Why the hell do you think I'm in such a hurry?" Caldswell snapped, breaking into a run when he reached the hall.

"He's going to genocide the planet," I said, hot on his heels. Montblanc might not be a core world, but it was still a huge colony with close to a billion people, all of whom were going to die if I didn't go to Reaper. "We can't just run!"

Caldswell stopped like he'd hit a wall and spun around. "We can and we are!" he shouted at me. "Don't you get it by now, Morris? Your plasmex bug is the key to preserving the whole of human civilization. You think I'm going to hand that over just to save one planet?"

I blinked at him, but the captain was already on the move again. "You want to be a martyr, you'll get your chance, but not here. Now come on."

I obeyed more out of habit than anything else. "We're going to get shot down," I said as we ran onto the bridge.

"Not if we get the lead out," Caldswell replied, vaulting over the rail to land in his captain's chair. "Speaking of which, why aren't we up yet, Basil?"

"Getting there, sir!" Basil cried. The aeon was in his pilot's nest, feathers puffed in agitation as he punched the engine controls with both feet and one wing claw. "We were still on the warm-up cycle when—"

"Just get us in the air," Caldswell said, cutting him off. "Nova, get ready to jump on my mark. Morris, hold on."

I hadn't even realized Nova had followed us until I saw her strapping herself into her tall chair with one hand while the other began punching numbers into the hyperdrive. Halfway through she gave up and started typing with both hands, but her harness kept buckling, the straps clicking together on their own. Plasmex, I realized belatedly, grabbing one of the bridge's many rails. Good thing, too, because a second later, Basil stomped the thrusters, and the *Fool* popped off the ground like a cork.

We weren't alone. Despite Reaper's warning, the air was suddenly full of ships as anyone who could scrambled to get off-world. We narrowly missed getting hit as another ship blasted into the air right behind us, and I had to hold tight as Basil rolled us port side, cursing at the top of his lungs.

"What did you do anyway?" he squawked, turning his head completely around to glare at me.

I opened my mouth to say this wasn't my idea, but Caldswell beat me to it.

"Just get us out," he ordered, buckling his harness.

Through the large windows of the redone bridge, I could see the ships all around us like an enormous school of metal fish. I couldn't remember ever seeing so many ships in the air at the same time before. But as we got higher and the atmosphere thinned, the tribe ships came into view, along with the fleet they'd brought with them, and suddenly, our rush didn't feel so big anymore.

"Sacred King," I muttered, eyes going wide as my suit's system counted the ships I could see. And counted. And counted. "Did Reaper bring his whole damn tribe?"

"We're not going to stick around to find out," Caldswell said. "Nova, I want a jump the second we're out of the planet's gravity well."

"But, captain." Nova's voice was so tiny I could barely hear it. "I don't even have the variables from the gate yet. We might—"

"Just do your best," Caldswell said. "One-minute jump, just enough to get us out."

"Yes sir," Nova whispered as she resumed typing frantic equations on the hyperdrive screen.

"Thirty seconds until we clear the atmosphere," Basil announced, his whistling voice frantic. "And...we've got a missile lock."

"Dodge it," Caldswell ordered. "We just need to get far enough to jump."

Basil ducked his head and hit the throttle. I grabbed the rail as the *Fool* banked hard, sending the stars I could now see clearly through the window spinning. We'd barely moved when the white tail of a missile shot past, missing us by less than a foot. A second later, a blast wave rocked the *Fool* as the cruiser below us exploded. My stabilizer took the bump in stride, but I sank to my knees anyway, hugging the bridge railing for dear life. Above us, the glare from Montblanc's sun had vanished, eaten by the enormous shadow of a tribe ship as it moved over our heads.

"Sir?" Basil said, his yellow eyes huge.

"Stick to the plan!" Caldswell ordered. "How long until we can jump?"

"Five seconds," Nova announced, her dreamy voice strained to a tiny thread. "Starting spin up."

As she said it, I felt the hum of the hyperdrive coil spinning to life, and not a second too soon. Above us, the huge dark shape of the tribe ship was firing on the escaping ships, shooting each one down with a volley from its thousands of missile batteries. I watched in a sort of horrified trance as whole waves of ships went down like sparks from a firework.

The sheer scale of the destruction was actually hard to get my head around. I'd never seen a tribe ship in action before. Now I finally understood why they were so feared. Nothing could stand up to that sort of firepower. The only reason we were still alive was because there were so many ships in the sky. Even a tribe ship took a few seconds to chew through that kind of target density. I just prayed a few seconds would be enough.

"Battleship coming up starboard," Basil said, head swiveling toward the glowing icon of the huge red ship flying through the projected map that surrounded his station. "Fast."

For the first time in this whole crazy flight, Caldswell paled. "Jump us now, Nova."

"Jump in three," she said, her pale hands hovering over the jump button as the coil spun faster and faster. "Two. One—"

The *Fool* jerked hard enough to throw me even with my stabilizer. My suit caught me with a roll, but I wouldn't have cared if I'd face-planted. I'd never been so happy to feel the bump into hyperspace in all my life. But as I righted myself, I realized something was wrong. There'd been no flash, no feeling of leaving dimensions, and this was certainly not the hyperspace stillness. Exactly the opposite—the whole ship was shaking, and I looked up to see the sky fill with explosions as the tribe ship fired.

"What was that?" Caldswell shouted.

"Something hit the coil!" Nova cried, her eternal calm slipping. "It's a line of some kind."

"A line?" I grunted, rolling to my feet.

No one answered; they were all staring at the main screen. I looked too, and my stomach sank to the floor. Up on the monitor was a shot from one of the rear cameras showing our hyperdrive coil, or what was left of it. The delicate machine had been skewered by a giant barbed harpoon attached to a metal cable as thick as my leg. At the other end was a xith'cal warship four times the *Fool*'s size. For a moment we both sat there, and then the *Fool* shuddered as they began to reel us in.

Caldswell cursed and hit a red button on his console. A second later, the *Fool*'s rear cannon fired, but it did no good. The shell stuck in the battleship's heavy shields like a splinter. Caldswell didn't even bother with a second shot. He jumped out of his chair and started for the bridge door. "Prepare for boarding," he announced.

That was music to my ears. Standing there, watching the fight in the sky, I'd been terrified. It had been so huge, so out of my control, but a boarding party was my game. Shooting xith'cal I could do.

But when I ran into the hall after the captain, Caldswell stopped and put out his hand. "Not on your life, Morris," he snarled. "I didn't just slag my ship so you could get shot by some rank-and-file xith'cal raider."

"Don't be stupid," I said. "What am I supposed to do? Hide in the—"

A huge pulse went through the ship, and my suit went dark. For a moment, I thought it was a phantom, but then I realized I was getting too fancy. That was a good old-fashioned EMP. The lizards had fried our ship.

By the time I had the Lady back on line, Caldswell was at the other end of the hall, and Rupert was with him.

After Reaper's message, I'd been too busy to wonder where Rupert was, but apparently he'd made it back to the ship just fine, and he'd been busy. He was standing beside the captain with two giant weapon cases in his hands. Both looked heavier than my suit could handle one-handed, and the front of each was neatly stenciled with the letters ATSM.

My breath caught. Anti-tank strategic missiles. Now *those* we could use. But before I could get close enough to ask what the plan was, the captain gave what looked like a final order and Rupert turned and ran, hefting the huge cases like they were full of straw as he swept down the spiral stair to the *Fool*'s lower level.

"Please tell me that's your trump card," I said, running up to the captain.

"Afraid I'm all out of those. We're playing this by ear now." He shot me a grim look and pulled out his com. When he spoke again, his voice sounded over the ship's system and in my helmet. "All hands to the cargo bay. Bring no arms. Prepare for surrender."

Excitement turned to horror as I watched the captain close his com and stick it back in his pocket. "You can't be serious."

"As a heart attack," Caldswell replied, walking into the lounge.

"I am not surrendering."

Caldswell didn't even dignify that with a look. "You'll do as I say. Use your head, Morris. We're caught tight. If we fight, we'll just end up caught and dead. So we're going to make the most of a bad situation. I need you to follow my orders exactly with no back talk, agreed?"

I didn't, but I also knew I couldn't take an entire xith'cal tribe by myself. So, grudgingly, I took my hands off my guns and followed the captain into the lounge.

By this point, Basil and Nova were right behind us. Hyrek was already there, waiting by the kitchen. Our xith'cal looked almost gray with fear under the orange emergency lights, but like everyone else, he was composed as he greeted the captain with a respectful nod. Rupert was nowhere to be seen, but that was to be expected. I just hoped he was as good with those tank killers as he was at faking being a Royal Knight.

Once we were all together, Caldswell told the rest of the crew what he'd just told me. To my surprise, no one argued, not even Basil. Every single one of them was looking at the captain with so much trust it made me feel a little ill, but then I suppose a bit of blind faith was a career necessity when you were one of Brian Cald-swell's permanent crew.

I hung back as Caldswell led his people down the lounge stairs to the cargo bay. This was partially because being on the ship again put me back in security officer mode, which meant it was my job to bring up the rear, but mostly I was mesmerized by what was going on outside the lounge windows. The enormous xith'cal battle cruiser that had shot out our hyperdrive coil wasn't reeling us in as I'd first thought. It was towing us, pulling the junked *Fool* like so much space trash toward the enormous shadow of the tribe ship.

When I'd seen the dead tribe ship floating in the asteroids in the Recant, I'd thought it was the biggest ship I would ever see. Now I realized what Hyrek had meant when he'd said Stoneclaw was a small tribe. The tribe ship in front of me was so huge I couldn't see the light of Montblanc's sun anymore. Reaper's ship was like a great black moon pricked with millions of tiny yellow-lit windows, and even though I knew the battleship must be towing us very quickly, compared to the huge curve of the hull before us, we didn't seem to be moving at all.

"Morris!"

The captain's sharp call made me wince, and I tore myself away from the window to join the rest of the crew in the cargo bay.

Mabel was already down there. Considering her real identity, I'd expected her to be with Rupert, but she was just standing with the rest of the crew. She wasn't even armed. Actually, the only thing she was carrying was a small cat crate.

"You're bringing your cat?" I blurted out.

"Of course I'm bringing her," Mabel said, shooting me a scath-ing look. "I'm not going to abandon her here. What kind of monster do you think I am?"

I couldn't answer that in present company, so I kept my mouth shut and got back to business. Since Mabel had chosen feline companionship over her gun, that left Caldswell and me as the only armed combatants. I had my usual load out, but all Caldswell had was his pearl-handled disrupter pistol, the one with two shots. That didn't seem very useful considering I was pretty sure there were going to be a lot more than two xith'cal, but Caldswell didn't look worried. He just stood in front of his crew, holding his ground while I checked and double-checked my suit and weapons.

After what felt like forever, I heard the unmistakable sound of a door opening. A huge one. With the screens out and no window in the cargo bay, I could only guess we'd been towed into a dock on the tribe ship itself. A minute later, my guess was proven correct when the artificial gravity grabbed us. With her thrusters dead and no one on the bridge, the *Fool* dropped like a stone, knocking everyone except myself and the symbionts to the ground as the ship crashed onto the floor. We were still being towed, though, and we scraped along the metal for several seconds before jerking to a stop.

While the rest of the crew picked themselves up, Caldswell motioned me over. I moved to stand beside him, but he motioned me closer still. Scowling, I leaned right into his face. "What?"

"Remove your helmet," the captain whispered.

"Why the hell would I do that?"

"If I tell you, it won't look real," he said. "Just do it. You can put it on again as soon as this is done."

The idea of facing a tribe ship with no cameras and nothing to protect my head made me panicky, but as I opened my mouth to tell the captain no, I realized I could hear xith'cal gathering on the other side of the cargo bay door. *Lots* of xith'cal. Way more than I could ever shoot before they took me down. I glanced back at Caldswell, but he was just standing there, looking at me with growing impatience.

With a long sigh, I reached up and popped my helmet. I didn't remove it completely, just hinged it back so it was hanging behind me, but that was still enough to make me feel like an exposed moron.

I didn't know any other word to describe a merc who removed her helmet seconds before an attack. I did it, though, because if my months on Caldswell's *Fool* had taught me anything, it was that the captain was a sneaky bastard. There was no way we were gunning down an entire tribe ship anyway, so I had nothing to lose by putting myself in Caldswell's hands. Except my head, of course.

"I hope you know what you're doing," I muttered.

"Just hold still and keep your hands off your guns," Caldswell said quietly, nodding for Mabel to open the cargo bay door. "And whatever you do, don't say a word."

That was not reassuring final advice, but it was too late now. Mabel had already unhooked the counterweight, starting the cargo bay's unpowered door rolling up toward the ceiling. As the metal barrier rose, Caldswell put his hands out in front of him, away from his gun. I kept mine clear as well, though it nearly killed me once I saw what was on the other side.

A sea of xith'cal was waiting for us. I'd never seen so many lizards in one place before, not even on the ghost ship. There had to be thousands of them packed into the cavernous landing bay, swarming the warship that had dragged us in like ants on a carcass.

They'd swarmed us, too. There were xith'cal on our ramp, xith'cal on top of the *Fool*'s flat roof, xith'cal putting out the electrical fires that had sprung up on our busted hyperdrive coil now that there was oxygen. There were so many xith'cal they started swimming together in my vision, but not before I'd noted that every single one was armed to the teeth and pointing their weapons at us.

At the front of the pack, though, one xith'cal was different. I now recognized the small bright-green lizard as a female, and though she was dwarfed by the males around her, she was clearly in charge. Like the Highest Guide back on the asteroid, she had a human slave on a chain. It was a middle-aged woman this time, probably another interpreter, but she didn't get a chance to interpret anything. The *Fool*'s ramp was barely half down before the female xith'cal sniffed deep and jumped back with a metallic shriek.

Something nudged me from behind, and both Caldswell and I looked to see Hyrek's handset held out between us.

She is screaming that you are the plague, it read.

Caldswell nodded and looked at me. "Ready?"

I frowned. "Ready for wha—"

Before I could finish, Caldswell's arm was around my throat and his gun was pressed against my temple.

I jumped on instinct, but Caldswell's arm clamped down tighter, holding me still. "Easy, Morris," he whispered. "Just roll with it."

I do *not* roll with guns pointed at my head unless I'm the one holding the trigger, but as much as I hated it, Caldswell's ploy seemed to be working. Down in the crowd, the female's shriek cut off like it had been chopped with a knife. In its place, the air filled with the click of claws on triggers as the whole room prepared to fire, and I gave myself up for dead. But before a single shot could go off, the female held up her hand and barked a command. Beside her, the human slave stepped forward.

"Do not shoot, Brian Caldswell, sworn prey of Reaper," the woman said, her voice shaking in terror. "Step away from the plague bearer."

"Hyrek," Caldswell said quietly.

Our lizard nodded and stepped forward, standing beside his captain much as the human slave stood by her xith'cal master. When he was in place, Caldswell lifted his chin. "Flesh of Reaper," he said, his captain's voice filling the room. "I have brought the woman as demanded. Call off the siege of Montblanc or I will kill her right here."

I nearly choked. Logically, I knew this had to be a bluff, but the captain didn't sound like he was bluffing. He sounded deadly serious, emphasis on the *deadly*.

Hyrek lifted his own snout and started to speak. I hadn't actually heard our xith'cal speak much, and the effect was surprising. His voice was deeper than the female's but clearly not male. It was its own thing, and the xith'cal reacted, hissing and snarling. Even the female bared her small fangs when she replied, and though her words sounded like spent bullet casings going through a shredder, there was no mistaking the scorn in them.

"What insult is this?" the slave woman said, completely failing to replicate the haughty disdain of her mistress's voice. "You bring a child to lay down terms to the great Reaper?"

Hyrek looked at the captain, but Caldswell only narrowed his eyes and tapped his finger on the trigger. The female xith'cal winced at the motion, and the huge male beside her leaned down to hiss something in her ear. The female shook her head and began speaking again.

"Your terms are accepted, sworn prey," the human slave woman translated. "We shall allow the weak planet to live. Now, give us Stoneclaw's weapon."

"I'm not done yet," Caldswell said, wedging the gun harder against my temple. "I also want a guarantee of safe passage for my crew and my ship."

This time, the female didn't even wait for Hyrek to translate before giving her answer with a squeal so sharp it made my ears ring.

"You are sworn prey," her slave said haughtily. "There can be no escape for you. The great Reaper will eat your flesh this day in glory."

"I never said me," Caldswell replied. "I said my ship and my crew."

As he spoke, the hard pressure of the pistol's muzzle vanished from my head. I blinked in surprise and turned just in time to see Caldswell step back and press the gun against his own temple.

"Sworn prey must be defeated in combat," he said, grinning down at the xith'cal as he tightened his finger on the trigger. "I already have your pledge to leave Montblanc alone in exchange for Deviana Morris, but if you refuse to swear safe passage for my people and my ship, I'll end this farce right here, and Reaper's disgrace will go unanswered forever. Are you willing to risk that, Highest Guide?"

The female gave Caldswell a scathing look, and then she turned to the male beside her. They talked for a long while. The male was clearly enraged, but the female just kept shaking her head. Eventually, they seemed to come to an agreement, and the female spoke to her slave, who repeated the words to us.

"We will swear safe passage for your crew and ship," the woman said. "But only after your death. You have been sworn prey for many years, Brian Caldswell, and great Reaper whose flesh we are demands your blood."

"I die and they go free without harassment," Caldswell verified. "This is your pledge?"

The female xith'cal nodded, and Caldswell lowered his gun. "Done."

I stared at the captain in amazement as he holstered his pistol.

"What?" he whispered. "I got the idea from you. And stop gaping, Morris. You'll give people the wrong impression."

"Didn't know it was wrong," I whispered back, folding my arms over my chest. "Didn't think you were the hero type, offering to die for your crew."

Caldswell grinned. "Don't give me too much credit. I knew I was dead the moment that towline hit, but if I couldn't double sell a sure thing to guarantee the safety of my crew, what kind of trader captain would I be?"

I couldn't even begin to answer that. Behind us, Nova was tearing up. Basil looked stricken, Mabel looked impressed, and Hyrek just looked overwhelmed. I was sure he would have said something, but Caldswell silenced everyone with a glare before turning back to me. "Better put your helmet back on."

My eyes widened, and I snapped my helmet into place just in time to see the xith'cal coming up the ramp through my side camera. But though they had us grossly outnumbered, the xith'cal stopped at the edge of the cargo bay, looking at me like they were afraid to come any closer. For a moment, I almost took that as a compliment to my reputation as a badass lizard killer before I remembered my new name among the xith'cal, "plague bearer." Too bad I couldn't just throw the stuff at them and run.

Our mini standoff lasted almost a full minute before the female made her way up the ramp. She must have left her human slave behind, because when she appeared, all she had in her hands was a thing that looked like a large white ball. She said something and pointed at me, then at the corner of the cargo bay. Such a simple command didn't require translation, but I still waited for Hyrek to tell me to move before I obeyed.

I fully expected her to order me to strip next, because what kind of idiot keeps a Paradoxian prisoner in her armor? But the female didn't say anything else. She just waited until I was in the corner, and then she lobbed the white ball at my face.

Despite the thousands of guns pointed at me, I very nearly shot the thing down on instinct. I caught myself at the last second, forcing my hands off Sasha as the white ball hit me in the chest. The moment it struck, it expanded, flowing over me until I was standing in the middle of what looked like a white gum bubble. Once it reached its full size, the bubble hardened instantly, much like Mabel's patches. Unlike a patch, though, this stuff wasn't brittle. It didn't crack when I pushed it, or even when I punched it. I would have tried shooting, but that didn't seem like a smart idea when the female was walking toward me with ten warriors.

She reached up to touch the bubble, tapping the white surface with her claws as she said something in her twisting-metal voice. Behind her, I could see Hyrek typing, and then a message appeared at the bottom of my camera feed.

She says it's completely shatterproof and airtight, Hyrek's message read. *She also hopes you have an air supply that can last you until you reach the lab.*

My eyes went wide as I sealed my suit. The female xith'cal laughed at the sound of my air lock and began commanding the warriors to pick up my makeshift prison. Outside, I saw Caldswell surrender his pistol before being hauled off by two very large xith'cal. The rest of the crew went without protest, including Mabel, and though they were clearly terrified, especially Basil, who was going on about how he was an old bird and couldn't be very tasty, the xith'cal didn't seem to be treating them roughly.

As the crew was escorted out, I felt a deep rumble under my feet. It was so huge, it took me a few seconds to realize that the tiny earthquake was actually the roar of the tribe ship's thrusters. We were leaving Montblanc. The xith'cal were keeping their word, apparently.

Once Caldswell and the crew had been led away, the warriors lifted my bubble and started down the ramp. I cannot begin to describe how bizarre it was to have xith'cal warriors bearing me on their shoulders like a noble in an old-fashioned palanquin. If they hadn't been carrying me to near-certain doom, I probably would have enjoyed it.

The crew had been marched out ahead of me, and by the time the slow-moving warriors carrying my bubble made it down the *Fool*'s ramp, Caldswell and the rest were gone. I kept my eyes open anyway, keeping all my cameras busy marking doors and vents, anything that might be useful later for an escape. I also kept watch for Rupert, but I didn't see so much as a flash of black. I refused to let it bother me, though. Rupert hadn't been taken with the crew, which meant he was undoubtedly already working on whatever plan he and the captain had made. He'd find me for sure, and together we'd bust this place wide open, get the crew, and get the hell out.

I was taking comfort in that thought when the jump flash washed over me.

———

In the movies, the inside of a xith'cal tribe ship was always a shadowy, terrible place filled with human skeletons. As it turned out, the truth wasn't too far off. There were no bones, but it was uncomfortably dark, and the hallways went on forever. Since I wasn't walking, my suit was having trouble drawing a map as the xith'cal warriors carrying my bubble turned again and again, and by the time we reached our destination, a large, well-lit room lined with what appeared to be medical sterile storage, I was utterly lost.

Wherever this place was, it was clearly a female room. The ceiling was so low the males carrying me had to duck to fit. There were dozens of females standing clustered around clean metal tables with projected diagrams hovering over them like ghosts. They hissed when the warriors entered. The warriors hissed back, causing the female who'd met us in the dock, the Highest Guide, to roar. Everyone shut up after that, and the males kept their heads down as they carried my bubble to an air lock at the far side of the room.

The Highest Guide opened the air lock and stepped back, motioning for the warriors to place me inside. The lock itself was pretty large, but it opened into a small room with glass walls roughly half the size of the bunk I'd shared with Nova. There was barely enough room to fit the bubble, and I got rattled like a nut in its shell as the males wedged me inside.

When I was finally in, the Highest Guide closed the air lock. The moment the seal clicked, my bubble began to dissolve, leaving me standing inside the glass cell. One prison to another wasn't much of an improvement, but at least I wasn't being carted around anymore. I tried to feel happy about that as I examined my new cage.

It didn't take long. The prison beyond the air lock was basically a clear glass box at the end of a larger room that looked like an observation area. The setup made me feel like I was on exhibit at a zoo, though I didn't think they'd be bringing classes of baby lizards down to see me.

There were two doors I could see, the air lock I'd come in through and a second, larger door on the far side of the observation room. The only furniture was a large box set into the wall across from me. The low light and the thick, smudgy glass of my prison were messing with my cameras, so I couldn't make out details, but the box seemed to be made of metal, and I could pick up a faint heat signal inside it.

That was a little creepy, because on my scanner, it almost looked like there was a person in there. The box was about the right size, too, like a coffin. But these morbid thoughts weren't helping, and there was absolutely no reason I could think of for the xith'cal to keep me in a room with a coffin, so I forced my eyes away.

The observation room had been built to accommodate male xith'cal, but my prison was human scale, which meant my ceiling stopped well before the room's did. Unlike the walls, though, the ceiling of my cell wasn't clear, so I could only guess that the vents up there led into some kind of closed air recirculating system meant to keep in contagion. That made sense, but what I couldn't figure out was why a clearly dangerous bioweapon like myself was being kept in a glass box like some kind of exotic pet.

There was no window in the air lock behind me, but I could hear the lizards moving in the other room. I leaned against the glass on the opposite side of my cell, waiting for them to come in and start the interrogation, but no one came. Minutes turned into hours, and still I was left alone. I'd fully expected to have been subdued, stripped out of my armor, and cut into alphabetically arranged pieces by this point, but I hadn't seen so much as a lizard snout since they'd shoved me in here. It was almost like they'd locked me up and forgotten I existed.

You would think I'd be ecstatic at this turn of events. I wasn't being vivisected or put in jars or any of the other horrors my brain had imagined. The worst things I'd had to endure so far were boredom and the fact that I was getting hungry, but as the hours built up, so did my anger.

I hate, hate, *hate* being helpless, and helpless was what I felt at the moment. I'd steeled myself to face anything, to fight to the death, and instead I was locked up with nothing to do. The xith'cal must have taken the crew's coms, because I couldn't raise anyone. Not surprising, but it pissed me off to no end to know they considered Nova and Basil a greater threat than me. They weren't even taking me seriously enough to bother removing my guns, which I took as a personal insult.

By the time we exited hyperspace somewhere around the beginning of the third hour, I'd gotten mad enough to fire half of Sasha's clip into the glass walls, which was how I'd learned they were exceptionally bulletproof. Not that it mattered. Even if I'd shattered them, I had nowhere to escape to. I was alone and lost in a tribe ship the size of a major city. I couldn't even play hero because I had no idea where Caldswell and the crew were being held, assuming Caldswell hadn't been eaten already. I was trapped, useless, and helpless, and it was driving me *crazy*. It was even worse than when I'd been lost in the mine. At least there I'd been able to walk. Here I couldn't do anything except pace and brood. I was doing just that, and working myself into a rare fury in the process, when I felt the telltale prick of pins and needles.

Anger turned to fear in a flash. I knelt in the corner of my clear cage and yanked off my gloves. Sure enough, my fingers were solid black, like I'd dipped them in coal dust, and the stain was still growing. It blossomed before my eyes, sweeping down my hand and up my arm under my suit. But even though I couldn't see it moving anymore, I could feel the pins and needles crawling up my arm nearly to my elbows before finally slowing down.

"Shit," I whispered, shoving my hands back into my gloves so the xith'cal, who were almost certainly watching, wouldn't see. "Shit, shit, *shit*."

Why was this happening *now*? Had the xith'cal pumped something into my cage to trigger the virus? It was possible, but up until I'd taken off my gloves, I'd been sealed into my suit, which ruled out anything airborne. A plasmex attack then?

Since my seal had already been broken, I shoved up my visor. The bitter taste of the arsenic-heavy air made me feel queasy, but I didn't have time to worry about it. My cameras couldn't pick up plasmex, but my eyes could, and if I was under attack, I wanted to see it. As my visor went up, though, the black stuff on my hands shrank to a minor concern.

The walls of my cell were no longer clear. When I'd had my

cameras on, I'd seen plain, slightly cloudy glass. Now, looking with my naked eyes, I saw the truth. The walls of my cell were covered in a fractal pattern of glowing plasmex so thick and bright it hurt to look at. The patterns spilled out into the observation room as well, spiraling over the walls, floor, and ceiling until I felt like a fly caught at the center of a giant, glowing, mathematically inclined spider's web. But while the fractal patterns came together around my cage, they started at the mysterious box on the wall.

I pushed my face against the glass, peering through the glowing patterns. I still couldn't tell what the box was made of, but I could clearly see the thing inside it now. More than see, actually. The shape was glowing through the box like the sun through paper, filling the room with light. But the brightness brought me no comfort, because the shape was a girl's silhouette, one I knew far too well.

I jumped back from the glass like I'd been burned. There was a daughter of Maat in that box that began the net of plasmex, and I was standing in the middle with my hands black as sin. I could have already killed her, but I didn't see the inklike stain of the virus spreading through the patterns.

Since it didn't seem like I'd infected her, at least not yet, I began to pace around my cell. This could be my break. I didn't know how or why Reaper had nabbed a daughter, but if Maat had reached me through Ren, maybe she could reach through this girl and break me out again.

Feeling like a right idiot, I moved to the edge of my cell that was closest to the box and called. "Maat?"

I got no answer but silence, and the feeling of idiocy deepened, but that didn't stop me from calling again. "Maat!" I shouted, pounding on the glass with my gloved fist. "Maat! Wake up!"

Nothing. I pushed off the glass with a curse, turning around to start pacing again, and nearly ran into the dark-haired girl standing right behind me.

My suit jumped me back automatically, landing in a crouch at the far edge of my cell. Maat's too-bright eyes followed the movement, but she didn't comment. She just stood there with her arms crossed over her chest, glaring at me.

She looked slightly different than the other times I'd seen her. The white hospital gown was gone, replaced by the same drab, simple clothes Ren had been wearing when she died. This, plus the way her skin seemed to glow in the light of fractal patterns around us, gave me the uncanny feeling that I was speaking to a ghost.

"Maat," I said when I found my voice at last. "You came."

The girl said nothing, and I bit my lip. I wasn't sure what was going on, but if she wasn't going to talk, I'd best get straight to the point.

"I need your help," I said. "The xith'cal have me trapped, they have your daughter, too. They're using her for something. I don't know what, but it can't be good, see?" I pointed at the patterns. "If you can blast me out again, I swear I'll get her as well. I'll set us both free, promise, I just need you to get me started."

I finished with a smile, but Maat's scowl only deepened. *Why would Maat help you?*

I winced. I'd forgotten how cold and hateful a whisper in my mind could be.

I asked you for one thing, Deviana Morris, Maat said quietly. *All Maat wanted was freedom for freedom. But you betrayed me.*

"What?" I said. "No! I tried to—"

LIAR!

Maat's roar tore through my head, sending me to my knees.

Do you forget? The voice pounded against my skull, and I felt the awful sensation of a hand in my mind again, shuffling through my brain. *Maat sees your memories, idiot. Brenton gave you the chance to free Maat, but you denied him! You ran away, ran to the Eyes. You even made a deal with **that man!***

She moved forward with each word until she was almost standing on me, her little fists clenched at her sides. *Liar!* she screamed, her mad eyes filling with tears.

"I didn't betray you!" I yelled back, finally getting my head back together. "That deal was my best shot at helping you. And Brenton wasn't coming to set you free, he wanted me to *kill* you."

Exactly! Maat roared so loud my eyes crossed. *He was **loyal**! He kept his word! You are a **traitor**!*

The echos of her rage were still battering me when Maat collapsed. *All Maat wants is to rest*, she whispered, curling up on the floor and covering her face with her bony hands. *The watching Eyes, they'll never let Maat die. Never never. Only you could free me, but you betrayed Maat.* She curled tighter. *Betrayed, betrayed, betrayed.*

Her words faded into babbling after that. I tried to reach out to comfort her, but my hands passed right though her shoulders. She didn't even notice, so I leaned back on the glass wall to think.

I was pretty sure the daughter in the box was Brenton's. Enna was the only daughter I'd seen who was thin enough to match the glowing profile I saw. That actually gave me hope. Enna had been on Reaper's asteroid, and if she was here, then maybe Brenton was still alive as well. I was trying to think how that could help me when I realized the light in the room was getting brighter.

The other two times Maat had come to me, the phantoms had followed. This time was no different. When I looked up, the room was full of glowing bugs crawling on the fractal patterns of plasmex that surrounded my cage. Maat's crying must have called to them, because more appeared with every silent heave of her chest. As always, nothing got close to me, but the rest of the room was filling up so fast I could barely see the daughter's glowing outline anymore.

That couldn't be good. I needed to stop Maat's weeping before she attracted something bigger. I was trying to figure out the right thing to say when Maat suddenly stood up.

It doesn't matter, she said, sweeping to her feet as fast as she'd collapsed. *Maat found a new ally, one who will not betray. Already, he got you for me, and now, with Maat's help, he will end it for me as well.*

My whole body went cold as the full implication of what she'd just said clicked in my head. "It was you," I whispered. "*You* told Reaper about me."

He already knew about the virus, Maat said with a sneer. *Maat just told him where to find you after the lelgis left.* Her tear-streaked face pulled up in a haughty smile. *Brian stole me from Reaper, you know, back at the beginning. That's why Reaper hates him. Of course, Maat wasn't Maat then…*

Her smile vanished as her voice trailed off, and she glared at me bitterly. *I begged Brian to kill me then, too. He refused, but at least he didn't lie about it. But it doesn't matter. Maat will win in the end.*

Her words chilled me to the bone. I wasn't sure how much of that was crazy talk and how much was real, but my eyes had already drifted to the patterns on the walls of my cage. Patterns that ran to Maat's daughter, who I now knew was willingly working with the lizards.

"What do these do?" I demanded, pointing at the web of plasmex.

Maat smiled wide, the same horrible, too-wide, doomed smile Ren had given me in the lounge so long ago. *She swallowed the spider to catch the fly.*

Her words were singsongy nonsense, but I refused to let her madness derail me. I stepped forward, thrusting my hands at her face. My gloves hid the blackness, but I knew the stain was still there. I could feel it prickling, the pins and needles like little insect feet crawling up my arms. "Did you do this to me?"

Maat actually laughed at that, a jittery, mad sound. *If Maat could make you bloom, she would have done it hours ago.*

"So if you're not making this stuff spread, what's all this for?" I demanded, jerking my head at the glowing patterns.

Maat shot up on her tiptoes, getting in my face despite being almost a foot shorter than I was in my suit. *Maat and Reaper made a bargain,* she said, eyes dancing. *The xith'cal dare not get near you as you are now. A very poor weapon, very unstable. But even in your tiny plasmex, Stoneclaw's virus is kindling.* She reached out, resting her fingers just above my elbow, right on the very edge of the pins and needles. *See how far it's spread.*

I jerked away, but Maat just laughed. *When the blackness covers you completely, you will die. But Maat, clever spider, made a web.* She looked up at the plasmex patterns. *Maat will catch your death as it kills you and finish what Stoneclaw couldn't. Maat will give Reaper the weapon he seeks, and when it is done, we'll both be free, Deviana.*

"We'll both be dead!" I shouted.

Maat turned back to me with a soft smile. *Exactly.*

I opened my mouth to tell her she was crazy, but Maat beat me to the punch by proving it. *Do you know how long I've waited for death?* she whispered, folding her ghostly arms over her chest. *Maat doesn't even know anymore how long she's been alive. Their lives, my daughters, they tangle inside me. I see my father killed in front of me, and though I know it's not my father, I remember.* Her eyes filled with tears again. *Oh, Papa.*

The words shot through me, because when Maat said them, her voice in my head went breathy and broken, exactly like Ren's.

Maat can't even remember which of those faces is her real father anymore, she murmured. *But it doesn't matter. They're all dead. The Eyes take them all away and tell Maat she makes a great sacrifice. But no one ever asked Maat if she wanted to sacrifice, and I'm so tired.*

Her tiny voice just about broke my heart, but as much as I felt for her right then, I couldn't let her do this. "I know we've done you wrong," I said, trying my best to ignore the pins and needles that were now creeping up toward my shoulders. "I want to make things right, Maat. Read my mind and see for yourself. But it can't end like this. Reaper is our enemy. If you finish Stoneclaw's virus for him, he'll use it to enslave everyone."

Maat's hands clenched to fists. *Do not tell me what I can and can't do,* she hissed. *Maat and her daughters have sacrificed a thousand lifetimes to save humanity, now humanity will sacrifice to save us.*

She stepped away, staring at me with so much hate I could feel it on my skin, sharp and jagged as a serrated knife. *You will all suffer,* she hissed. *And Maat will not care, because Maat will be dead. Maat will not hurt, not anymore. I will be free, just like you promised, and there is nothing you can do about it.*

"I won't let you!" I shouted.

Let me? Maat sneered. *What can you do? You can't even control yourself enough to slow the spread of the corruption.* She shook her head. *You're already dead, Deviana Morris, you're just too stubborn to know it.*

My answer to that was to swing at her head, but my fist passed through her without even a tingle, and Maat laughed. *Bye bye, rabbit.*

I roared, a mindless bellow of rage, but it was too late. Maat was gone, leaving only the glowing web she'd woven to catch my virus. The virus that was now up over my shoulders and spreading across my chest with alarming speed.

I dropped to my knees with a curse. All around me, the phantoms that had followed Maat were starting to back away, and for once, I knew why. My whole body was on fire with the virus, my skin crawling wherever the black stuff spread. The plasmex web was already starting to glow, and I realized this was it. I was going to die.

The thought hit me like a slap in the face, and I gritted my teeth. No. I had not survived this long and fought this hard to go out like a chump now, dying on my knees to a virus. Maat had taunted me that I couldn't control myself enough to stop the spread of the corruption, but that implied a way existed. I just had to find it.

Panting against the needles crawling down my chest, I forced myself to ignore my body and focus. What made it spread? I thought back to all the other times it had appeared, looking for a common thread, but the only thing I could remember was that I'd been upset each time before the black stuff appeared.

That couldn't be it, though. If the virus spread every time I got mad, I'd have been dead days ago. Now that I thought about it, though, I hadn't just been mad when the virus appeared. I'd been furious, the kind of superhot rage I really had to work up to, just like I'd worked myself up over being locked in this box right before the stain had appeared on my fingers...

My eyes went wide. That was it. The virus fed on my *rage.* And with that realization, I slammed my eyes shut and focused on calming down.

Taming my anger isn't exactly a skill I've spent much time developing. Back when I was a recruit, my commanders used to lecture us constantly about the danger of rage, but I'd never really bought their warnings. In my experience, anger made me stronger, not weaker. Now, though, for the first time in years, I went back to my training and clamped down, forcing my mind to be still.

I didn't do very well. Even when I added in the stupid breathing exercises, I was just too mad. Mad at Maat for selling out all of humanity to Reaper just so she could escape, mad at being trapped, mad at the stupid black bullshit I could now feel spreading over my stomach. I was also scared, and not just of the death I could feel breathing down my neck. If I failed here, Maat would die, too. Caldswell hadn't explained why that was so terrible, but he'd been willing to let me shoot myself rather than even talk about freeing her, so I was pretty sure it was bad on an epic scale. There was also the part where Reaper would be in possession of Stoneclaw's completed virus, which was a catastrophe I didn't even want to think about.

So failure was not an option, but I still couldn't seem to calm down. And the more I failed, the more upset I got, and the more impossible my task became.

When the virus had eaten half my body, I decided it was time to switch tactics. Clearly, I needed to work on my anger management, but there was no time for learning curves. So I gave up on trying to stomp down my rage and focused on harnessing it instead.

This went much better. I'd always considered my anger an ally, after all, so it was no surprise that once I stopped fighting it, we got along great. I started with Maat's claim that I couldn't do anything. That my lack of control was letting the virus eat me alive, letting her win. That thought fanned my anger even hotter, but instead of letting it burn, I focused it into the useful, pointed fury of my battle rage.

All at once, my mind stilled. The fear vanished, and everything grew very clear. I was no longer an angry, terrified woman trapped in a box. I was a weapon, a soldier, an avenging fury who was going to smash this whole place to bits, and as the battle rage settled over me, the pins and needles began to fade.

With my armor on, I couldn't check to make sure if the black stuff was receding, but when the last of the tingling vanished from my fingers, I didn't feel sick anymore. I felt focused, ready for the fight as I turned to face the bulletproof wall of my cell and dropped my visor. I couldn't see the plasmex patterns through my cameras, but that didn't matter. I knew they were there, and that knowledge was all I needed as I launched Elsie from her sheath.

Trapped, was I? Nothing I could do, eh? We'd see about that. It was time I taught Maat and her lizards exactly how destructive a Paradoxian could be.

Smiling a deadly smile, I brought my fist back, firing Elsie's thermite as I did. The blinding light filled the chamber as I shifted all of my suit's power to my arm. And then, when we were both primed and burning, I punched forward, slamming my white-hot blade into the glass as hard as I could.

CHAPTER
14

Elsie hit with a crash I felt to my boots, but even with her thermite burning full tilt, the wall didn't crack. I wrenched my arm back and hit it again, using my targeting system to slam Elsie's point right back into the tiny nick I'd gouged the first time. The boom of my burning blade against the glass was deafening, and by my third hit, I could hear the xith'cal females shrieking on the other side of the air lock.

I ignored them, focusing on the glass. My fifth hit opened a tiny hole, and when I landed my seventh, I was rewarded with a loud crack as Elsie's blade finally punched through.

Stop!

With my visor down and cameras on, I couldn't see Maat, but I could feel her clawing hand in my mind. *You'll ruin everything*, she hissed. *Stop this!*

"Try and make me," I growled as I wedged Elsie against the bottom of the hole I'd punched and leaned on it, using my weight to force her blade down.

Slicing the wall proved easier than piercing it, but it was still slow going, and I'd lost a lot of time. Whatever this glass was made of, it took all my suit's strength to cut through it. But my thermite was roaring now, and every inch felt easier than the last.

The racket on the other side of the air lock was getting louder. Maat was yelling, too, banging on my mind. I could even feel her hand on my spine, but for some reason her pulling wasn't working.

Maybe I was doing whatever I'd done when I'd resisted Brenton's girl, or maybe her link through Enna was too weak to maintain the web she'd spun and throw me around at the same time.

Whatever the reason, I didn't care. As soon as I'd figured out Maat couldn't hurt me, I stopped worrying about her. I ignored the xith'cal, too, focusing only on the cut, because if I couldn't finish that, everything else was for nothing.

I'd managed nearly a full circle by the time my thermite finally burned out. I scraped the brittle, burned crust of the spent thermite off Elsie's edge and retracted her, stepping back at the same time. Then, bracing one foot against my cage, I kicked off, launched myself at the hole I'd almost finished cutting.

My suit hit the glass so hard I felt the blow through my stabilizers, but the wall didn't crack. It bowed, though, and I raced back across my cell to kick off again, slamming my shoulder into the side I'd loosened. This time, the impact pushed the half-cut hole out far enough for me to get a foot through, and I braced, using my leverage to crack the glass the rest of the way. The final inches broke with a sharp snap, and I tumbled forward, my suit rolling me to my feet in the middle of the observation room just as the xith'cal warriors began pouring through the door.

As soon as they saw me, though, I knew something was wrong. I've faced down a lot of xith'cal in my day, and these males weren't acting like the ones I was used to. Normally, xith'cal are chargers, trusting their superior size and weight to bowl over opponents, but these were hanging back, watching me with wary yellow eyes.

They were afraid of me, I realized with a start. I was the plague bearer, and I was out of my protective box. Even the females shrieking orders from the back were keeping well away, and I felt my face break into a feral grin. This was going to be *good*.

With a battle cry that would have made my drill sergeant proud, I launched myself at the xith'cal. I didn't bother drawing my gun, I couldn't have shot them all anyway. Instead, I relied on surprise and their own terror, and the result was better than I could have hoped.

The xith'cal dove shrieking out of my way. I bowled past them, kicking anything that got in front of me. But though I was feet shorter and half their weight, none of the big males tried to grab me as I shot out the door, knocking over the females in the process.

The door led into a room much like the one they'd brought me through earlier. The ceiling here was much higher, though, and there were weapons against the walls as well as sterile storage. A mixed-gender room. More important, one that had two exits, a big freight dock, and a smaller door that opened into a long hall.

The smaller exit was closer, so that was the one I picked, sprinting across the room as fast as my suit could go. There were several females in my way, but they were in an even bigger hurry to get away from me than the males had been. Even so, it was only a matter of time before one of the lizards finally got over its fear of the plague and made a grab for me, so I pushed my suit harder, darting between tables covered in heavy, complicated-looking scientific equipment as I raced toward freedom.

I made it almost halfway before my luck gave out.

I was ducking under a machine that looked like a giant centrifuge when I spotted the Highest Guide standing in the freight door holding another of those cursed white balls. Like hell was I getting hit with that again, and by the time she'd raised her arm to hurl it at me, Mia was already in my hands. My fully charged plasma shotgun whistled to life with a beautiful sound, and when it hit its highest pitch, I ducked out from behind my cover and fired a white-hot burst straight into the Highest Guide's chest.

Hyrek had said that females weren't warriors, but the Highest Guide was still a xith'cal, and she jumped out of the way of my blast with admirable skill. Still, Mia isn't a precision weapon, and fast as she'd jumped, it wasn't enough to avoid getting hit completely. The burning plasma struck the Highest Guide across her side, and she went down screaming as the white fire engulfed her. The flames went out a second later, probably smothered by plasmex I couldn't see through my cameras, but the damage was done. The ball she'd been prepping to throw at me was lying on the ground in a gooey melted heap, and I was running again, legs pumping as I shot toward the little door.

I didn't have a plan. My goal at this point was just to get to the hall and play things from there. But when I was nearly to my exit, I caught sight of something huge charging up behind me in my rear camera. That was all the warning I got before a claw grabbed my leg.

The xith'cal yanked me off my feet like a doll, and I went down hard only to find there was no ground to go down to. I was hanging upside down in the grip of the largest lizard I'd ever seen other than Reaper himself. He had to be twelve feet tall and he was covered in scales as black as a symbiont's. There was a mantle of some kind draped across his shoulders too, which was odd. Most xith'cal wore no clothes. It was probably a rank insignia of some sort, I thought bitterly as I struggled in his grip. He was certainly big enough to qualify for something like that in a race that valued strength above all else.

Unlike the others, this xith'cal didn't seem scared of me at all. He held me at arm's length, dangling me high off the floor from one hand while he used the other trying to pry Mia out of my grip. I shot him for his trouble, but the burning plasma didn't even seem to tickle him. He just squeezed my leg tighter, and my alarm blared as my suit began to buckle.

That was the last straw. *No one* messed with my Lady Gray. Snarling in rage, I dropped Mia and sprung Elsie again, swinging up to dig her point straight into the xith'cal's wrist.

Punching through xith'cal scales is notoriously difficult. If I hadn't had a hardened tungsten spike, I probably wouldn't have gotten through, but my suit is strong where it counts, and I was hitting a joint, where the scales were softer and smaller. The stab landed perfectly, my blade sliding between the huge xith'cal's wrist bones like a wedge. The second I was in, I swung to the side, using my weight as leverage to snap the warrior's joint.

That got his attention. The xith'cal roared in pain and flung me away. I flew through the air like a missile, slamming into the far wall so hard I saw stars. Thanks to my suit's amazing shock system, I didn't break anything, though from the ache in my ribs, it had been close. I did break something on the wall behind me, though, because an alarm began to scream as I fell to the floor in a heap.

I was pretty punch-drunk from the hit but I forced myself up anyway, brandishing Elsie to take the next enemy, but it wasn't necessary. The xith'cal weren't looking at me anymore. Instead, they were scrambling for a big metal cabinet in the corner. I had no idea what for, but before I could think of a good guess, I heard something metal slam down behind me.

I whirled around with a curse. The exit to the hall I'd been running for was now covered by a heavy fire door. The large freight entrance the Highest Guide had been standing in was sealed as well, but it wasn't until my suit warned me that the air outside was rapidly filling with a neutral gas that I realized what had happened. Those doors weren't down for *me*. The thing I'd broken on the wall had been the fire alarm, and since this was a lab inside a spaceship, they used a heavy gas to smother the flames instead of precious water. No oxygen, no fire.

My face spread into a huge grin. Different as we were, xith'cal still needed to breathe, and every lizard in the room, even the huge one, was rushing for the air masks. And as I watched them scramble, a beautiful plan fell into my mind.

I reached over my shoulder and grabbed a grenade from my string. My ordnance was low since I worked, or had worked, on a spaceship, but it was still plenty for what I needed now. Using my targeting computer to line up my shots, I lobbed my entire grenade payload in rapid succession, not at the xith'cal, but at the metal cabinet in the corner where the masks were stored. My bombs exploded in blinding flashes, knocking lizards back and blowing masks everywhere.

The resulting chaos was so perfect I couldn't have planned it better. Everywhere, male and female xith'cal were scrambling to grab the scattered masks, but their motions got slower and slower as the flame-retardant gas filled the room. By the time the smoke from my grenades was forced down as well, the air was completely unbreathable, and I was the only thing left standing.

Grinning inside my sealed suit, I hopped over the xith'cal bodies and scooped Mia off the ground. Sliding her back into place over my shoulder, I hurried back across the room toward the door that led to my prison. I didn't have much time, but now that I had a chance, there was one final piece of business I wanted to take care of before I left.

The door to the observation room had sealed like the others when the gas came on, but a blast from Mia opened it again. I couldn't see the daughter's glow with my visor down, but I could still make out her heat signature inside the box. I crossed the room and grabbed the lid, tearing the box open with my suit's strength, but though I'd braced for the worst, the thing locked inside still took me by surprise.

It was a daughter, there was no doubting that, but she was so thin she barely looked human. She was naked, hooked up to a dozen strange xith'cal machines with a tube down her throat, which explained why she hadn't suffocated yet. They'd shaved her head, and her eyes were closed in sleep, but her face was screwed up in pain and her body was heaving, crying without making a sound, just as she had in Brenton's arms back on Falcon 34.

"Enna," I whispered, brushing my gloved hand over the girl's bald head. She didn't stir at her name, or when I reached down to pick up her hand. Her fingers were so thin they felt like twigs in my grip.

I dropped her hand with a soft curse and moved up to cradle her fragile head. Then, gently as I could, I reached into her mouth and began working the tube out of her throat. I'd barely gotten an inch free before I felt an invisible hand grab my wrist.

What do you think you are doing?

"Stopping you," I said, pushing against Maat's hold. "I can't leave any of this virus for Reaper, and I won't leave this poor girl either."

I couldn't see Maat through my cameras, but I could feel her cold fury like a knife against my throat. *So you would kill my daughter?*

"She's already dead," I said, staring down at Enna's emaciated body. "If not for these machines, she'd have moved on a long time ago."

The grip on my arm tightened, and I turned to glare at the empty air where I could feel Maat standing. "Why are you stopping me? She's clearly suffering, and you're the one who's always talking about death as freedom."

Maat's death, Maat hissed. *This girl is Maat's link here. You will not sever her.*

I arched an eyebrow. "So the Eyes aren't the only ones using the daughters as tools."

I DO WHAT MUST BE DONE! Maat roared, making my head ache. But quick as her anger came, it vanished, replaced by despair.

Please, she whispered, her grip softening on my wrist. *You can end both our suffering right now. You know how to activate the virus. Give it to us. The daughter's plasmex is Maat's. If you infect her here, we will die at last, and a direct infection will kill her too quickly to leave Reaper with a viable sample. We'll both win, don't you see? So please. Please, Deviana, set us free.*

I took a deep breath. It wasn't like I wasn't sympathetic to Maat's situation. But as much as I wanted to end her suffering, I couldn't do it yet. Not before we had another weapon against the phantoms, and not before I was sure I wouldn't be killing all her daughters in the process. "I will set you free," I promised her. "No matter what Caldswell says, as soon as this virus works, I promise I'll come to you."

Save your false promises, Maat snarled as her hand landed in my mind. *Maat will take it from you if you do not—*

She never got to finish. The moment she touched my mind, my other arm, the one she wasn't holding, shot up and grabbed the daughter's neck. With my suit's strength, breaking it was nothing. Enna's spine broke like chalk under my fingers, and Maat's presence vanished.

I removed my hand slowly, looking down at the girl's still, abused body. Rupert's memories welled up at the sight, but I didn't need them. I understood how he felt well enough on my own now. Whoever Enna had been before, she hadn't deserved this. Someday, I promised myself, I'd get the Eyes to tell me who her parents were so I could offer my apologies. It was a stupid promise that I'd probably never be able to keep, but making it gave me the strength to walk away, stepping over xith'cal bodies as I made my way to the door.

I fully expected to find an emergency team waiting when I hacked my way through the lab's fire door. Or worse, a full band of warriors come to recapture me, but there was no one. The hall outside the lab was empty, and that scared me more than running into Reaper himself.

The whole setup screamed trap, but I couldn't hang around waiting for it to spring, so I set off down the corridor, jogging at a steady pace with Sasha ready in my hand. I kept my eyes locked on my cameras for any sign of the hammer I knew was about to fall, but I didn't see so much as a flicker of movement. This entire section of the tribe ship seemed to be empty.

Paranoid and jumpy, I put my back to the wall as I tried to figure out my next course of action. I wanted to go find the crew, but I had no idea where they were or how to find out. Even if I could take a xith'cal hostage and make them tell me, I wouldn't be able to understand it. Also, tribe ships were huge. The crew could be miles away and I wouldn't even know.

Standing around definitely wasn't an option, though, so I decided to just keep moving until I spotted something better. I focused on getting as far from the lab as possible, turning corners at random and keeping out of sight of the cameras. I'd just spotted a long, low hall that looked like it might lead somewhere interesting when I saw something behind me.

I turned and fired before I could think, shooting a three-shot spread. Sasha's bullets caught the thing in the chest, sending it flying. I flew after it, pinning it to the ground with my suit before my brain could catch up. From the size, my gut reaction was that it was a female xith'cal, but as I brought my gun up to shoot it in the head and finish it off, I realized that the black-scaled thing beneath me wasn't an alien at all. It was a symbiont.

The black glossy eyes stared at me for a second, and then Rupert's familiar accented voice sighed. "We really have to stop doing this."

"Shit," I said, scrambling off him. "I'm sorry, did I hurt you?"

It was a stupid question. If Sasha's bullets could hurt symbionts, my life would have been a lot simpler. That didn't stop me from examining Rupert's chest for injuries, though. When I was satisfied I hadn't broken anything, I slugged him in the arm as hard as I could. "What the hell were you doing, sneaking up on me?"

"I wasn't," Rupert protested, rubbing his arm. "I'd been looking for you for a while when I heard the alarms. Emergencies and Devi tend to go together, so I came over here to check it out. I'd just spotted you when you shot me." His chest flexed, and the scales covering his head fell away, revealing an almost sheepish expression. "I was coming to rescue you."

I couldn't help a grin at that one. "Well, you're about fifteen minutes late," I said, offering him my hand. Rupert took it, and I pulled him up, though his weight made me stumble. I always forgot how much heavier he was than he looked. "Where are your big guns?"

"This way," Rupert said, running down the hall back in the direction I'd come. "I left them with Mabel."

I ran after him, matching his pace with effort. My suit is fast, but symbionts can *move*. Fortunately, we didn't have to go far. A few turnings down, Rupert ducked into a small room I'd dismissed as a dead end and opened a panel on the wall. He motioned me inside, and I went, ducking into the dark. When I came up again, I was nose to snout with a xith'cal. Fortunately, it was the one I liked.

"Hyrek!" I cried. "What are you doing here?"

"Mabel sprang him when she escaped, along with the rest of the crew," Rupert said, coming in behind me and replacing the panel. "We couldn't navigate this place without an inside man."

Once again, I am reduced to translator, Hyrek typed into his com. Clearly, Mabel had also gotten everyone's stuff back.

I looked at Rupert in his symbiont scales and then at Hyrek. "I'm guessing you're in on this, then?"

One does not work for the captain as long as I have without picking up a few things, Hyrek replied.

"I'm always the last to know anything," I grumbled, looking around at the place Hyrek had been hiding. It looked like we were in some kind of maintenance tunnel, but the scale was wrong for xith'cal. I could stand, but Rupert had to stoop, and Hyrek was bent nearly double. Also, it was filthy, the walls smeared with dirt and grease like hundreds of people passed through here regularly, which seemed odd for a tunnel inside a wall. "What is this?"

A slave road, Hyrek replied. *They run all through the ship. But we need to get out of here quickly. This whole area has been locked down for quarantine.*

"They're treating your escape as an outbreak," Rupert said. "If they didn't need you alive, they'd already be spraying the whole sector with neurotoxin."

Hyrek shot me a wary look, and I raised my hands in surrender. "I didn't plague anything," I said. "And I'm not going to, either. That shit is dangerous. Let's just get out of here. I'll tell you what happened when we're safe."

Hyrek nodded and started down the tunnel, clicking his handset as he went. A second later, a message appeared on my camera as he patched himself into my suit. *This way.*

Before I could follow him, Rupert's arm slipped around my waist. "I'm so happy you're all right," he whispered, his voice warm as he hugged me tight.

He let me go before I could tell him to get his claws off me, which was *absolutely* what I'd been about to say, even though the phrase forming on my tongue had felt more like *I'm glad you're okay, too.* But that couldn't have been it, because I wasn't saying that sort of thing to Rupert anymore.

Fortunately, my near miss went unnoticed. Rupert was already jogging down the tunnel after Hyrek, his black clawed feet as silent as falling leaves on the grubby floor. I followed a few seconds later, keeping my eyes firmly on my sensors and absolutely not on Rupert's muscles as they shifted under the smooth scales on his back, which for some reason didn't seem nearly as alien or creepy as I remembered. Not that I was looking, of course.

Considering how busy I was not looking, it was a very good thing the tunnel was empty. The slave area must have been evacuated for quarantine, too, because I didn't pick up so much as a flicker of a heat signature until the tunnel we were following let out into what looked like a storeroom. It was only after Hyrek slowed down that I saw the first sign of life. Three of them, actually.

Directly opposite our tunnel, three thin, filthy men were sitting on crates watching what looked like a gladiator match on a battered screen set into the wall. If it wasn't for all the xith'cal writing, I'd have thought it was a Paradoxian game, but none of the figures fighting on the floor of the huge stadium were wearing armor. I was zooming in with my own cameras to try and see what sort of blood sport was awful enough to qualify as xith'cal entertainment when the bird's-eye shot of the fight vanished, replaced by a close-up of Caldswell.

I barely stopped my squeak in time. The captain was standing tall at the center of the arena, facing down three xith'cal warriors alone and apparently unarmed. His face and clothes were bloody, as was the sand at his feet. All around him, the massive stands were packed with roaring lizards. The three lizards in the arena roared back, digging their claws in for a charge. That was all I saw before Rupert pulled me behind a wall of boxes.

"They're slaughtering him," I hissed, yanking my arm out of Rupert's grasp.

"I know," Rupert said calmly. "But there's nothing we can do. The captain's spectacle is actually the only reason we've been able to move through the ship so freely. Let's not waste it."

I didn't like it. I didn't like it one bit. Caldswell and I had our differences, but he'd always been a brave man. He didn't deserve much, but he'd definitely earned a better end than being tortured to death for the xith'cal's amusement.

That said, Rupert had a point. It wasn't like I could help Caldswell anyway, so though it sat wrong in my gut, I followed Rupert down a little tunnel hidden behind the boxes, out of sight of the glassy-eyed human slaves watching the captain's death. Hyrek was already waiting at the end, holding open a little door much like the one we'd used to enter the slave road.

We came out in a hangar. It was tiny compared to the huge dock the *Fool* had been towed into, but it was still big by my standards. This was clearly a nonmilitary facility, though, because all the ships here were blocky and unarmored. They were also surprisingly small.

Female ships, Hyrek typed at my questioning look. *This is the bay for the laboratory division, the one that is currently shut down for fear of you. As a result, we were able to secure a ship with limited effort.*

My eyes went wide. "We're escaping in a xith'cal ship?"

"No other choice," Rupert replied. "The *Fool* has a harpoon through her hyperdrive coil. She's also in a hangar that's under guard by a full troop of warriors."

I was still staring when the closest ship, a boxy planet hopper a quarter the size of the *Fool*, opened up, and Mabel jumped down right in front of me. Like Rupert, she'd clearly given up all pretense. Her mechanic's coveralls were gone, leaving her in scales up to her neck. Her graying, curly hair was pinned back tight, and her face was set in a serious scowl that left no trace of the pleasant, easygoing engineer. "Found her, I see."

"She found us, actually," Rupert said, nodding at the ship Mabel had hopped out of. "Are we ready to go?"

"As ready as we'll ever be," Mabel replied with a shrug. "Basil and Nova have things more or less worked out, and as soon as Hyrek joins them to translate the last few sticking points, we'll be good to fly."

"Fly?" I said, incredulous. "That's your plan? Just fly out? They'll shoot us on sight."

Mabel scowled, but Hyrek beat her to it. *Actually*, he typed, *Devi brings up a valid concern. Even with the distraction of the captain's execution, if we try to launch from a quarantined dock, the security turrets will almost certainly fire on us.*

I'd been thinking more of what would happen if we flew a xith'cal ship into human space, but that was also a good point. "Can't you override them or something?"

Hyrek shot me a cutting look. *I am a butcher turned surgeon for the lesser races. The security system for a tribe ship can only be handled by females who've completed five years of training. Overriding it is completely beyond my skill set.*

"Right right, I get it, you're a doctor, not a hacker," I said. "Fair enough, but what are we going to do?"

"We could take out the turrets," Mabel said.

I shook my head. "No way we could get them all. Have you seen this thing fire? It's a ball of guns."

"They're outside, anyway," Rupert said. "To disable them from here, we'd have to take out the firing stations, which are beyond the quarantine zone. We'd be up to our eyes in xith'cal as soon as we hit the first one."

Perhaps a distraction? Hyrek typed. *Something to keep them too busy to fire at us?*

"We can do something about that," Rupert said, looking at Mabel, who smiled and reached back into the ship. When her clawed hand reappeared, she was holding the two enormous missile cases I'd seen Rupert carrying back on the *Fool*.

"Charkov and I can play decoy," she said, handing one of the cases to Rupert. "Hyrek, you get Morris out. She's the only thing that matters."

"What?" I cried. "No way. I have a better plan. Hyrek, how do we get to that arena?"

Rupert turned on me. "Absolutely not."

"You haven't even heard what I want to do," I protested, but Rupert just crossed his arms over his chest.

"I don't care," he said. "You know how important you are." He paused there, but the unspoken words hung in the air anyway, and I knew he wasn't just talking about the virus. "We are not going to do anything that puts you at risk," he continued at last. "And you are absolutely not getting within a mile of that arena or Reaper."

I fixed Rupert with a glare that should have made him cower. He didn't, of course. He just held his ground and glared back, which was exactly the wrong thing to do. Rupert should have known about me and challenges by now.

"How much longer do you think this area will be under quarantine?" I asked. "A weapon does no good if you can't use it. As soon as they get brave enough, they're coming in to get me, and then we're all lizard food. I'm certainly not going to hang around here while you go off and be a hero, so you have a choice: you can either hear me out and be helpful, or you can get out of my way."

I could almost see Rupert's hackles rising, but I held my ground. When it was obvious I wasn't backing down, Rupert sighed. "Fine, what is your plan?"

"Charkov," Mabel said warningly, but Rupert held up his hand. I expected Mabel to bite his head off for that, but she just backed off, a sour glare on her face, and that was when I realized that Rupert outranked her.

I was digesting that bit of new information when I realized Rupert was still glaring at me, and I got to the point. "I can get us a distraction like nothing you'd believe," I said. "But once it goes, we have to leave quick, and that will be a lot easier if we take the head off the tribe."

"That sounds a lot like you mean to take out Reaper," Rupert said suspiciously.

"I do," I said. "And get Caldswell, and get out alive."

"Caldswell?" Mabel said, eyes going wide. "Impossible. Brian's dead, Devi. He knew it from the moment we got hit, and he would not thank you for trying to save him if it put you in danger."

"I don't care what he thinks," I snapped. "I put a gun to my head to get that man to agree to meet my demands, and like hell am I abandoning all that work." I turned back to Rupert. "You heard what he promised. Is there another person in the Eyes with the power to make all of that come true who would have agreed to work with me?"

Rupert set his jaw. "No."

"*Rupert,*" Mabel hissed, but Rupert shook his head.

"I'm not lying to her anymore," he said calmly. "You saw Commander Martin's order, he wanted her sedated and restrained. Commander Caldswell disagreed. He wanted to work with Devi, and so do I. I'll take full responsibility for whatever happens here."

Mabel stared at him hard, and then she held up her hands in surrender. "Have it your way, but the captain is not going to like it."

"Then he can bitch to me," I said. "If Caldswell dies, I go right back to square one, and personally I'd rather die here fighting xith'cal than go back to the Eyes as a glorified virus holder to be sedated and restrained. Anyway, I'm the best weapon we have against the xith'cal right now. They can't risk killing me or getting near me, which means I'm our best ticket out, and I'm not leaving without Caldswell."

My determination must have been clear on my face, because Rupert's shoulders slumped in defeat. "Fine," he said. "I'm listening. What kind of distraction do you have that can free us, kill Reaper, and save the captain?"

From the tone of his voice, I could tell he didn't expect to like my answer. And he was right. He didn't.

"Don't be such a lead weight," I scolded as we followed Hyrek's directions down the slave roads.

We'd been jogging for fifteen minutes, but we were still only halfway to Reaper's arena. Even though I'd been in one before, it was easy to forget just how huge tribe ships were. Hyrek had said the arena was close, but "close" on a tribe ship meant nearly fifteen miles of tunnels. If I hadn't had my suit and Rupert hadn't been an inexhaustible alien monster, it would have been impossible.

"This is a terrible idea," Rupert grumbled. He'd insisted on taking point, despite the fact that I was the one with the gun. I'd thought it was kind of sweet until I'd realized what a slow pace he set.

"Too late to change your mind now," I reminded him. "In for a shot, in for the bottle."

Rupert huffed. Despite his speech to Mabel, he'd flat-out refused my plan the first time I'd explained it, but no one had been able to come up with anything better before the alarms sounded to signal the end of the quarantine. After that, it had come down to fly out and get shot, fort up in the bay and fight the xith'cal until we were overwhelmed, or try something crazy. Since only one of those didn't necessarily end in death, Rupert had ordered Mabel to guard our escape and struck off with me through the tunnels. He'd been grumbling ever since.

"Just stick to the plan and everything will be fine," I said. "Now"—I pulled up my density monitor to study the knot of turns coming up ahead—"which way, Hyrek?"

Second left, scrolled the text on my screen. *Then down the ladder, skip the first two passages, and follow the one that leads up.*

"Such a useful lizard," I said before reading the directions out loud to Rupert.

Maps are freely available on the tribe ship grid, Hyrek typed. *Though if you wish to think of me as all knowing, I will not disabuse you of the notion.*

"And so modest," I added, rolling my eyes.

Try to keep away from the corridor coming up on your right, Hyrek warned, ignoring me. *It leads to the slaughter rooms. Wouldn't want you passing out.*

I wasn't afraid of a little blood, but I kept my eyes ahead all the same as we walked by the grim door. It was the tenth such room we'd passed. Hyrek had always been careful to warn us they were coming, and though I acted tough, I was grateful to him for it. Killing is one thing, but human slaughter is something else entirely, and I'd learned from my curious glancing into the first room that I had no stomach for it.

All the slave roads so far had been the same as the first: small, dirty tunnels running through the tribe ship like capillaries. Given the amount of grime on the walls, I'd expected them to be crowded, but apparently all the slaves had been rounded up into the main pits near the ship's core to watch Caldswell get slaughtered. According to Hyrek, the point of this was to keep the imbalance of power and their own helplessness fresh in the slaves' minds. There were a few slaves left in the tunnels tending to jobs that couldn't be put on hold, but they were as enraptured as everyone else by the gruesome spectacle on the screens, and we were able to sneak past them no problem.

I'd floated the idea of getting the slaves on our side, but Hyrek had nixed that instantly. Any slave, human or the aeons they kept in the feed pits, would reap huge rewards for reporting us, which meant none of them could be trusted. Still, I was happy they were all tucked away down in their bunkers. I knew what was coming, and I wanted the humans as far as possible when it hit.

All in all, the journey was much less hairy than I'd expected. The xith'cal's complete dismissal of the "lesser races" they enslaved meant there were few cameras in the slave roads and no guards. In the end, we were able to make it all the way to our destination without a single fight.

According to Hyrek's map, we were now in a tunnel that passed directly beneath the arena. It looked so much like every other slave road so far, I was a little worried we'd missed a turn, but then as we walked, I began to hear the roar of the screaming crowd through the metal over my head, and I knew we were in the right spot.

"How's our boy doing?" I asked, scanning the tunnel's ceiling with my density sensor for the place where the metal was thinnest.

Not so well, Hyrek replied.

"Not so well how?" I said, but before Hyrek answered, Rupert waved me over. He'd moved down the hall a bit and hopped up on a pipe to pry a panel off the ceiling. I jumped up to join him, putting my head through the opening he'd made. At first, I wasn't sure what I was looking at, and then I realized that Rupert had pried the bottom off a ventilation grate. Through the metal mesh, I could see straight into the arena itself, and Hyrek was right. It wasn't good.

I didn't know how long Caldswell had been in there. It had

been almost half an hour since I'd seen him on the screen, but I was willing to bet he'd been fighting a lot longer. The captain was panting and pale, and his clothes were soaked through with blood and sweat. When I'd first seen him, he'd been facing off unarmed against three xith'cal warriors. Now they had him fighting some kind of huge, hairy, sharp-toothed animal I didn't recognize.

At least he had a weapon now, a heavy xith'cal knife that was way too big for him. For all that, though, he handled the oversized blade deftly, waiting on the alien to charge before stepping aside with blinding speed and planting the knife neatly in the beast's spine like he'd been doing this all his life. If I hadn't already guessed he was a symbiont, that little stunt would have clinched it for me.

"Why hasn't he transformed?" I whispered.

"He is old," Rupert whispered back. "The symbiont heals, but the change is hard on the body. Caldswell doesn't do it unless he must."

"I'd say we're past must," I muttered, leaning closer to Rupert to get a better view as the captain yanked his knife out of the dying creature's back. "I wonder why Reaper hasn't killed him yet?"

"He is sworn prey," Rupert said, his voice disgusted. "That means spectacle. Caldswell humiliated Reaper, and pride must be paid."

"So they're toying with him," I said, looking up.

At the far end of the arena, a huge, brightly lit box hung suspended high above the bloody sand, and Reaper was sitting on it like an idol on an altar. Even this far away, I was struck again by the size of him. If I hadn't known for a fact Reaper was a xith'cal, I'd have sworn he was a different species entirely from the warriors that stood crowded around him.

"All right," I said with a deep breath. "Let's get this show on the road."

Rupert might not have liked my plan, but to his credit, he didn't waste time now. We were getting the first missile ready when the crowd's screaming kicked up a notch. When I jumped back on the pipe to see why, my breath caught. "Rupert!"

He was beside me in an instant, and I heard him mutter something that sounded like a curse. Now that Caldswell had killed the huge beast they'd sicked on him, his next challenge was being brought in through the gate on the arena's far side. The captain watched the rising barrier with calm acceptance, the knife easy in his hands. But Caldswell had never been nearly as good at bluffing as Rupert, and when his face flashed up on the xith'cal's huge screens, I could see the hints of fear. When I looked back at the arena gate, I saw why.

Something was coming out of the dark, dragging chains behind it. It walked jerkily, like it was sick, but it wasn't until it stepped into the light that I realized the thing was a symbiont. One with broad shoulders and a stocky build I recognized all too well.

"God and king," I whispered. "That's *Brenton*." I frowned at his shambling steps. "What's wrong with him?"

"They've enraged his symbiont," Rupert said quietly. "The alien part of us was taken from the xith'cal initially. It still responds to several of their drugs."

"Why would they drug him?" I asked. Having spent a day in the man's company, I was pretty sure Brenton would jump at the chance to kill Caldswell all on his own, no drugs needed.

"Because they mean this to be the end," Rupert said. "When Brenton went rogue, he was one of the two best fighters the Eyes had ever produced. Caldswell was the other, though for my money, I'd have bet on the captain every time. Now, with the drugs and Caldswell wounded?" Rupert shook his head.

"Then we'd better get a move on," I said, hopping down. Rupert could finish setting up the missile. It was time for me to do my part.

Ever since the incident with Maat, the little phantoms had been following me. I hadn't seen them at first since I'd had my cameras on, but once Rupert had agreed to my plan, I'd pushed up my visor to check on them every few minutes. I pushed it up again now, and there they were, a little cloud of light drifting just out of reach.

"Remember what I said," I told Rupert as I sealed my helmet again. "Don't get near me once I start. And don't touch me, whatever—"

I cut off as Rupert's arms circled around me, hugging me tight through my armor.

"What did I just say?" I snapped, struggling, but Rupert only hugged me tighter.

"Just in case," he whispered, leaning down to press his scaled mask gently against the side of my neck.

He didn't say anything else, but he didn't need to. His body said it all as it wrapped around mine. I've been held by a lot of men in my life, but not a one of them had ever come close to making me feel as precious, loved, and wanted as Rupert could with a single gesture, and it took an extraordinary act of will to pull away.

"Rupert," I said when I finally managed to step out of his arms, doing my best to form my breathy voice into a warning.

"I know," he said, cutting me off. "But I'm not sorry."

His hands settled on my shoulders as he spoke, turning me gently but firmly until we were standing face to face. For a second, I was staring up at his alien mask, and then his chest flexed, and the scales receded to reveal Rupert looking at me with the same defiant determination that had prompted Caldswell to grumble that I'd ruined his best Eye.

"I meant every word I said before," he said, trailing his black claws down my arms to gently cup my hands. "You're what's most important to me, and I will not lose you. Remember that before you decide to do anything stupidly brave, because I will come after you, and there's nothing you can do to stop me."

I stared at him for a second, and then I started to laugh. It was horribly inappropriate, but I couldn't help it. He just looked so serious, like if I ran into that arena and started randomly shooting lizards, he'd run in right after me without even hesitating. And that stopped my laughter, because as he looked down at me, I realized he would. I might not be ready to trust him on a lot of things, but right now, I knew to my bones that Rupert would follow me anywhere.

"I'll keep that in mind before I jump off any more cliffs," I said. "Now shove off and let me work."

Rupert leaned over, dropping a quick kiss to the top of my helmet. Before I could react, he was gone, his scales folding back over his face as he returned to his missile. I stared after him for several seconds, and then I shook myself like a dog and got back to the task at hand.

I strode down the hall for several dozen feet. Then, when I'd put what I judged as a safe distance between myself and Rupert, I sat down and pushed up my visor. As always, the phantoms had followed. They were all around me now, drifting through the dark, dirty walls of the slave road.

I looked around until I found a nice fat one, and then I stopped, taking a deep breath. Back in the hangar, I'd treated this part of the plan like a given. My confidence had been vital. If I'd shown any hesitation, Rupert would never have agreed. Now that we were down to the wire, though, I had to face the fact that I wasn't sure this would work at all. I'd only done it once, and not on purpose. Still, no one got anywhere by not trying, so I shoved my worries aside, closed my eyes, and focused on getting mad.

It didn't take much. I'd been fighting my rage since I'd realized it was what made the black stuff spread. But it's not my nature to hold back, and the moment I stopped trying, the righteous fury came roaring back like a furnace.

I bared my teeth, thinking about how Maat had sold us out even after I'd put my life on the line to save her daughters. That made me more sad than angry, though, so I thought about Caldswell instead, how I'd risked everything to get him on board, and now those idiot xith'cal were butchering all my hard work. That got me going nicely. Nothing pisses me off like having my sacrifices undermined.

And Brenton. I could hear him up there, roaring like one of the xith'cal as he strained against his chains. The sound made me furious. He might be nuts, but Brenton was up there because he'd stayed behind so I could get out, and I wasn't about to let him die for some lizard's amusement. I wasn't going to die here either. Neither was Rupert. I wasn't giving those lizards a goddamn thing.

By this point, I'd worked myself up so well that I didn't even notice the pins and needles until they were racing up my arm. The black stuff spread faster than ever before, passing my elbow in seconds to shoot up my biceps and over my shoulder. When I could feel the crawling edging down toward my chest, I snapped my eyes open.

The phantoms must have known something was up, because while my eyes had been closed, they'd all drifted away, but not far enough. The one I'd had my eye on earlier was still floating about ten feet down the hall, a fist-sized semitransparent blob with a dozen tiny kicking legs. I took careful note of its position as I slid off my glove. The moment my ink-black skin was free, I jumped.

Every time I'd grabbed at one of the little phantoms, they'd run away before I could touch them. I'd never made a serious try, though. Now I was serious as the grave, and the bug didn't have a chance.

I flew at the blob like a bullet, snatching it out of the air with my bare blackened hand. The little phantom was surprisingly soft against my palm, its surface cold and slick and slimy as a mud skink in winter. For a moment, it was surprisingly difficult to hold on to, but the phantom's struggles stopped when the stain of my sickness began to seep into its body.

Just like the phantom on the asteroid, I could see the blackness curling through its frosted-glass body like ink dripped in water. But this phantom was much, much smaller than the one in the cave had been. My blackness ate it in seconds, and as its light died, the emptiness bloomed in my mind.

It was only for an instant, but an instant was all I needed. The second the darkness fell, I reached out with that strange otherness, straining far and fast. It actually was much harder than I'd expected, like trying to throw a knockout punch with an arm you haven't used in ten years, but I didn't have the luxury of failure. I'd suggested this plan, I was going to see it through, and I reached out with all my might, throwing myself into the dark as hard as I could.

I was still reaching when the phantom died. I could actually feel it dissolving in my hand, and as it fell apart, so did the emptiness, but not before I felt them. Just like before, they were there, waiting for me. I didn't have time for more than an impression, but what I got was enough. They'd seen me, and they were coming.

I slammed back into my body with a gasp, looking up to see Rupert right in front of me. His scales hid his worried expression, but I could hear his fear just fine. "Devi!" he cried when he saw my eyes open, but I was already scrambling away from him.

"Stay back," I warned, throwing up my hand, the one that was still gloved. My blackened right hand I kept pressed against my chest. Rupert's eyes flicked to it, and his mouth tightened to a thin line.

"Just stay back," I repeated. Brenton had said symbionts were resistant to plasmex, but I didn't know if that mattered to the virus, and I wasn't taking any chances. I could smell the rot of my sickness now, and I didn't want that anywhere near him. When I was sure he'd stay away, I closed my eyes and focused on calming my anger, pushing my mind down until the pins and needles faded. It was much easier now that I wasn't trapped, and when I opened my eyes a minute later, my hand was clean.

"Devi."

I looked up to see Rupert standing over me, his fists clenched. I didn't know if it was safe for him to be so close yet, but I couldn't do anything to stop him as he reached down and pulled me to my feet. "Are you all right?"

"Fine," I breathed, letting myself lean into his chest. I wasn't as disoriented as I'd been when I'd woken up to three dead xith'cal and Brenton screaming in my face, but I wasn't ready to trust my feet just yet. "Guess that looked scary, huh?"

Rupert's silence was answer enough. "Please don't do that again," he whispered, pulling me a little closer.

"I'll try to keep it to a minimum," I promised, absently running my gloved hand over the scales on his back I'd admired earlier. They were surprisingly smooth, my foggy brain noted, like a snake's. "Did it work?"

Rupert pulled away. "I don't know," he said. "I haven't—"

The rest of what he said was drowned out by a deafening alarm. A split second later, the floor shook under my feet as something crashed into the tribe ship. Something big.

"Hyrek!" I shouted, dropping my visor back into place.

When there was no answer for several seconds, I started to get worried, but then Hyrek's text filled the bottom of my screen. *The next time you suggest a plan, remind me to say no.* Before I could ask what he meant by that, a new camera feed patched into my suit, looking out through a small port window at the fleet of beautiful fishlike ships that now surrounded the tribe ship.

"And there's our ticket," I said with a grin, shoving my glove back on. "Go time!"

Rupert didn't need to be told twice. He was already kneeling over the missile he'd set up. "On three," he said as I got in position behind him. "Two. One."

Rupert hit the charge, and the missile launched, slamming into the ceiling of the slave road. The blast was so big I couldn't see anything for several seconds, but when the hot white smoke started to clear, I saw the huge hole we'd blown in the arena's floor.

The explosion had knocked us both over, and though Rupert got up first, I was right behind him. Together we jumped through the hole, Rupert with the second missile, me with my gun, landing on the sandy floor of the arena with enough smoke left to cover us. I could hear the xith'cal all around me, their alarmed screeches like tearing metal in my ears, but I didn't pay them any mind. As soon as my feet were steady, I charged forward, throwing myself in front of the shocked, panting Caldswell just as Brenton's crazed symbiont began to charge.

CHAPTER

15

I'd always said I'd shoot myself if I ever got roped into an arena fight, but to be fair, I don't think I could have envisioned this. The bloody sand was soft beneath my boots as I skidded to a stop, the lights overhead like small suns as the alien crowd roared, literally. But my attention was on the alien in front of me, the one that had once been human.

Brenton charged with a roar of his own, launching at me with terrifying speed. Now that I was close, I could see the tube in his neck where they'd drugged him. They must have used a lot, because though he was fast as ever, the Brenton I knew would never have tried such a straightforward attack. He charged me like a bull, leaving me a good two seconds to jump if I wanted. But I didn't jump. I held my ground, leveling Sasha until I'd lined up a perfect shot.

When Brenton was only a foot away, I fired. Sasha's round struck him square in the head, right between the eyes just like Rupert had showed me. Of course, Sasha wasn't a disrupter pistol, but I didn't want to kill Brenton this time. I only wanted to blow him back, and there, at least, I succeeded. Sasha kicked him hard, and Brenton flew backward as fast as he'd flown at me, landing in the sand across the arena. I shot him again when he hit, trusting my targeting system to line up a shot that would get the tube on his neck. My pistol jerked in my hand, and I saw the tube go flying as the sand exploded around Brenton's head.

I lifted my gun, scanning the arena for the next enemy, but all I saw was Caldswell gaping in my rear cam like he'd just seen me raise the dead. "Morris?" he got out at last. "What the hell are you doing here?"

"Saving you," I said, grabbing his arm. "Come on."

The captain was normally faster on the pickup, but all the fighting must have left him a bit punch-drunk, because he just stood there staring at me like my words made no sense. I didn't have time to explain it again, though. The crowd was already getting louder as two more doors opened on either side of the arena, letting in a wave of warrior xith'cal. High overhead, Reaper was on his feet in front of his throne, roaring out orders loud enough to rattle my suit.

The sight of him almost made me drop my gun. Seeing the tribe leader on camera had been scary enough, but that was nothing compared to seeing him right above you. It wasn't just his size, either. That was nothing new, but I hadn't expected the *feel* of Reaper. Even though he was standing on his balcony almost fifty feet away, his presence was like a force of nature, a huge, undeniable gravity far larger than any physical size or charisma could account for.

I'd heard the xith'cal speak of their leader in awed tones plenty of times, but I'd always thought that whole "Reaper's flesh" thing was just propaganda. Now, I realized it was much, much more. Reaper's power was plasmex. A *lot* of plasmex, and he was using it with ruthless efficiency, soothing the panic even as another lelgis cannon strike shook the tribe ship. And when his huge, yellow eyes swept down to meet mine, I felt his control land on me.

I bared my teeth in response. Wrong merc to mess with, pal. "Rupert!" I shouted. "Do it now! Take out the head!"

Caldswell whirled around in surprise. "Rupert?"

The word wasn't out of his mouth before Rupert ran up beside me, our final strategic anti-tank missile hoisted on his shoulder. There was no countdown this time. He took one second to line up the shot, and then the missile exploded off him in a blast of burning smoke.

Since it wasn't aimed at a ceiling this time, I could actually watch the missile go. It streaked across the arena, flying so fast Reaper didn't have time to move. He didn't have time to do anything except stare as the missile shrieked through the air to land in his chest.

The explosion knocked me off my feet. I hadn't realized until it blew how much stronger this missile was than the other. The explosion had blown Reaper's entire platform down in a ball of black, billowing smoke. The wreckage landed in the sandy arena with a crash that sent a wave of sand flying into my face. For two heartbeats, all I could hear was the echo of the crash bouncing around the arena, and then every lizard in the place went insane.

If the xith'cal had been screaming before, I had no idea what they were doing now. The stands exploded into violence as the xith'cal began attacking one another with astonishing ferocity, ripping and clawing and biting like animals. The sheer magnitude of the carnage was so shocking I couldn't do anything except watch in stunned silence for several seconds before I finally got it together enough to scramble back to my feet. "What the hell is going on?"

Caldswell stared at me in disbelief. "You killed Reaper."

"And that caused all this?" I threw out my hand at the slaughter going on in the stand.

"The tribe leader keeps order within the bloodlust," Caldswell said. "It's how they..." His voice faded as he shook himself. He blinked a few times, wiping the blood off his temple. When he turned back to me, he looked much more aware. He also looked pissed as hell.

"*What do you think you're doing?*" he shouted. "You were supposed to be getting out of here!"

"I don't take orders from you!" I shouted back.

Caldswell's arm flung out, pointing at Rupert, who was brushing the ash from the blast off his shoulder. "He does! What the hell was that, Charkov?"

Rupert's smooth answer made me proud. "A missile, sir," he

said crisply. "Our last one. We should go. It is foolish to waste time arguing here."

"This is not over!" Caldswell bellowed, but he started running toward the hole we'd made in the arena floor. "What's our exit?"

"Hyrek's got us a ship," I said. "Let me grab Brenton and—"

I didn't get to finish, because at that moment, Brenton grabbed me.

He must have recovered from the shot during the chaos, because the bastard came out of nowhere, taking me off my feet before my cameras had even registered him. We flew across the arena in a tangle that unfortunately landed with me on the bottom. But as I'd noted before, this Brenton was nowhere near as clever as he normally was. Though he landed on top, he didn't pin my legs, and the second he got me down, I kicked him off. My suit flipped me back to my feet on the upswing, and I came up gun first, pegging Brenton in the chest.

Sasha's bullet didn't even get through his scales, but the force pounded him back into the sand again long enough for me to get the advantage. I jumped on him, getting him in a headlock. Symbionts might be tough bastards, but under all that armor and strength, they were still human, and they still needed to breathe. I twisted him tight, putting all my weight into the arm I was using to pinch his neck, but I was still barely holding him. I glanced at my cameras, scanning the arena for Rupert in the hopes I could get him to come help me deal with this craziness, and that's when I realized that the arena had gone still.

Without letting my grip on Brenton slack, I jerked my head up. It wasn't my imagination. The arena was silent, the xith'cal frozen like someone had hit pause. Only Rupert and Caldswell were moving, and they were backing away. A second later, I saw why.

Something was stirring beneath the smoking wreckage of Reaper's box, the broken metal shaking like there was an engine rumbling under it. Then, without warning, the pieces exploded out as Reaper shot to his feet.

As he rose, the pressure of his presence rose, too. The strength of it was enough to make my body go slack, and I almost lost Brenton. I recovered at the last second, bashing the mad symbiont into the sand again, but I was sorely tempted to toss Brenton and run.

I'd never seen Reaper fight. Never seen him do anything actually except sit around, give orders, and survive a missile to the chest. But even if I hadn't witnessed that last part, my instincts were enough to tell me that Brenton was now the lesser threat by several orders of magnitude.

Fortunately, though, the xith'cal wasn't looking at me. All his attention was on Caldswell, and as he stared the captain down, his shoulders began to shake with a horrible, deep, metallic sound. Laughter, I realized belatedly. Reaper was *laughing.*

His huge snout opened, showing thousands of yellow teeth sharp as shrapnel as he began to speak. The words were so deep they vibrated in my chest, and though I had no idea what the giant lizard was saying, Caldswell must have, because his shoulders stiffened.

"Devi!"

I glanced at my camera to see Rupert skid to a stop beside me. I hadn't even seen him run over, but he was with me now, his knee on Brenton's chest, pinning him down. "Let's go!" he hissed.

"Can you understand that?" I said, pointing at Reaper.

"No, Caldswell's the one who understands xith'cal," Rupert said, tugging on my arm.

He's telling Caldswell that he is impressed by his final blow, but it failed all the same, scrolled the text across my camera.

I gasped. I hadn't realized Hyrek was still watching. "What else?" I asked, ignoring Rupert's growl.

Your weapon is mine, sworn prey, Hyrek translated. *Call your puppet squid off, or I will use her to destroy you all.*

I frowned. Puppet squid? Caldswell must have thought the same thing, because the captain grinned wide as he glanced at me. I could almost see him putting two and two together as he remembered my earlier threat to call the lelgis if he betrayed me, and when he looked back at Reaper, his face was so cocky even I wanted to punch him.

"The lelgis aren't here for me," he said, folding his arms over his bloody chest as the tribe ship rumbled under the lelgis' fire. "You'd better look to your tribe, Jorek, while you still have lizards left."

Reaper hissed, and a roar rose from the stands, half rage, half shock. Even Hyrek's text looked excited when it scrolled over the screen.

He used Reaper's old name! The words flew by. *That is the greatest insult. Tribe leaders abandon their names when they become the flesh of all. Caldswell must be suicidal to say such a thing to Reaper's face.*

Or calculating, I thought. Reaper looked ready to eat the captain right there, but as Caldswell held his ground, daring him, his hand was behind his back, waving at us to run. Rupert saw it too, and he tightened his grip on my arm, yanking me off Brenton. But before he'd gotten me to my feet, Reaper attacked.

For such a huge lizard, he could certainly move. His head snapped down like a trap, jaws plunging to devour Caldswell whole. If the captain hadn't been a symbiont, that would have been the end. Even my Lady couldn't have evaded Reaper's teeth. But Caldswell was faster than death. He dropped and rolled just in time, and as he came up, the change rippled over his body.

I was used to seeing symbionts change by this point, but Caldswell's shift still took me by surprise, mostly because it was so *fast*. Rupert and Brenton both took seconds to cover their body in scales. Not many, but you could see it happening. Caldswell changed like a flipped switch. One moment he was human, the next he was perched on claws as long and deadly as any I've ever seen, leaving shredded clothing behind as he dove out of the way of Reaper's next attack.

For a supposedly injured old guy, it was a pretty impressive sight. Caldswell was so fast my cameras had trouble tracking him. Good thing, too, because Reaper was tearing after him now, and with every move, the huge xith'cal seemed to be growing even bigger as the lizards in the stands began to chant.

He's drawing on the strength of the tribe. Hyrek's message flew by in frantic bursts. *You have to get out of there before he gets any stronger.*

"Devi!" Rupert shouted at the same time, tugging my arm so hard I stumbled. "Let's go!"

Even Brenton seemed to have caught what was going on. Maybe it was because I'd shot the tube out of his neck, cutting off the drugs, or maybe Reaper was just that scary, but Brenton seemed to be coming around. He still wasn't talking, but his symbiont wasn't fighting us anymore. Like me, he was staring at Caldswell and Reaper and the double ring of warrior xith'cal that now circled the arena.

I felt Rupert tense as his head swiveled, taking in our position. I didn't have to look because my suit had already laid it out for me. The xith'cal that had charged into the arena when we'd blasted through the floor hadn't stopped coming while Reaper had been making his speech. The arena was thick with them now, and though they'd spread out to give their tribe leader room to fight, I had no illusions they'd let us run. I also didn't see how we could take them all.

Rupert must have come to the same conclusion, because he moved closer to me. For a second, I thought he was about to remind me that this fiasco was my idea, but whatever his other failings, Rupert had always been tactful, and all he said was, "How do you want to do this?"

I blew out a long breath to put off admitting that I had no idea. Originally, I'd planned to escape using the chaos of a lelgis attack for cover and the death of their tribe leader to wreck the chain of command, but while the lelgis part had worked just fine, how was I supposed to know that asshole lizard could survive a missile to the chest? Now, though, no matter how I cased the situation, I couldn't find our out. There were just too many of them, and we were too deep into the tribe ship. Even if we could break free of the warriors ringing us in, we'd have to fight our way back over fifteen miles of enemy territory to get to our ship. Rupert and I were good, but we weren't *that* good.

And just like that, the feeling hit me in the gut. That cold, sinking tightness that comes when you know you're completely screwed. Reaper was already a good five feet taller than he'd been when the fight started, and Caldswell's escapes were getting narrower every time. Another few swipes and it would all be over. Caldswell would die, Rupert would die, the crew would get caught and die. Even goddamn Brenton would die, and I'd be a xith'cal weapon until I died too, a quiet, traitor's death in a xith'cal lab where even the king's death guides couldn't find me.

My fists curled into tight balls. Rupert saw the motion, and his calm voice grew hard. "Devi?"

"No," I said.

I felt him tense. "No what?"

"I'm not dying like this," I snarled. "I'm not giving these lizards a goddamn thing."

As the words left my mouth, the pins and needles of the black sickness spread up my arms like wildfire. I welcomed them. I'd been trying very hard to avoid this, but right now I was having a hard time caring about the consequences. For once, I hadn't come looking for a fight. Reaper and Maat had captured me, sought to make me their weapon. Well, they were about to see just how dangerous a weapon I could be.

Rupert still had a death grip on my arm, but it didn't matter. One thought was enough to pop my armor's sleeve, leaving Rupert holding the pieces as I ripped away and charged straight at Reaper. I heard Rupert start running after me a second later, but for once, he was too slow. I'd thrown everything I had into this charge, and I launched into the air on my second step, shooting up toward the distant lights before flipping and coming down straight at Reaper with my soot-black arm held out in front of me like a spear.

As I fell toward the huge xith'cal, I could feel my rage coalescing. Sharpening, just like it had back in the glass cell. I was still furious, but it was a directed sort of fury. Like the battle drugs, but better. Even time felt slower, leaving me plenty of space to put my mind in order for what was likely to be my final hurrah.

One of the blessings of being a mercenary is that you have a much greater chance than most to pick the manner of your death. I'd always hoped mine would be glorious, but this was even more spectacular than I'd envisioned. My only sadness was that no one back home would ever get to see it, which was a real pity, because this would have wowed the Devastators for sure. That was fine, though. After everything that had happened, a glorious death was good enough for me. And when I got to the warrior's gate of heaven, I'd be able to hold my head up high and tell them that Devi Morris had died as a Paradoxian should, taking her enemy with her.

That thought actually made me a little sad. I didn't want to waste the virus, but honestly, it was probably better this way. The speed of the lelgis' response had made me realize that my plan to use the virus to free the daughters was likely a pipe dream. It didn't matter how secret the Eyes kept me, the lelgis would have found me the first time the virus killed a phantom, and that would have been that. Caldswell wouldn't even have to betray me to bring the squids down on us with all their blue fire.

It seemed so obvious now that I felt like a complete idiot for not realizing it earlier, but it was far too late to change things. And anyway, this wasn't such a bad end. I hadn't killed Maat or her daughters, and I'd get to take out Reaper, which was more than the Republic Starfleet had ever been able to manage. Even better, I'd be making a chance for Rupert and the rest to get out. No, not bad at all, I decided, and that final thought was enough to put a smile on my face as I slammed my black hand down on the ridged scales of Reaper's unguarded neck.

I felt Reaper's plasmex before I felt him. It was like diving headfirst into a pool of voices, all of them roaring. My senses expanded in an explosion, and suddenly I could feel them, every xith'cal in Reaper's Fleet like they were my own body. Reaper's flesh, indeed. For one second, I was there with Reaper, part of his enormous presence, and then, like poison dripped in a well, the blackness began to spread.

When I'd killed the phantom, it had made me empty, but the deaths of the xith'cal filled me to bursting. I couldn't begin to count how many there were, but I felt each one like a needle digging into my skin. Like the phantom, I could feel their pain, but this was worse, because unlike the phantom, the xith'cal weren't actually dying. They were rotting, curling up like bits of fruit left out in the sun. If I'd been a real, trained plasmex user, I probably could have explained it better, but even though I was swimming in the stuff, I didn't know plasmex from potatoes. All I could figure out was that the virus killed the most important part of the xith'cal but left the rest intact, dead but alive, and it was killing me, too.

I couldn't feel the pins and needles anymore. I couldn't feel my own body at all, actually, but I could feel the virus in my mind. It was like suffocating, only instead of air, I was being cut off from something I hadn't even known my body needed. Plasmex, I guessed. This must have been what Maat had warned me about. The corruption had finally spread all the way, and now the virus was going to kill me. But even though I knew what was happening, I couldn't do anything except sit and wait as the xith'cal shriveled up one by one until I was alone in the emptiness once again.

By the time the last one flared and died, I was deep in the blackness. If my first trip here had been dipping my fingers in a pond, this was diving to the bottom of the sea. I didn't even know which way was up, or if the concept of up existed anymore. I was starting to wonder if I was dead when the image entered my mind.

After so much nothing, the sudden jumble of sensation made me jump. It was like someone had shoved a video feed directly into my consciousness and was playing everything at double time. For several seconds the chaos was overwhelming, but then, slowly, the images merged into meaning, and the meaning into something like words.

You should not be here, death bringer of the mad queen.

That was paraphrasing. Really, it was more like the jumpy, terrified feeling of trespassing somewhere where trespassing got you lynched mixed with the sense of reckless use, like I was a loaded gun in the hands of a toddler. The feelings were so complex and intense, it took me several seconds before I could answer.

"Who are you?" I said, turning toward the presence of the others in the emptiness, the others who had always been here. "And where is here?"

This time, their answer couldn't be shaped into words. I got the feeling of motherhood and guardianship combined with that sense of smallness you get when you stare too long into the void of space. This was followed by a concept of infinity that nearly broke my mind with its hugeness, and yet I felt like I was part of it, a tiny speck floating in a greater oneness.

I rolled my eyes as the thoughts left. Great, now I sounded like Nova. But the weird image talking gave me an idea.

"You're the lelgis, aren't you?" I said, or thought I said. It was hard to talk when you had no vocal cords to vibrate or air to resonate sound.

We are all, came the answer, followed by another shot of that intense sense of belonging to the infinite.

"Right, gotcha," I said. "What do you want from me?"

That time, the answer was simple: a quick, bloodthirsty image of my death. But gruesome as the sight was, it gave me hope. After all, if the weird things in the dark wanted me dead, that must mean I was still alive somewhere.

"So why don't you do it, then?" I said, crossing my nonexistent arms over where I thought my chest should be. Taunting giant invisible things might not have been the smartest move, but if they hadn't squished me yet, there had to be a reason, and I wanted to know why.

You are shrouded in darkness we cannot pass. This time the words reeked of poison and toxicity and a strong warning to stay away. *But you are the death of all. We must end you lest you end the endless.* The feeling of oneness and infinity bloomed in my head again for a single moment before it cut out. This was followed by images of lelgis ships hunting through space like sharks through the sea. *We will find you, death. The mad queen will not have you.*

I didn't understand that last bit. The phrase "mad queen" was very specific, but the sensation that came with it was a mix of sickness, fear, and pity. "Who is the mad queen?"

The one they made who is like us, the lelgis replied. The feeling of sickness and pity was back in force, but this time it came with an image: a girl bound to a wall with her face covered in a metal mask and sickness hanging around her like a fog.

"Maat," I whispered, more to myself than to them, and then, "Hey! I don't serve her."

She seeks to use your death as her own, they said, and again, I felt the sensation of reckless use. *But the mad queen must not die. It is for this we made agreements with the humans, but for you, all pacts are discarded.*

With the words came a feeling of broken promises and an image of a man standing before a circle of alien figures so enormous I couldn't comprehend them. But that wasn't what got me. What got me was that I recognized the man.

It was Caldswell. He looked about a decade younger and he was wearing a Republic officer's coat, and at his side was Maat. The real Maat, not a daughter. I couldn't say how I was so sure, but I knew it was her without a doubt. She was kneeling on the ground, clutching Caldswell's sleeve and begging him, pleading with tears in her eyes for him not to do something. Before I could figure out what, though, the image vanished.

We come, the lelgis said. *Go now, death bringer. Never return.*

I was about to call bullshit on that when something hit me. It felt like I'd fallen ten stories and landed face-first on the ground, but instead of stopping, I was blown back through the emptiness. I flew forever, going faster and faster and faster. And then, like a bullet breaking through ice, I crashed back into my body.

I woke with a start to find myself pinned tight against something hard that was moving very quickly, bouncing up and down through somewhere dim and gray. It was so weird that if it wasn't for the Lady's familiar heads-up displays scattered across my vision, I'd have worried I was still dreaming. I shifted experimentally, testing my fingers. My left hand felt fine, but my right felt very odd. I spent several seconds in confusion over this before I realized my right arm felt funny because it wasn't armored.

"Well, look who's come to," said a smug, familiar voice. "Welcome back to the party, Morris."

I closed my eyes with a groan. Oh goody, we'd saved Caldswell. I opened my eyes again and looked around, actually using my cameras this time, and I saw that the world was bobbing up and down because Rupert was carrying me on his back. Caldswell was behind him, still in symbiont form and looking worse for wear but on his feet. He had a shape on his back too, a black scaly one. Brenton.

I shifted my position, moving my hands up to grip Rupert's shoulders. As I did this, I noticed that my naked arm was clean again with no sign of the black soot. Relief flooded through me. I hadn't realized how scared I'd been that I'd broken myself for good until I saw my normal skin.

"Put me down," I said, looking at Rupert, whose scale-covered head was right beside mine. "I can run on my own."

"No," Rupert snapped with a vehemence that made me flinch.

"You scared him good back there," Caldswell explained. "We couldn't get you to wake up, and that black stuff was almost up to your neck." He shook his head. "Trust me, you should just let him carry you."

Rupert's grip tightened possessively on me as the captain spoke, and I couldn't tell if I was touched or annoyed by that. A bit of both, I decided in the end. But Caldswell was right, I wasn't up for fighting Rupert. Now that I thought about it, I wasn't sure if I was up for running, either. My skin might look fine, but my body felt like it had been chewed up and spit out.

"What happened?" Because I wasn't sure how much of my dream was dream and how much was real.

"I'm not sure," Caldswell said. "I was busy trying not to get my head bitten off, so I didn't see where you came from. You just appeared on top of Reaper's shoulder, perched up there like a little silver bird, and the moment you touched him, Reaper stopped."

"He died?" I asked.

"No, he stopped," Caldswell repeated, his voice going grim. "They all did, every single lizard. It was like someone pulled the plug on the whole tribe. I've never seen anything like it, but we didn't stick around to spectate. We got you and ran."

I took a long breath. So much for the dream theory. "You didn't get near the black stuff, did you?"

"No," Rupert said. "We stayed back until it faded." His voice was tight, and I could tell that had not been his decision. "I have your Lady's arm piece, by the way," he added. "But I couldn't put it on while you were unconscious."

"*Really?*" When Caldswell had said they'd run, I'd thought for sure that the armor I'd shed to get away from Rupert was gone forever, so when he told me it wasn't, the relief was almost too much to bear. "Thank you!" I cried, wrapping my arms around Rupert's neck so hard I would have broken it if he'd been human.

Caldswell made a choking sound, but I ignored him, reaching out my bare hand. Rupert slowed down just enough to hand me the pieces he'd been carrying. I snatched them from him and put them back on with frantic glee. Elsie's blade had been attached to my right arm, after all. If I'd lost her, that would make two blades I'd sacrificed to xith'cal, which was simply unacceptable. "How much farther?"

"We're almost there," Rupert said, his voice much less angry now. "We made much better time with no lizards to worry about."

"So they're really all dead?" I asked.

Caldswell shook his head. "No. Learn to listen, Morris. I said they stopped."

"What he's saying is that the xith'cal aren't moving," Rupert clarified. "But they're not dead either. They just stopped where they were."

Cold dread began to curl in my stomach. "They won't be like

that for long," I whispered. "This is about to become another ghost ship."

"We figured as much," Caldswell replied. "That's why we're hustling. What I want to know is why the lelgis have stopped firing."

I had no idea why the lelgis would stop shooting, considering they'd told me in no uncertain terms they were coming to kill me. I didn't like the sound of it at all, though, and I messaged Hyrek for an update.

They backed off and stopped firing about five minutes ago, Hyrek reported. *Now they're just sitting out there. We haven't seen any of Reaper's tribe either, and all the ship feeds have gone dead. What's going on?*

"Just get ready to fly," I said, pulling up the map of the slave roads my suit had drawn on our first trip through. "We'll be there in two minutes."

"Who are you talking to?" Caldswell asked.

I turned so I could grin at him. "Hyrek," I replied, tapping my helmet. "Onboard computer and com, reason number eight hundred and one why powered armor is better than a symbiont. The crew knows we're coming, and they're getting the ship warmed up for us right now."

"Good work, Morris," Caldswell said, and though he was no longer my captain, I couldn't help feeling smug.

Sure enough, we made it back to the little dock right when I said we would. It was empty, just like Hyrek had said. The ship Rupert had commandeered had its ramp down, and Mabel was waiting for us when we ran up.

"Everything's ready to go so far as I can tell, sir," she said, scowling at the shape on Caldswell's shoulder. "Who's that?"

"Brenton," Caldswell replied, marching up the ramp.

"Wonders never cease," Mabel said as the captain unceremoniously dumped Brenton's unconscious body just inside the door.

"Let's get moving, people!" Caldswell shouted, striding toward the front of the ship.

Mabel gave Rupert and me an appraising look, then she smiled and turned to follow Caldswell. I had no idea what that smile meant, but it hadn't looked smug. If anything, I'd have said she looked relieved, but before I could think more about it, Rupert hopped up the ramp as well and set me down. Despite my fears, I was able to stand without help, mostly. I had to grab the door in the end, but I hid my wobble by making like I was leaning in to take stock of my surroundings.

The ship wasn't actually as small as it had looked from the outside, and it was definitely a female ship. The ceilings were much too low for male xith'cal, though they were still high by my standards. Also, unlike the raiding ships I'd spent my career busting up, it was clean. Everything was clinically neat and orderly, from the little hall we were standing in to the labs that opened off it. A science vessel, then, and a nice new one at that. Or it looked new to me. I'm not much of an engineer in my own race. Xith'cal equipment was way above my pay grade.

I was still getting my bearings when arms wrapped around me, and I stumbled into Rupert. He'd dropped the scales over his head while I wasn't looking, and he was hugging me like he was afraid I'd vanish. "Take off your helmet," he whispered.

I didn't bother arguing. The moment my helmet clicked, Rupert pulled it off and dove at me, his lips slamming into mine. It was a brutal, desperate kiss. Rupert was always intense, but this was different. He radiated fear and need as he clutched me tighter, making my suit creak, and as his power overwhelmed me, I started to realize just how badly I'd scared him.

Finally he broke the kiss, lifting up just enough to whisper against my lips. "Don't ever do that again."

"Not planning on it."

"I'm serious, Devi," he growled. "Never again. Promise me."

"I'm not promising anything of the sort," I said, pushing away. "I do what I have to do, Rupert. And we are *not* back on kissing terms."

Rupert closed his eyes and leaned his forehead against mine with a frustrated sound. "We'll talk about this later."

I didn't see what there was to talk about, but he was right. This was not the time. The ship was already spinning up. Rupert and I pulled apart, and he handed me back my helmet. I put it on as we walked to the front to see what we were up against.

The xith'cal bridge was surprisingly similar to every other bridge I've been on. There were the usual consoles against the walls and the pilot's station up front facing the view port. Nova was sitting off to one side on a padded stool that was way too big for her, doing math on a touchscreen that took up an entire wall. The numbers must not have needed translation, because she was deep in an equation, though she did look up to give me a shaky smile when I stepped in.

Caldswell, still in symbiont form but with the scales off his head, had already occupied the captain's chair. Mabel was nowhere to be seen, which probably meant she was back with the engine, but Basil and Hyrek were standing on either side of the captain. All three of them were staring at a big display screen covered in xith'cal chicken scratch and a big, round shape surrounded by a red cloud. As I got closer, though, I realized the haze on the screen wasn't a cloud. It was dots, thousands of little red dots so close together they blended into a whole.

"Let me guess," I said, pointing at the big round thing. "That's the tribe ship"—I moved my finger to the thousands of red dots—"and those are the lelgis."

"We're doomed," Basil moaned. "The xith'cal were fighting them before, but then everything stopped. Now they're just sitting out there like hawks waiting for us to leave the nest."

"Flying into that is not an option," Caldswell agreed. "We're just going to have to jump from here."

"Are you crazy?" I shouted at the same time as Basil's terrified squawk. "We can't jump from inside a tribe ship! Every bit of debris is a variable in the jump equation, right? Even if we had a gate all to ourselves, which we don't, we couldn't figure a safe jump from a dirty floor inside a ship filled with atmosphere. The margin of error from the dust in the air alone is enough to get us lost in hyperspace for a hundred years!"

"You'd rather die to lelgis?" Caldswell asked, hitting a button on the enormously complicated panel beside him. "And we *do* have a gate to ourselves. Xith'cal tribe ships have hyperspace computers that provide far more accurate computations than our own gates can manage."

"I thought we couldn't get into the xith'cal computer," I said.

We couldn't before, Hyrek typed at me. *But there's no one left to stop us now, is there?*

I stared down at the captain, who was sitting in the chair, working the xith'cal console like an old hand. "How do you know all of this?"

"Before my current employment, I was one of the captains the Republic Starfleet charged with stopping the xith'cal," Caldswell replied. "I picked up a few things." He glanced at Nova. "I'm sending you the jump coordinates now. How fast can we fly?"

"I've already got all the ship's variables in, I think," Nova replied, biting her lip as she fed the captain's coordinates into her wall of incomprehensible math. "I've never worked with a system like this before." She turned and flashed us a nervous smile over her shoulder. "Will a fifteen percent margin be acceptable?"

"I'll take those odds," Caldswell said, tapping a xith'cal-sized button at the top of his console. "Hold on tight."

I felt the familiar vibrations of a hyperdrive coil spinning up. Xith'cal coils must have been better than ours, though, because the jump flash washed over us almost immediately, and as it finished, the whole ship tipped.

There's usually a little bump when you enter hyperspace. This time, though, it was more like a mountain. The xith'cal ship lurched and rolled, dumping us sideways before the gravity cut out. But the turbulence lasted only a few seconds before the stillness of hyperspace took over, settling everything. The gravity came back a few moments later, dropping us to the floor.

"Where are we going?" I asked, pushing myself up.

"Dark Star Station," Caldswell said, pulling himself to his feet. "The lelgis can track a ship through hyperspace, so we can't outrun them with a jump. All we can do is go somewhere they won't follow."

I almost choked. According to Brenton, Dark Star Station was Eye headquarters, and Maat's prison. "I can't go there," I said quickly.

The captain looked at me, but I held my tongue. He might be sitting around in his scales like it was no big deal, but saying Maat's name in front of the crew still felt too dangerous for words. Fortunately, it didn't seem necessary. Caldswell was already on the move. "I figured you couldn't," he said, hopping out of his chair. "That's why we're dumping you first."

"Excuse me?" I said, but Caldswell was already jogging off toward the rear of the ship. "What do you mean, dumping?" I demanded, running down the hall after him.

"The only reason we were able to jump before they blasted us was because the lelgis didn't want to risk getting near the infected tribe ship," Caldswell said. "But even though they didn't see us leave, they certainly felt us. Jumping from inside got us a head start, though, and I intend to make the most of it."

By this point we'd reached the rear of the small ship. It was a crowded storage area not unlike the *Fool*'s cargo bay, but much smaller and mostly taken up by what looked like an escape pod, which Caldswell immediately started unhooking.

"The coordinates I gave Nova were for two jumps," Caldswell said, hitting the winch that lowered the emergency ship. "The second is to the Dark Star. The first is to a nice, crowded little Republic cash system just inside civilized space."

My eyes went wide. Cash systems were nothing but automated farming planets. They normally didn't even have defense grids, much less anything that could stop the lelgis. "Why the hell would you do that?"

"Because that's where you'll be getting out," Caldswell answered,

jumping down to the lower bay where the tiny ship was now waiting. "We're going to stop, dump you, and jump again before the
lelgis can catch up. With any luck, they'll be too busy chasing the
target they expect to look for one they don't."

"Hold up," I said. "You're going to leave hyperspace, kick me
out in the middle of nowhere, and then jump again in the hope the
lelgis keep chasing you?" Caldswell nodded, and I gaped at him.
"That's a terrible plan!"

"Terrible plans are what we've got," Caldswell said, opening the
emergency ship's glass canopy. "Get in."

I didn't want to do any such thing, but I didn't want to stay here
and fight with Caldswell either. So, with a long breath, I jumped
down onto the lower deck beside him and hauled myself into the
tiny alien escape pod. I was trying to figure out how I was supposed to sit on the xith'cal's strange, long bench seat when I realized
Rupert was getting in, too.

I hadn't even seen him come into the back bay, but he was here
now, dumping a black nylon duffel bag on the floor by my feet
before plopping down in front of me, sliding between my legs on
the long seat that had been built to hold one female xith'cal, not two
people, one of whom was wearing armor. I was trying to get enough
room for my knees when Caldswell handed Rupert something else.
I was about to point out there was no way that thing was fitting
when I recognized the sleek metal box.

"My armor case!" I cried, snatching it out of his hands.

"I grabbed it off the *Fool* before I left," Rupert said, and though
his voice was all business, I could hear the pride in it. "I thought it
would be useful."

I was so happy to see my case that I didn't even care that it took
up all the room I had left. If Rupert and Caldswell hadn't both
been looking, I might have hugged it. As it was, I wedged my case
into the back of the tiny ship and leaned against it.

"Don't let her do anything stupid," Caldswell ordered as he
closed the glass flight canopy over our heads.

I gave the captain a nasty look, but he'd already left, getting clear of the little ship as Rupert started the tiny engine. His head was still bare, which I took to mean that our escape pod had air for now, but I sealed my suit anyway, just in case.

"Can you even fly this thing?" I said as he settled his hands on something that looked sort of like a flight stick. "I thought you couldn't read xith'cal?"

"It's a simple ship," Rupert answered with a shrug, reaching up to flip a row of switches along the cabin's top. The first three toggles seemed to do nothing, but the fourth sealed the ship with an audible pop. "See?" Rupert said, looking back with a smile. "Best guess works."

That did *not* make me feel better, but I didn't get a chance to voice my opinion. Not three seconds after Rupert sealed our ship, the jump flash rolled over us again. I'd barely recovered from the feeling of being pulled back into time-space when the floor opened and our little ship was sucked into the vacuum of space.

We didn't fall. Falling is impossible when there's no down, but we did tumble out, and it was awful. We hurtled out of the ship, spinning like a pinwheel into the void. After what felt like hours, but was probably only a few seconds, Rupert turned on the thrusters, evening us out far below the stolen xith'cal ship.

But while we'd been spinning, Caldswell had been working. High above us, the hyperdrive was flaring back up. The door we'd dropped through hadn't even finished closing before the ship vanished again, flashing and fading as Nova jumped them back into hyperspace.

I'd never seen a jump done so hot on the heels of another, gate or no, but like all Caldswell's crazy plans, there was a good reason. Seconds after the stolen xith'cal ship vanished, four lelgis cruisers rippled into existence in the most beautiful hyperspace flash I'd ever seen. It was like they simply coalesced out of light, and the moment they appeared, they started circling.

Even though I knew it wouldn't do a bit of good, I held my breath, staring up at the hunting lelgis ships through the escape pod's glass canopy and praying as hard as I could that they wouldn't spot us. We were very small, small enough to look like space trash, and Rupert had cut our lights. He was holding as still as I was, and that made me feel a little better as we sat and waited.

For once, though, it seemed luck was on our side. After fifteen endless seconds, the lelgis fleet vanished as beautifully as they'd arrived. The enormous ships slid back into hyperspace like all of space was only oil floating on the surface of a sea of light. For a moment, I swore I could actually see the brilliant eddies spinning in their wake, and then the ships were gone, leaving nothing but emptiness behind.

I waited another five seconds before I let out my breath, flopping back as far as I could in the cramped little cabin. Rupert relaxed too, his shoulders slumping. Then he was back to business as he reached out to check the escape pod's bare-bones console.

"We lost some time on that jump."

I stiffened, though I shouldn't have been surprised. I'd done three ungated jumps now in less than three days. It had to catch up with me sometime. "How much?"

"Not centuries," he said. "But I won't know for sure until we check in with the Republic's standard clock, which we can't do in a xith'cal ship."

That made sense. "So what now?"

"We find somewhere to land," Rupert said. "This emergency vessel has limited fuel and no hyperdrive, so unless we set down and get another ship, we're not going anywhere."

"We have to land a xith'cal ship on a Terran planet?" I said, horrified. "What's your plan for not getting shot?"

"Luck," Rupert answered, turning the ship out into what looked to me like the endless black void. "And rank. We'll figure something out. Right now, my objective is to get you somewhere safe until I hear from Caldswell."

"*If* we hear from Caldswell," I muttered.

Rupert actually chuckled. "You'd be surprised. Brian Caldswell tends to land on his feet. He'll get through."

I believed that; what I couldn't figure out was how I was going to keep avoiding the lelgis. The captain might be leading them on a merry chase at the moment, but I knew they were always waiting for me in the black space on the other side of the virus. The moment I killed a phantom, even by accident, they'd find me. I slumped against my armor case, wondering grumpily what Caldswell had meant when he'd said the lelgis wouldn't go to the Dark Star. Was it because they were afraid of the Eyes, or because Maat was there?

It had to be Maat, I decided. So far as I'd seen, the lelgis weren't afraid of anything except my virus and the one they called the mad queen. That thought brought back the image the lelgis had shown me of Caldswell standing with Maat before the enormous creatures I was now sure were lelgis queens. He'd talked with them before they'd burned Stoneclaw's ghost ship, too, right after I'd gotten bitten. That had impressed me at the time. Knowing what I knew now, though, the idea that the lelgis hadn't killed us all just for being there baffled me. What kind of deal did Caldswell have with the squids, anyway?

"Devi?"

I blinked and looked up to see Rupert staring at me over his shoulder. "I said we'll be at a planet in a few hours," he repeated softly. "Do you want to get some sleep?"

"Sure," I said, leaning back on my armor case again. The idea of sleeping under these circumstances was absurd, but I did mean to make good use of the silence. I had a lot to process, after all. But the business on the tribe ship must have busted me up more than I'd realized, because the second I relaxed, sleep took me. And when I dreamed, I dreamed of that infinite oneness the lelgis had showed me being slowly devoured by darkness that came from my hands.

Suffice it to say, I didn't sleep well.

ACKNOWLEDGMENTS

I can't end this book without acknowledging my wonderful parents and parents-in-law, for without their constant help and support, no writing would be done at all. Thank you for loving us.

extras

meet the author

Alyssa Alig

RACHEL BACH grew up wanting to be an author and a super-villain. Unfortunately, supervillainy proved surprisingly difficult to break into, so she stuck to writing and everything worked out great. She currently lives in Athens, Georgia, with her perpetually energetic toddler, extremely understanding husband, overflowing library, and obese wiener dog. You can find out more about Rachel and all her books at rachelbach.net.

Rachel also writes fantasy under the name Rachel Aaron. Learn more about her first series, The Legend of Eli Monpress, and read sample chapters for yourself at rachelaaron.net!

introducing

If you enjoyed
HONOR'S KNIGHT,
look out for

HEAVEN'S QUEEN

by Rachel Bach

Prologue

Commander Brian Caldswell, commanding officer of the little-known and terribly named Joint Investigatory Spatial Anomaly Task Force, stood on the bridge of the Republic battle cruiser he'd requisitioned from fleet command an hour ago, staring out through the huge observation window at the void beyond, a void that should have been a thriving planet of nearly sixteen billion people, and wondering how everything could have gone so wrong so quickly.

Seven years now they'd been fighting the phantoms. Seven years of working constantly, of never seeing his wife, of missing his daughter grow up. But in those seven years, they'd never failed. They'd never missed an alarm or failed to save whatever colony planet the phantoms had chosen to nest on. Even these past eighteen months, when the phantom attacks had grown so frequent it didn't seem possible to catch them all in time, somehow Caldswell's team had always pulled it off. Always, that was, until yesterday.

"It's pointless to feel guilty."

Caldswell kept himself from jumping just in time, sliding his eyes over to look at his partner. John Brenton was right beside him, his arm almost brushing Caldswell's shoulder, and Caldswell hadn't heard a thing. *Damn creepy symbiont*, he thought with an angry breath. Dr. Strauss wanted to put one of those things in him, too, but that wasn't happening. Caldswell had spent the first fifteen years of his career running slave-freeing missions against those damn lizards, like hell was he going to let the doctor shove one into his brain.

"Even if we'd left the second the gravity alarms went off, the planet would have already been completely destabilized by the time we'd finished the jump," Brenton went on, staring down at the small knot of refugee ships that huddled in the battleship's shadow, the ten thousand people who were all that remained of the Republic core world of Svenya. "The only thing we can do now is make sure it never happens again."

"And how do you suggest we do that?" Caldswell said quietly, glancing over his shoulder.

Behind him, Maat lay on the floor, curled up in a ball on Brenton's coat. Dr. Strauss, the universally renowned plasmex doctor who was now Maat's caretaker, was on his knees beside her, gently trying to cajole her into getting up. Maat didn't even seem to hear him. She just lay there, her dark eyes glassy and empty but still afraid. That made Caldswell want to pull his hair out, because it meant they were probably going to have to drug her again.

As a powerful plasmex user rescued from the pits of a xith'cal lab, Maat had always been unstable, but they'd never had to drug her until this year. With the added workload, her fits were rapidly getting out of control. They'd had to drug her nearly unconscious just two days ago, and Caldswell never would have ordered it again so soon, but the moment they'd arrived at Svenya she'd gone into hysterics, nearly killing their entire crew before Brenton managed to get her with the syringe. She'd screamed the whole time, babbling about a god, a monster that spanned the sky. At the time, Caldswell had thought she was raving, but that was before he'd heard that the phantom they'd come here to hunt had destroyed an earth-class planet in less than a galactic-standard day. Now, he wasn't so sure Maat was wrong.

"She's strong," Brenton said earnestly, staring at Maat. "She'll snap herself out of this."

"And what if she can't?" Caldswell asked. "What if this thing really is as huge as she claims? Our biggest phantom was what, fifty feet?"

"Forty-five," Brenton said. "But she handled it."

"And yet she went to pieces at the sight of this one," Caldswell said, nodding like Brenton had just made his point for him. "Did you see the ships it destroyed? Huge freighters crushed like tin cans. Damn thing must be miles long, and it's *still* out there."

With Maat out of commission, Caldswell had been forced to track the phantom by sending scout ships to fly until they hit the phantom's aura and blacked out. As spotting methods went, it was only slightly less inaccurate and dangerous as randomly shooting the cannons until they scored a hit, but Caldswell had to know if the thing moved. Svenya had been the largest colony in this system by far, but her sister colonies still numbered in the millions. If the monster made a move toward one of them, Caldswell needed to know. Not, of course, that he knew what he'd do if that happened. "Maybe we should try nuking it again."

Brenton scoffed. "The nukes don't work on the little ones. A phantom this size wouldn't even feel it." He shook his head. "Maat's power is the only thing that can touch them."

"You tell me, then," Caldswell snapped. "We've got a monster capable of destroying a planet in a day just sitting there, only we can't see it, can't track it, and can't fight it. Just the sight of it was enough to scare our only viable weapon into a coma, and fleet command is expecting me to report in by the end of the hour that we've got this under control. So you tell me, John, what do we do?"

"Tell the truth," Brenton said. "Tell them we don't have it under control because something like this *can't* be controlled. Our best bet is to evacuate all the remaining colonies and close off the system. It's never been proven phantoms can travel faster than light. If we give it enough space, we might never see it again in our lifetime."

"There's also no proof that they *can't* travel faster than light," Caldswell snapped. "Seven years and we still know jack shit about how they move. We don't even know if this monster is the only one of its kind. The phantom population has been going up exponentially all year and we can't even say why, or where they're coming from. For all we know, this is the new normal."

The end of humanity, Caldswell thought with a cold clench. He'd always thought the xith'cal were the worst threat to mankind, but the lizards were nothing on this enemy, the monster they couldn't see coming. "We have to do something," he said, turning back to the empty window. "Find some way to block it in or—"

He cut off as a deep rolling scream rattled through the ship. The noise was more like pressure than sound, squeezing his mind in a way Caldswell recognized too well. It was the phantom's scream, but he'd never heard one this deep and huge. The ship lights flickered, giving in to the phantom's electrical current wrecking aura before Maat's power canceled it out.

"It's getting closer," Caldswell said as the scream faded. "Ben!" he called, turning to the doctor. "How soon can you wake her up?"

Dr. Strauss shook his head wildly, making his wispy, white blond hair fly over his paper-pale face. "It would be unwise in the extreme to disrupt her harmony now," he said. "She's still in trauma from being put under, and from whatever she saw. If you bring her up now, the chance of long-term damage is exponentially increased."

As the doctor spoke, the lights flickered again. This time, though, only the low-energy emergency lights came back on, and Caldswell swore under his breath. "Do it," he snapped. "We'll deal with the consequences later."

"We don't even know if she'll be able to do anything," Brenton said, grabbing Caldswell's arm. "Are you really willing to risk damaging her? Our only weapon?"

"If that thing catches us while she's asleep, we're all dead for sure," Caldswell said, jumping into the gunnery control seat. Phantoms couldn't be killed by physical objects or energy attacks, but they didn't like them. If he could just find a hard spot and land a hit, maybe he could buy them some—

The battleship lurched beneath him as something crashed into the port side. Something enormous. Even at low power, the thrusters righted them immediately, but Caldswell had had enough.

"Wake her up!" he shouted, punching the button to authorize live fire on all guns. Before he could shoot, though, another scream ripped through the bridge, sending a stab of pain right through his head. His first thought was that another phantom had joined the attack, a much smaller one, but then he saw Maat lurch to her feet, her mouth open as she screamed again.

"They're coming!"

As always, Brenton got to her first. "Easy," he whispered, pulling her into his arms. "Who's coming?"

Maat buried her face in his chest, and Caldswell felt a twinge of guilt. She was nearly twenty now, but when she did that, she looked just like the little girl they'd rescued so long ago. The little girl they should have been protecting, not using like this.

"Who?" Brenton asked again.

Maat's whole body shook with a sob. "The ones who speak in the dark."

Brenton glanced at Caldswell, but the commander just shrugged. Maat said cryptic shit all the time. But before he could try and guess what this particular riddle was about, a flash outside put everything else out of his mind.

Light bloomed in the empty space that had been the colony of Svenya, pushing through the darkness like all of reality was just oil floating on water. Caldswell had never seen anything like it, though he knew enough to guess it must be some kind of hyperspace exit. As for the ships that came through, however, Caldswell couldn't guess at all.

They looked like deep-sea fish, their flat bodies marked with gorgeous blues, greens, and purples that glowed with their own light. They dwarfed the midsized battleship Caldswell had brought, but they moved with a grace that belied their hugeness, an effortless natural motion that Caldswell had never seen in any machine. If it wasn't for the fact that he could see obvious doors in their sides and prows, he would have sworn the giant vessels were *alive*. Whatever they were, though, they were beautiful. So beautiful Caldswell could have stared at them forever, but he couldn't, because the final shape that blossomed out of hyperspace dwarfed the rest completely.

If the mystery ships had been huge, this thing was gigantic, as large as any of the xith'cal warships Caldswell had fought, only this, he was sure, was no ship. Unlike the others with their rainbow colors, the last thing to exit hyperspace was as black as the void behind it. Once the hyperspace flash faded, Caldswell could only catch glimpses of its surface in the reflected light of the other ships: a wide pointed head framed by millions of tendrils, a shiny shell-black surface, and deep, terrible pits that could have been eyes or mouths or something else he couldn't even imagine. He was still staring at it when the other ships opened fire.

Caldswell grabbed the console on instinct, because from where he was sitting the beautiful ships seemed to be firing straight at him. But the brilliant beams of blue-white fire never hit the Republic ship. Instead, they struck the invisible mass of the phantom floating between them.

For one terrifying moment, the entire sky was ablaze. For the first time ever, Caldswell saw the whole of the phantom's body as the alien's fire lit it up from within. The thing was even bigger than he'd imagined, and he'd imagined big. Miles, he'd guessed, maybe hundreds of them. Now, with the truth spelled out in fire, all he could think was that he'd been a fool. The phantom's snakelike body stretched from one end of Svenya's dust cloud to the other. It was as big as a planet, bigger even than the enormous black monster commanding the attack, and it wasn't going down.

The creature burned for nearly thirty minutes, thrashing in agony, taking out several of the beautiful fishlike ships in the process. It was only by pure luck that it didn't hit the battleship again. The unknown aliens kept up their fire the entire time until, at last, the phantom's body gave one final shudder and started to disintegrate. That was all Caldswell saw before the fire snuffed out and the phantom vanished, invisible once again, though he knew if he could somehow reach out there, he would still feel it falling apart.

All through the attack, Maat hadn't moved. She was still clinging to Brenton, her eyes locked on the light show outside. When it finished, however, she collapsed into a sobbing heap. Dr. Strauss was at her side at once, helping Brenton move her into the captain's chair. Caldswell was about to go over as well when the voice spoke into his head:

Enemy of our enemy.

The words weren't words exactly, not like he knew them. They were more like impressions, meanings layered together to form something richer than language. For a moment, Caldswell thought he was imagining things, but then Brenton and the doctor snapped their heads up as well, looking around as if they'd heard it, too. Meanwhile, Maat began to cry harder.

Outside, the beautiful alien ships were coming toward them with the huge black shape at the center. They moved so fast there was no chance to run even if Caldswell had wanted to. But he wanted no such thing, and he walked back up to the prow of the bridge as the aliens came to an abrupt halt just outside of docking distance.

Who speaks for all?

The words brushed over Caldswell's mind like impatient fingers, demanding to know who was in command. He could see from Brenton's face that he'd felt it, too, but Caldswell was commander here, so he was the one who answered. "I am."

Any worries he had that it wouldn't be able to hear him vanished when he felt the presence in his mind focus, the impressions growing louder and clearer, like the speaker had turned to face him. *Enemy of our enemy*, it said again, only now the words implied kinship and cooperation. *We offer you aid.*

"And we appreciate it," Caldswell replied. "Thank you. We never could have killed that thing on our own."

We know this, the alien said dismissively. *And now you know it, too. You are dead without us.*

Caldswell fought the urge to scowl. "What kind of aid are you offering?"

Protection, the voice said, the word itself a wall. *The universe has been torn open and the corruption is seeping through. This attack was only the beginning. More are coming.* "More" was the word Caldswell's brain supplied, but the alien's impression was infinitely larger, an endless flood.

"How many more?" he asked.

Countless, the voice answered. *More than either of us can fight.*

Caldswell nodded. "So you want to work together."

Amusement trilled through his thoughts like a swirling feather. *We do not fight unless forced*, it answered. *Violence is a risk we cannot take. We are vital, therefore, we cannot be allowed to end.*

"Is that so?" Caldswell said, folding his arms over his chest. "Then what exactly would we be getting out of this aid if you won't fight?"

Survival, the alien replied with the feeling of an open hand. *We are lelgis, those without end, and we offer you our knowledge and the opportunity to save your race. We will show you how to forge the weapon that can kill the ones you know as phantoms, and in return, you will hunt them until we are all safe.* The voice paused, letting this sink in. Just before Caldswell told it to go on, it added, *We also require an offering.*

"What kind of offering?" Brenton said, making Caldswell jump. He hadn't realized the others could hear this as well, but Brenton was glaring murder at the black alien. "You seem to be getting the sweet end of this deal while we do all the work."

Without us, you will die, the alien called lelgis said lightly. *You need us, and to aid you, we require the one called Maat.*

"What?" Brenton shouted, but Caldswell put out his hand.

"Explain," he said.

She has the potential to be like us, the lelgis said, the words carrying the implication of great power. *Give her to us and we will forge her to be the tool that saves us all.*

Caldswell could feel Brenton's rage building from across the room, so he made sure to speak first. "What would that entail, exactly?"

The enormous black lelgis moved a little closer. *She will stop the flood in our stead*, it said, offering up the picture of a door closing. *Without a wall, the corruption will overwhelm us all, and this poor place will be but the first in a plague of death. But with her, we can stop them. A single sacrifice so that all may live.*

Caldswell bit his lip, trying to think this through, to tease out what was really going on. Before he could, though, the alien spoke again. *This offer will be tendered only once, enemy of our enemy. Accept and save your species, refuse and perish.*

"Don't do it, Brian," Brenton said, suddenly beside him. "Don't even think about it. We can't trust them. We don't even know what they are."

"You saw what they killed," Caldswell said. "You're not wrong, but without them we'd be dead right now."

"Maat is our only weapon against the phantoms," Brenton said, his voice rising. "You can't just give—"

"Maat is breaking!" Caldswell yelled, turning on him. "You know that damn well. Even if she wasn't, do you really think we can keep going like we have been over the last few months forever? Some of us need to sleep, Brenton, and we can't guard the entire universe with one girl. Not at the rate the phantoms are multiplying. We need a better solution, and if they're offering one, we'd be suicidal idiots not to hear it out."

"So you'd just give her over?" Brenton shouted. "Sacrifice her to some alien—"

"Yes!" Caldswell shouted back, jabbing his finger at the dark where the phantom had died. "If it means something like this never happens again, I'd give them my own daughter!"

Caldswell regretted his words as soon as they were out of his mouth, but it was too late. The alien voice was already crooning in his head.

Good, it whispered, petting him with their approval as the aliens turned their fleet around. *Follow.*

"Do it," Caldswell ordered, ignoring Brenton's horrified look. Moments later, the battleship took off after them, following the aliens into the dark.

Once the ship was moving, Caldswell stomped over to Brenton to take Maat from him, but the symbiont wouldn't let go. Maat was trembling in his arms, staring at Caldswell with terrified eyes. "I can see what they want," she whispered, her voice breaking like glass. "Don't let them take me." Tears appeared in her eyes. "*Please*, Brian, don't do this."

When he didn't answer, she flew into a rage. As Brenton and Dr. Strauss fought her back to the chair for sedation, Caldswell slumped in his own seat to watch the lelgis fly. He knew Brenton wouldn't stop fighting him on this. Brenton always took Maat's side, but it didn't matter. Caldswell had made up his mind. If the lelgis could give him the weapon that had burned that monster out of the sky, or any weapon that could reliably kill phantoms on the scale they needed to be killed, then he would pay any price. He would climb up on the altar with Maat himself if they wanted, so long as they gave him the power to stop the goddamn tragedies.

After all, he thought, slumping down, *what were a few more deaths compared to the billions of lives already lost? What was anything, so long as no more planets died?* Nothing, he decided. Nothing at all.

Five days later, Maat was given to the lelgis as promised, and at the far corner of the newly restricted zone that had been the Svenya system, construction began on the prison that would later be known as Dark Star Station.

STE

BACH
Bach, Rachel.
Honor's knight /

STELLA LINK
05/14

VISIT THE ORBIT BLOG AT

www.orbitbooks.net

FEATURING

BREAKING NEWS
FORTHCOMING RELEASES
LINKS TO AUTHOR SITES
EXCLUSIVE INTERVIEWS
EARLY EXTRACTS

AND COMMENTARY FROM OUR EDITORS

WITH REGULAR UPDATES FROM OUR TEAM,
ORBITBOOKS.NET IS YOUR SOURCE
FOR ALL THINGS ORBITAL.

WHILE YOU'RE THERE, JOIN OUR E-MAIL LIST
TO RECEIVE INFORMATION ON SPECIAL OFFERS,
GIVEAWAYS, AND MORE.

imagine. explore. engage.